A Touch of Forever

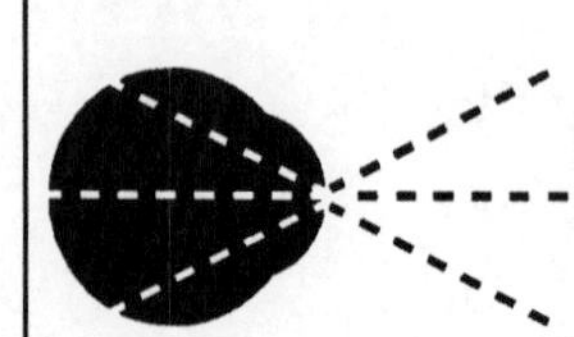

This Large Print Book carries the Seal of Approval of N.A.V.H.

A Touch of Forever

Jo Goodman

THORNDIKE PRESS
A part of Gale, a Cengage Company

Thorndike Press, a part of Gale, a Cengage Company.

Thorndike Press® Large Print Romance.
The text of this Large Print edition is unabridged.
Other aspects of the book may vary from the original edition.
Set in 16 pt. Plantin.

LIBRARY OF CONGRESS CIP DATA ON FILE.
CATALOGUING IN PUBLICATION FOR THIS BOOK
IS AVAILABLE FROM THE LIBRARY OF CONGRESS

ISBN-13: 978-1-4328-6207-7 (hardcover alk. paper)

Published in 2020 by arrangement with Berkley, an imprint of Penguin Publishing Group, a division of Penguin Random House, LLC

Printed in Mexico
Print Number: 01 Print Year: 2020

This one's for the wonderful folks on the
sixth floor of Weirton Medical Center
who dedicate themselves to
helping and healing others.
I finished this book between physical
therapy, medication delivery, and the
ignominy of needing assistance to get out
of bed, bathe, and groom.
To a person they were kind,
and that is a gift I shall always cherish.

Chapter One

Frost Falls, Colorado
September 1901

Back in New York, they called him the black sheep. Not to his face. Or rarely to his face. But he'd heard it whispered in a pitying sort of way in the free-spirited Bohemian circles where his family was revered. Roen Shepard didn't mind particularly. Depending on one's view, he supposed it might even be true. It was certainly his family's view; although the appellation was couched in humor, not pity. They were dreamers. He was not. He'd been stewed in creative juices since birth. Musicians. Painters. Poets. Novelists. Surrounded by so much talent and imaginative genius, something should have inspired him. Nothing had.

He'd never been afraid to try, and so, encouraged by his parents and grandparents, by his siblings and cousins, by his tutors and teachers, he tried his hand at every sort of artistic endeavor.

He was fair to middlin' on the piano if there weren't too many sharps or flats, and if he wasn't required to sing at the same time. For a while, he thought painting might be his forte. He could put a still life on canvas that looked exactly like the bowl of fruit on the table in front of him. It was politely pointed out to him that he represented the fruit too accurately. A photograph would do just as well, his mother said, and that would not do at all. He wrote bad poetry and even worse prose. He'd once revised the first chapter of a proposed novel sixteen times before his father kindly took the pages and burned them.

The differences between him and his family were not only artistic ones. There were physical differences as well, so many of them, in fact, that his brother and sisters teased him mercilessly that he was a foundling adopted by their parents in one of the impulsive, magnanimous gestures they were known for. As he was the only child with green eyes, chestnut-colored hair, and a clumsy, loose-jointed frame that took years to grow into, it was easy to believe the foundling story no matter how often his parents reassured him it was not the case. As for the dissimilarity in appearance, it was all on account of his being a change-of-life baby, his mother told him, although she neglected to furnish an explanation for what that meant.

Thinking about it now, Roen smiled to himself. He was still a fish out of water at family affairs, but as an adult, he'd come into his own. At twenty-nine, he was content with the features that set him apart. He was more athletic than graceful, which made him a better baseball player than a dancer, and at a hair above six feet, he stood half a head taller than all his male relatives. He could joke, before his family did, that he had physical stature if not an artistic one. He could also have pointed out that he was not possessed of the same fiery temperament as the rest of the Shepards, but they would have said he lacked their passion and wouldn't have understood that he was thankful for it.

Roen studied the drawing he had made in his sketch pad, reviewed the calculations, checking and rechecking his work on the elevations, and, once satisfied, closed the book with a pleasant thump.

It was only then that he became aware that he was not alone, and he guessed that he hadn't been for some time. Roen could acknowledge that upon occasion he had an extraordinary eye for detail while being oblivious to the whole. This was one of those occasions.

He looked up from his sketch pad and turned his head in the direction of his visitor. He merely raised an inquiring eyebrow.

A lesser man might have flinched at being caught out, perhaps even been unseated from his hunkered position on the rocky outcropping where he was perched like a bird of prey, but Clay Salt didn't twitch. Roen estimated the boy was eleven, maybe twelve, so that explained both his curiosity and his lack of embarrassment.

"Are you done now, mister? Seems like you might be. Didn't want to disturb you none while you was working, so I just settled down to watch. I never seen the like before, what you were doing. That much fascinated I was."

Roen had no recollection of anyone ever being fascinated by what he did, and he looked for mischief in young Clay's eyes. What he saw were a pair of dark brown eyes, earnest in their direct gaze and without a shred of guile.

"Did you follow me up here, Clay?"

Now Clay flinched. "You know who I am?"

"Uh-huh. Why does that surprise you?"

"Well, you're new to town. You've hardly been here more than a minute."

"Three weeks. People are friendly, and I've been to your church twice. Saw you there with your mother and your brother and sisters. Between the minister and Mrs. Springer, I believe I was introduced to every parishioner."

"Yeah? Not us."

"No, that's true. I misspoke." Clay and his family sat at the back of the church and were the first out the door both Sundays. Out of the corner of his eye he had seen them fleeing — that was the word that came to mind — while Mrs. Springer was pumping him for information under the guise of welcoming him to Frost Falls. "I'm pleased to make your acquaintance now."

"Are you? Ma said I should leave you be, that your work is too important to suffer the children."

Roen's cocked an eyebrow again, this time with a challenging curve. "Suffer the children? Did she say that?"

Clay shrugged, unabashed. "Something like that."

"I see. So you are in defiance of your mother's wishes right now."

"Not really. You didn't know I was here until you were done so you didn't have to suffer me at all."

"True, and I admire your logic even if you are splitting hairs." Roen saw one corner of the boy's mouth lift at what he perceived was a compliment, and for the first time Roen had a hint of the rascal that resided within. He was gratified to see it. Until this moment, Clay Salt had seemed unnaturally self-possessed. Roen opened his sketch pad to the page he had just completed and held it up. "Do you want to get a closer look?"

In answer, Clay clambered down from his rock and closed the ten yards that separated them. Roen handed him the book and waited for the inevitable disappointment that would shadow Clay's features. It wasn't disappointment, though. It was puzzlement.

"What is it?" asked Clay. He turned the pad sideways as though an angle might offer clarity. "I mean, I see it's numbers. I know numbers. But these other scratchings? Looks like a hen stepped in ink and walked across your paper."

Roen tugged on the pad so that Clay had to lower it for him to see. He regarded his work with fresh eyes. He huffed a laugh and ran a hand through his chestnut hair: Δ h Σ D g. "So it does."

"What does it mean?"

"It's part of the formula to measure the

refraction and curvature of the earth."

"Huh."

"I need a lot of precise measurements to know where I can recommend that Northeast Rail lay down new track."

"Huh."

"You know the earth is round, right?"

Clay's lip curled. " 'Course I know."

"Good. And because there's a curve, a straight line isn't exactly straight, and air refracts light that further distorts the line, so what you see isn't as precise as my equipment and calculations can be."

Clay returned the pad to Roen and pointed to the upper-right-hand corner of the page, the only part that made perfect sense to him. "You drew the landscape over yonder, and that double line winding through it, those are tracks, aren't they? You reckon that's a place to put down rail?"

"It might be."

"Huh. That's Double H land. Hard to imagine Ol' Harrison Hardy will sell to the railroad. He's cussed cranky even when his lumbago isn't bothering him."

"Good to know, but that's a problem for another day. Right now I need to pack up and get back to town before dark."

Clay looked at the sky. "Dark's coming on

fast, but I'll help you, and I know the way back day or night."

CHAPTER TWO

Lily Salt did not raise her voice when her older boy attempted to make a stealthy entrance into the kitchen. Neither did she turn around from the stove, where she was stirring a pot of chili. "Clay Bryant Salt."

"Yes, ma'am. I'm going to oil that hinge first thing tomorrow."

"Won't help you. I suppose I know when my son's been wandering and when he's home."

"Chili smells good." He sidled up to the stove and bumped her affectionately. "Better than good, I'm thinking. Might be excellent."

"I am not mollified. Not even a little." But she bumped him back while she continued to stir. "Go tell your sister it's time to set the table and then you wash your hands. Help Ham and Lizzie, too."

When Clay took a step sideways but didn't leave the kitchen, Lily was immediately suspicious. She swiveled her head in his direction. He was tall now, as tall as she was, and she hadn't quite gotten used to it. It pained her some to look him in the eye. He had his father's eyes and coloring, though in every other way he was nothing at all like his father. Still, the eyes. "What is it?" she asked.

Clay pointed to the kitchen door, where Roen Shepard stood framed in the opening.

"I beg your pardon, Mrs. Salt," Roen said, removing his hat and holding it in front of him like a penitent. "I wanted to see your son home safely. I'm Roen Shepard, the engineering surveyor employed by Northeast Rail."

Lily indicated that Clay should take the long-handled wooden spoon. "Stir," she said. She thought he was glad to have the spoon in his hand and not hers, though she had never once raised it against him. There were memories of his father not easily erased. "I know who you are, Mr. Shepard." She crossed a few feet to the table and rested one hand on the back of a chair. She did not close the distance between them.

Roen did not inch into the room, nor did he back away. Lily Salt was regarding him warily, with the innate stillness of a rabbit in the wild sensing something feral in her midst. In deference to what he perceived as distress, he remained rooted where he stood.

It was in the back pew of the Presbyterian Church that Clay's mother had made her first impression on Roen Shepard. He'd been sitting five pews ahead on the aisle when a cloth ball rolled between his feet. He picked it up, looked around for the owner, and passed it back to a harried mother with a child set to squall on her lap. The squalling was averted, and he was grateful for that, but more grateful that his backward search had afforded him a glimpse of the woman who later became known to him as Lily Salt.

She looked to him as composed and serene as any Madonna rendered in oils by the great artists of the Renaissance. That she was flanked by two boys and two girls, who could only be her children, made her calm seem preternatural. She had the smile of the *Mona Lisa,* which was to say it was more a smile of imagination than it was of reality, but when he turned away, that perception of her smile lingered.

She wore a wide-brimmed straw sailor hat trimmed with a black ribbon and tilted forward as was the fashion. Her hair, what he could see of it then, was rust red, but her older daughter had hair like a flame and made him suspect that this was Lily's color in her youth.

When he caught sight of her escaping the church with her children in tow, Roen knew himself to be mildly intrigued. He was saved from expressing any measure of curiosity by Mrs. Springer's account of the congregation, their lineage, their talents, and their foibles. Amanda Springer was a wellspring of information, most of which he later learned from the minister could be taken as gospel.

So here he was facing Lily Salt, age thirty-four, a widow whose husband had perished in a fire almost two years earlier, mother of four children, seamstress employed in the dress shop owned by Mrs. Fish, and doing well enough on her own that she had no interest in inviting a man into her life, though according to Mrs. Springer, a number of men had tried.

This last was rather more than Roen had expected or even wanted to hear, since he had no interest in such an invitation, but Amanda Springer, once sprung, said what was on her mind. All of it. Her husband, an affable man who tended bar at the Songbird Saloon, seized on the opportunity to disengage her at the first sign she was winding down. Later, Roen rewarded Jim Springer's strategy by buying him a drink at the saloon, though he never explained the reason for his generosity.

At the risk of Lily Salt turning tail and fleeing her own kitchen, Roen offered a slim, apologetic smile. "Your boy was a help to me," he said. At the stove, Clay glanced over his shoulder and gave Roen an appreciative eyeful. Roen ignored him. "Thought it was the least I could do to see him home."

Lily's slim hand, the one that curved over the back of a chair, tightened so her knuckles stood out in stark white relief. Her chin came up. "I reckon Clay knows the lay of the land a mite better than you do even with all of your fancy instruments."

Clay stopped stirring and stared openmouthed at his mother. "Ma!"

Roen thought Lily appeared more surprised by her temerity than she was regretful of it. Her lips parted but she had no words. It fell to Roen to supply them. "You're correct, Mrs. Salt. Clay was a better escort to me than I was to him, and I'll be taking my leave now."

"Ma!" This time Clay's cry was plaintive. "I invited Mr. Shepard to take supper with us."

"Did you now?" she asked without taking

her eyes off Clay's guest.

"I did. He's been taking his meals regular at the hotel and I figured home-cooked food would do him right." He jerked his chin in Roen's direction. "You can see for yourself that some meat on his bones wouldn't come amiss."

Lily's eyes did not stray from Roen Shepard's angular face, but it was impossible not to note that her son was correct. The man standing in her doorway probably filled out a black coat and tails just fine, even excellently, but his blue chambray shirt drooped some at the shoulders. The butternut leather vest was loose across the chest, and his denim trousers looked as if they would benefit from a belt *and* suspenders. Someone needed to take him in hand. That thought flitted uncomfortably through her mind, but what she said was, "The Butterworth serves excellent food."

She stepped back to the stove, took the spoon from Clay, and set it aside. "Go do what I asked you to do."

Uncertain, Clay nonetheless hurried from the kitchen.

When he was gone, Lily pointed to the pegs to the left of the door. "You can hang your hat there."

Roen did as he was told and closed the

door behind him. Lily was already turned back to the stove when he was done. Her thick hair was neatly arranged in a braided coil at the back of her head. His eyes settled on the fragile nape of her neck as she bent to her work. "What decided you?" he asked.

"It's the least I can do to make amends for my son pestering you."

"Oh, but he didn't."

Lily picked up a folded towel and used it to open the oven door. She removed a pan of cornbread, but not before she gave Roen Shepard a jaundiced look that said she knew her son as well as her son knew the lay of the land. It was gratifying that he accepted that silent reprimand and said nothing in return.

The warm fragrance of cornbread was wafting through the kitchen as Hannah came rushing in from the hallway. She skidded to a halt, closely followed by her younger sister Lizzie, and the pair of them held up their hands to show they'd been washed clean. Droplets of water flew from their fingertips as they shook them out. Whatever admonishment Lily meant to say when she opened her mouth to speak came to nothing as Hannah interrupted her mother.

"So you *are* here!" she said, addressing

Roen Shepard. "Clay said you were but I didn't know if I could believe him. He likes to play tricks. Say hello, Lizzie, to Mr. Shepard."

Lizzie, at five, was a practiced coquette. She gave Roen a sidelong glance and a sweet smile while tilting her head just so. Her curls, the color of sunshine, swung to and fro when she righted her head. "Hello." Then she sidled closer to her sister, where she sought the protection of Hannah's gingham skirt.

"Hello, Lizzie. Hannah. What a pleasure it is to see you again."

Lily set the pan of cornbread on a warming plate on top of the stove. "Set the table, Hannah. Bowls and spoons. Lizzie, take your seat." To Roen, she said, "How do my girls know you?"

Hannah answered before Roen could. "We see him in church, Ma. Same as everyone."

Lily recognized the truth in that, but she also recognized there was something left unsaid. "I was speaking to Mr. Shepard."

Roen hadn't moved more than two feet into the kitchen. His place at the table was not clear to him, and he waited to be invited to sit or asked to help. "They introduced themselves when we were in Hennepin's mercantile."

Lizzie plopped herself into her chair and swung her feet under the table. "He bought us a bag of licorice whips and horehound drops."

Lily frowned deeply. "Why would you do that? No, Lizzie, I don't want to hear from you. I want to hear from Mr. Shepard."

Lizzie clamped her lips closed and regarded Roen sorrowfully. She had told the truth but her mother's expression led her to believe it wasn't the right answer.

Without the least regret, Roen said, "It appears I overstepped, and that certainly was not my intention. Indeed, my intention was to move them along. As I'm sure you're aware, Mr. Hennepin has a large selection of candy and your girls could not decide between the peppermint, the butterscotch, or the horehound drops. It was amusing at first, and then it was painful. I had an appointment, you see, and needed to be on my way, and Mr. Hennepin was giving the girls their due, as a good shopkeeper should. I chose the horehound candies for them and added the licorice whips because I wanted one myself. And that's how it came to pass. They were grateful and I was on time for my meeting with the town council."

He thought he saw Lily's lips twitch, but whether she was amused or skeptical, he couldn't say. After a moment she nodded once and the subject was closed. Lizzie's sigh of relief was audible and Hannah actually winked at him. If Lily noticed either girl's reaction, she did not comment.

"Can I help?" Roen asked as Hannah set bowls on the table.

Lily pointed out a chair. "You can sit yourself there. Ham will sit beside you. The girls opposite. Hannah. See what's keeping your brothers."

He assumed from the position of the chairs that it meant Clay sat at one end and Lily at the other. Roen went around the table but stood behind his chair rather than sit down.

Lily cut the cornbread and placed the warm pan on a trivet on the table. As she ladled chili into the bowls, Hannah reappeared with her brothers on her heels. The boys held up their hands for inspection, and when Lily pronounced them fit, they moved to the table.

Unlike his whip-thin older brother, Ham was a sturdy boy with a cherub's face and deviltry in his eyes. Roen noticed he wasn't wearing shoes and his hands were considerably cleaner than his feet. As soon as Ham sat, he leaned over to the empty chair designated for Roen and patted the seat.

"This is you here, Mr. Shepard. Beside me." With the unaffected aplomb of a six-year-old, he held out his hand and announced, "I'm Hamilton Salt, by the way, and I am glad to make your acquaintance."

Lily regarded her younger son with suspicion and then her gaze slid sideways to Clay. He made a show of shrugging just as if he hadn't been helping Ham master that introduction.

Roen solemnly extended his hand and shook Hamilton's. "It's a pleasure."

"You can sit now," said Ham.

"I am waiting for your mother."

"Oh." His mouth screwed up to one side while he considered this as Lily returned the chili pot to the stove.

Roen skirted the table and held out Lily's chair for her. She stared at it and then at him. A vertical frown line appeared between her eyebrows. She sat slowly, hesitantly, almost as if she anticipated the chair being pulled out from under her. That didn't happen. Roen pushed the chair closer to the table.

Ham watched this all with naked curiosity. "She'll just get up again," he said. "She always does."

"Hush," Lily whispered, and under the table, Hannah kicked him.

"Ow!" He glared at his sister. "Why'd you do that?"

"Because Lizzie's legs are too short."

It was true, but it was hardly the answer Ham was looking for. He settled into his seat and tucked his legs under him. He was quiet until Roen took his seat and then he announced, "We pray now," and bent his head over dimpled hands folded into a single fist.

Roen bowed his head. The prayer was familiar, one he had learned as a child, but he chose to mouth the words rather than give voice to them with the rest of the family.

As soon as every "amen" was said, Ham reached for the pan of cornbread. Lily lightly tapped him on the back of his hand with the bowl of her spoon. "I should let you burn your fingers. We serve our guest first." She slipped a turner into the pan and removed a square of cornbread. Roen raised his chili bowl toward her and she set the bread neatly on the lip. She did the same for Ham and herself and then let Hannah serve Lizzie and Clay.

"Go on," Lily said, tipping her head in Roen's direction. "Tuck in." She saw him nod, but she also noticed he did not take his first bite until she had. She acquitted him of suspecting that she was trying to poison him. His reticence was born of good manners, and while she was grateful for what he was demonstrating to her children, it made her distinctly uncomfortable. She wasn't used to this deference and doubted that she deserved it.

Lily's throat felt thick. She choked down the first mouthful of chili and was grateful that no one noticed her distress. It faded with the second bite and was nothing at all by the third.

"There's plenty more," she told Ham as he shoveled chili and cornbread into his mouth. "Slow down."

"It's good, Ma. Real good."

"I'm happy to hear it. Now slow down."

Out of the corner of his eye, Roen saw Ham dutifully slow the lift of his spoon to his mouth but not the size of his bite. Aware that Lily Salt was watching him now, Roen took care not to smile. Amusement would not have been appreciated just then.

"Your chili is excellent," he said. "A family recipe?"

"No. Mrs. Butterworth's. If you take your meals at the hotel, you've met her."

He nodded. "Ah, yes. Ellie. The owner's wife."

Clay spoke around a mouthful of cornbread. "She's the sheriff's mother. Did you know that?"

"I believe she mentioned that," he said, his voice a tad dry. "Several times."

"Well, she's that proud," said Lily. "And no one faults her for it. Sheriff Ben is good people."

"I've had the pleasure." Roen guided another spoonful of chili to his mouth. The aroma teased his senses. "He welcomed me, took me around to meet the shopkeepers and the gentlemen who manage the land office."

"Dave and Ed Saunders."

"Yes. The brothers. They've been helpful providing me with maps and plotting boundaries."

Clay said, "Mr. Shepard was looking at Double H land this afternoon, but I told him that Ol' Harrison Hardy isn't going to fool with the railroad."

Lily raised a single eyebrow and regarded her son with a seriously set mien. "Maybe. Maybe not. That's business between Mr. Hardy and Mr. Shepard."

As a reprimand, Roen thought it was a mild one, but nevertheless Clay ducked his head and nodded.

Lily served another square of cornbread to Roen. "How long will you be staying in

Frost Falls, Mr. Shepard?"

For all that the question was politely posed and made with an offering of sweet cornbread, Roen had the sense that if his answer was more than a few more days, it would be too long. Unless she was anticipating that he would be a frequent dinner guest, Roen couldn't imagine why it mattered. "It's never clear this early," he said, hedging. "It's hard to project a timeline at this juncture, and Northeast Rail has hired me on to see this through."

"But roughly," said Lily.

"I'll know better inside of six weeks."

"Oh."

Roen could see nothing in the placid composition of her delicate features to indicate that she was aggrieved; yet he couldn't shake the feeling that she was. Her children, on the other hand, appeared to be delighted.

Hannah said, "So you'll hardly be a visitor to Frost Falls. More like regular folk."

"I suppose that's true."

"Oh, it is. Especially since you're staying in Sheriff Ben's house, or what used to be his house, and not taking a room at the Butterworth."

Lily frowned at her daughter. "And just how do you know so much about it?"

Hannah shrugged. "It's like you say. Everyone here knows everything."

Lily felt her cheeks warm. It was her own voice she heard in Hannah's ironic tones. Her daughter was a perfect mimic. "Yes, well, you don't have to repeat everything you hear."

"No, ma'am."

Roen said, "Northeast Rail is renting the sheriff's house for the duration of my stay. I spend a lot of time in hotels and railroad cars, so this is a welcome change."

Clay said, "Sheriff Ben likes having someone living in the house. He told me. I work for him sometimes. Me and my friend Frankie Fuller. Odd jobs mostly. I'm real good at a lot of things. So is Frankie." He tilted his head to the side as he regarded his guest. "You ever have a need for an odd jobber?"

"Clay." Lily said his name quietly, without inflection, but he nevertheless sat back in his chair as though pushed. "This is supper, and Mr. Shepard is your guest. You can talk business after over cigars and port when the rest of us retire to the front room."

Her response was so unexpected that Clay's jaw went slack. Hannah stared at her mother. Lizzie and Ham looked at each other with identical frowns. For his part,

Roen threw back his head and gave a shout of laughter.

Lily took this all in, nodded faintly, satisfied, and smiled in a way that suggested she had swallowed a secret.

Chapter Three

Roen Shepard wasn't sure why Lily's *Mona Lisa* smile came to him off and on that evening and again the following morning as he took his seat in church. Because of Ham's chatter and Hannah's shushing, Roen was aware when the Salts took their usual place in the last pew. He didn't turn to acknowledge them, presuming that Lily would not appreciate the attention. She struck him as an isolated individual and one who was not unhappy about it. Her children, on the other hand, were creatures of the never-met-a-stranger variety, and he couldn't help but wonder if they took after their father in that regard. Except to tell him that Jeremiah Salt had operated a forge and perished in a fire, Amanda Springer had nothing else to say about the man, and Roen hadn't minded in the least back then. Now, upon meeting the family, he found that he was curious.

No one spoke of Jeremiah Salt at supper. They either thought Roen already knew the story or didn't think the absence of a father and husband was important enough to mention. As with so many things he contemplated from time to time, the matter of Jeremiah Salt was likely to remain as persistently annoying as a pebble in his shoe. He wished to hell he knew why.

His interest in a dead man didn't make sense to him. He generally concentrated on the living. He'd learned early on that his job was made easier when the locals understood what he was doing and how the railroad figured to improve their lives and their livelihood. There were always skeptics and folks who resisted change, but he was a good listener and made it a practice to look for compromise. Clay's information, offhandedly offered, about Harrison Hardy and the Double H land was something worth knowing early, and Clay Salt, at twelve years old, was likely a superior source of intelligence to Amanda Springer. He genuinely meant to be helpful. Certainly he lacked the older woman's guile.

Maybe, Roen thought, that's why he wanted to know what sort of man Clay's father was. In his experience, it never hurt to know how far the apple fell from the tree.

When the service was over, he turned toward the back of the church. As expected, Lily and her children were among the first to leave, pausing only long enough to pass pleasantries with the minister. Roen didn't realize he was staring after them until Ben Madison nudged his elbow and spoke so softly that only he could hear.

"Careful Lily doesn't take notice of your interest."

Surprised, Roen gave a small start. "What?" He blinked, collected himself, and turned his head to the sheriff. "Oh. I was hoping Clay would look back this way. He asked me if I had need of an odd jobber."

Ben flashed a quicksilver grin and repeated dryly, "Odd jobber."

"That's what he said, which I took to mean a person who does odd jobs. He told me you hire him and another boy for that purpose."

"Uh-huh. Frankie Fuller. Good workers, the both of them. Why, do have some work for him?"

"I've been thinking I might. I have some modest regrets about firing my last assistant. I've never worked with anyone as young as Clay Salt, but I could train him, and I have a feeling he'd be a quicker study than Joe Watson was."

Ben looked around and saw the congregation had thinned considerably. He picked up his hat from where it lay on the pew and set it on his unruly thatch of carrot-colored hair. "You want to join me at the hotel for dinner? My wife had to make a call on Bob Washburn this morning and she told me that she expected to be there a spell. I'm on my own. We can talk about this idea you have for Clay there. I'd like to hear more."

"All right. I'd like that. Thank you."

After making their farewells to the minister, Roen and Ben headed diagonally across the wide main street to the Butterworth Hotel. Ellie's greeting was equally enthusiastic toward both men, though Roen thought her green eyes sparkled a bit more brightly when she regarded her son. She was a handsome woman in her fifties, and all indications were still there that she had been even lovelier in her youth. She had a warm smile and a lively energy that transcended her fine features and made the most curmudgeonly of hotel guests uncommonly good-natured.

Ellie seated them next to a window that faced the side street and their respective homes. The house Roen rented from the sheriff was a pleasant two-story frame home painted white with blue shutters, while the house next door where Ben lived with his doctor wife was similarly constructed but butter yellow from the top to bottom.

Ben took off his hat before his mother cuffed him for wearing it to the table. Grinning cheekily, he hooked it on the spindle of the empty chair on his left. Ellie told them the specials, they ordered, and then she left them alone.

Ben leaned back and stretched his long legs under the table. He looked askance at Roen. "She likes you. I can tell. Maybe you already noticed that her good opinion goes a long way around here. She accepts you, folks accept you."

"I did notice. And, well, I like her."

Ben nodded. "Most days I like her just fine, especially when she remembers not to hug me within an inch of my life in public. It's not dignified, I say, but that point is lost on her."

"I imagine your mother harbors worry and pride in equal measure every time she sees you, and probably just as often when she doesn't." Roen looked pointedly at Ben's holstered weapon. "Your position in Frost Falls is not precisely without hazard. Have you had occasion to use that?"

"My Peacemaker? I have."

"There you go."

Ben's blue eyes narrowed ever so slightly.

"Has Ellie been talking to you?"

"Maybe you haven't noticed, but your mother talks to everyone."

"You know what I mean. About me. Has she been talking to you about me?"

Roen was saved from answering by the arrival of a young woman carrying a pot of coffee. He moved his cup and saucer a few inches to the side to make it easier for her to pour and thanked her when she'd finished. She offered a small smile that was as timid as her downcast, almond-shaped eyes and then moved to Ben's side to pour.

"Mornin', Fedora. Smells like the coffee's fresh."

"It always is for you."

He chuckled and raised his cup to Roen. "There are benefits to having my mother here." He looked up at Fedora, who was standing at his elbow waiting for his approval. Taking a careful sip of the hot brew, he told her it was excellent. She left as silently as she'd come. Ben watched Roen's gaze slide sideways as he watched her go.

"You've met Miss Chen, haven't you?" asked Ben. "Or should I have introduced you?"

"No, I know who she is." He picked up his coffee cup but didn't drink. He regarded Ben over the rim. "I'm not sure she's spoken above a dozen words to me in all the time I've been coming here. I'm fairly certain she avoids my table. That she attended me today has everything to do with you. At first I thought she was merely shy, and that's part of it, but I'm coming to the opinion that it's more than that." He took a mouthful of coffee that was pleasantly warm all the way down and set his cup aside. "I've been wondering if I've done something to offend her."

"The truth?"

"Please."

Ben also set his cup down. He said candidly, "Your presence here offends her."

Roen's dark eyebrows arched symmetrically as his head reared back a fraction. "Here? In this hotel?"

"Here. In Frost Falls."

"What? Why?"

"It's not you specifically. It's who you represent."

"Northeast Rail?"

"More generally the railroad. Any railroad." Ben nodded as he watched Roen's features clear of confusion. The penny had finally dropped.

"Because she's Chinese," Roen said flatly.

"Good. You noticed. I was beginning to question your powers of observation."

Roen's mouth twisted sardonically and allowed that to speak for him.

"Sorry," said Ben.

"You're not."

"Maybe a little."

"That's more like it." Roen lifted his cup and drank. "I take it Miss Chen's family came here when the Central Pacific was hiring."

"Hiring," Ben repeated without inflection. "That'd be the word they used. The fact that they paid a wage is all that kept it from being slavery. That's not a widely held view, but it's my view. It's a sure thing that Fedora has the same perspective."

"She was born here?"

"Yes, not in Frost Falls, but in the country. Her grandfather and father came here back in the sixties. Her grandfather was killed working for the Central. Her father survived, married, and raised his family somewhere in Utah until they were all but driven out. They resettled in Colorado; Mr. Chen took up with the railroad again, this time the Union Pacific, and now with his two sons. The way I understand it is that a few years later, Fedora was the only family member to survive an outbreak of influenza that ran rampant through the railroad community."

Roen exhaled slowly. The tightness in his chest eased only marginally. He said quietly, "It must have been extraordinarily difficult for her."

"Yes."

Roen waited, but it was all Ben would say on the matter. "Thank you for telling me. It probably won't matter, but I'll tread even more carefully."

"You're right. It probably won't matter, but it won't hurt. She hasn't been here long, less than a year, and there are folks who aren't happy about it. Some don't want her serving them, so she's naturally skittish. Ellie won't have it, though there's not a lot she can do about it."

"I suppose even her good opinion has its limits."

"I guess it does. Can't say that it stops her from pushing at those limits. My mother has Fedora firmly under her wing, which is not bad, all things considered." Ben's eyes shifted from Roen to a point beyond his shoulder. "Here she comes," he said under his breath.

Roen didn't know if Ben meant his mother or Fedora. The wisest course was not to inquire and risk being overheard.

It was Fedora Chen who approached their table balancing two plates heaped with roast beef, potatoes, and carrots on one forearm and carrying the coffeepot in her other hand. She set the pot down and then carefully placed the plates in front of Roen and Ben. Both men thanked her. Her response was the same small smile accompanied by downcast eyes. She poured more coffee, swept the pot away, and disappeared.

Ben savored the aroma of the beef as he lifted it to his mouth. He swore he could taste it before it reached his tongue. "So tell me about this conversation you had with Clay Salt. I reckon it happened when he followed you out to your work site yesterday."

Roen didn't try to hide his surprise. "You know about that?"

Ben shrugged modestly. "I try to keep abreast of the comings and goings of folks, particularly the rascals."

"Clay is certainly one of those."

"Is he? I was talking about you."

Roen laughed and swallowed at the same time. "You might have waited until I cleared the potato to say that. I almost choked. Your wife warned me that you like to amuse yourself."

"She did? Of course she did. She thinks I'm a rascal, too."

"True."

"So about Clay . . . he stopped by my office to see if I had something for him to do. I didn't, so he said he was going to go out to where you were working and watch, see what he could learn about surveying. I told him not to pester you. Did he?"

"No. I didn't know he was there until I was getting ready to pack up. How did he know I'd gone out?"

"He lives close to the livery. You hired a pack horse, didn't you?" When Roen nodded, he went on. "I imagine he saw you leave. Truth is, I think he would have been disappointed if I'd had work for him. He was so clearly wanting to be on his way that he was twitching in his shoes." Ben speared two carrots. "What is it that you think he can do for you?"

"Pack and carry. Keep the horse settled. Help me sight my marks. Act as a guide, a scout, if you will. The Saunders brothers provided me with good maps, but sometimes what I'm looking for hasn't been recorded yet. Clay indicated that he knows the area. He could be an asset."

"Clay would tell you he knows every crater and hillock on the dark side of the moon if he thought it would get him a job with the railroad."

"Hmm. Well, I'm an independent contractor. He'd be working for me, not Northeast."

"Close enough." Ben paused to get Fedora Chen's attention when she passed through the door from the kitchen to the dining room. He asked her for bread and butter when she reached the table and then spent the next thirty seconds alternately listening to her apology and promising her that her oversight did not mean she would be fired.

"I'm not sure she believes you," said Roen when she'd finally left, hurrying away as though hungry dogs were nipping at her heels.

"I'm sure she doesn't. She will, though . . . eventually."

They ate in silence for as long as it took the basket of warm bread to arrive accompanied by a small plate of sweet cream butter. It was not Miss Chen, but Ellie who delivered the bread and butter. She placed both on the table and then looked from Ben to Roen and back to Ben. She did not need to set her hands on her hips to communicate that she was aggrieved.

Ellie looked around quickly to make certain she had not attracted notice. Nevertheless, she spoke in a tone not much above a whisper. "What did you say to her?" she asked her son.

"Me? I asked her for bread and butter."

Ellie turned her head and arched an eyebrow at Roen. "Then what did you say to her?"

Roen was glad he'd set his knife and fork down. He raised his hands, palms out.

Ben said, "Not a word, Ma. He didn't say a word."

"Then why is she sobbing into her apron? Mrs. Vandergrift has no patience for her on a good day, and this is not a good day. The oven's too hot and the piecrusts aren't flaky enough to suit her. You know who she's blaming, don't you?"

"You?" Ben asked hopefully. He ducked when she swung, but he wasn't quick enough and she caught him on the back of his head anyway. He was grinning when he straightened. "You have to stop that, Ma." He rubbed the back of his head. "I'm going to arrest you for assault one of these days."

"Uh-huh. Behave yourself or I'll hug you. You decide." Ellie turned her gaze on Roen. His hands were still raised and she batted them down. She appreciated that he was struggling manfully not to laugh. "I suppose you don't give your mother reason to cuff you."

Roen answered with all the gravity he could muster. He did not want this woman doubting his sincerity. "I give her plenty of reason, but I duck and run better than your son."

Ellie smiled. "Good for you. Now. Tell me what happened. Not you, Ben. I want to hear it from Mr. Shepard."

"It's as Ben said. He asked for bread and butter. Miss Chen began to apologize profusely for forgetting to bring it to the table. Your son tried to reassure her that it wasn't a criticism and no harm was done. Ben promised her that her job was not in jeopardy."

"Oh, Lord." Ellie turned back to her son. "Did she mention being fired first or did you bring it up?"

Ben frowned slightly as he went back over the conversation. "I think I said it first. She was so distressed I figured that's what she was thinking."

Now Ellie did set her hands on her hips. "The next time you think you know what a woman's thinking, you remind yourself you have no earthly idea. Do you understand?"

"Yes, ma'am," he said dutifully. "No earthly idea."

"That's right. You planted that notion in Fedora's head."

"Is there something I can do to make it right?"

Ellie's hands fell to her sides. "You're a good man, Ben, but unless you're willing to escort Mrs. Vandergrift out of here before I have words with her, I'll take care of everything." She started to go, stopped, and turned back. "Is your meal satisfactory?"

It was Roen who answered. "Better than satisfactory. Quite as good as any fare I've had in Manhattan."

Ellie's eyes crinkled at the corners as her smile deepened. "Thank you. There's something I can tell the cook that she will find most gratifying."

When she was gone, Ben picked up his fork and waggled it at Roen. "As good as you've had in Manhattan? You understand I'm skeptical."

Roen shrugged. "It's true."

"Isn't Delmonico's in Manhattan?"

"It is, but I've never eaten there. Mostly I do my own cooking when I'm in the city, or if I'm having dinner with my family, well, there's some trial and error involved there. A lot of experimentation with spices. My mother is as creative a cook as she is a painter, but the food is often more interesting than good."

Ben hesitated as he raised his fork to his mouth. A small crease appeared in the space between his eyebrows. "Your mother's a painter?"

"Hmm."

"Shepard." Ben repeated the name mostly to himself, rolled it over on his tongue. "Anne Shepard?"

"Yes. You know her work?" Roen hadn't expected that. His mother was well known, even celebrated, in New York and Paris. But Frost Falls?

"I do. Jackson Brewer, the sheriff before me, took his wife to Paris a few years back and sent some postcards. One of them was of a painting that caught his eye in a museum he visited. He said he liked it especially because the artist was an American. His wife liked it because the artist was a woman. I still have it. Use it as a bookmark, if you want to see it."

"No. I know which one it is. *Children at Play.*"

"I thought it was called *Hide and Seek.*"

"That's the popular name for it. Mother simply titled it *Children at Play.*"

"Huh. *Hide and Seek* suits it better, if you don't mind me saying."

"I agree with you. So does my mother."

"It's a clever painting," said Ben. "Admittedly I've only seen the postcard, but besides the obvious children running to their hiding places, I was able to spot two more hiding in tree branches."

"There are five hiding. Even in the painting they are hard to see, but once found, you can't unsee them."

"Any of them you?"

"No," Roen said. The lie was force of habit. He was in several of his mother's paintings along with his brother, two sisters, and a cousin. She'd been interested in them as children but stopped painting each of them around the time they turned twelve. Since he was the youngest, he was last to disappear from her body of work.

"Do you paint?" asked Ben.

"Tried and failed. Too much detail and not enough imagination." He marveled that he could say this as a statement of fact, without rancor. That hadn't always been the case. "Good for practical applications like designing bridges but not for paint on a canvas."

"I don't know," said Ben, looking doubtful. "Seems like designing a bridge would take plenty of imagination."

Roen shrugged. "It's mostly math."

"Uh-huh. Right." Ben buttered a slice of bread and resumed eating. "Clay's pretty clever himself, but I guess you figured that out."

"I did. He had a lot of questions on the

way back to town."

"He's a good student. If he works for you, it can't interfere with his schooling. His mother won't approve it if it does."

"I'm not surprised. Mrs. Springer spoke to me about her."

Suspicious, Ben cheeked his bite of bread and asked, "She did?"

"She told me something about everyone. Cornered me in church the first time I attended."

Ben swallowed. "Gossip is Amanda Springer's specialty, best taken with more than a few grains of salt."

"I used a shaker."

"Good for you." Ben folded his bread and used it to sop gravy from his plate. "She must have failed to pump you for information, otherwise I'd have already known about your mother."

"I diverted her with railroad talk. Jobs. The men I'd be hiring, local and from neighboring towns. It's just good business. She told me she owns the butcher shop. An army marches on its stomach. Likewise, full bellies build railroads. Mrs. Springer understands that."

"She's a savvy businesswoman and an honest one. You can depend on her for fair prices and good product."

That was Roen's sense also, but he was glad to have it confirmed. "About Clay . . . what do you suggest is the best way to approach his mother? How much of a factor is the money that Clay will bring home?"

"Money's never much motivated Lily," said Ben. "Not that I've ever seen. She was a couple of grades ahead of me in school and smart as a whip, but she missed a fair amount because she took care of her mother — a woman who was perpetually ailing or claimed she was. I lost touch with Lily for a lot of years but caught up again when I moved from the ranch into town and became Sheriff Brewer's deputy. She does all right for herself and her family, but I know that what she cares about is that her children get a good education and make what they can of that."

"I can offer Clay a better than good education working alongside me."

Ben did not offer encouragement. He leveled serious eyes on Roen and said, "Then you better be ready to tell Lily about that."

Chapter Four

Lily Salt did not look up from her work when she heard someone knock at the front door. She continued to deftly rip out the side seam in Abigail Saunders's cornflower blue dress, the same one she had altered a month earlier. Abigail was increasing at what Lily considered an alarming rate, some of it on account of the baby, but most of it on account of Abigail's craving for crullers and her husband's indulgence in getting them for her.

"See who's at the door, Lizzie."

Lizzie, who was playing a memory card game on the floor at her mother's feet, leapt up and darted like a water sprite from the parlor to the door. Her cap of yellow curls bounced like springs. In preparation for greeting the visitor, she patted her hair before she set her hand on the doorknob.

"But don't let whoever it is in until I say," Lily called after her. "Unless it's Mrs. Fish."

"I know, Mama."

Lizzie turned the knob and pushed at the door. She positioned herself in the narrow opening and stared up at Roen Shepard, her eyes wide, her mouth parted in a perfect O.

"Hello, Lizzie."

Lizzie did not return his greeting. She shut the door on him and ran back to the parlor. "It's Mr. Shepard, Mama. What should I do?"

Lily's hand stilled. Her fingers tightened on the seam ripper but she did not set it aside. Mustering calm, she said, "That depends on what he wants. Did you ask him?"

"No."

"Then do that."

Lizzie hurried back to the door. Roen was standing exactly as he had been, just as if she hadn't rudely closed the door in his face. "Clay's in school," she announced.

"I thought he would be. Hannah and Ham, too, I imagine."

Nodding, Lizzie opened the door a little wider but made no move to invite him inside. "I'm supposed to ask why you're here."

"There's something I'd like to discuss with your mother. She's here, isn't she?"

Lizzie hesitated and then nodded. "She's working on a dress for Mrs. Saunders." She shut the door again and retreated to the parlor, where she parted the curtains at the front window and peered out at an angle where she could see Roen. "He's just standing there," she told her mother. "I told him Clay's in school and you're working, but he's just standing there."

"Lizzie, come away from the window before he sees you. What does he want?"

"He wants to talk to you."

"Yes, but what about?"

Sighing heavily, Lizzie went back to the door, this time dragging her feet. She stood in the opening and asked, "What about?"

Roen blinked. "Pardon?"

"Mama wants to know what about."

"Ah. Well, about a job. For Clay." This time when she began to close the door, Roen inserted his foot. "Please. Not again."

"All right, but you can't come in. Not yet. Not until Mama says you can."

"I understand."

Lizzie looked him over as if she could divine the truth of that, and then, deciding she could, she retreated and relayed the message to her mother.

"A job?" Lily frowned, puzzling over that. She set the seam ripper on the table at her side and nodded once to her daughter. It was hard to move her next words past the lump in her throat. "Go on. You can let him in."

Lizzie didn't immediately move. She watched her mother closely, saw the smile that was meant to assure but only made Lizzie's belly hurt. She couldn't have explained why that was exactly, just that it was. She said, "I'll be right here," and she couldn't know that saying that about broke her mother's heart.

Roen was still standing with one foot in the doorway when Lizzie returned. He regarded her with a single raised eyebrow and a glimmer of amusement playing about his mouth.

"You can come in," she said importantly. "Mama said so."

"Thank you." He stepped inside, closed the door behind him, and followed Lizzie into the parlor. He was struck immediately by the cheerfulness of the room, or perhaps dumbstruck. It was unexpected, given the homey practicality of the kitchen. Two tall windows fronted the parlor, and sunshine poured through the open drapery. Roen suspected that even on a dreary day, there was enough color in the room to suggest the arc of a rainbow. A plump, ruby velvet sofa sat just beyond the beam of sunlight so it was in no danger of fading. Two ball-and-claw chairs had damask seat covers in royal blue. The area rug, where Lizzie was already sitting cross-legged and turning over cards, was patterned in repeating prism shapes that reminded him of looking through a kaleidoscope. There was an emerald velvet overstuffed chair that complemented the sofa in design, if not in color. All of the pieces were gently worn, lending the parlor a certain warmth that did not require a fire in the fireplace. There were no photographs on any of the tables or arranged across the length of the mantel. In places where he might have seen them, there were short stacks of books. The family had an interesting assortment of histories, anthologies, and thick reference tomes, interspersed with dime novels and children's literature. Roen suspected the Salts were frequent visitors to the town's library because the breadth of the collection represented varying interests and a great deal of money. He took all of this in while standing under the wide archway, but it wasn't until his eyes alighted on Lily Salt that his attention was fixed.

She sat unmoving in a rocker, sunlight spilling over her shoulder, illuminating the cornflower blue dress spread across her lap and draping her legs. She was flanked by an end table on her left and a large canvas carryall on her right. The table held a lamp and an open box of spools. Pins poked a wrist cushion and needles lay safely side by side in a cardboard case. The carryall was overflowing with material, though whether it was fabric remnants or garments in need of repair, he couldn't tell.

Touched by the sun, Lily's hair was shaded more toward red than rust, and highlighted silver threads at her temples. He wondered at the silver because she was still a young woman and her coloring did not seem to lend itself to premature graying. She wore her hair loosely pulled back from her face and coiled in a topknot. It was slightly askew, but the effect was charming, not untidy. For some reason, Roen wanted to smile. He thought better of it when her chin came up as if she was daring him.

"Thank you for seeing me," he said. He had his hat in hand and bowed his head slightly. He did not assume he could take a seat and waited for an invitation or an opening where he could ask to sit.

"Pardon me for not getting up to greet you properly," Lily said. She indicated the table, the carryall, and Lizzie at her feet to show she was hemmed in.

Roen heard no apology in her tone and her gesture was merely an explanation. He had the sense that she was more at ease in the rocker than out of it, and as he had no wish to add to her discomfort, he graciously accepted her at her word. "Please, don't give it another thought. I don't hold with ceremony. As the intruder here, I am already out of bounds." He took Lily's silence as agreement. The cheerful parlor was decidedly chilly now. "I believe Lizzie explained why I'm here. Did she?"

Lizzie's head came up, proof she was listening to every word. "About a job for Clay."

Lily leaned forward and touched the crown of her daughter's head. Her fingers ruffled Lizzie's feathery curls. "Mr. Shepard knows you did," she said while pinning Roen in place with her narrowing, blue-green eyes. "You're a good girl."

Pleased with herself, Lizzie ducked her head to escape her mother's fingers and returned to the pretense of playing with her cards.

Lily sat back and folded her hands in her lap. "Well?" she asked.

Well, indeed, Roen thought. She was giving no quarter. There was nothing for it but to go straight to the point of his visit. "I have some work for Clay. He mentioned that he did odd jobs for the sheriff and it got me thinking. I spoke to Ben after church and he gave Clay good marks for his work."

"That was three days ago. You must be doing a powerful lot of thinking on it."

"I have," he said truthfully. "There's his age to consider. He's only twelve."

"Only?"

Roen thought it was interesting that she bristled on behalf of her son. She might have objections to Clay working, but for him to be dismissed because of his age was objectionable. "Twelve going on twenty," said Roen, seeking to regain a foothold.

"Yes, but you've spent very little time with Clay. I'm surprised you noticed." Her eyes kept him pinned. "Unless . . ." What she was going to say remained a thought.

Roen picked up the trail. "Unless I've had time with him that you don't know about?" he asked. "Is that what you were going to say?"

"It was. I didn't go on because I think I know my son. He would have told me or at least dropped enough hints to give himself away."

"I want to be clear," said Roen. "I haven't seen Clay since Sunday, and then only as you all were leaving church." His eyes purposely strayed to the nearest ball-and-claw chair. "May I?" he asked, indicating the chair with a sweep of his hat. It was a risk to pose the question; she might turn him down and turn him away. She didn't, though. Following a brief hesitation, she nodded. Roen slid onto the chair and carefully released a breath he hardly knew he'd been holding.

Lily arched an eyebrow. "Are you all right, Mr. Shepard? If I may be frank, you look ill at ease, and I thought, what with you wearing a suit today and presenting yourself in a parlor instead of a kitchen, you'd be comfortable in your skin. I'm not sure you are."

Roen regarded her with equal candor. "You're not wrong. I know I am not welcome, so I would say that accounts for it. Perhaps a suit of armor would improve my comfort, but what I'm wearing now is inadequate to the task."

Lily felt heat rush to her cheeks, but she did not look away. In her lap, her folded hands tightened. "I deserve that because it's true," she said quietly. "You are not welcome. I don't know you and I don't care to know you. You're simply passing through. As I'm sure you're aware, I've been a widow almost two years, and you are not the first snake oil salesman or whiskey drummer or railroad front man to make a fuss over one of my children in order to insinuate himself into my life. I'm not flattering myself; there is nothing flattering about the attention I've received. You can deny that is your motive, and perhaps you'll be stating the truth, but I won't believe you. History is an excellent teacher and I am a good student."

Roen carefully considered his words before he spoke. He was comfortable with his silence. Lily Salt, he observed, was not. Her clasped hands had loosened and she was tapping her fingers ever so slightly. "Ben Madison told me you and he were in school at the same time. He said you were whip smart, and I have no reason to doubt the truth of that since I'm still feeling the sting. I am not going to deny an interest in you since, as you have indicated, it would be a waste of breath. I have an urge to apologize on behalf of all the salesmen and railroad front men, but upon reflection, I believe it would be an insult to you. You have demonstrated beyond any doubt in my mind that you are eminently capable of keeping any man at arm's length."

His eyes dropped to the tic in her cheek as she clenched and unclenched her jaw. He didn't think she realized she was doing it. If they had been playing poker, it would have been a tell. In a way, it still was. For all that her words were cutting, he believed they were a bluff. That muscle working in her exposed her vulnerability.

"I don't know where this leaves Clay. I have a genuine offer to propose, and Ben led me to believe you would consider it. That makes me wonder if Ben knows about the men who come calling on you."

"He knows," she said. "There's not much that happens in Frost Falls that Ben doesn't know firsthand. He's run a couple of my would-be suitors out of town, and it gave him pleasure to do so, but if he encouraged you to bring your offer to me, then he's coming to understand that I'm able to manage with out his help or he thinks well enough of you that he's anticipating I'll come around to a similar opinion."

"Why can't it be both?" Roen meant the question sincerely, but he didn't expect a response. He observed that her fingers ceased their drumming and there was no more movement in her cheek, but it was not until she unclasped her hands and set them on the arms of the rocker that he thought she might have stopped seeing him as a threat.

"Tell me about your offer of work for my son."

Roen merely nodded, careful not to show any pleasure in his small victory. "Of course," he said, and launched into an explanation of the duties Clay would perform as his assistant. "He'll act as my guide some of the time. You said yourself that he knows the lay of the land. His familiarity is firsthand knowledge, but I'll be teaching him how to read the maps that Dave and Ed Saunders provided for me as well as the ones I brought from New York. This is more than simply getting to a place. I have to factor elevation, slope, and the roadbed before I can confidently recommend a route to the company. There are other considerations such as the location of depots, drainage, and right-of-ways. I can teach Clay all about that as I go forward. Trestles will have to be constructed where none exist now. The Rockies present challenges like no other, but Northeast is only looking for a new spur to Stonechurch. Northeast doesn't want to cross the range, only put down rails that match the gauge of the track coming up from Denver."

"Why not lay the new rails along the same route as the one that already exists?"

"That was the first question I had to answer. I spent most of my first week here on horseback riding alongside the tracks, and that was after taking the train to make my initial observations. The answer is that there are too many places where the route isn't wide enough to accommodate a second, wider track, and tearing up the current track to lay new rail would disrupt service for months."

When Roen saw Lily nod her understanding, he went on. "Northeast didn't lay the rails that go through Falls Hollow and on to Stonechurch. The track was laid for expediency, to get the silver ore from the mines to Denver. The rails hug the mountains, which made sense because the engines at that time could not climb the steeper grades. Narrow gauge was often used because of the difficult terrain, but there was no uniformity in the track gauge among the competing railroads so the cars had to be offloaded at various switching points. All of those companies are bankrupt now, most of them bought out by Northeast. Northeast entered into an agreement with Stonechurch Mining to improve service to the business and the town."

"Stonechurch Mining *is* the town," said Lily.

"You've been there?"

She shook her head. "Reputation is all I know about it."

"Well, it's true. What is good for the mining operation is good for the town, and Northeast is eager to increase its presence here in Colorado." He saw Lily looked doubtful, but he didn't know why. "Do you have questions?"

"Is your work dangerous?"

"Maybe, if I poke my eye with a pencil that I'm trying to put behind my ear."

"Blasting?" she asked.

"That's a long way off, and Clay wouldn't be allowed anywhere close to it."

"If my son's curious enough, he'll find a way."

"Then I'll keep him on a leash." He smiled slightly as he said it, and she smiled as well. Small inroads, he thought. He was also learning the lay of the land.

"I'm guessing that you'll want him during school hours," said Lily. "It's starting to get dark earlier."

"Yes, but I won't ask him to accompany me every time I go out. He'll take care of the particulars, getting the horses from the livery, packing my instruments, and recommending a route when I tell him what I want to see." Roen moved the hat in his lap to a nearby table. He leaned forward and rested his forearms on his thighs. "I am going to teach him about building lasting structures, Mrs. Salt. There will be book learning; he'll have to study. There will be calculations, formulas. He'll be using basic algebra, geometry, and trigonometry. If he shows aptitude, there will be calculus."

His posture was meant to engage Lily, but he watched her press her lips together. Uncertainty returned to her eyes.

"I don't know what that is," she said.

"Calculus?"

"Yes. And the other thing you mentioned before that."

"Trigonometry."

She nodded.

"They are methods of mathematics for assuring the correct height of a bridge, how much weight it can support, and whether it can be built at all. Mathematics is used to factor the cost. I don't want to climb canyons if I can connect them at the gap."

"Clay has a head for numbers."

"I thought he might. He was interested in the ones I showed him. He didn't understand what he saw, but he seemed keen to learn."

"The symbols intrigued him. He took out a book from the library, but what he's learned so far is the Greek alphabet."

Roen chuckled. "Many of those letters are used as mathematical symbols. He's making a good beginning. I had no idea." He sat back in his chair. "Does he get his aptitude for math from his father?" The question was hardly out of his mouth when he saw Lily bristle. Before he could correct what he now realized was a mistake, she was making sure he knew he was wrong.

"Why do you assume that?"

The way her delicate chin jutted forward, Roen knew she was daring him to lie to her. He didn't. "There was only one woman in my applied mathematics class at the Institute and only a handful in the general student population."

"So you take those impoverished numbers as evidence that women do not possess the aptitude for mathematics when it is more likely that what they lack is opportunity."

"I won't make that error in judgment again." He paused a beat, and because he couldn't seem to help himself, he added on a dry note, "Not in your presence at any rate."

One corner of Lily's mouth lifted in a scornful smile. "Did you mean for me to hear that?"

"I suppose I did, since I said it."

"Are you reckoned to be a wit back in New York?" she asked pointedly. "Or a half-wit?"

"The latter," he said without hesitation. "I accept it."

The other corner of Lily's mouth tilted upward, and scorn was no longer there in the shape of her lips.

"You ought not to look amused," he said. "I am not to be encouraged. Everyone in my family says so."

"Indeed, you are not."

Roen watched her primly set her lips. It should have put him off, but the effect of that butter-wouldn't-melt mouth was incongruent with the gleam in her eye. He preferred to study the gleam and, for once, ignore her mouth.

"It's you, then, who has a head for figures," he said.

"Yes. And little opportunity to advance my learning." She said this without heat or bitterness. It was merely a statement of fact.

"And if you had the opportunity?"

Lily shook her head and waved the question aside without answering.

"Mrs. Salt?" he asked. "If you had the opportunity?"

"I save my dreams for my children," she said quietly. "I have lots of reasons to hope there."

Roen guessed she was already regretting saying as much as she did because her eyes slid sideways and she stirred uncomfortably in the rocker. Fearing she would put him out before the matter of Clay's job was settled, he did not press the question again.

To that end, he asked, "Do I have your permission to propose the job to Clay?"

"I'd like some time to think it over."

At least she was not saying no out of hand. Roen took that as a very good sign. "How much time do you need?"

"I'll send a note round to your house tomorrow. There's no call for you to come here."

He was disappointed, but upon reflection he realized he should have expected that she would not invite him back. "Of course. If you agree, where should I discuss this with Clay?"

"If I agree, Mr. Shepard, I'll send Clay with the note. If not, it will be Hannah at your door."

So either way, he could anticipate a visit before the headmaster rang the school bell. "Very good," he said. He swept his hat off the table and started to rise.

"Another moment, if you will," said Lily.

Roen sat.

"When would you want Clay to begin?"

"The day after tomorrow, if that's agreeable to both of you." He thought she would ask about compensation, and he waited for the question. When she didn't, he told her what he was prepared to offer for a day's wage.

"That's between you and Clay," she said. "And don't assume he will accept your offer out of the gate. He negotiates all the time with Ben. Every cent is dear to him, and what he doesn't insist that I accept, he saves. My son has an account at the bank, and Mr. Washburn, the manager, told me he's the youngest customer he's ever had."

It was not a boast that Roen heard but a mother's rightful pride. "Is he saving for something specific?"

"I'm not sure. He doesn't say. It doesn't matter, though, because it's his money."

Lizzie looked up from her cards. "Sometimes Clay buys candy for me, and once he bought me a pink ribbon for my hair."

"Then he's a good brother," said Roen.

Lizzie nodded. "He saved Ham in the fire. He tried to save me and Hannah, but then Sheriff Ben saved him and us."

One of Lily's hands snaked out and touched her daughter's head. Roen had no difficulty recognizing the gesture as a caution.

Lizzie screwed her bow-shaped mouth to one side and ducked out from under Lily's palm. "Everyone knows," she said in protest of the warning. "Mrs. Springer tells everyone our business. You said so."

Lily withdrew her hand. "And did I not also say you don't need to repeat everything you hear . . . or overhear?"

Lizzie's capitulation came with an audible sigh. "Yes, ma'am."

"I'll know you mean it if you remember it."

"I'll remember if we talk about it sometimes." In an aside to Roen, she said, "We never talk about it."

Roen said nothing.

Neither did Lily. Her hand returned to the rocker arm, and her grip was white-knuckled.

Roen stood, and this time Lily did not stop him. "I'll wait for your decision tomorrow. Thank you for hearing me out, Mrs. Salt. Good day, Lizzie."

Lily acknowledged his final words with a brief nod and nudged Lizzie to show him to the door. She heard him thank Lizzie and then he was gone. Lily reached for the seam ripper on the side table and bent her head to the work in her lap. It was a clear signal to Lizzie that there would be no talking about it now either.

Chapter Five

Roen was drinking coffee at the kitchen table when the knock he was expecting finally came. He was tempted to look out the window to see who was standing on the porch, whether it was Clay or Hannah, but he went straight to the door instead. He was still questioning the wisdom of putting his job proposal to Clay. Perhaps it would be better if it were Hannah waiting for him. That would be the end of it. Full stop.

The odd but undeniable attraction he felt toward Lily Salt would remain just as it was: a curiosity.

Roen opened the door. He had a glimpse of Clay's palpable excitement before the boy stopped shifting his weight from side to side and came to soldierlike attention.

"Ma said I should come here before school, that you were expecting me."

"And that's all?"

"Uh-huh. You got maybe something for

me to do? Like Sheriff Ben does? That's what I'm figuring. I told her that's probably what it was, but she never said one way or another. Silent as a spinx about it."

"Sphinx," said Roen. "Silent as a sphinx."

"Yeah, sure. One of those."

"Exactly." Roen looked over the top of Clay's head in the direction of the schoolhouse. "Do you have a few minutes before the bell?" When Clay nodded, Roen invited him inside. "This way. I was having coffee in the kitchen. Did you have breakfast?"

"Yes, sir."

"Good." Roen led the way through the parlor and his office to the kitchen at the back of the house. He pointed to the chair at a right angle to the one he took. His coffee was cooling quickly and he wrapped his hands around the mug and drank before he spoke. "I was going to suggest that we talk at the library after your school day is finished, but I suspect you won't be able to concentrate if you don't know something now."

"That's a fact," said Clay. "I sure do appreciate you suspicioning that."

Roen hid his grin behind the mug and lowered it only when he was sure he could school his features. "Yes, well, we are not so different that way." He observed that Clay seemed pleased to hear it. Roen was not so sure that it was a compliment to either of them, but he did not point this out. "Here's what I'm proposing, Clay. I want to hire you as my assistant. My odd jobber, if you will. You'll work for me mostly when school's out but there'll be occasions when you will have to miss class. That's missing class, not missing classwork. There will be plenty of that, and you'll have to keep up with all of it."

"You talked to my ma, didn't you? That classwork is her idea. Sounds like what she would say."

"I did speak to your mother, and she was clear about your education being important. I agree with her. I'm not hiring ignorance. You learn, or you leave." Roen didn't have to ask if Clay understood. The boy swallowed hard as he nodded his agreement. "Good. There are a number of ways you can be of help to me." He listed the requirements as he had explained them to Lily, this time ticking them off on his fingers. Not only did he have Clay's full attention, but it also seemed that the boy was committing every tick to memory. When he'd finished, he asked, "Do you think you can do all that?"

There was no hesitation. "Yes, sir, though

I admit that it's got me baffled some that *you* think I can."

"Let's just say you made a good first impression."

"Huh. That's interestin'. Ma says that first impressions count for something. I guess I never figured how true that was seein' as how I get so few chances to make a first impression. What I mean is, darn near everyone in Frost Falls knows me already."

Roen chuckled. "They've known you since the cradle. Is that it?"

"Yep. Bald and wrinkled and red in the face. There's probably some that still see me that way."

"It's a cross we all bear."

Clay regarded Roen suspiciously. "Are you funnin' with me now?"

"A little."

Clay thought about that. "I reckon it's okay as long as I know it and you don't mind me funnin' with you now and again."

"I don't mind."

Nodding gravely, Clay said, "Sheriff Ben doesn't mind either. I guess I wouldn't want to work for someone who minded." He added quickly, "Not that I wouldn't, you understand, just that I wouldn't want to."

"I understand. Then it's settled? You're going to work for me?"

Clay sat up a little straighter in his chair and placed his folded hands on the table. "I sure want to, Mr. Shepard, but we have to talk wages. I'd be disappointed in myself if I didn't mention it."

"I'd be disappointed in you, too." He told Clay what his daily earnings would be regardless of the number of hours. "That's for the first month. You show me that you can do what I think you can, and I'll double that."

Clay stared at him. "I don't feel right not telling you that you're offering me a man's pay."

"I know what I'm offering. I hope I know what I'm getting. Just the same, it's probably wise not to tell anyone."

"Sure, and I won't. Don't want to give folks cause to think you're foolish."

Roen almost choked as he swallowed the last of his coffee. He set the mug down. "No, we don't want that. Thank you."

Clay cocked his head toward the front of the house. "D'you hear that? School bell." He pushed his chair away from the table, stood, and then suddenly sat again. "Are we done?"

"Yes."

Clay jumped to his feet. "I sure am grateful, Mr. Shepard. You won't be sorry."

"I don't believe I will." Roen expected the boy to go then, but Clay took only a single step backward before he stopped. "Is there something else?" asked Roen. Clearly there was something niggling at the boy. "Go on. What is it?"

Clay's shoulders rose and fell on the breath he took in and slowly released. Still, he spoke in a rush. "Do you like my mother?"

"What?" Roen had heard the question but he hardly understood it. "How's that again?"

This time each word was carefully enunciated. "Do you like my mother?"

"Yes. I like her fine."

Clay shook his head. "Hard to find a person who doesn't like her. What I want to know is if you *like* her."

"I think what you want to know is whether I offered you the job because of your mother."

He considered that. "No. That's not it. I want to know if you like her. I don't think she made a good first impression, but I still have to wonder."

Roen's eyes narrowed ever so slightly. "Why did you invite me to dinner, Clay?"

Clay was spared an immediate reply because the schoolmaster rang the bell again. "I should go."

"You should answer my question. Let me help you out. Did you invite me to dinner so I could meet your mother?"

Shrugging, Clay said, "Hannah said it was the only way to make an introduction. It was her idea. You can ask her. She's been conjugating on the idea since you bought her and Lizzie that bag of candy at Hennepin's."

"Cogitating."

"What?"

"She's been cogitating . . . never mind. Has Hannah encouraged you to do something like this before? Maybe with a traveling salesman or a whiskey drummer? Maybe with another railroad front man?"

Clay stared, jaw sagging. "You know about them?"

Roen hedged. "I may have heard something."

"Mrs. Springer, I bet. Well, Ben ran them off, or my mother did, and not one of them was Hannah's idea. Mine neither. In fact, it's on account of men passing through, trying to take up with our ma, that Hannah thought she should do something. If you're known to be on the trail, it'd keep others away."

Roen felt as if his own jaw might sag. "That's your plan?"

"Like I said, more Hannah's plan."

"Good Lord."

"Uh-huh. She's somethin'."

"Somethin'."

"Can I go?"

Roen held up an index finger. "In a moment. Why me? Hannah didn't hatch this scheme solely because I bought her horehound drops and licorice whips."

"No, sir. You're right about that. She hatched it when she saw you in church. She liked your profile, at least that's what she told me. I don't see it myself, but then you can hardly expect that I would. Nobility in your profile, she said. Especially your nose." Clay squinted as he studied Roen's nose. "I guess I see that."

Roen had an urge to run his index finger down the bridge of his nose. Long and downward sloping at the tip, it was yet another feature that distinguished him from the rest of his family. His mother had remarked on more than one occasion that it was a nose that belonged on a coin. He did not thank her for the observation.

"And then there was the fact that she saw you in church," Clay said. "None of those other fellows ever went to church, and I think one of them might have been Catholic." He added this last in hushed accents as if imparting a terrible secret. “Can’t say for sure.”

“Then perhaps you shouldn’t say at all.”

Admonished, Clay shifted from foot to foot.

Roen took pity on him. “Go on. Go. We’ll talk again after school. Chores first.” He watched Clay flee the kitchen and braced himself for the sound of the front door being slammed in the wake of the boy’s haste. Instead, he heard it being quietly closed. Roen smiled. “I’ll be darned.”

Chapter Six

Roen stepped aside and held the door to allow a woman to exit the sheriff's office before he entered. It was only when a little yellow-haired girl squeezed herself out between the doorframe and her mother's skirts that Roen recognized that the woman was Lily Salt. She was wearing a straw boater pitched at a forward angle so that it shaded her eyes. It was the same hat she wore to church, but on this occasion, she'd embellished it with a yellow ribbon band and a spray of delicate blue wildflowers that he thought were forget-me-nots.

Keeping the door open with a foot, he tipped his hat. "Good afternoon, Mrs. Salt."

Lily looked up, startled. "Oh. It's you. Forgive me. I was woolgathering." She touched the top of Lizzie's head. "It's Mr. Shepard, Lizzie. Say hello."

Lizzie was already beaming. "I saw him right away, Mama. Hello!"

"Hello, Lizzie. You're looking very fine today. Is that a new dress?"

She twirled like a top, showing off her apple green dress with the miniature bustle in the back. "It was Hannah's dress first but Mama cut it down and made it all new for me. I love it." She hugged Lily's legs and thus prevented any forward movement.

Lily's tentative smile was apologetic. "Lizzie, I can't take a step. Mr. Shepard must have business here and we're keeping him from it."

"I do, but it can wait. I'd rather escort two lovely ladies to the drugstore for a fountain drink."

"That's kind of you." Her narrowed blue-green eyes said it was unfair of him. "I must decline. Lizzie and I are on our way to Mrs. Fish's to pick up a pattern and material. It's my job, Mr. Shepard."

Roen heard what she didn't say. Something along the lines of, *I'm doing my job, why aren't you doing yours?* Still thinking about what Clay had told him that morning, he discovered he had just enough rascal in him to persevere. "We'll pass the dress shop on our way back."

"Need I point out that we'll come to it before Mangold's drugstore?"

"Huh. How about that."

"Mama?" Lizzie's hugged her mother's legs a little tighter. "I would surely like a fizzy drink."

Roen held up his hands as though the gesture could absolve him of responsibility. He knew the moment Lily relented because her lips parted and she blew out a shallow breath. He grinned.

"You understand I am not amused."

"I understand." Roen couldn't rein in his grin, and when it deepened, a small dimple on the left side of his mouth was revealed. He did not miss that her gaze dropped to it. He didn't know why women found it fascinating; some were moved to comment on it, others to touch it. Most recently that woman was Victorine Headley, but as she began to take a proprietary interest in his dimple, Roen found fewer and fewer reasons to smile. Thinking about Victorine was a sure way to sour his mood, so he stopped and gave all his attention to the woman with an expression that could best be described as mulish. "We should go." He held out a hand to Lizzie, and the child immediately released her mother's legs and put her fingers against his palm. "See? That's much better." He reversed direction and escorted Lizzie forward, leaving Lily little choice but to follow. It was only a few steps before she came abreast of them.

Lizzie rattled on about what flavor fizzy drink she wanted. She didn't ask for an opinion and neither adult offered one. As near as Roen could make out, it would either be root beer and seltzer water or ginger beer mixed with the same. When they were seated at one of the small round tables close to the fountain bar, Lizzie ordered a cherry fizzy.

Roen did not anticipate sharing a chuckle with Lily Salt after having shamelessly used her daughter to engage her cooperation, yet a chuckle was precisely what they shared as their eyes met over Lizzie's small head. He liked the sound of it bubbling on her lips, the way it came up from her throat and mingled with his deeper, rumbling laughter. There was harmony, real harmony, in their agreement.

Dolly Mangold, the druggist's wife and blender of specialty teas, waited for the quiet laughter to subside. She plunged into the awkward silence that followed and took two orders for root beer fizzy drinks before she retreated behind the fountain bar.

Lily watched her go. A thin vertical crease appeared between her eyebrows.

"What is it?" asked Roen.

Lily darted a sideways look at Lizzie, who

was blowing humid breaths on the glass tabletop and then dragging a finger through the condensation. She quickly shook her head.

Roen said, "Lizzie, why don't you belly up to the bar and watch Mrs. Mangold make our drinks?" Lizzie's head came up so quickly Roen feared whiplash. She didn't leap away from the table, though. She looked to her mother for permission.

"You can go," said Lily, "but don't make a nuisance of yourself with a hundred questions."

When the little girl climbed onto a barstool and was out of hearing range, Roen put the question to Lily again. "What is it?"

"I shouldn't be here. You know I didn't want to come with you."

"But you did."

"You were walking away with my daughter. That wasn't right."

"Or fair," he said. "Not right. Not fair. But you're here, and that was the goal."

"Why?" She leaned in and her voice dropped to a whisper. "Dolly Mangold is not a gossip of the caliber that Amanda Springer is, but that doesn't mean she won't tell a friend that she saw me here."

"Surely there's nothing strange about that."

"With *you.* She'll tell someone I was here with *you.*"

"The best way to deal with that is to make it a habit. Then it won't be out of the ordinary. People don't comment on the ordinary, have you noticed?"

Lily's nostrils flared slightly as she inhaled. "Mr. Shepard. I don't appreciate you making light of my concerns. I think I know the mind-set of folks here better than you. Even if you stay a year, you're still only passing through. I live here. Will always live here. It would be a kindness if you would take that into account. The next time you make to walk off with my daughter, I will holler bloody murder."

"Bloody murder? That's an awful expression. Do you read dime novels? I believe they're still popular. I used to read Nat Church's adventures. That sounds like something he would say."

"Mr. Shepard."

"Yes?"

"I mean for you to take me seriously."

"Hmm. Why didn't you holler bloody murder when we were standing in the sheriff's doorway? Seems as if that would have been the time to do it. He was right there, sitting behind his desk, nursing a cup of coffee and watching the goings-on with what I would call a peculiar level of interest. I think he would have gotten up if you had hollered. But you didn't. Why is that?"

Lily didn't — couldn't — respond. She stared at him instead.

Roen went on conversationally, "Anyway, I don't think you holler."

A muscle jumped in her cheek. "Perhaps not, but I can scream, Mr. Shepard, and right now you're making me want to scream."

He nodded slowly. "I've heard that before. My piano teacher. He *did* scream, but then he was dramatic about taking his seat on the piano bench, so it was to be expected. You are not dramatic, Mrs. Salt."

Lily leaned back the few inches necessary to sit up straight again. Beneath her emerald green shawl, she squared her shoulders. Her gaze was direct, unflinching. "What is it that you want from me?"

"Company."

"Really? Company? Not a sparring partner?"

Roen turned his head to greet Dolly as she approached with their drinks. "Ah, that didn't take long. Thank you, Mrs. Mangold."

"Dolly," she said, setting a drink in front of each of them. "We discussed this before.

I'm Dolly to nearly everyone. I hardly know how to answer to the other."

"Dolly, then. I'll keep that in mind."

"See that you do." She winked at him as she took a step back from the table. She wiped her hands on her apron and spoke to Lily. "Lizzie wants to drink her fizzy at the counter. It's fine with me if you say the same."

Lily nodded. "Thank you, Dolly. You're good with her."

"Wish I saw her more often. She reminds me of my Sarah when she was just a little thing. Same hair. Always jabbering when something caught her eye. Don't you be a stranger either, Lily." Dolly looked from Lily to Roen and back to Lily. Her smile remained unremarkably pleasant, but the look she leveled on Lily was significant.

When she was gone, Roen said, "What was that?"

"What?"

"That look she gave you. What was that?"

"I'm sure I don't know. She winked at you. What was that?"

"That? I'm sure I don't know." Roen positioned the paper straw in his drink toward his mouth, bent his head, and sipped. "It's good. Go on. Try it."

Lily did. There was no point in not appreciating this special treat. "It's delicious. Lizzie told me the bubbles tickle the back of her throat but I didn't know what she meant."

Roen's eyebrows lifted. "This is your first time?"

She nodded and took a second sip. "The fountain bar is relatively new. Mickey and Dolly installed it at the beginning of summer. Clay brought his sisters and brother here several times. I came once, but I ordered tea. I suppose I thought that fizzy drinks were for children."

"What do you think now?"

"I think I was wrong."

Roen cocked his head to one side as he studied her. Lily's face was a near perfect oval, and her features — except for her nose, which was a fraction left of center — were symmetrically aligned. Her eyes were focused on her drink so he could see the curve of her long lashes. They were a shade darker than her rust-colored hair, which was mostly hidden by her hat. He had to call on the memory of Lily sitting in the rocker with the sun glancing off her shoulder and bare head to bring the richness of that color to mind. He was not an artist, as anyone in his family would attest, but he saw details with the eye of a camera lens and held on to them just as clearly.

She glanced up just then and caught him staring. Roen didn't look away. That unnerved her, and for that he was sorry, but he did not regret having eyes on her in the first place.

"If it is your desire to make me uncomfortable, Mr. Shepard, then please know that you've succeeded and have done with it."

"Not my desire, Mrs. Salt. I apologize for that. Did you know my mother is an artist?"

"I'm not certain what that has to do with anything, but I learned of it today when I was speaking with Ben. He told me. I gather she is quite famous."

"Well known, I would say. And also well regarded. You have an interesting face, Mrs. Salt, of the kind my mother would want to paint. I was thinking about that." It was not a complete fabrication, for somewhere at the back of his mind the thought had been there. He watched Lily touch the bridge of her nose in a self-conscious gesture. Before she dwelled on that, he pointed to his nose and then turned sideways so she could better see the outline of his face. "My mother tells me that I have a profile for coins. Ancient coins. Roman coins. The ones someone discovers in old shipwrecks or archeological digs. Are you familiar?"

She nodded as he faced forward. "I've seen drawings in books."

"And?"

"And your mother is correct. I imagine she meant it kindly. It's a noble profile."

That brought Roen back to his early morning conversation with Clay. He'd been repeating something Hannah shared with him. *Nobility in your profile,* she'd said. *Especially your nose.*

"You shouldn't infer too much from that, Mr. Shepard. I was commenting on your nose, not your character."

Far from taking offense, Roen chuckled appreciatively. "Perhaps you would make a good sparring partner after all."

"You had doubts?"

"A few, but you've put a period to them." He thought she might bristle, but she appeared oddly satisfied that he knew she could give as good as she got. "I'm not at all sure why I desire your company, Mrs. Salt, but I've not changed my mind about that."

"There's a pity. You recall that I have four children. They are the company I keep."

"I haven't forgotten. The oldest is going to work for me, and the youngest is slurping a cherry fizzy at the counter. Ham doesn't like to wear shoes, and Hannah also thinks I have a noble profile."

"What?"

"Hmm?"

"What did you say about Hannah?"

"Oh, that. She told Clay that I have a noble profile. He told me. I suspect it's because she saw me in church." He smiled crookedly. "She is not yet as clear as you in distinguishing a noble proboscis from nobility of character. You should probably explain that to her."

"Oh, I certainly will."

Roen shrugged as he reconsidered. "She's bright, though. She could come to it on her own."

Lily sat up just that much straighter and looked him squarely in the eye. Her fingertips tightened on her glass. "I won't chance it."

"The wiser course. Do you always take it?"

"Does anyone?"

"I was asking about you."

"No, then. I submit being here with you as evidence of my own folly."

"That cut me deeply."

"I doubt that. You didn't flinch." Lily allowed herself to relax and turned her head toward the counter. "Lizzie. You're slurping air now. Stop, please, and come over here."

Lizzie turned on her stool. "May I have another?"

"No. And don't beg. It's unbecoming."

Sighing audibly, Lizzie pushed her glass away from the edge of the counter and slid off the stool. She sat at the table in the chair she had vacated earlier and eyed the root beer fizzy her mother had not finished. "May I have a taste of yours?"

"A sip," Lily said firmly. She lowered her glass in front of Lizzie so her daughter could easily find the straw. Lizzie quickly stole two sips before she looked up and revealed her most impish grin. "You are the very devil," said Lily.

"I thought Ham was the very devil."

"He's not here, so it's you."

Lizzie was not at all disturbed to hear this. She looked over at Roen. "I'm the very devil."

"Seems that way."

Her eyes fell on his half-finished drink. "May I have a taste of yours?"

Lily intervened. "Lizzie. You forget your manners. No, you may not have any of Mr. Shepard's drink."

Roen shrugged helplessly. "Your mother says no." When Lily cast a narrow, accusing look his way, he said, "I would have told you no even if your mother hadn't."

Lizzie was disappointed but resigned. "Can we go to Mrs. Fish's now?"

"You read my mind," said Roen. He removed some coins from his jacket pocket and placed them on the table. "Shall we?" He rose, helped Lizzie down from her chair, and then stood at Lily's side while she rose. "Thank you, Dolly," he called over his shoulder as they exited. When they'd reached the boardwalk, Lizzie separated herself and skipped ahead. "Well?" he said to Lily. "That wasn't so terrible, was it?"

"It isn't over." She lifted her chin to indicate a figure farther down the walk. "That's Mr. Hennepin sweeping in front of the mercantile. And across the street, Maxwell Wayne just stepped out of the bakery. His bones reliably predict the weather, but right now he's more interested in us than he is in the change in air pressure. We're coming up on the butcher shop. There will be people in there. There always are, and they'll see us through the front window. Do you begin to comprehend my concern?"

"I'm not sure. What do you imagine people will be whispering?"

"Whispering? That's too subtle for some folks. They'll be saying I'm taking up with you."

"Are you?"
"No!"
"You seem firm on that."
Lily gritted her teeth. "I am."
"Then they'll figure that out. It's not the end of the world."
"No, merely the end of my reputation." She greeted Mr. Hennepin as they passed the mercantile and paused long enough to exchange pleasantries.
"That was brave of you to step up that way," Roen said once they were out of earshot. "The way you explained it to me, I fully expected him to call you a Jezebel."
"How old are you, Mr. Shepard? I ask because you put me in mind of Clay, and as you know, he's twelve."
"Ah. Not a compliment, then. I'm twenty-nine."
"So I have five years and four children on you. I suppose that's why my perspective on life is more serious than yours."
"I don't find everything amusing."
"Then it's me."
"Sometimes it is."
"Well, at least that's honest." She waved to Maxwell Wayne across the street. He waved back and then slipped inside his bakery. "What do you take seriously?"
"My calculations."

"I'm not sure I understand what you mean."

"The integrity of the things I design depends on the soundness of my calculations. I take that seriously. Very much so. When it's done correctly, math is reliable."

"And people aren't?"

"I didn't say that."

"But it's true."

"Mostly it's true," he said.

Lily stopped walking as Lizzie took a left turn into the alcove that marked the entrance to the dress shop. "We're here," she said. "Please don't follow us inside. You have business with Ben, I believe. You should see to that."

Roen agreed, albeit reluctantly. "I asked Clay to come by after he finished his chores. If that's satisfactory with you, that is."

"It's fine."

"I spent the morning poring over maps. I have a route planned for Saturday. That's when I'll need Clay for the day."

"All right."

"All right," he repeated. His eyes lingered on her mouth, and her smile faltered. He was definitely sorry for that. He reached for the door and held it open until Lizzie and Lily were inside, then he raised a hand to acknowledge Mrs. Fish before he backed out of the alcove and headed down the street to find the sheriff.

Chapter Seven

As near as Roen could tell, Ben Madison hadn't twitched since he'd last seen him. He was still behind his desk, still nursing a cup of coffee, still leaning as far back in his chair as gravity would allow.

"Please tell me that's fresh coffee," Roen said as he sat in a visitor's chair opposite Ben.

"Fresh ten minutes ago," said Ben, raising his mug. "You want a cup?"

Roen shook his head. "Just had a root beer fizzy."

One of Ben's fiery eyebrows lifted in a perfect arch. "You were at Mangold's drugstore?"

"Uh-huh."

"Alone?"

"No. With Lily and Lizzie Salt. Mrs. Salt had root beer same as I did. Lizzie had the cherry."

"They were on their way to the dress shop."

"That's where they are now. We parted ways at the entrance."

"Huh. I knew you were a pretty persuasive fella when I heard you speak to the council and later at the town hall. You sold them on Northeast's plans for new rails through here, but better than that, you sold them on you. That's not easy to do."

Roen offered a modest shrug.

"Of course, Lily Salt didn't attend the town hall meeting, so she didn't see what I saw. How'd you get her to go to the drugstore with you?"

"I used Lizzie. She begged prettily when I suggested a fizzy drink, and her mother gave in. Reluctantly, I admit. Most definitely against her better judgment. She told me the next time I take Lizzie by the hand to lead her away, she'll holler bloody murder."

"She said that?"

"Almost verbatim."

"She doesn't holler."

"That's why I thought. She barely raises her voice. I can admit that I find it a little unnerving. I'm more familiar with loud and chaotic."

"Family?"

Roen nodded. "And neighbors. The entire

neighborhood actually. But I can appreciate the bucolic charms of Frost Falls, and the quiet of the surrounding country."

Ben chuckled. "You need to visit some of the ranches. There's nothing quiet about bleating sheep and bellowing cattle."

"I won't have to take your word for it. It's my intention to ride out to a few of the homesteads on Saturday. I'm taking Clay with me."

"Then you cleared it with Lily."

"That's what I came here earlier to tell you. Just happenstance that I bumped into her. I spoke to her yesterday when the children, save for Lizzie, were in school. It required some convincing and reassurances, and she didn't give me an answer until this morning when she sent Clay to my door. That was her way of telling me she is willing to let him try out the job. If Hannah had showed, it would have meant I'd have to find someone else."

"I'll be darned," said Ben. "I reckon I can tell you now that I didn't hold out much hope that you'd be successful, but I didn't want to discourage you."

"What you mentioned about Clay's education, that was helpful. I think it may have been what swayed her to give her approval."

"I'm glad to hear it, though I'm thinking

you shouldn't be too confident that you have her full approval. She has doubts. That's why she was here earlier. She never mentioned that she'd already given you her permission. I didn't press for more information than she was prepared to disclose. I gathered that you and she had had a conversation, but I figured it was preliminary. She had some questions about you, things she was probably thinking she should have asked before she sent Clay out this morning. That's how I know now that she was entertaining doubts."

"What kind of things did she ask?"

Ben set the coffee mug on his desk before he dropped his chair to all four legs. He stretched his legs, took the mug in hand again, and drank. "I guess there's no harm in telling you. Basically she wanted a character reference. I reminded her I hadn't known you but a few weeks and that we only crossed paths now and again, mostly about railroad business. She still wanted my impression, so I gave it to her."

"She sets store by first impressions," said Roen. "I have that from Clay."

"I had a favorable one to give her. Told her you were a good tenant, that you spend a lot time in your office working because I could still see the lamps burning when Ridley and I were retiring for the night. I repeated some of what you told the council that she wasn't there to hear. Information about you graduating from that technology school in Massachusetts and you being steadily employed by different railroad companies since you left. I thought that spoke to your independence and figured she'd appreciate that, her being independent herself."

"Did she ask about my family?"

"Yes. But I could only tell her that your mother was a famous artist. Until you told me your family was loud and chaotic, I didn't know anything else."

"That's fine. We're very different, my family and me. Was there anything else?"

"I believe I mentioned that you weren't a frequent visitor to the Songbird and that when you drank, it wasn't to excess."

Roen's eyebrows puckered. "You and I have never been in the Songbird at the same time."

Ben shrugged. "I asked around. There are things I like to know, too. If there's trouble in town, it generally can be traced back to whiskey shots and beer chasers at the Songbird."

"Not the Nightingale?"

"Oh, so you know about our brothel."

"The first time I stepped foot in the Songbird, the owner made it a point to tell me things about Frost Falls that the council and Mrs. Springer did not."

Ben flashed an uneven grin over the rim of his mug. "That's sounds exactly like something Buzz Winegarten would do. And it'd tickle him to share that tidbit when he knows Amanda Springer would never. The two of them have a long history of trading barbs. She's the head of the temperance movement, and he operates the saloon."

"But that's her husband that tends bar there, isn't it? Or did I misunderstand?"

"Oh, no. You have it right. Another bone of contention. But in answer to your question about the brothel, I rarely get a summons to go there. I've learned that men tend to argue more over their drinks than they do their ladybirds, and Mrs. Morrison — God bless her — sees that it remains that way. She doesn't suffer fools or foolery."

Ben tipped back his mug and drank. When he'd finished off his drink, he returned the mug to his desk. "You sure I can't get you a cup?"

"I'm sure." Roen thought Ben might rise to pour himself another, but the sheriff stayed put. It would have been better if he had, for Roen found himself on the receiving end of the man's considering gaze. Roen wondered if prisoners were subjected to the same stare and how quickly they confessed to real or even imagined crimes. He took the offense, inviting the question that Ben seemed to be formulating. "What is it you want to know?"

Except for a single arching eyebrow, Ben had no immediate response. He remained silent, thoughtful, making no attempt to hide the fact that he was taking measure of the man sitting opposite him. It was an effective prelude to interrogation, and it might have worked here if the door to his office hadn't opened suddenly and produced his wife on the threshold.

Both men got to their feet as Dr. Ridley Madison walked determinedly into the room. Her take-no-prisoners entrance was a counterpoint to her petite and slender stature. She had a delicate build but strong features, with sharply intelligent brown eyes and a bold mouth, which was now set in a tight, straight line. Without a word in greeting, she set her medical bag and two packages wrapped in brown butcher's paper on the long bench against the wall. Wanted notices were posted above it. She gave them no attention. It was only when her hands were free that she turned to finally acknowledge that she was not alone.

"This is a stroke of luck that you are both here," she said. "Please, sit. I fully intend to."

Roen moved to his right and forfeited the chair where he had been sitting, as it was closer to Ridley. He waited until she was comfortably situated before he took his seat. Ben offered his wife coffee, but when she declined, he dropped back into his chair and regarded her expectantly. "Well?" he asked.

"Indeed. You might very well ask that."

"I thought I just did."

"This is not the time to amuse yourself. I am here on important business."

Roen observed that Ben did not look particularly contrite although the effort was made.

"Perhaps if you told us what it is . . ." Ben let the suggestion lie there and waited for Ridley to pick it up.

She did, but not before she took in a breath and then released it slowly, calmly. "Did you know that Mr. Shepard was seen escorting Lily up and down the boardwalk? Parading her is the way it was put to me. The wags have the tale already, and they are not being kind. It hardly matters that it's repeated out of concern for her; there is an element of shaming in the retelling. Lily will be mortified when she learns of it."

"First," said Ben, "yes, I did know. I was preparing to discuss that in more detail with him when you came in. Second, how will Lily learn of it if no one tells her?"

"Oh, Ben." Ridley shook her head sorrowfully. "It's inevitable that someone will think they're doing her a favor by telling her, or at least it will be presented in that fashion. Truly, what you don't know about women could fill a book."

"Ellie said pretty much the same thing the other day."

"She's right." Not desiring to belabor the point, Ridley turned her attention to Roen. "What is your interest in Lily Salt? Better yet, what are your intentions, Mr. Shepard?"

It occurred to Roen that the doctor had every bit the same skill as the sheriff when it came to interrogation. "Mrs. Salt asked me a similar question, and I told her I would be pleased to have her company." When Ridley subjected him to a jaundiced look, he added, "I am not using 'company' as a euphemism, Dr. Madison. I mean just that. Company."

"Hmm. Then you know there is a brothel a block off Main Street."

"The Nightingale. Yes, I'm aware."

Ben broke in. "Buzz told him about it."

She sighed. "Of course he did. Did he tell you that the locals don't go there? They scratch that itch in Liberty Junction or over in Harmony. Men from both those places come here."

Roen wasn't sure what he was supposed to say to that. "I'll keep that in mind, I guess."

"My wife sees to the ladies at the Nightingale," said Ben by way of explanation. To Ridley, he said, "And that's plain speaking even for you."

Ridley considered and dismissed it. "Sometimes plain speaking is what's called for. Did I offend you, Mr. Shepard?"

Roen shook his head.

"Very well. Then I shall try harder."

Ben rolled his eyes while Roen merely chuckled.

Ridley went on as if she hadn't seen or heard either man's reaction. "Are you married?" She looked sideways at her husband. "Do you even know if he's married? Has a fiancée? A sweetheart?"

"I believe I mentioned I was getting around to that when you came in."

"Well, we're getting to it now." She turned back to Roen. "Are you, Mr. Shepard? Married, that is?"

"No. No fiancée. No sweetheart."

"No mistress?" asked Ridley.

Thinking of Victorine Headley made Roen hesitate and Ridley seized on that.

"A mistress, then." She pretended she didn't hear her husband's audible, much-put-upon sigh. "Can we expect that she'll be joining you?"

Roen held up a finger. "A point of clarification, please?"

"Go on."

"You're asking this because . . . ?"

"Because Lily Salt is dear to me. So are her children. I don't want anyone to make trouble for them, and it seems to me you're already stirring the pot."

"Have you put these questions to anyone before me?"

"No. My husband ran off those ersatz suitors before I had the opportunity."

"I see. Doesn't it ease your mind that he hasn't run me off?"

"Not entirely, no."

"And what of Lily's judgment? Do you not have regard for her opinion? She hasn't run me off."

"I am getting the impression that you stick like a fly in molasses."

"I enjoy her company, Dr. Madison. I'd like to see more of her. If that's sticking like a fly in molasses, then that's what it is. I am not interested in romantic entanglements. The correct answer to your unseemly question about a mistress is that I recently ended that arrangement. I would be more dismayed than you if she were to show up in Frost Falls, but I will tell you that it is not outside the realm of possibilities."

The gold flecks in Ridley's brown eyes glittered as she considered not only what he said, but also what he didn't say. "Lily's company is a safeguard, isn't it? You chose her quite deliberately, I imagine, because you learned very quickly that she's a widow with four children who has even less interest in romantic entanglements than you. I saw Amanda Springer bending your ear in church your first Sunday here, and I'm familiar with the bent that conversation takes. I don't think it matters to you how Lily's companionship is perceived by others as long as it keeps the keenly interested at bay and allows you to go about your work."

"I am not so Machiavellian as that, Doctor, though I am perhaps that selfish." He saw her eyebrows climb her forehead. "You look surprised. Did you think I would deny it? There's proof you don't really know me." Roen stood, nodded to Ridley and Ben in turn, and politely took his leave.

Ben looked at his wife, one eyebrow

raised. "So much for sticking like a fly in molasses. You ran him off."

"No, I didn't. He didn't walk away angry. He simply said his piece and walked away. I don't think he was bothered a whit by anything I said, though I can't say the same for you."

Ben rubbed behind his ear. "You were rather more candid than I expected."

"It was all for Lily."

"I think he's a good man, Ridley. We should take him at his word."

"I want to, but how can any of us know? She's still vulnerable, Ben. Sudden movements make her flinch. I've seen it."

"Perhaps we should tell him why we're so protective."

Ridley shook her head. "No. If he's a man who raises his hand against a woman, then he already knows about Lily. Men like that seem to instinctively know who can be terrorized."

Chapter Eight

Ham skidded to a halt just inside the parlor. Hannah and Clay were right behind him and stopped as quickly when they saw their mother lying on the sofa with a damp compress across her forehead. Lizzie had Lily's stocking feet in her lap and she was running her fingertips back and forth across the tops of them. Sometimes Lily would curl her toes.

"Mama doesn't feel well," Lizzie said.

"It's all right, Lizzie," said Lily. "I'm better now." She lifted the compress, raised her head a few inches, and smiled at her returning children. The fact that the smile was wan and not warm did nothing to reassure them.

Hannah rushed to her mother's side and replaced the compress as Lily's head fell back. "Stay right there. Shall I send Clay for Doc Madison?"

"No. No doctor. It's nothing. An upset

stomach. I took some bicarbonate of soda."

Hannah wasn't sure what an upset stomach had to do with the compress on her mother's head, but she didn't ask. Instead she looked to Lizzie for whatever explanation a five-year-old could offer.

"I think it was the fizzy drink," Lizzie said importantly. "We almost didn't make it home before Ma loosed that fizzy and then all of her lunch in the kitchen sink. I had a cherry fizzy but I kept it down. I can't say if Mr. Shepard did because he went on to Sheriff Ben's and we stopped at Mrs. Fish's. He had the root beer, too, you see."

They didn't see, but the three of them made a concerted effort to figure it out. They finally pieced together a story that made sense to them, and Clay and Hannah, with their better understanding of the root of their mother's distress, exchanged meaningful glances over the tops of Ham and Lizzie's heads.

Hannah removed the compress from Lily's forehead and gave it to Ham to dampen with fresh, cooler water. "Lizzie, go help Ham before he makes a mess."

Lizzie clambered off the sofa, careful not to disturb her mother more than she had to.

"Ma?" Clay approached the sofa. "We

know it wasn't the fizzy."

Lily opened one eye. "Do you?"

"You don't have to pretend it was. Maybe you shouldn't have spent so much time with Mr. Shepard. Couldn't have been easy for you."

"Lizzie was there."

Hannah asked, "I don't think that matters much. Was he unkind, hurtful?"

"No, Hannah. He was a gentleman."

Hannah blew out a breath that ruffled the fine hair at her mother's temple. "I am very glad to hear it. I hoped he would be."

Lily saw an opening there to mention the noble profile but she let it pass. There would be other opportunities. "It's been a long time since I've been out of the house all of an afternoon." She mocked herself with a small smile. "I don't think I'll do that again for a while."

Clay said, "But it's good, isn't it, to go out?"

"Mm. Maybe."

Ham and Lizzie returned just then. There was a tug-of-war for the compress until Hannah snatched it from them and laid it gently across Lily's brow. "I'll start dinner, Ma. There's soup, and I can make biscuits. I'll be careful with the stove."

"All right, but call if you need me." Lily

eyed Clay. "Don't you have chores to do and somewhere to be?"

"I don't have to go see Mr. Shepard."

"You do. He's expecting you, and I'll be just fine. Hannah's making dinner, and Ham and Lizzie will keep me company."

Clay was reluctant to leave, but in a battle of wills, she would always win. She was strong in ways he wondered if he would ever be.

Roen opened the door to Clay exactly an hour after he'd seen students fleeing the schoolhouse. "Let me get my maps. We're going to work at the library."

"Yes, sir. I'll wait right here."

Roen hesitated. "Did you get something to eat after school?"

"No. But it's all right. Hannah's warming soup and making biscuits. She'll keep some back for me to have when I get home."

"There's a jar of sugar cookies in the kitchen that my housekeeper left with me." Martha Rushton was also Ben and Ridley's housekeeper, and they were generous to share her time and her cookies. "Go on. Help yourself while I get what I need."

Clay's pockets were stuffed with cookies when they met up again on the porch. Roen noticed the dusting of sugar around the boy's mouth and the bulge in his cheeks and figured he was filling up now and taking the rest home. He gave one of the rolled maps to Clay and carried the other two under his arm. "Careful you don't crease that. I like a smooth map."

"Yes, sir." The words were mushy, confirming the mouthful of cookies.

Smiling, Roen clapped Clay lightly between his shoulder blades. "C'mon. Let's go."

The library was a nondescript but generously sized wooden frame building situated on Main Street between the leather goods store and Maxwell Wayne's bakery. According to Amanda Springer, the money to erect the library was an early gift to the town from its founder, the father of the current owner of the Twin Star Ranch, Thaddeus Frost, and the grandfather of the owner of the neighboring property, which had yet to be named, Remington Frost. There was some connection there to the sheriff, but Jim Springer pulled his wife away before she expounded on that theme. Roen had never asked about it, and no one else had offered the information without invitation.

Some of the floor-to-ceiling shelves inside the library sagged under the weight of the books, but when Roen looked around, he could see that even after so many years, filling all the shelves was still a work in progress. Books were expensive, and lending them out shortened their life expectancy. It was one of the reasons dime novel adventures were still so popular. Stacks of them required very little space.

Roen nodded to the librarian as he paused at the front desk. Out of the corner of his eye, he saw Clay do the same. "Where is the best place to unroll these maps so we can study them? It's Miss Fletcher, isn't it? I'm Roen Shepard with Northeast Rail."

Miss Dorothea Fletcher offered an awkward smile while she patted her walnut-colored hair, ostensibly to make certain the pins were holding it in place. She flushed when she discovered her missing spectacles were nesting there, and the flush deepened when the earpieces tangled in her hair as she tried to remove them, making the pins superfluous. She left them to sit crookedly on her head and held out a hand to Roen. "It's a pleasure to meet you, Mr. Shepard. Of course I know who you are. I was at the town meeting for your presentation."

Roen took her hand, gave it a gentle shake, and released it. "You know Clay."

"I do." She eyed the boy sternly. If her spectacles had been in place, she would have bent her head and looked at him from over the rims. "You have books overdue, young man. I don't suppose you have them with you."

Clay shifted uncomfortably and shook his head.

"Tomorrow. Bring them by." To Roen, she said, "There's a large table at the back. You can use that. If you need to use some books to weigh down the corners of your maps, help yourself. Just return them where you found them."

"Indeed I will. Thank you."

They found the table shoved indecorously between two stacks. History and geography faced each other on the shelves. There was only a single chair, and Clay set down his map to find another one. Roen had all three maps unrolled and smoothed across the table by the time Clay returned with a chair and a lamp.

"Good," said Roen. "You found a lamp. It's hard to see anything back here without one."

"I can get another if we need it."

"Mm. We'll try this first." He took the oil lamp and placed it where it would be the most helpful. "Put your chair over here next to mine."

Clay did as directed. He sat on his knees

and leaned forward over the table. "Did you notice that she got all twitchy?" he asked, looking at the map and not at Roen.

"Who?"

"Miss Fletcher. She got twitchy when you spoke to her. I only seen her like that once before, and that was when Scooter Banks from over at Twin Star came in to get a book for Mr. Frost. She got twitchy then."

"Is that right? No, I didn't notice."

"Huh. I bet that's because it happens to you a lot on account of your noble profile and you being a good-lookin' fella. Sally Clark says you look fine in a suit, like the kind of gentleman we don't often see around here except at weddings and funerals."

"Clay. Who is Sally Clark?"

"She's Hannah's friend. I like her okay, but she gives herself airs. You know what I mean?"

"I know someone like that," he said, thinking of Victorine. "Are you done? We have work."

Clay smiled guiltily. "Done."

"All right. Do you know what you're looking at?"

"I'm not sure."

"Find a reference point. Some feature on the map that you're familiar with."

Clay took his time and eventually pointed

to the cross-hatching that indicated train tracks. They appeared and disappeared as they wound around a mountainside. "These tracks are climbing up to Butler's Ridge. It's a fair piece from here, and I've only been that way once. Shouldn't it be marked?"

"We can mark it now. I made this map to evaluate your skill at seeing the land in a different way." He took a pencil from inside his jacket and wrote "BR." "Can you find Smith's Run?"

Clay used his index finger to trace several lines that represented creeks, falls, streams, and runs. He closed his eyes as he visualized the landscape, and when he saw it clearly, he grinned and pointed out the tributary that meandered in the southwest corner of the map. "Smith's Run," he said. "I got it right, didn't I?"

"You did. Are you sure you've only been out that way once?"

"Pretty sure. My pa took me with him to Stonechurch when he was lookin' to buy some silver for a special piece of jewelry. Commissioned, I think he called it."

"That sounds right."

"He owned the forge back then. Ma sold it after the fire and now Bertie Graves owns it, but he doesn't do specialty pieces like Pa did. Not that Pa did a lot of pieces like that. Mostly he did regular forge work. Horseshoes. Wheel rims. Nuts and bolts. Tools."

"I see. It was good of him to take you."

Clay shrugged. "I suppose."

Roen looked down at the boy's bent head. He didn't know how to interpret Clay's response, and following it up with a comment or question did not seem respectful. He said, "Can you locate Butler's Gorge?"

"That's easy." Clay followed the ridgeline until it dropped away. He outlined the steep walls of the gorge. "The tracks wind down one side and up the other."

"They do. That's why I want to build a bridge across it."

Clay looked up then, wide-eyed. "You mean it? A bridge there?"

Roen nodded. "A trestle bridge. It takes a train better than an hour to negotiate that gorge now. With the bridge, it will be able to cross in mere minutes. Here, let me roll this up and I'll show you."

When the second map was revealed, all the indicators and the legend were in place. Clay set his elbows on the table and studied it. It was not a map of what was, but of what could be. There was a different route for the tracks, and the gorge was filled with the crisscross tripod frames peculiar to erecting trestles. He looked up at Roen, his expression skeptical.

"What?" asked Roen. "You have something to say, I collect."

Clay pointed to the bridge. "Can a train really cross that?"

"If it's built to my specifications, it can. This is not a new design. The Central Pacific couldn't have reached Promontory Point without bridges like this. This one is going to be framed using a combination of timber and iron."

"It's awfully high and long."

"It is. The trestles you're familiar with cross the river, but the engineering is basically the same."

"If you say so."

Roen chuckled. "I do. And I'm going to show you some calculations to prove it."

Clay put his head in his hands. "This is the schoolwork you talked about it."

"It is, but we're not going to do that today. I want to show you another map." He rolled up the planning map and tied it off with twine. The final map showed a different topography than the first two. "This is one of the maps I received from the land office. Ed Saunders copied this from the original, but I'm not certain he was as meticulous as I need him to be. This shows approximately ten square miles. You recognize it. This is the area I was surveying while you were spying on me."

"I wasn't spying," Clay said before he thought better of it.

Roen gave him the gimlet eye.

"Well, maybe I was. But it wasn't for nefarious purposes."

"Nefarious. Do you even know what that means?"

"Wicked. Evil. *Nat Church and the Nefarious Ninja.*"

"I should have known. Is that one of the books Miss Fletcher mentioned that's overdue?"

"Yes. There'll be a fine, but I want to read it again. Anyway, the fine goes toward buying more books so I'm actually helping the library."

Roen decided against arguing with that logic. He pointed to the map again, specifically to a boundary line that defined two properties. "This area to the north, where I want to lay track, is what you told me is owned by Mr. Hardy, but I think the initial survey of the land was off by more than half a mile. Whether that's because of inadequate instruments or incompetency, I don't know, and it doesn't matter. I think this strip, something like a panhandle, is actually part of the Twin Star Ranch."

"Huh. Maybe it's like you thought at first. Mr. Saunders might not have copied it carefully."

"Or the original is incorrect. We're going to find out on Saturday."

"We are?"

"We are. Can you finish your chores by eight?"

"I can finish them by seven if you want."

Roen appreciated Clay's eagerness, but he said, "Eight's fine. I'll arrange to have the horses paid for and available. You bring them here and help me pack. We'll be gone almost all the daylight hours so eat breakfast and I'll have Ellie Butterworth pack something for us to take along. Dress for the weather because we're not coming back for coats or slickers."

"Yes, sir. I reckon this would be a good time to tell you I'm not that good of a rider. Only been on a horse about half a dozen times. Three of those times, Ben was leading me."

"How is that possible?" asked Roen. "I thought everyone out here was born knowing how to ride."

Clay snickered. "I bet you thought there were regular saloon fights and shoot-outs."

"Not regular. I know it's not the Wild West."

"Uh-huh."

Roen clapped the boy gently on the back of his head the way he'd seen Ellie do to Ben. Clay grinned up at him, so he knew no harm was done. "All right. We're finished here." He started to roll the last map, but Clay put out his hands to take it, and Roen let him.

Clay tied off the twine and held the roll loosely under his arm. "Can I ask you something?"

Roen did not know what was coming, but Clay's attempt to sound casual about it meant it was probably important. "Go ahead."

"You treated Lizzie and Ma to fizzy drinks this afternoon."

It wasn't a question. Roen nodded anyway.

"Lizzie was real fond of her cherry fizzy, but the root beer didn't settle so good with my ma. You had root beer, too, and you looked fine when you came to the door."

"That's because I was fine. What do you mean, it didn't settle so well with your mother?"

Clay hesitated, rubbed his ear. "I ought not to be telling you, but it's pertinent to what I'm going to say later."

"You can't get to later if you don't get to now."

"Ma was stomach sick when she got home, and she was still not feeling good when me and Hannah and Ham came in from school. She was lying on the sofa with a wet cloth on her forehead, so it was easy to figure that she was ailing."

"You said Hannah was making dinner. That's why, isn't it?"

"Hmm."

"And now we're to the later part," said Roen. "What is it you want to say?"

"Don't really want to say it, but I got to. Hannah and I don't think it was the fizzy that disagreed with Ma. We think it was you. Now Ma didn't say that. She never would. Fact is, she said you were a gentleman, which we figure is probably true. It's just that it doesn't make much difference to how Ma feels about you, so we're thinking you should probably stay away. Church is fine; it can't be helped unless you was to become a Methodist and worship there."

"That is not going to happen."

"Didn't think so." He shrugged. "You could sleep in on Sunday mornings. There's plenty who do."

"Clay. Are you saying your mother was ill because she spent part of an afternoon in

my company?"
"Um, yeah. That's what I'm saying."
"Did you ask her?"
"Sure, but besides blaming the fizzy, she said it was because she hadn't been out of the house much and not for so long a time. Probably seems peculiar to you, but she's not exactly lying about it."
"But it's not the whole truth either, is that it?"
"That's it. She doesn't get twitchy like Miss Fletcher does. Ma gets . . ." He paused, searching for the right word.
Roen supplied it. "Skittish?"
"Yep. Skittish."
"You seem to know a lot about it."
"I guess I should. I been with her all my life."
There was no refuting that. He wondered if Lily had an inkling of how her children looked after her. "Is it just me who makes her skittish?"
"Mostly you. She's her steady self around people she knows, like Ben and the doc. Mrs. Springer can set her teeth on edge but that's because Ma knows her too well, if you take my meaning."
Roen refrained from saying that he understood perfectly. Instead he asked, "Does she need Dr. Madison to visit her?"

"She says not."

"All right. Careful, you're crushing that map. Here. Let me have it."

Clay gave it over. "I'm sorry."

"No harm done. Let's go. I'll walk you home."

"But —"

"I heard everything you said. I don't have to go inside. I'll stop at the door. I'm not promising that I'll always do that or that I'll walk to the opposite side of the street if I see your mother coming. I'd like to hear this from your mother, but I'll respect your wishes for now."

"They're Hannah's wishes, too."

Roen nodded and placed his hand at Clay's back and gave him a nudge. "And I had such hopes that my noble profile would carry the day."

"Show it off to Miss Fletcher," said Clay. "Bet she twitches."

Chapter Nine

Deputy Hitchcock Springer entered the Butterworth's kitchen by the back door. He made sure that Mrs. Vandergrift saw him wipe his muddy boots on the mat. She was as particular about her kitchen floor as she was about her pastries. Grinning at her, he tipped his hat. A steady stream of water poured from the brim. "Sorry. It's raining bulls and bears out there this morning."

The cook waggled a pancake turner at him. "Isn't the expression 'cats and dogs'?"

"Cats and dogs is a cliché. I aim to use my own phraseology."

Ellie Butterworth came into the kitchen through the swinging dining room door. She looked Hitch over head to toe and shook her head. He was as lean and ropy as a steer after a two-hundred-mile cattle drive, but she knew for a fact that he ate three square meals a day because he took at least two of them at the hotel. She pointed to a stool at the heavy butcher block table. "Take off that hat and slicker, Deputy, and sit. You're as wet as a pair of knickers after a good drubbing."

Hitch wasn't sure he cared for the comparison, but there was no denying he was wet through and through. He hung the slicker and his hat on a peg by the door, where they dripped water in an alternating tattoo. He ran his fingers through his sandy hair to settle the spikes and then took out a handkerchief and wiped his damp brow.

"Breakfast?" asked Ellie, seeing him eyeing the flapjacks Mrs. Vandergrift was expertly turning on the griddle.

"No, thank you, ma'am. I'm here on jail business. Need a breakfast for Billy Nelson. He got himself in another tussle at the Songbird. Sheriff put him in a cell for drunk and disorderly so he could sleep it off, and he's going to let him go after he's fed. Pancakes and molasses would be just the thing. Maybe a couple strips of bacon to go with it."

Mrs. Vandergrift took a militant stance, setting one fist on the ample curve of her hip while she continued to flip pancakes. "If you ask me, seems like the sheriff is operating a hotel for wastrels. George Hotchkiss has a lie-in there a couple or three times a month. About time Ben got wise to it."

Ellie began plating pancakes and bacon to take into the dining room. "You know better than to criticize my boy in my hearing, or you should. Leave him be. I'm not the only one saying he's doing a fine job, and breakfast for the prisoners isn't charity. Ben has a fund for that."

The cook harrumphed her disapproval and left it at that.

Ellie started to excuse herself to take out the filled plates when Fedora Chen rushed in from the dining room. Hitch jumped to his feet, but in his eagerness to greet her, he knocked Ellie's tray out of her hands. To his credit, he stretched both arms and tried to corral the tray, the plates, and one of the flying flapjacks. His feet tangled. The stool at his back wobbled and fell, landing with a thump at Mrs. Vandergrift's feet. She jumped out of the way but not so far that she couldn't swipe at his bony ass with her turner. He yelped because the hit surprised *and* stung, and it was at that point he knew all was lost. He stopped flailing and braced himself for a fall. The tray landed with a dull thud, but the china crashed and clattered. The flapjacks did nothing to cushion his fall while the crispy bacon crackled as he crushed it.

As near as Hitch could tell, it was a full ten count before anyone spoke. That was ten long seconds of complete humiliation at the feet of Fedora Chen, when all he'd meant to do was make a good impression.

Fedora's glossy black braid fell forward over her shoulder as she dropped to her knees beside the deputy. "Mr. Hitch?" His head was turned away from her. She touched him lightly on the arm when he didn't stir. "Mr. Hitch? Are you all right?"

Hitch groaned. He didn't want to face her, but he didn't have an alternative. The flapjack under his nose was suffocating him.

"This is your fault, Chen," Mrs. Vandergrift said in harsh tones. "You came in here like your hair was on fire, and you can see what came of that. The boy was trying to show you some manners, though I can't say he knows them or that you deserve them."

Ellie had been watching and listening in openmouthed astonishment. Now her jaw snapped shut with an audible click. "That is enough, Mrs. Vandergrift. This is no one's fault. It was an accident. I dare you to tell Amanda Springer her son doesn't know his manners." She put a hand on Fedora's shoulder. "Pick up what you can and then fetch a broom and mop. I'll help Hitch."

"I can get to my own damn feet."

"Language," Ellie said mildly. "You're still representing the sheriff's office. Here. Take my hand."

Hitch ignored the outstretched hand as he rose to his knees. He peeled an oddly shaped piece of flapjack from his cheek and shook it off his fingertips. It wasn't easy. The molasses made everything sticky. He sat back on his haunches, and when Ellie handed him a damp kitchen rag, he took the offering. What he wanted to do was bury his hot face in it, but he only wiped it down and handed the rag over.

"Sorry, Ellie. Mrs. Vandergrift." He brushed Fedora's delicate hands aside when she would have picked up a broken piece of china. "My mess, Fedora. I'll clean it up."

Fedora kept the dish shard she was holding and looked up at Ellie for direction. Her face was pale, but her small chin didn't wobble and her eyes were dry. "Mr. Shepard came in while you were back here."

Ellie heard Fedora's statement as an explanation for why she'd hurried into the kitchen. She was fleeing the dining room. "You didn't leave him standing at the entrance, did you?"

"No, ma'am." She hardly noticed that Hitch was gently removing the piece of broken china from her hand. "I showed him to his usual table even though it's Saturday and he's never come on a Saturday before. He asked for flapjacks, eggs, fried potatoes, and bacon. I poured coffee for him. Mr. Shepard said he had plans to ride out toward the Double H this morning if the rain stopped."

Ellie blew out a breath. "Oh, Lord, that's right. I clean forgot it was Saturday. He asked me if he could have some provisions for the outing, and I assured him he could." Her eyes darted to the cook. "Mrs. Vandergrift?"

"I'll get on it straight away once my floor is cleared of all this rubbish."

"Doing it now," said Hitch, picking up the pace at which he was picking up the pieces.

Ellie helped Fedora to her feet. "Mop and broom, Fedora. Hitch is proving he can take care of this."

Nodding, Fedora gracefully skirted the mess on the floor on her way to the broom closet. When she returned, Hitch was setting the tray piled with the detritus of his fall on the butcher block. There was a short battle of wills as he tried to take the broom from her, but Fedora held on and he settled for the dustpan and eyed the damp mop that she leaned against the table.

Mrs. Vandergrift watched them with

pursed lips and raised salt-and-pepper eyebrows. Disapproval did not improve her appearance, and she would not have been offended to hear it. Shaking her head, she turned back to the stove and began pouring batter onto the sizzling griddle.

Ellie did not miss the cook's censure. She was grateful not only that Mrs. Vandergrift did not voice it, but also that Fedora and Hitch did not see it. "Empty the dustpan on the tray, Hitch, then carry it out. Bring the tray back. Fedora will finish the mopping and I'll wipe down the butcher block." Her assignments were meant to avoid a tug-of-war over the mop, and they worked as planned. Hitch returned from the outside at the same time Fedora was at the broom closet. Ellie wanted to believe they took advantage of a few moments in passing away from the cook's disapproving eye, but she wasn't sure that Hitch had the gumption or that Fedora even knew there was an attraction.

"Rain's slowed," said Hitch, taking up the stool again. "Did Mr. Shepard say what he was going to do out by the Double H?"

Ellie surreptitiously nudged Fedora. The girl was waiting at attention for Mrs. Vandergrift to plate the food and pass it to her. When Fedora didn't move or respond, Ellie said, “He’s speaking to you.”

Fedora’s narrow shoulders and slender frame twitched as she came out of her trance. “Oh. Pardon?”

Hitch repeated his question.

“A survey.”

“Huh. I thought he’d been over that section of land.”

“I don’t know about that. He said he was doing a survey and was taking someone to help him.”

At the stove, Mrs. Vandergrift snorted. “That no-account George Hotchkiss, I’ll wager.”

Ellie sighed but otherwise ignored the pointed interjection. “I didn’t know where he was going until Fedora told us,” she said to Hitch. “He didn’t offer that information when he asked about provisions, and I guess I wasn’t interested enough to ask. Now, if he’d mentioned that he’d hired someone, I would have wanted to know about that.”

Hitch shrugged. “Seems like Mr. Shepard had a lot to say to you this morning, Miss Chen, or does he always ramble on when you’re at his table?”

“I don’t usually wait on him.”

Which wasn’t an answer to his question. He let it go. “How’s that jail order coming, Mrs. Vandergrift? Billy will be wondering what's keeping me. If he's up. I made coffee before I left to tempt him."

"I have it right here," the cook said. She set a full plate of flapjacks and bacon on the tray and covered it with a blue-and-white kitchen towel. "You make sure you bring back that dish. I reckon you know we're down three. Can't keep losing them."

"Yes, ma'am." He started off to get his hat and slicker, but when he turned, he saw that Fedora was holding both out to him. She was a head and a half shorter than he was and had to raise her arm to keep his slicker from dragging on the floor. He took it, thanked her, and shrugged into it. Droplets of water still fell from the sleeves. He was careful with his hat, adjusting it until it sat on his head in the preferred position. Hitch was working out his parting words to Fedora, which wasn't easy with Ellie standing in front of him looking a little amused and Mrs. Vandergrift standing at his back with a turner in her hand. He just about had them set in his mind when the cook interrupted in chilly, authoritative accents.

"I've got plates for you, Chen. Take them. Get them out of my way."

Fedora had a brief, apologetic smile for Hitch, or at least he imagined that she had. He held on to that glimpse of her sweetly tentative smile on his walk back to the jail. He could almost dodge the raindrops now. Clouds were parting and east of town he made out a glimmer of sunshine. If his luck held, maybe there'd be someone else in a cell tonight who'd need a meal from the Butterworth.

"How is your mother?" Roen asked. He'd been holding on to the question until they reached the place he had in mind to begin the survey. For most of the journey he'd been occupied keeping an eye on Clay, who had not exaggerated his lack of riding experience. The boy's concentration was so focused on staying in his saddle that he had a difficult time with conversation. Roen dismounted first and then made sure Clay was able to do the same without mishap. The boy was lithe and light on his feet, and there was no awkwardness at all. That was youth, Roen thought, not familiarity, and he was reminded that there was a lot about youth to recommend it.

Clay took the reins of their riding mounts and led the horses to a scrub pine where he could tether them. Roen began to remove his instrument case and tripod from the packhorse.

"Did you hear what I said?" asked Roen

when Clay came back to get the pack animal.

"You asked about Ma. I was thinking on how to answer."

"You have to think about it? Is she all right now or isn't she?"

"In between, I'd have to say. Not exactly one or the other."

"I don't understand."

"That's what I was figuring, so I didn't answer right away." Clay removed the canteens but left their provisions on the horse. He led the animal over to the others. "I wasn't being rude," he called over his shoulder.

"I realize that." Roen handed Clay the tripod. "You think you can set that up?"

"Sure. Show me where you want it."

Roen walked about twenty paces ahead and drew an X in the damp soil with the toe of his boot. "Right here." When Clay had the tripod in place, Roen set the wye level on it and removed the telescope. He peered through it, locating a point in the distance to be his marker in the crosshairs. He handed the telescope to Clay. "Have a look. You might have to make an adjustment for your eye. Just turn this dial until everything's in focus. That's a wye level on the tripod. It measures elevation."

While Clay was doing that, Roen took out his compass and turned it in the direction of the line he wanted to survey. True north was to his left. He was facing northeast. According to his map, he was close to the Double H's boundary line. He returned the compass to the case. "Has Dr. Madison been to the house?"

"No." He continued to look through the telescope, moving it across the tree line. "I can see the needles on the loblollies. Ain't that something?"

"Indeed. Do you think the doctor should visit her?"

"Don't see the point. She's not sickening for anything. She's just not herself, or rather she is, but not in a good way."

As an explanation, it left a lot to be desired. Roen wondered if he should offer to call on her. He hardly had the thought before he rejected it.

"Hannah says she's grieving." He handed the telescope back to Roen. "I don't know about that. My sister has peculiar notions sometimes. I have to remember she's only ten."

It didn't sound all that peculiar to Roen. "Perhaps she's grieving for your father."

"Don't think so."

"Aren't you coming up on the time of year

he died?"

"That's still a few months away." He looked around. "So what do we do now?"

Roen recognized that the subject of Lily Salt was closed. "I need my notebook. It's in the case. I have a pencil here." He produced it from his coat pocket. When Clay came back with it, he set the telescope in the level again and then showed Clay how to record the elevation. He exchanged the level for a transit to measure horizontal and vertical angles, explaining the process to Clay as he went. When the information was recorded, Roen told Clay to get the chains from the packhorse.

"For measuring distance," he said. "This is an engineer's chain. One hundred feet long with one hundred links. There are tally tags every ten feet. Careful. It's a little heavy. Hold this end while I walk it out."

The process of measuring, recording, walking, and comparing calculations to the map was repeated throughout the morning. They packed up once to find shelter under an overhang of rock while they waited for another round of rain to move on. It was as good a time as any to open the leather bag of foodstuffs Ellie Butterworth had packed for them. Clay ate with gusto. Roen, only a little less so.

"I guess the only person who makes better fried chicken than Ma is Mrs. Vandergrift," said Clay.

"Your mother makes fine chili and cornbread."

"She does. She's good at a lot of things. You know she works for Mrs. Fish, sewing new things and mending others."

Roen had removed his coat to sit on and now Clay was giving his garments a critical eye. "What is it?"

Clay shrugged. "I was thinking that Ma could do something about your workin'-outside-of-town clothes. Take them in maybe or just start over. That shirt doesn't fit you proper and your vest gaps. Your trousers hang kinda funny."

Roen pointed to his head. "Do you want to say something about my hat?"

"No. A felt derby's fine, but I like the kind of hat ranchers wear better. Sheriff Ben wears a Stetson."

"I know."

"Your boots are good."

"Thank you. It might interest you to know that the valise carrying my working-outside-of-town clothes went missing in Saint Louis. I put in a request to have the case sent on to me, but it hasn't arrived. These clothes were the best I could do at Hennepin's mercantile. I had more success at the leather goods store."

"Huh. That's too bad about your clothes, but I guess losing them was better than losing your instruments."

"I carried those with me."

Clay nodded. "Good thing you did. We gonna start again?"

"Soon as you finish the pie."

"There's pie?"

"Mm-hmm. Apple. I smelled it when Mrs. Butterworth was packing our bags." He took it out, unwrapped it, and gave it to Clay. "Go on. I only asked for the one piece. It's for you." Roen began to clean up while Clay made short work of the pie.

Clay wiped his hands on his trousers when he was finished, ignoring the handkerchief Roen held out for him. "Don't want to get it dirty." He stood, picked up their bags, and carried them to the horses. "Did you see that?" he asked. The bags were still in his hands. "Something moved over there." He jerked his chin to the left.

Roen followed the movement with his eyes. "I don't see anything."

"Caught it out of the corner of my eye. Not close. Way over there." Clay hung the bags over the packhorse. "Can I look through the telescope?"

"Sure. Isn't it likely to be an animal?"

"Coyote, maybe, but I'm thinking something taller. With something that glints."

Roen gave him the telescope, and Clay stepped away from the animals. Roen threw his coat over a saddle and followed, squinting as he tried to see what had captured Clay's interest. They saw the flash at the same time. Roen pushed Clay to the ground at the exact moment something hot and stinging creased his upper arm. It was followed immediately by the report from a rifle.

"Someone's shooting at us!" Clay made himself as small as he could against the ground.

"Roll," said Roen. "Toward the horses. Now!"

Clay hugged the telescope to his chest and did as directed. He stopped when he was lying between two of the animals. He watched as another shot hit the ground less than an arm's length from Roen. "He's shooting at you, not me!"

"Run back up to the shelter where we ate. I'm not moving until I know you're safe. Go!"

Clay scrambled to his feet but stayed low. He ran in that crouched position to their picnic shelter. There was a third shot, but now Roen was on the move. He reached the overhang seconds after Clay. They sat there, catching their breath and bracing for another shot in spite of the fact that they were well protected for the moment. If someone came after them, they were fish in a barrel.

"What do we do now?" asked Clay. "You don't have a gun, do you? I didn't see that you packed a gun."

"Because I didn't. As a rule, surveying does not require one."

"Bet this changes your mind."

Roen didn't have an answer for that. He clapped a hand over the wound in his arm. Blood was beginning to seep through his shirt.

"Hey! You're hurt." Clay moved closer to get a better look.

"It's nothing. A crease. I'm trying to decide if I was lucky or if it was a lucky shot."

Clay frowned. "What do you mean?"

"I mean that whoever was doing the shooting intended to run us off, not kill us."

"Maybe I should find out, make a run for my horse, and ride back to town. I could bring Sheriff Ben here. If no one shoots at me, then we'll know. He'll see he's run me off."

"That's about as brave a plan as I've ever heard and about as foolish. No. You're not riding out, not without me, and not until we're sure that it's safe."

"How we gonna know that?"

Roen released his arm and found his handkerchief. "You can give up that telescope now." The boy had a death grip on it. "And thank you for taking such good care of it." When Clay handed it over, Roen draped it with the white hanky. He crab-walked to the opening of their cramped shelter and raised his makeshift white flag above the overhang and waved it.

"You're surrendering?" Appalled, Clay's dark eyebrows laddered his forehead. "Even Custer didn't surrender."

"Custer died. I'm taking you back to your mother in the same shape she sent you to me."

"What about you?"

"I'll be fine." He continued to wave the flag in a broad arc. "This is nothing."

"How do you know? You been shot before?"

"As a matter of fact, I have." Roen recalled the event more clearly than he liked. It was a consequence of ending his arrangement with Victorine as she'd had definite expectations regarding their relationship that did not agree with his. "And no, I'm not telling you about it, so don't ask."

"I'd tell you if I'd been shot before."

"You haven't been shot now. There is no *before* about it." Roen lowered the telescope. "I'm going to step out. You stay put."

"But —" He stopped because Roen was already ducking out from under the rock ledge. Clay cringed in anticipation of another shot as Roen began to rise, but when it didn't come, he crawled to the entrance and tried to look up. "What's happening?"

"Nothing's happening. There's no one here and no one coming. You can come out. We're leaving."

For once, Clay was at a loss for words.

Chapter Ten

Lily heard the familiar screech of the back door swinging open. Despite his good intentions, Clay still hadn't gotten around to fixing it. "About time you're home," she said, turning away from the sink, where she was scrubbing out a pot. She used her apron to dry her wet hands and brushed rusty tendrils of hair made damp by the hot water. In spite of the fact that Clay was late arriving home, Lily had a ready smile for her son when he stepped into the kitchen. That smile faltered but didn't fade when she saw Roen Shepard step into view behind him. Good manners kept it in place. That, and a stronger constitution than she generally credited herself with.

"Mr. Shepard," she said. Her voice was steady, and the annoyance she felt was absent from her tone. Lily rested her gaze on Clay, who she observed was not quite looking her in the eye. "What is it? What's happened?"

Clay dug his hands into his pockets while he shifted from one foot to the other.

Lily recognized the signs pointing toward obfuscation. "Take off your coat and sit at the table. I saved dinner for you. It won't take but a few minutes to heat up the stew. You can use that time to think about whether you want to tell me a story or tell me the truth."

Clay sighed. He looked back at Roen as he began to slip out of his coat, but his mother cleared her throat in a way that warned him he was on his own.

"Come inside, Mr. Shepard. There is plenty of stew."

"I don't want to impose. I'm here to make certain that Clay tells you about our adventure, but after seeing how well you have him in hand, I think my presence is unnecessary."

Lily was rather more intrigued than she wanted to be. "I'm not letting you leave now. Coat on the rack and take a seat."

"I'd like to keep my coat on if it's all the same to you."

"I reckon that's your prerogative." She turned to rekindle the wood in the stove while Clay and Roen went to the table. It was tempting to look over her shoulder to see if she could catch them communicating in some fashion, but she resisted because she realized she wanted to believe that Roen Shepard had her son's best interests on his mind.

Lily removed the stew pot from the warming drawer and set it on the stove. She gave it a stir before she finally turned around. Clay was sitting opposite Roen. He was staring at the tabletop, his head bent like a penitent. Roen was staring at him. "Are you prepared to begin?" she asked. "The stew will be ready to eat in about five minutes. That should be enough time to tell me the truth." The implication was that a story would take much longer.

Clay lifted his head and looked at this mother. "I'm real sorry that I'm late. Mr. Shepard wanted me to go home straightaway once we got into town, but I figured he was paying for a full day's work and I thought I should give it to him."

"Admirable," she said dryly.

"Uh-huh. I thought it was proper. Mr. Shepard wasn't so sure, but I wore him down. Well, not so much wore him down as I wouldn't leave his side."

"I see." But of course, she didn't.

"I told him we should see Doc Madison first thing. He had other ideas. Wanted to unpack his work gear and make sure it was all undamaged. We left our last site in a hurry and didn't have time to look things over."

"Mm-hmm."

"Right. So we did that and then we argued about whether we should see the doctor or the sheriff. I was still of a mind that it should be the doc, but Mr. Shepard, well, he's my boss, so we went to the sheriff's office. Turned out it was a good decision because the doc was there."

"Two birds, one stone."

"That's what Sheriff Ben said. We made our report while the doc tended to Mr. Shepard. Afterwards, we took the horses back to the livery, and here we are."

"And here you are," Lily said softly. Her gaze swiveled to Roen Shepard. She could find no evidence that pointed to Ridley's medical attention, but then he was still wearing his coat. She was thoughtful as she regarded her son again. "Do you think I'm satisfied with your explanation?"

"It's the truth."

"I believe you. It's just not the *whole* truth."

"Oh." He had a short reprieve as Hannah, Ham, and Lizzie chose that moment to rush into the kitchen carrying cards and clamoring for Lily to tell them who had the better hand.

"I've been teaching them poker," she explained somewhat sheepishly. "I was bored with Old Maid." Lily thought Roen's chuckle rumbled too pleasantly in her ear for her peace of mind. She busied herself examining the hands her children thrust in her direction. "Ham's full house is better than two of a kind, girls. Now, go on. No more interruptions."

After they ran off, Lily rose from the table, stirred the stew, and then portioned it out into two bowls. She placed the bowls in front of Clay and Roen and added a plate of bread, which she put between them. "No ceremony," she said, taking her seat once more. "Eat up. Clay, I know you can talk with your mouth full so don't let that stop you now."

Clay's dark sideways glance was suspicious. "Are you funnin' me?"

"Where do you come by these expressions? No, that doesn't require an answer. Yes, I was funnin' you."

Clay nodded, swallowed. "You probably want to know what happened after we rode out this morning."

"That would be a good start." She listened attentively to her son's description of the work he performed for Mr. Shepard. It was clear not only that he was learning some useful skills but also that he was proud of his contribution. She did not want to dismiss his account by hurrying him along, but it required extraordinary patience on her part.

"So we were packing up after we ate," Clay said, "and I saw something moving off to my left. Not close, mind you. Probably wouldn't have noticed it at all except that there was this glint, like something caught the sunlight and reflected it. Mr. Shepard didn't see it so I asked if I could look through the telescope. He handed it over and that's when someone took a shot at us."

Lily's lips parted but no sound emerged.

"Uh-huh," said Clay. "You heard me right. I'm not hurt, Ma. Not a scratch, but Mr. Shepard got hit when he flung out an arm and pushed me to the ground. I'd guess you'd say he was a hero."

"I prefer to reserve judgment," Lily said calmly.

Clay nodded as if he'd expected that. "Now you know all of it. The whole truth like you asked for." He tucked into his stew again and spoke around a hot mouthful of it. "Good stew, Ma. I told Mr. Shepard that the fried chicken Mrs. Butterworth packed for us was the second best I ever had. Yours being the first, of course."

"Of course." Lily's mouth lifted in a wry slant. "Do you think flattery is going to change my mind?"

"Change your mind about what?"

"You know very well."

He did. "I'm not gonna stop working for Mr. Shepard, Ma. I'm not. I told you he pushed me out of the way. And it was probably an accident that he got hit. That's what he and Sheriff Ben think, and I'm inclined to believe they're right."

"You don't want to argue with me now, Clay." Out of the corner of her eye she saw Roen surreptitiously shake his head at her son. It explained why Clay's mouth snapped shut. "I don't require your assistance, Mr. Shepard."

"How well I know," he said. "I simply didn't want to hear him argue either."

Lily couldn't quite tamp down her smile. "Would you like something to drink? I have tea. Coffee if you prefer. I don't keep beer."

"Tea, please."

Lily got up and put on the kettle. She leaned back against the sink while she waited for the water to heat. "Is this the first someone's taken a shot at you?"

"While I'm conducting a survey it is."

"What are you not telling me? Someone's taken a shot at you but not while you were going about your work?"

"That'd be the gist of it."

"Are you going to explain that?"

"No."

Clay spoke up. "He wouldn't tell me any more either, Ma, but he's been shot before, not just shot at."

"Is that right?" She wasn't certain whom she was addressing at that point, but they nodded their heads simultaneously. "What was the purpose of surveying that particular parcel of land?"

Roen explained his theory about the map being inaccurate. "We were on our way to proving that some of the land that Harrison Hardy claims belongs to the Double H is actually Twin Star property."

"Thaddeus Frost and Mr. Hardy have been neighbors and neighborly for years. If it's not a bone of contention for the two of them, why make it one? Why is it important to you?"

"It's not personal, Mrs. Salt. It's business. Mr. Hardy might have no legal right to sell the property even if he wanted to. Mr. Frost is potentially more amenable to an arrangement with Northeast."

"You think so?" She laughed under her

breath. "What did Ben say when you told him that? You did tell him, didn't you?"

"He chuckled, same as you."

Lily started to respond to that and thought better of it. She extended a hand and touched Clay on the shoulder. "That bowl's empty, son. You're going to erase the ivy pattern next. Pass it here and go in the parlor with the others."

Clay's mouth flattened and then turned down, but he got up and surrendered his bowl and spoon. His displeasure was further marked by his heavy footfalls as he left the kitchen.

Lily waited until she saw he had turned the corner into the parlor and was well out of earshot. "Some things aren't for his ears," she said, "even if he thinks they should be. Do you know about Ben's connection to Twin Star and Thaddeus Frost?"

"Not really. I had the sense that he wanted to explain it to me, but then he looked at Clay and seemed to think better of it. Probably for the same reason you sent Clay out of the room."

"That's Ben. I don't think he'd mind me telling you. It's not exactly a secret but it's not for children either. I'm surprised Mrs. Springer hasn't bent your ear about it already."

"She started to. Mr. Springer pulled her away."

"He's had a lot of practice." The kettle started to roil and Lily attended to it first, pouring hot water over the tea ball in the ivy-patterned pot. She set the teapot on the table and took out two cups and saucers from the china cupboard. "Most people believe that Ben is Thaddeus Frost's son. Ben doesn't make that claim. He probably doesn't know for sure but that doesn't stop folks from speculating. Mr. Frost raised Ben beside his own son and treated Ben as if he were a son so I tend to think the distinction of bastardy versus legitimacy is an unimportant one. Ben's mother was a housekeeper at Twin Star for more than twenty years, and she helped care for Remington when his mother died of childbed fever. Ben was born sometime after that. You can see why people wonder about something that's not their business."

Lily judged the tea had had enough time to steep and she poured for both of them. "Sugar? I don't have milk. Lizzie had the last of it at dinner."

"Sugar, please. I don't take milk."

Lily carried the sugar bowl to the table and let Roen serve himself. She sat then and drew the sugar closer to her cup when he was finished. "I'm telling you this to explain why Ben chuckled when you brought up Twin Star. I think he was letting you know that Thaddeus Frost isn't likely to be any more amenable to an arrangement with the railroad than Mr. Hardy. Ben is close to all the Frosts so you have to figure he'd have at least an inkling of how Thaddeus would respond to an overture from you."

"Hmm."

"That's all? Hmm?"

Roen slowly stirred his tea. "It's a lot to take in. I suppose I'm thinking that Ben had opportunities to tell me and didn't. I'm wondering now how he feels about the railroad passing through Frost property. It'd be personal to him."

"Yes, it would, but probably not so that he'd take a shot at you," she said, deadpan.

One corner of Roen's mouth twisted in a quirky grin, though he matched her arid tone. "Probably not."

Lily said, "Thaddeus settled a tract of land on him, the same as he did Remington, but Ben seems to be settled here in town and I haven't heard that he intends to move to the ranch anytime soon. It wouldn't suit his wife anyway, at least not while she's practicing medicine."

Roen nodded, thoughtful. "Do you think he would accompany me to see Mr. Frost?"

"I don't know, but I imagine you'll want to find out what Ben thinks about the railroad on Twin Star land first, and you'll also want to ask him what he thinks Remington's opinion would be. Don't misunderstand; Thaddeus Frost is his own man. In the end, he's the one you'll have to convince."

"Before I do that, I have to discover who owns that strip of land I was surveying today."

Lily picked up her cup, sipped, and then set it carefully on its saucer. She looked steadily at Roen, her expression grave. "You understand you'll be doing that without my son's assistance."

"I'm very well aware. I explained that to him on the ride back to town. He had objections."

Her mouth curled in a half smile. "I'm certain he did."

"There are ways in which he can still assist me, if you will permit it, but I will not allow him to accompany me out of town even when the work site is miles beyond where we were today. You can take me at my word, Mrs. Salt. Today's little adventure is not something I wish to repeat and not because I was shot."

Lily appreciated that Roen Shepard did not avoid looking at her. His gaze remained direct, sincere, and he tolerated her taking his measure. "All right, Mr. Shepard. I will take you at your word." Could he possibly know how difficult it was for her to say that? Unlikely. He struck her as someone who was used to being trusted, and undoubtedly he had earned that reputation among his colleagues and from the company that employed him, but what did he really know about making and keeping promises to the mother of a headstrong boy? Lily released a breath she didn't know she was holding as she realized she had just agreed to find out.

"Thank you," said Roen. "I appreciate your confidence."

"Don't disappoint me." Even to her own ears it sounded vaguely like a threat. Roen must have heard it the same way, she thought, because he blinked rather like an owl. Rather than dwell on the moment so that it required an apology, Lily forged ahead. "What did Ben have to say about the shooting? Does he suspect Mr. Hardy?"

"No. Not Mr. Hardy himself, but I understand he has four sons and that any one of them might have found my presence objectionable. I'm going to ride out to the

Double H with Ben tomorrow and introduce myself. None of the Hardys came to town for my presentation so this is an opportunity to put the facts before them."

"Or get yourself shot again. You could let Ben go alone, you know."

"I could. I suspect he'd prefer it, but he left it up to me. I don't believe there was intention to do harm. The purpose was to run me off, and it worked. Whoever was doing the shooting might not realize he hit me. It's merely a graze."

"Let me see."

"I don't think —"

"Mr. Shepard." Lily spoke his name in the firm and patient manner of one who would not be ignored or dismissed. He must have recognized the tone because he sighed and began to remove his coat. She observed him wince several times but declined to draw attention to it. When he finally shrugged off the coat so that it lay over the back of his chair, she had her first glimpse of the bloody rent in his sleeve and the bandage that covered his injury under it. "How many stitches did Ridley give you?"

"Five."

Amused, Lily looked away from his wound to examine his face. "A graze doesn't require stitches, Mr. Shepard."

He grinned sheepishly. "I realize that. Now. You tricked me."

"If you'd like to think that . . ." She offered an innocent, elegant shrug. "If you take that shirt to Mrs. Fish, she'll pass it on to me for repairing."

"Or I could give it to you directly."

She shook her head. "It's not done that way."

"Appearances. Yes, I understand. Very well, I'll take this shirt and another that I purchased at Hennepin's to Mrs. Fish."

"What's wrong with the other shirt?"

Roen lifted one of the drooping shoulder seams. "It looks like this."

"Oh." Lily felt herself begin to smile and quickly raised her teacup to hide it.

"It's all right," said Roen. "Your son's already pointed out the flaws in my work attire."

Lily was genuinely appalled. "He did what?"

"He spoke the truth. You can't fault him for that." Roen explained how one of his bags did not follow him when he changed trains in Saint Louis. "He also told me he prefers a hat like the sheriff wears to my derby."

"Clay is a bit too free with his opinions."

Roen shrugged. "Maybe, but he's not wrong."

Lily's lips parted, but the thought that was on the tip of her tongue stayed there. She bit her lower lip instead.

"Go on," he said. "I can see you want to say something. Is it the hat?"

She shook her head.

"Well, it's not the boots. Clay had a favorable view of my boots."

"Trousers," she said on a thread of sound. "You might consider dropping off the trousers when you bring the shirts."

"Right. The trousers."

Lily caught the wry twist of his mouth and the even wryer twist in his tone. "You're not offended?"

"Offended? No. Humbled, certainly. In New York I have a reputation as a natty dresser, although I make no effort at it and take no pride in it."

She was amused. "I can see that. You as a natty dresser, I mean. Black silk evening suit with spoon-shaped coattail. White tie and vest. Top hat."

He put out a hand as if he could ward her off, but a rueful chuckle accompanied the gesture. "Please. You have to stop."

Far from stopping, Lily leaned forward and asked with earnest curiosity, "Do you attend the opera? I think you must attend the opera."

He sighed. "Only when my sister is in the production and only when she is one of the featured performers. I love Artemis, but I do not share her passion for the opera."

"Artemis Shepard? The coloratura soprano? She's your sister?"

"One of them. I suppose I need to stop being surprised that members of my family are known in what they would call parts unknown."

"I read about her in the *Rocky.* She was in Chicago with the opera company, and the paper sent one of their reporters to interview her. The reporter was effusive in his praise of her performance. He called it a triumph, I believe."

"She makes quite an impression," said Roen. "Onstage and off."

Lily heard something in his tone that she couldn't quite identify. "Aren't you proud?"

"Yes. Artemis is extraordinarily talented, and she is not above regularly reminding me. I'm her brother, remember. Her *younger* brother. I love her, but I don't always like her. She's Artemis James now. She keeps her maiden name for the stage. Robert James is her third husband, so you can see that remaining a Shepard is a practical choice."

"You must find Frost Falls provincial. I don't even know what a coloratura soprano is."

"When no one is shooting at me, I find Frost Falls close to perfect, and coloratura is fancy singing. Lots of trilling. When I want to needle her, I tell her she warbles. She throws something at my head, I duck, and we're good again for a couple of months."

"Your mother and sister are vastly talented. Is that true for everyone in your family?"

"My sister Apollonia is a concert pianist who regularly tours Europe. My brother is Rand Shepard, the writer. He has eight novels published. You have one of them here. I saw it on your mantel."

"Beckwith's Ghost."

"That's it. Is it overdue at the library? Miss Fletcher told Clay that he had a book out that he needed to return."

"It might be due, but he brought it home for me. I suppose that means I have to pay the fine." Lily smiled a shade guiltily. "It supports the library, you know."

Roen managed not to choke as he was swallowing his tea, but it was a narrow thing.

"Are you all right?" she asked.

"Mm." He cleared his throat. "I'm good. Clay said much the same thing about the book fines."

"Oh, I see. I'll speak to him. I don't want him to think that paying the fine justifies the crime."

Roen arched an eyebrow. "The crime?"

Lily blinked. "Pardon?"

"You said you don't want him to think that paying the fine justifies the crime. Crime seems a rather harsh characterization for overdue books."

She had spoken carelessly, she realized, lulled into a sense of well-being by easy conversation with comfortable company. She would have to be on her guard. There were things she could never say and he could never know. It begged the disturbing question: When had Roen Shepard's presence at her kitchen table become comfortable?

Chapter Eleven

The visit to the Double H was unproductive. Harrison Hardy seemed surprised to hear about the shooting, and Roen decided he was either a fine actor or telling the truth. He was less certain about Hardy's four sons, but they weren't about to break ranks. If any one of them had done it, then he wasn't saying, and no one was going to point fingers.

Ben Madison escorted Roen back to town by way of the Twin Star Ranch. Thaddeus and Remington Frost were interested in what Roen had to say about the property lines being drawn up wrong but not eager to make the correction for the benefit of the railroad. Roen did not bring up eminent domain. That was an option of last resort as far as he was concerned, although he wasn't sure his employer, the government, or the Stonechurch mining operation would agree with him.

During the weeks that followed, Roen made regular surveys of the country outside of Frost Falls but stayed clear of the property that he considered in dispute. Clay Salt remained helpful in a limited capacity and gradually accepted that his role had changed. He still acquired the horses from the livery, packed them, and picked up Roen's provisions from the Butterworth. He studied the maps and the proposed routes, and saw familiar territory with fresh eyes. As far as Roen was concerned, the boy was a sponge, absorbing everything Roen could teach him with an eagerness that was exciting but occasionally exhausting.

The first significant snow fell early in November. The temperatures dipped dangerously low even for the natives, and Maxwell Wayne complained that his bones ached as fierce as the wind that howled through the center of town.

When Clay showed up on Roen's doorstep after another burst of snow, shovel in hand, Roen thought it was because the boy wanted to earn some money for clearing a path from the porch to the street. It turned out that Clay already had an arrangement with Ben to do that, and his purpose at the door was to resume his math studies. Roen suggested they return to it the following evening or even in a few days and that Clay go back home before winter swallowed him whole. That's when Roen was pointedly reminded that winter hadn't yet arrived and that he'd better get himself a coat fit for the weather. Roen invited him inside.

"Your enthusiasm for trigonometry does you credit," Roen said, taking Clay's outerwear as he peeled it off in the entranceway. "But wouldn't you rather spend the evening reading a book? An adventure story? A mystery?"

Clay dropped to the floor, removed his snow-covered boots, and massaged his toes through his thick woolen socks. "Is that what you were doing?"

"As a matter of fact, I was. Someone finally returned *Beckwith's Ghost* to the library. I decided I should read it." He hung Clay's things on the coatrack and toed the boots aside so they weren't blocking the door. "We'll work in the front room tonight. It's warmer there."

Clay stood and followed Roen into the parlor. He sat on the end of the sofa closest to the woodstove and warmed his hands while Roen went to get paper and pencils. When Roen returned, Clay reached in his pocket and pulled out a piece of paper that was folded into quarters. "I got that problem you gave me a couple of days ago right here. It was a real head scratcher. Took me some time, but I think I got it."

"Let me look." Roen set the paper and pencils on a side table on top of *Beckwith's Ghost* and took Clay's offering before he sat down. He unfolded the paper, smoothed it out over his knee, and examined it for errors. There were none. It was hard not to be aware that Clay was anxiously awaiting the verdict. "Excellent work," said Roen. "But I don't think it's yours alone, is it? Who helped you?"

Clay hung his head. "Ma," he whispered.

"Are you embarrassed?"

"Ashamed I didn't get it on my own and embarrassed you figured it out."

"I see. There's nothing wrong with asking for help. How much of it did your mother do?"

"Most —" He stopped, shook his head. "All of it. I had to teach her some about tangents and cotangents, sines and cosines, but then she took to it like a cat to a mouse. Played with the problem like she was enjoying herself." He glanced up at Roen. "She's real smart, isn't she?"

"She is. Do you understand how to solve the problem now?"

"Uh-huh. She showed me. I had to do it

on my own. I guess I brought the wrong paper. She'll be tickled when I tell her she got it right."

"I think she probably knows that she did."

Clay shrugged. "Maybe. What are you going to show me tonight?"

"I guess that depends on what your mother wants to learn."

"Oh, you figured that out, too."

"None too quickly, I think. You've been teaching her all along."

"Best I can. I had to get some books for her from the library." He hesitated. "You don't mind?"

"Mind? No, of course not. Teaching her probably helps you."

"It does. Kinda cements it in my mind. At least sometimes it does. Sometimes, like with this problem, she has to teach me."

"How is your mother?"

"Fine."

"I haven't seen her except in passing, and she passes quickly. I managed to thank her for altering my clothes. That was the extent of our conversation, and the talking was mostly on my end."

"You still like her, though, right?"

"Yes, of course."

"Good, because Hannah and I have been thinking you ought to come around again.

It's been a long time. I think maybe since you were shot."

It had been exactly that long, but Roen did not confirm it. "You and Hannah think too much. It can't be good for you."

"What? Oh, you're funnin' me again."

"I'm not sure I am. Regardless, I am not showing up at your house again uninvited."

"I invited you."

Roen clarified, "The invitation needs to come from your mother."

"Well, that's not going to happen. She says she doesn't have a lot of use for company, even when it's the minister."

"That's my point, Clay. I'm not going to trespass on your mother's privacy."

Clay sighed heavily and plowed his fingers through his coal black hair. "This is a conundrum worse than any problem you ever gave me."

Roen didn't laugh because he knew Clay was serious, but he couldn't stop his lips from twitching. He cleared his throat and tamped down his smile. "I can't fix your conundrum, but I can give you a harder problem."

Three days later, Clay's conundrum became Roen's when he received a telegram from Victorine Headley while he was enjoying a late lunch at the Butterworth. He gave young Frankie Fuller a nickel for delivering it and hoped the boy hadn't heard him swear under his breath when he saw who it was from. Except for him, Deputy Hitch Springer, who was waiting for a tray to take back to the jail, and an older couple in town for their daughter's wedding, the hotel's dining room was deserted. Roen was aware the arrival of the telegram brought attention to his table. "Business," he said in response to their inquiring stares. He said it so matter-of-factly that he almost believed it himself. He waited until the others were no longer looking in his direction before he opened it. The message was brief and everything he feared.

FOUND YOU STOP
ARRIVING WEDS STOP

Obviously she had found him. The telegram delivery confirmed that. Victorine wanted to underscore her triumph. She'd switched weapons, abandoned her palm pistol in favor of driving a knife in his back.

Wednesday. If he could believe her, she was going to arrive on Wednesday, but that was a very big "if." The best he could hope for was that she was merely funnin' him and wouldn't arrive at all. It strained his thinking to imagine her in Frost Falls. She lived on Fifth Avenue north of Fiftieth Street in an impressive — some would say imperious — gray stone mansion overlooking Central Park. The whole of the Butterworth Hotel, grand by Frost Falls standards, was not much bigger than the coach house at the back of the property. Where on earth did she imagine she would be staying?

Victorine came from transportation money. First, shipping. Later, railroads. Her father was rumored to be investing in the development of automobiles though no one had ever seen him ride in one of the horseless carriages. Their popularity was still a novelty, but Roen suspected that if the rumors were true, Victor Headley's interest would take the automobile from novelty to necessity. Victorine's father was no one's fool.

It was Victor Headley who had introduced Roen to his daughter. Reluctantly, Roen thought now. Victorine had forced the introduction when she sailed into her father's study and interrupted negotiations on the contract Victor was proposing to Roen. "This is why I don't like to work at home," Victor had said, but because he smiled warmly at his daughter as he said it, Roen thought he had a father's happy tolerance for the intrusion. He learned later that he was under a misapprehension. Victor Headley suffered his only child's presence but did not embrace it. According to Victorine, that warm, welcoming smile was for Roen's benefit.

Recalling that she had been in his bed when she offered that explanation, Roen knew why he had found it easy to believe. The shot that nearly unmanned him made him question everything. Sighing, he folded the telegram and slipped it inside his jacket. He looked down at his plate. He'd finished only half the serving of chicken and gravy over biscuits, and now the whole of it appeared to be congealing in a cold, unappetizing fashion. No longer hungry, he pushed the plate away and leaned back in his chair.

"You don't like it, Mr. Shepard?"

Roen's head snapped up. He'd been staring at the pattern of cabbage roses on the far wall. Fedora put him in mind of a hummingbird the way she seemed to hover beside his table. She watched him, her dark eyes wary. Nothing about that had changed since she'd first waited on him. Roen thought if he moved unexpectedly, she would dart away. "I liked it just fine, Miss

Chen, but I'm done. Please extend my compliments to Mrs. Vandergrift. I'd like a beer, though, no more coffee."

"Yes. Yes, of course." She cleared the table.

Roen anticipated that she would leave then. When she didn't, he slowly raised a questioning eyebrow. He watched her take a breath, pause, then take another before she found the courage to speak.

"Is he looking this way?" She mouthed the words more than whispered them.

It could only be the deputy or the man sitting with his wife to whom she was referring. Roen casually let his gaze roam without focusing on any of the occupants. Hitchcock Springer was certainly looking this way. In answer to Fedora's question, he nodded. For the life of him, he couldn't tell if she was pleased or disturbed.

"Thank you. I'll bring your beer."

Roen watched her make a graceful turn and dart away. The deputy's eyes followed her. If Hitchcock Springer wasn't lovesick, then Roen needed a new word for what he was seeing. He wondered if he had ever looked at Victorine like that. He didn't think so. She'd never provoked that feeling in him, and he would wager everything he had that it had been the same for her. There was mutual attraction, some shared interests, and a reciprocated need for companionship. None of it justified a proposal. He never once entertained the idea of marrying her, and he would have sworn it was not something she wanted either, yet when he ended their arrangement, she spoke as if marriage was exactly what she expected. He knew she had been unfaithful; she didn't deny it. It was the odd sense of relief that he felt that told him it was time to step away.

It came to him gradually that Victorine Headley wasn't who he thought she was, though in fairness, perhaps she would say the same of him. He began to understand that she was attracted to him in part because he was working for her father. She was the princess and he was the help. Over time he also recognized there were no common interests. She pretended to share his enjoyment for walking or skating in the park, milling with the artists in Greenwich and the rabble in the Bowery, or sailing on the Hudson, in which she was expected to help with the sails. He, on the other hand, made no secret of the fact that he did not like fancy dress balls, theater openings, or dinners with fifteen courses and fifty people at the table. He went because it was important to her. She was headstrong and spoiled and had a dog-in-the-manger view of people and things. Once she laid claim to someone or something, what became important was that no one else had it.

She'd aimed her gun at him only after she'd learned he'd gone riding in Central Park with Mary Ellen Glidden. His arrangement with Victorine had ended three weeks earlier, but Roen had time to reflect on what she'd done while he was convalescing in his parents' home. He came to understand that Victorine had merely bided her time in anticipation of an opportunity. Mary Ellen Glidden was the catalyst for revenge. The whole affair was tawdry enough that his brother was contemplating using it in his next book.

From time to time, Roen wondered if he should have reported the incident to the police instead of arriving at the hospital with the claim that he'd shot himself while cleaning his pistol. No one questioned him so he stayed with his story. The hospital doctors and matrons were familiar with his family, the talent and the eccentricities, and that was enough to assure that he was believed. Hadn't his mother once shot a blank canvas when she couldn't find inspiration? And his father had severed the head of a sculpture nearing completion with such passion that bits of flying marble embedded in his forehead, cheek, and neck. Artemis flew at her second husband with a barber's razor during a rehearsal of *Figaro,* and the poor man required thirteen stitches in his arm.

Roen had overheard the nurses giggling and whispering behind his bed screen. They seemed to be disappointed that his injury didn't arise from artistic temperament. Even in this, he was the black sheep.

Sometime during his musings, Fedora Chen had reappeared with his beer. He'd hardly noticed. Hitch was gone now but the couple had been joined by their daughter and her fiancé. They were talking excitedly about the upcoming wedding, Roen supposed. He picked up his beer and took a long pull. At the back of his mind, a thought niggled. He tried to hold on to it but it proved elusive. He finished his beer and ordered another. Alcohol had a way of loosening provocative thoughts, especially ones that weren't his own. It was someone else's idea first; he was sure of it. Ben's? Clay's? Something Mrs. Springer had said?

Fedora brought his second beer. He drank slowly, trying to remember where he'd been when he heard the idea. The hotel? The drugstore? The sheriff's office?

He set his mug down with a satisfying thump. It was the sheriff's office, and it was the sheriff's wife who had definite ideas of her own. "Lily's company is a safeguard, isn't it?" she had said. "You chose her quite deliberately because you learned very quickly that she's a widow with four children who has even less interest in romantic entanglements than you. I don't think it matters to you how Lily's companionship is perceived by others as long as it keeps the keenly interested at bay and allows you to go about your work."

Victorine Headley certainly qualified as the keenly interested. And she would never allow him to go about his work.

Roen pushed back his chair, stood, and said good day to Mrs. Springer when he passed her in the foyer on his way out. He considered telling her where he was going and why just to see the shock on her face, but he kept his destination and his purpose a secret.

That was only fair to Lily Salt. In spite of what Ridley Madison thought, it did matter to him how her companionship was perceived by others. It mattered a great deal.

Chapter Twelve

Lily was comfortably ensconced in her rocker when someone knocked at the front door. There was a pile of mending on one side and fabric for a new gown on the other. The navy blue skirt in her lap required hemming, but she hadn't begun so she set it aside, intending to go to the door herself. Clay was already on his feet and hurrying to the door when she was only halfway out of the rocker. Shaking her head, she resumed her position.

"Is he expecting Frankie Fuller?" she asked Hannah.

Hannah was curled on the sofa and didn't look up from the book she was reading. "Don't know, Ma."

"The way he raced to the door, I thought . . ." She shrugged, bent her head to the task of searching for the right color thread for the hem, and didn't look up as she calmly admonished Ham to stop teasing Lizzie.

"But you didn't even see me," he protested.

"I don't need to see you. You're making your sister squeal and that's enough for me. And, Lizzie, don't you stick your tongue out at him." She smiled to herself as her youngest children fell silent. Her pleasure did not last long. The quiet allowed her to hear Clay and their visitor at the door.

"It's Mr. Shepard," said Hannah, closing her book around her finger as she looked toward the doorway.

"Yes. I'm aware now." Lily threaded a needle and then called to her son. "Let him in, Clay. It's too cold out to keep someone standing on the doorstep." When there was no movement at the door, she looked to Hannah, who was craning her neck for a better view.

"Clay slipped outside. I don't think he heard you."

Lily sighed. "They are both going to get frostbite." By Lily's count, it was a full minute before the door opened again. She heard more than one pair of boots stomping at the threshold to shake off clumps of snow. Clay had his arms folded across his chest and his hands under his armpits for warmth when he came to the parlor entrance. A shiver rippled through him followed by chattering teeth. "Don't just stand there, Clay. Go to the stove and warm yourself."

"It's Mr. Shepard," he said. The announcement was unnecessary as it happened because Roen was already behind him.

"You, too, Mr. Shepard," said Lily, nodding toward the stove. "Hannah will take your outerwear as soon as you're warm."

Roen removed his gloves and unwound his gray woolen scarf and gave them to Hannah as he passed her on the way to the stove. He opened his coat to let the warmth seep in and then extended his arms so that his hands hovered inches above the top of the stove. In a few minutes he was sufficiently warm to shrug out of his coat and remove his hat. He passed both to Hannah.

"May I?" he asked, pointing to the overstuffed armchair.

"Of course." Lily glanced at Clay, who was still at the stove and did not appear to have any intention of moving without direction to do so. "Clay, go to the kitchen and put on the kettle. Make a pot of tea, please, and bring the service in here. Take Ham with you. You can play a game of cards with him while you're waiting for the water to boil."

Lily thought Clay might protest, but he surprised her by taking Ham by the hand and leading him off. Hannah reentered the parlor just then, having dealt with Mr. Shepard's garments. Lily directed her to take her book, her sister, and her sister's doll upstairs. Hannah did as she was told but in a dramatic fashion, dragging her feet and sighing with much feeling.

Lily watched them go, her amusement in check, and then set her blue-green gaze on Roen Shepard. Her raised eyebrows served as a question. She waited for an explanation.

"Am I so obvious, then?" Roen asked.

"If you only wanted to speak to Clay, you'd have already done it and you would be on your way. Instead, you're still here, and I take that to mean you want to speak to me. Alone is better, I think. A precaution, really. I can't predict what you're going to say."

"Then I *am* obvious."

"But not predictable."

"A fine distinction, but I appreciate it."

Lily nodded, waited, and when he said nothing, she prompted him. "So?"

Roen blew out a breath. "So," he said heavily. "I have a proposal for you, and I'd like you to hear me out and give it serious consideration."

"Another proposal? Is this about Clay again? Have you changed your mind about wanting to take him out with you?"

"This is not about Clay. I just went through that again with him. That's why we were standing out in the cold. He didn't want you to hear." Roen held up a hand, palm out. "Please don't say anything to him about it. He doesn't ask as often as he used to, and my answer is always the same. In his place, I'd want to press just as hard."

"All right. I won't caution him again about pestering you."

"Good."

"So, if your proposal is not about Clay, then what is it about?"

"You."

Lily blinked. "Me?"

"Yes. I am proposing an arrangement in which you agree to marry me but never have to."

She stared at him. "What?"

"I admit it sounded better when I was only thinking it."

"You're mad."

"Probably."

"Not probably. Certainly."

Roen pushed fingers through his thick hair and left furrows in their wake. "Will you hear me out?"

"I'm not sure I should. I fear you'll make the ridiculous sound reasonable."

"No, I'm fairly sure it will still sound ridiculous."

His easy agreement caught her off guard. She didn't want him to amuse her. She didn't want him to make her smile. Lily clenched her teeth and felt a muscle jump in her cheek. That was better. "Very well," she said after a moment. "Go on."

"I'm not sure I should," he said, parroting her. "I'm asking you to hear me out, not do battle."

Lily chose not to respond to that. "Clay will be back with the tea soon. It would be for the best if you were to begin now."

Nodding, Roen took a moment to collect his thoughts and then plunged into the explanation that began and ended with Victorine Headley. He was forthright about his involvement with Victorine, sparing himself nothing in the telling. He shared all the ways he was mistaken in his assumptions about her and how she felt that she'd been used and then cast off by him.

"Victorine thought my interest in her was predicated on my interest in her father's empire. I can honestly say that wasn't true, although I understand why she doesn't believe me. She has no experience being the one put aside, except perhaps by her father, and while she appeared to graciously accept our end as inevitable, her rage asserted itself a few weeks later when she heard that I'd gone riding with Mary Ellen Glidden. Victorine did not consider Miss Glidden her social equal, which further enraged her. It was then that she acted on what she perceived as her humiliation. She arranged for me to go to her home under the mistaken belief that the invitation was from her father. I was waiting for him in his study, the same place I met Victorine, when she entered. I was not happy to see her, but I was considerate of her feelings and offered to wait for Victor elsewhere. That's when she —"

"Shot you," Lily said.

"Yes."

"Hmm. I understand why you didn't provide any details when you were here for dinner. Thank you for not sharing them with Clay when you were out at the Double H."

"I have some notion of what discretion entails."

It was true, she thought, at least where her children were concerned. Discretion was no part of his repertoire when he escorted her to the drugstore for fizzy drinks. She'd told him there would be comments, and there were. "There's more, I presume. I don't believe you've arrived at the end of your story."

"There's more," he said.

Lily merely raised her eyebrows.

"I received a telegram while I was at the hotel. It was from Victorine. Would you like to see it?"

"No. I believe you. Tell me."

"Her message read, 'Found you. Arriving Wednesday.' "

"Pithy."

"Yes."

"Do you believe her?"

"I decided I can't risk *not* believing her."

"Do you expect her to arrive with her derringer?"

"I never said it was a derringer."

"She shot you in her father's study, I presume at close range, and if she'd used something more powerful, say, a forty-five or a thirty-eight, you and I would not be having this conversation. Not that a palm pistol can't kill you, but your chances of recovery are improved if it's a peashooter."

"It didn't feel like a peashooter."

She smiled indulgently. "No, probably not. Where did she shoot you?"

"I'd rather not say."

"The groin, then."

Roen's head reared back. "The inner thigh."

"But she aimed for your groin."

"You are rather more frank than I could have imagined."

"Have I shocked you?"

"I think you have. You are not at all predictable, Mrs. Salt."

Lily accepted that as a good thing. She caught movement out of the corner of her eye. "Ah. Our tea has arrived." She waved Clay in. Ham followed on his brother's heels. "Will you pour, Clay?" She set her sewing aside in the event she had to help him. It was an unnecessary precaution. He didn't spill a drop, and after adding sugar to Mr. Shepard's cup and a dollop of sweet cream to hers, he passed them their respective cups. "Thank you. Mr. Shepard and I still require privacy. I would like you and Ham to go upstairs. You can play cards or ask Hannah to read to you, but whatever you do, please do it quietly."

Clay's eyes darted to Roen then back to his mother. "Has he given you a headache, Ma? He has problems that will give you a headache."

"Does he? Well, they haven't yet," she said, knowing very well that she and Clay were talking about a very different set of problems. I'm fine. I *am.* Go on."

Clay took Ham by the shoulders and turned him around so he faced the stairs. "You heard Ma. Let's go." He gave his brother a nudge and then they were off, running out of the parlor and then racing up the steps.

Lily held her breath until she heard them pounding down the upstairs hall. "I always think Clay will throw Ham out of the way to reach the top first."

"Huh. I was thinking it would be Ham who did the tossing. The boy's built like a freight train engine."

Lily conceded the truth of that. She did not mention that of all her children, Ham was most physically like his father. The similarities ended there. Ham had a sweet disposition. He made mischief, but he was never cruel. "My children won't amuse themselves indefinitely, Mr. Shepard. Perhaps you should continue."

Roen took a sip of tea and then set the cup down. He leaned toward Lily, rested his forearms on his knees, and folded his hands together. "I don't know that I would have considered this proposal if Dr. Madison hadn't suggested it. That's not to say that she's aware that I mean to act on it or even that she would approve. The opposite is more likely true."

"You're telling me it was her idea but she would not approve."

"That's right."

"And this has to do with the arrangement you mentioned at the outset. The one where I agree to marry you but never have to."

"Correct. You called me mad."

"And my opinion has not changed. I imagine you believe that marriage will remove you from Miss Headley's crosshairs. What evidence do you have to support that?"

"Only that she's never had an affair with a married man. Never showed any interest in one. She doesn't pursue what someone's already claimed. She covets what she thinks will tweak her father's nose but not what will force his hand to disown her."

"He would do that?"

"I don't know. She thinks he would. That works to Victor's benefit. It keeps Victorine from acting too rashly."

"And shooting was not a rash act? Why isn't she in jail?"

"I didn't press charges, and Victor never learned of it. I left the house without assistance and the cabdriver waiting for me took me to the hospital. I have always assumed Victorine had a plausible explanation for staff brave enough to inquire. The shot wasn't loud, no one saw me leave, so there is a possibility that there were no questions."

"Your family?"

"Took it in stride."

"Why do you think she's coming here?"

"Not because she wants to kill me."

"I agree. So why?"

"She wants a marriage proposal. She indicated that was what she was expecting to hear when I broke it off."

"So if you're married, you can't very well propose to her."

"That's right."

Lily pressed three fingers to her temple and briefly closed her eyes. "I believe I have the beginnings of a headache, Mr. Shepard."

"I'm sorry. Can I get you something?"

"No. You can tell me how this would work exactly. You have a plan, I suppose."

"I do. You and I will take the train to Liberty Junction, where we'll have lunch at the Boxwood Hotel. We will introduce ourselves as Mr. and Mrs. Shepard to anyone who asks, and after we take a leisurely walk through town, we'll catch the late afternoon train and return to Frost Falls. People in Liberty Junction will believe we are married and people here will learn we eloped."

"That's your plan?"

"It probably needs refining."

"Mm-hmm."

"And you have to agree. It hinges on that."

"I'm glad you realize it." Lily kept her gaze steady on Roen. He did not look away. She suspected it was easier for him than it was for her. Her heart was racing. "How do I benefit if I agree?"

"I am encouraged you haven't said no."

"That may be, but it is not an answer to my question. You never considered that I might ask for something in return."

"You're right, I didn't. I suppose I was relying on your compassion."

"Not a good idea, Mr. Shepard." She tilted her head to one side. "Well?"

"Tutoring," he said.

Lily's brow puckered. "How's that again?"

"I'll tutor you. Clay showed me the work you did on that problem I gave him. You thought it through with no instruction."

"No instruction from you. Clay explained some things to me first, and I had a book."

"You're being modest. You proved you're capable of understanding complex calculations."

"I solved a single problem. It wasn't very

difficult."

"So say you. I recall sitting in this room speaking to you about what I would be teaching Clay. You were interested. Not just for Clay, I thought, but also for yourself. You took offense when I asked if he got his head for figures from his father."

"Yes, I remember."

"That head for figures came from you, and later you told me that you had little opportunity to advance your learning."

"Good Lord. You're as bad as Lizzie, recalling everything I say and repeating it back to me, mostly in ways I don't like to hear it."

"I won't be put off, Mrs. Salt. I'm offering you that opportunity you didn't have. When I look around this room, I can't help but notice the books. You enjoy learning, I think. They are not all for your children's benefit."

She put up her hand. "Stop talking, please."

Roen's jaw snapped shut with such force that he surprised a short laugh out of her.

"I think you must be used to getting your way, Mr. Shepard, else you wouldn't be so persistent toward that end."

"Does that mean —"

She shook her head, cutting him off.

"That was merely an observation and not meant to be construed as acceptance of your proposal."

"I see."

"I don't think you do. You've only thought this through as it relates to your situation, which is understandable but selfish and shortsighted. I admit that your offer to tutor is tempting; I only wish it had been inspired by your comprehension that I deserved to be compensated in some fashion. That compassion you were depending upon does not come cheaply."

Roen was quiet for a few long moments. "I believe I prefer to be shot by anyone rather than taken to the woodshed by you. I take it you have more terms."

"I do."

"All right. I'm listening."

"I am thinking of my children. You left them entirely out of your equation. I can't be part of your scheme when it involves lying to the children. I wouldn't accompany you to Liberty Junction without them in tow, and unless we engaged in some elaborate farce, Hannah and Clay would certainly know there were no marriage vows exchanged."

Roen pressed three fingers to his temple, mirroring Lily's earlier distress. "I believe I have the beginnings of a headache."

"As well you should. How much time did you spend developing your plan?"

"About as long as it takes to walk from the Butterworth to here."

"Ah."

"I had two beers before I set out."

"That explains it, then. Ben told me you weren't a drinker."

Roen let his hand fall to the arm of the chair and rest there. "You know, Mrs. Salt, I graduated at the top of my class, two of my bridge designs were written about in scientific journals, and I can confidently say that I am on the high side of fair to middlin' when it comes to intelligence, but here, right now, I can only claim to be a fool. Victorine Headley deserves me. You do not."

Lily's gaze dropped away from his. She stared at his hand resting on the arm of the chair. He had long, slender fingers with nails that were clipped and buffed. A pianist's fingers, she thought, though she didn't know why. She'd only ever seen Buzz Winegarten at the keys of his player piano. Perhaps Roen had an artist's hand like his mother. She could see it curling around a paintbrush and moving with deliberation from palette to canvas. Then she saw his hand as it truly was, an instrument in the service of his considerable intellect and imagination, scrawling numbers and formulas across a blank page that would become manmade wonders when applied in the three-dimensional world.

"You proposed a marriage of fiction," she said, still looking at his hand.

"Yes."

"I want to propose a marriage in fact."

CHAPTER THIRTEEN

"Mrs. Salt?" Roen bent his head to catch her eye. She was staring at his hand. When she didn't look at him, he wiggled his fingers. That seemed to lift her out of her trance.

"Hmm?"

"Did I hear you correctly? You want a marriage in fact?"

She said nothing for several seconds. "Yes, that's what I want. A legal marriage. I require nothing for myself beyond a certificate. No church ceremony. No marital bed. No ring. For my children, I require that you assist in providing for their care and demonstrate respect for me in front of them. When your work requires you to move on, we can arrange to be divorced."

"Those are your terms?"

She nodded. "I would still like to have the tutoring, but that is up to you."

Roen searched Lily's face and could find

no hint that she was anything but serious. Still, he needed to hear it again from her. "You're sure?"

"I am. I know what I'm offering is not what you were proposing, but I cannot agree to the arrangement you want. You have not said whether you can agree to mine."

"No romantic entanglements," he said, more to himself than to her. It was how Ridley Madison had characterized his interest in Lily Salt. *She's a widow with four children who has even less interest in romantic entanglements than you.* The terms by which Lily was agreeing to help him certainly bore that out. "I accept your terms."

Lily laid a hand against her midriff and sank her teeth into her lower lip.

Roen moved to the edge of the chair cushion in anticipation of Lily requiring his help. "Are you all right? There's no color in your face."

She smiled weakly. "There's no breath in my lungs."

"What can I do?"

Lily shook her head and waved him back into his chair.

Roen sank back but didn't take his eyes off her. She looked as if she'd been poleaxed. "Did you think I would say no?" he asked.

She inhaled deeply through her nose and released the breath slowly through parted lips. "I suppose I did."

"Do you want to change your mind?"

"No. Do you?"

"No." He noticed her cheeks were regaining their modest color. Lily had skin as smooth as her namesake but only when she was troubled was it as pale. He wondered if she'd had freckles as a child, maybe a light spray across her nose and cheeks that faded as she grew older. Hannah had that freckle spray, and Hannah bore the most resemblance to her mother. "Will you tell me about your particular terms? Why do you want a husband?" He watched her eyebrows lift in surprise and knew then what was coming.

"Did you misunderstand, Mr. Shepard? I don't want a husband. Wasn't I clear? I want a father for my children. Even if you only fill that position for a short time, it will be a good experience for them."

Roen wasn't as sure, but he didn't argue the point. "There isn't much time to arrange a ceremony."

"I know, so you are fortunate that Frost Falls is on Judge Miner's circuit and that the judge will be here Friday. That gives you all day tomorrow to make the arrangements."

"Yes, the arrangements. What are those exactly?"

"Your sister Artemis was married three times. Weren't you paying attention to any of them?"

Roen gave a shout of laughter that pushed Lily back in her rocker. She had to set her feet down firmly to stop it moving. "Sorry," he said.

She regarded him narrowly. "I don't think you are."

"Probably not. Not really. You have a rather biting sense of humor that I appreciate."

"I wasn't trying to be humorous."

"I know. You have a gift for it."

"Truly, Mr. Shepard, we will —"

"Roen, please. We're engaged."

Lily sighed heavily. "Roen, then. We will never be ready by Friday if you keep leading me down wayward paths. Conversation with you takes odd turns."

"All right. You were going to tell me about the arrangements."

"We will have to secure witnesses," she said. "Ben and Ridley will do nicely, I think, but you'll have to ask. You can send them here if they balk. It will be a shock and they might require convincing."

"What do I say to them?"

"The truth is best. They won't believe that we're marrying for love, so you shouldn't try that one on."

"Then I should tell them about Victorine."

"Heavens no. That sordid melodrama belongs in one of your brother's novels."

Roen opened his mouth to speak and then thought better of it. He let her go on.

"You can say that I was questioning whether I was doing right by my children to remain unmarried. Tell them we had the conversation while discussing Clay's education. You can add some detail here and there. You'll do what you do best."

"Make the ridiculous sound reasonable?"

"Exactly that."

Roen thought he should be offended, but he was learning that, with Lily, he was not. "What else?"

"You ask Ben to make sure Judge Miner makes time for us. I'm unaware of any criminal cases that he's hearing, so it shouldn't be a problem. I want this to be a private affair. Explain that to Ridley and Ben. The children will also bear witness. That assures our marriage will not remain a secret for long, but I don't want people gathering to observe the ceremony, and I certainly don't want a fuss following it."

"Not even a little fuss?"

"No. Why? Do you?"

He shrugged. "I like cake."

Laughter sputtered on Lily's lips. "All right. I'll bake a cake. Any particular kind?"

"Almond."

"Then I'll order it from Maxwell's bakery. His almond cake is better than mine."

Pleased, Roen asked, "Do you want flowers? I know that Dolly Mangold has a little greenhouse behind the drugstore because she uses flower petals to flavor some of her teas."

"Flowers. No. I don't think so."

"What about bouquets for Hannah and Lizzie?"

"Oh. Unfair of you to use them, but yes, two small bouquets would be appreciated. The girls would like that."

"Do you want to change your mind about a ring?"

Lily's fingers curled into light fists. "No. I never had one. It isn't important."

"You have lovely hands."

"I wish you hadn't said that. It's a lie. You must have noticed that my fingers are crooked."

"I didn't." He'd given an enormous

amount of attention to her *Mona Lisa* mouth. "Show me."

Lily's fists tightened.

Roen's eyes dropped to Lily's clenched hands. "Is that what you really want to do?"

"I thought you were being kind not to ask about them, but now you're telling me you're just blind."

He said nothing and continued to regard her expectantly.

Lily's mouth flattened. The creases at the corners of her eyes deepened. She held out her fists, splayed her fingers, and kept them there until Roen waved them down. "See?"

"Actually, I don't. The knuckles on the third and fourth fingers of your left hand are perhaps larger than the others, and the pinkie on your right hand curves left, but I think what you see is what your hands looked like when your fingers were broken, and what you feel is the pain that accompanied it. I would suppose that more than three of your fingers were damaged, so that means they healed remarkably well. What I see are capable hands and that makes them not only lovely, but also interesting. I would be pleased if you would allow me to mark the occasion of our wedding with a ring."

When she didn't respond except to take a

calming breath, he added, "I wouldn't expect you to return it if we divorce."

"You mean *when* we divorce."

He shrugged. "If you prefer."

Lily shook her head. "It feels wrong. Let's not argue about it. You agreed to my terms. That was one of them."

"You're right. I won't bring it up again. Is there anything else? You have a gown?"

"I have something suitable. You?"

"A suitable suit."

"Good. I'm assuming that you know we will live here. There are three bedrooms upstairs. One for the boys, one for the girls, and mine. You can keep your belongings in my room but you'll have to sleep on the sofa."

Roen's eyes slid sideways as he regarded the overstuffed piece of furniture. He wondered if it would swallow him. "It looks short."

"It won't be if you curl on your side."

"Of course. Curl on my side." What curled was Roen's lip. "Won't the children find it odd for me to be down here? You and your husband shared a bed, didn't you?"

"Yes."

"Then?"

"If they ask, which I doubt, I'll tell them you snore."

"You have answers for everything."

"I'll take that as a compliment, although I'm not sure you meant it that way."

"Mm."

"I think we're done here."

"Are we? What about the kiss?"

"The kiss?"

"I think that's the customary conclusion to the ceremony. Even a civil one."

"Customary, perhaps, but not required. Ben and Ridley won't expect it since you're going to explain it's not a . . . not a . . ."

"Love match? Is that the term you're searching for? Somewhat old-fashioned, isn't it?"

"It doesn't matter. It serves."

"So it's no to a kiss."

"Yes, it's no."

"Now I could go either way, but Hannah is a romantic. She'll expect it."

"What makes you think my daughter is a romantic?"

"Besides the fact that she's commented on my noble profile?" He turned his head sideways to emphasize the aquiline shape of his nose. When he turned back, she was shaking her head rather sadly at him. "Forget my profile. I saw what Hannah was reading. Did you?"

"I didn't notice."

"It was a Felicity Ravenwood adventure. Something about taming a beast. I only caught a glimpse of the title when she closed the book. The cover told me all I needed to know. Hannah is a dyed-in-the-wool romantic."

"She was reading about Alice's adventures the other day."

"Finding her way, then. It doesn't mean she won't expect a kiss."

"You're enjoying this, aren't you?"

"A little. You didn't stipulate that there couldn't be kissing."

"I'm stipulating it now."

"Too late. There will be kissing." He said it lightly. There could be no mistaking that he was teasing, and yet what he saw in her face told him that she hadn't heard it in the vein it was intended. He was put in mind of the first time he'd stepped into her kitchen, when there had been such wariness in her expression that he thought of her as a creature in the wild and himself as a feral beast. She had been so still on that occasion, and she was that still now. "Are you afraid of me?" he asked.

"No."

Perhaps if she had not said it so quickly, or perhaps if there had been a modest change in her countenance, he might have believed her. "I was teasing, Mrs. Salt. Clay would say I was funnin' you. I can't promise that I won't do it again, only that I won't do it about this. There will be no kissing." Whatever breath she had left seemed to be stuck in her throat. "You can breathe now."

She did, sipping the air as though through a straw.

"Better," he said. "Take another."

She nodded and sipped again.

"It would help if you would enlighten me. I don't know your mind, and you obviously don't know mine. That will come in time, or I hope it will." When she said nothing, he took a different tack, offering what he thought was the likeliest explanation. "Did you take what I said to mean that I would insist on kissing you?"

"You said there will be kissing. What interpretation am I to take from that except that there will be kissing?"

"You heard the words and took no account of the tone. Did you think I would force you?"

"You said it yourself. I don't know your mind."

"Did *he* force you?"

Lily was quiet, then, "This is a bad idea. I don't know what I was thinking. You're not mad. I am."

Roen held up a hand as though he could interrupt her thoughts. "Wait. Don't do this. Think. Perhaps we're both a little mad, but you know it's a fair, even good, arrangement. Your children will think so. Hannah and Clay have been trying to find ways that you and I might cross paths. Were you aware?"

Her eyes widened, providing the answer without having to say a word.

"I didn't think so," he said, lowering his hand so it rested on his knee. "Your older children have their own ideas about who they judge would suit you. For a while, I was their choice, and I have to tell you I was flattered."

She shook her head as if she didn't believe it or didn't want to.

"It's true. All of it."

Lily spoke quietly as if it would hurt too much to say the words any other way. "You said you were their choice for a while."

"Mm-hmm. They changed their minds."

"Do you know why?"

"The short of it is that I made you sick."

"What?" Lily frowned deeply.

"Perhaps I'm doing it now. Are you sure I can't get you anything? A headache powder?"

She touched the twin creases between her

eyebrows with her fingertips and smoothed them away. "No. I'm fine. Confused, but fine."

"Do you recall accompanying me to the drugstore for fizzy drinks?"

"Very well."

"Then you might also recall that you were not feeling well afterward. I have this information from Clay, and he and Hannah both knew it was not the fizzy that caused your distress. You were not yourself for days, I believe. Hannah told Clay you were grieving. They concluded that I needed to stay away."

"Grieving? Hannah said that?"

"According to Clay she did. He was inclined to believe her."

"Hmm."

"Was she right? Were you grieving?"

Lily stared straight ahead and didn't answer.

"Clay said I make you skittish."

"My son tells you things he knows nothing about."

"I'm not so sure that's true. He observed that I make the librarian twitchy."

Lily's hand flew to her mouth. She hid her bubbling laughter behind it.

"I know," said Roen. "It made me laugh, too. Not in front of Clay, mind you, but later when I thought about it."

Sobering, Lily lowered her hand and picked up her teacup. The tea was cold now. She sipped it anyway. "You have good instincts where Clay is concerned, and I've glimpsed the same with his brother and sisters."

"I wish those same instincts were as sharply honed with you."

"Yes, I'm sure you do." She fell silent, holding her teacup in both hands but not drinking from it again. "Why me, Mr. Shepard?"

"Roen," he said.

She didn't bite at the dangling bait and continued doggedly instead. "Why put your proposal to me instead of any of the other unmarried women in Frost Falls?"

"Miss Fletcher, for instance?"

"Well, yes. Or Mrs. Fish's daughter. Or Cerise Palmer."

"Do you mean to name every unmarried woman? Don't forget Miss Renquest. If not for the fact that she's nearing ninety, I would have gone to her home first."

"Please . . . *Roen* . . . answer my question."

"I already explained that Dr. Madison gave me the idea."

"And that's the whole of it? A stray comment in a conversation prompted your proposal?"

"Dr. Madison's comment presented itself as a solution to the problem of Victorine Headley, but that doesn't go to the heart of your question. The truth is, Mrs. Salt, I find you intriguing. I have from the first time I saw you in church. You sat in the last pew, your children on either side of you, and there was such calm about your person. Then I saw your smile, just a slip of a thing really, but it — are you familiar with a da Vinci painting called the *Mona Lisa*? Perhaps seen a reproduction of it in an art book?"

Lily shook her head.

"Well, she's famous for her smile, and the way you looked in church put me in mind of her. You don't smile nearly enough, but the hint of it sometimes hovers at the corners of your mouth, and I find myself wondering what secret amusement you're hiding." Roen lifted an eyebrow as Lily set her teacup down and pushed back in the rocker. "Ah. I think I've made you skittish."

"You haven't."

"True, you haven't tried to bolt, but do you want me to go on?"

"I've heard enough."

"Then you don't want to know that I genuinely like you."

"No."

"Or that I think you're attractive."

She touched her left temple. "I have gray hair here." She moved her hand to her right side. "And here."

"Silver wings."

Lily let her hand fall away. "That's ridiculous."

"It's poetry."

"*You're* ridiculous."

"I might be, but it doesn't change the fact that you're smiling right now. *Almost* smiling."

She rolled her lips inward, suppressing that almost smile, and shook her head. "I don't know what to make of you."

"I know."

"I have my children to consider. You could be good for them, but what will it be like when you leave?"

"You brought up divorce," he reminded her. "I didn't."

"What's the alternative? You meant for this to be a temporary arrangement."

"Did I? I don't recall saying that." Roen saw Lily blink. "If it suits us, it doesn't have to be. When my work takes me to other locations, there's no reason you and the children can't come."

"Like gypsies, you mean?"

"If you like. I was thinking you'd enjoy seeing the country outside of Frost Falls. Ben said the former sheriff here took his wife to Paris, so folks do get out."

"You don't work in Paris."

"You know you're being too literal. My point is that people leave Frost Falls to visit other places. Why can't you?"

Lily leaned forward, and asked earnestly, "Are you remembering all of my conditions?"

Roen ticked them off. "A marriage certificate. No church ceremony. No ring. You require that I assist in providing for care of the children and show you respect in front of them. I will also show you respect when they're not around, but that's what I expect of myself."

"You left something out."

"I did."

Her expression turned cynical. "You did."

"It must be that piece you said about the marital bed."

"I said no marital bed."

"Uh-huh."

"You agreed to it."

"I did."

"Did you think it would be something we could renegotiate at a later date?"

"Are you telling me we can't?"

"I don't like to say never. What I *am* saying is that you shouldn't hold out hope."

"All right, but that's my prerogative. I'm an optimist."

"You're delusional."

"It's a fine line."

"Not from where I'm sitting. What about romantic entanglements? I thought you were opposed to them."

"Not opposed. I said I wasn't interested. I meant at this time. Victorine left an unpleasant taste in my mouth."

"Understandable. What if your interest changes and I'm in the way?"

Roen sighed. "Can we leave that for another time? Can we not get married first?"

"You know that's not sensible."

"Nothing about this is sensible, but that doesn't mean we can't make it work. Take a risk with me, Lily."

Chapter Fourteen

"I will," she said. And with those words, her part of the ceremony was done. Lily listened as Roen repeated his vows after each of Judge Miner's prompts. There was more weight to his speech than hers. She'd heard the trembling in her voice even if no one else had. Roen had taken her hand in his, so she was fairly certain he'd felt the tremble at her fingertips. It calmed her, his hand. That was unexpected. So was the gentle brush of his thumb against her cheek after the judge pronounced them husband and wife. He would have been surprised to know that she thought about kissing him just then. Mercifully, the thought passed.

Lizzie threw her arms around her mother's legs and hugged her hard. Lily smiled indulgently and ruffled her daughter's hair. Hannah joined her sister, halting any forward progress Lily intended to make. Clay and Ham stepped forward and gravely shook Roen's hand.

Ridley corralled the children so Lily and Roen could thank the judge and look over their certificate. Ben took a copy to register it.

"It's done," Lily said after the judge had excused himself.

Roen nodded. "Was it painful for you?"

"The opposite. I hardly felt a thing."

He chuckled. "Just so you remember it."

There was no chance she would ever forget it, especially the brush stroke of his thumb on her cheek. If she had been alone, she would have covered the spot with her palm. She imagined that she still felt its warmth, but she wanted to touch it and know it was real.

He was so handsome. She allowed herself to appreciate that now and even acknowledge that it played some small part in her decision. She wondered if he knew. Probably. It was her experience that men generally knew if they were kindly featured. Women, not always, even the pretty ones like Ridley Madison. Lily looked at Ridley now, her arm linked in the crook of her husband's. She was listening to Hannah, chuckling at something she'd said, but then she glanced up and saw Lily watching, and she asked Hannah and others to wait by the door.

Lily wished she hadn't done that. Sometimes she needed her children to serve as a shield, no matter that she despised herself for it. Now was one of those times. She liked Ridley, admired her, but the doctor did not shy away from conversations that could be painful. Lily feared that one such conversation was in the offing. Without thinking, she slipped her arm under Roen's.

"Thank you for standing up for us," Lily said, addressing both Ridley and Ben.

Ridley said, "Roen must have mentioned we had reservations."

"Ridley," said Ben. "It's done now."

"It's all right," Lily said. "Roen did tell me. It's what I expected, which is why I appreciate you respecting my wishes. That meant a lot to me, that you trusted me to know my own mind."

"Don't make us regret it, Lily." Ridley looked meaningfully at Roen. "Don't *you* make *her* regret it."

"No, ma'am."

When Ridley merely continued to stare at him, Ben said, "How come you don't say anything when he calls you ma'am? I seem to recall that when I did it, you made it a point to tell me you were a doctor, not a ma'am."

"True, but he's younger than you."

"Not younger than I was then."

"He's better looking than you. That counts for something."

Ben affected a hurt look that was so out of proportion to the slight that Roen and Lily both laughed. Tension broken, precisely as he'd intended, Ben said, "Someone told me there's almond cake at your house."

"Indeed, there is," said Lily. She released Roen's arm and took Ridley's free hand in hers. "You'll join us, won't you?"

Ridley gave Lily's fingers a light squeeze. "Of course. We love almond cake."

Victorine Headley turned away from the bleak, white landscape outside her private rail car. The sumptuous interior of the car no longer cheered her. She felt as trapped as she imagined the passengers in the utilitarian cars ahead of her were feeling. They were crowded on wooden bench seats like cattle. The one time she had to go forward in search of a porter depressed her. That wretched man was apologetic in the extreme when she came upon him, and to her credit, she thought, she had not berated him publicly. She gave him the sharp edge of her tongue when he arrived later carrying her luncheon.

Her father had warned her that the weather on the plains could be unpredictable when she told him what she wanted to do. Wind built snowdrifts so high and deep they brought the most powerful engines to a halt, and a stopped train was vulnerable to being buried. It wasn't that she didn't believe him; she simply believed it could not happen to her.

It galled her that she was wrong. By now her father would have heard what happened. It would amuse him. The oddest things amused him, and most of them because they occurred at her expense. It was not her fault that her mother had died giving birth to her any more than it was her fault that she bore her mother's Nordic features. Her father could barely look at her, let alone tolerate being in her presence for extended periods of time.

It wasn't fair, it just was.

Victorine ran a brush through her hair. When it crackled with static, she smoothed the flyaway strands with her palm, then gathered a shock of it to examine in the lamplight. Her hair was so pale as to be almost colorless. It was the lamp's flame that added gold and a hint of orange to the threads. Some people said that her hair was her finest feature, but they didn't know her well, and she suspected they said it because her hair made her easy to spot in a crowded restaurant or ballroom. Her sisters at Barnard told her it was her figure they all envied. She was tall and svelte and looked like the women in the fashion plates they favored. Victorine didn't disagree with her female friends, but she preferred to hear her admirers wax poetic about her eyes, comparing them to the translucent waters of a lagoon or the shimmering blue center of a flame.

It was not particularly comforting to recall what acquaintances, friends, and admirers said about her, not when she was more than a thousand miles from the heart of the city and was unlikely to hear praise in a similar vein anytime soon. Roen had never been free with compliments, and Victorine had no expectation that had changed in her absence. Shooting him had added a layer of complication to their somewhat unorthodox relationship. She had not been allowed to see him during his recovery, though whether that was at his request or his parents', she wasn't sure. Her purpose in visiting had always been to make amends, to explain what had pushed her to such a mad end. He bore some of the responsibility; she wanted him to concede that as well. It wasn't fair that she should bear the weight of that near tragedy on her shoulders when it was an accident born of misunderstanding.

She would explain that to him, and all would be well. She'd been rehearsing what she would say and how she would say it since before leaving Manhattan. The silver lining of being trapped in a snowdrift was the opportunity to further refine her speech. She had some regret about the telegram she'd sent, primarily because it was done on a moment's impulse when the train stopped in Chicago. Acting on impulse was something she had vowed to do less, but since she'd made that promise impulsively, it was hard to know how badly she should feel about breaking it.

The private investigator that she'd hired to find Roen cautioned her against sending word that she was on her way. He didn't know her well enough to realize that she was inclined to act the opposite of advice. He should have kept his counsel to himself.

Mr. Martin Cabot had a seat three cars forward. She'd paid for him to accompany her but not associate himself with her. She thought of him as a ghost companion, someone who would remain peripherally aware of her movements but not interfere unless her safety was at issue. There had been little contact between them since leaving New York, which was exactly what she desired, but Mr. Cabot had inserted himself into her view when she went to send the telegram. That brief conversation was the longest they'd had and came close to being their last conversation. She still didn't know why she hadn't ended his employment right there. It consoled her to imagine he was likely dwelling on the same thing and regretting his decision to pocket the extra funds she gave him for a sleeping berth in favor of sitting up and catnapping the entire trip.

One of Mr. Cabot's assets, which he pointed out in his interview, was that his countenance was unremarkable. There was no particular feature that attracted notice. He was average in all things, from his height to his weight to his gait. He was clean-shaven, kept his nondescript brown hair trimmed above his collar, and wore no spectacles except for reading. He dressed conservatively, no plaids or stripes or colorful vests. He wore black with the sobering style of an undertaker. Mr. Cabot did not smile overmuch, nor did he keep people at a distance with a grim aspect. He was polite but not obsequious, friendly but not chummy.

The confidential nature of his work meant that his recommendations were largely anonymous. Victorine recognized two names that were not and she made subtle inquiries. She was satisfied with what she'd learned and hired the man, whose very age placed him in the middle of an average life expectancy.

Except for the incident in Chicago when he had overstepped, Victorine was satisfied with Mr. Cabot's performance. He'd located Roen, which had been the purpose of the exercise. It wasn't that Roen Shepard had set out to disappear once he'd recovered, but that he'd managed to keep the details of his exit a secret from her. All of her inquiries ended in frustration. His parents offered no information and discouraged her efforts. Artemis did not deign to see her even though Victorine was a devoted supporter of the opera company. Apollonia was out of reach and likely out of touch in Vienna, and Rand Shepard had turned the tables on her and wanted information about her affair for his new book.

She knew that Roen no longer had a contract with her father's company, but that was only one of many possibilities, and Roen did not contract solely with the railroads. He had experience with government contracts at every level, and although it had pained her to go to Brooklyn, she had accompanied him across the East River on a bridge of his design. She was no longer sorry that she had pretended interest in his drawings for proposals requested by Albany and Buffalo. The field was wide open because he was immensely capable. Still, she suggested to Cabot that he begin with the railroads. She had been paying enough attention to what Roen said that she knew the railroads were his first love.

Victorine gave her hair a few more hard pulls with the brush before she tossed it aside. She picked up *Peterson's* fashion magazine and idly thumbed it, pausing at last over the plate of an ivory satin and lace gown with puffed sleeves and yards of fabric in the train. She remembered packing a pearl choker with her jewelry that would be the perfect complement to the gown. She wondered if there was a seamstress in the frontier outpost that was Frost Falls with the talent to construct her wedding gown.

She aimed to find out.

Chapter Fifteen

Lily helped Roen make up the sofa. She snapped a sheet over the cushions, and they tucked it in together. He added the quilts and woolen blanket that she had directed him to carry down from the linen cupboard while she wrestled a pillow into its case.

"I think I'll be plenty warm," he said. Taking the pillow from her, he plumped it and then tossed it on what he decided would be the head of his new bed. "Do you have enough coals for the bedroom stoves?"

She nodded and looked sideways at him. "Are you sure you won't allow me to sleep here?"

"We already decided the sofa would be mine."

"Yes, but I'm realizing it was petty of me to insist on that."

"Change of heart?"

"I suppose. I was never so aware of your height until we were standing in front of

Judge Miner."

"It was the hat."

That made her smile. "No, it wasn't, but it begs the question of where you found a top hat."

"The milliner's. She designed it for Mrs. Frost, Thaddeus's wife, but it was never picked up. I purchased it, removed the elaborate silk bow on the brim and the scarf that served as a chin strap, stretched it some, and that was that."

"You looked quite elegant, I thought, but I was relieved that you didn't put it on until we were in the town hall. That hat suited you, but it doesn't suit Frost Falls."

"I remind you that it was intended for Fiona Frost, and she lives on a ranch in the back of nowhere."

"She's Fiona Frost," Lily said as if that explained everything. When Roen looked at her blankly, she added, "Fiona Apple?"

"The actress?"

"I've heard it said that she was."

"I met her when I visited Twin Star but I didn't recognize her."

"It's been some years since she was on the New York stage."

"Yes, but I've seen some of her plays. She was the toast of Broadway. I don't believe I didn't recognize her."

Chuckling, Lily patted his arm. "You can make it up to her by giving her the gift of that hat. I can reattach the bow and scarf."

"I could," said Roen, though he hardly knew what he was agreeing to. He was looking down at her hand on his arm and immediately regretted pulling her attention to it. She withdrew it as if scalded. To fill the awkward moment that followed, he told her where he put the hat.

"Clay will help you move your belongings here in the morning."

"He already offered. Ben offered up his deputy to do the same."

Admiring Ben's cheeky delegation and feeling a little sorry for Hitch, Lily could only shake her head.

Roen asked, "Shall we have tea?"

"Oh, I should have offered."

"I'm not a guest any longer. I live here. I'll make the tea. I'm not entirely helpless in the kitchen. I took most of my meals at the hotel because it was convenient, not because I can't cook."

She followed him into the kitchen to make sure he could manage the stove. He fired it up with expert efficiency. Her husband had had the knack for it as well, but then he operated the forge so he knew something about building a fire. He knew nothing about cooking and never showed the least interest. She'd never minded because it was her job and she not only accepted it, but did it well.

Lily was contemplating what she would or could tell Roen about her husband when he dropped into the chair on her right and startled her out of her musings.

"Deep thoughts?" he asked.

"Mm."

"Regrets?"

"No. I promised myself I wouldn't have any and I don't. You?"

"Not a one."

"The sofa?"

"All right. One."

"We could take turns, you know. Daily or weekly. Whatever suits."

"Let me spend at least one night on the sofa and I'll let you know."

She nodded. "Clay asked me what he should call you. I distracted him until I could speak to you. We didn't discuss it."

"He asked me the same thing. I told him you and I would talk about it. What did he call his father?"

"Father."

"Not papa? Not pa?"

"No. He might refer to him as 'pa,' but he

called him 'father' when speaking to his face."

"I'd rather the children stopped calling me Mr. Shepard, but Roen is too informal."

"And disrespectful," said Lily. "I won't abide that."

"I don't like pa. Papa makes feel as old as my father. What about da?"

"Da?"

"The Irish use it."

"We're not Irish."

Roen affected an accent he'd perfected while working with Irish laborers. "Sure, and I have a proper bit of the blood in me veins from me sainted mother's side."

"Da," she repeated, trying it out.

"Short for 'dada.' Why use two syllables when one will do?"

"Of course. I think it's fine if you like it."

"It's more important that I remember to answer to it, but I like it well enough." He rose and got out the cups, the saucers, and the ivy-patterned teapot and set them on the table. He waited by the stove for the water to boil. "What is your nightly routine?" he asked.

"I go to my room soon after the children are abed. Sometimes I fall asleep reading to Lizzie and stumble off to my room later. Not often, but now and again, I sit in the front room and do mending and hemming until I nod off and prick myself with a needle. What about you?"

"I am usually up quite late. That schedule suits me." He glanced up at the ceiling. "I don't hear anything moving up there."

"I'm not surprised. They were exhausted from excitement and Ben's extensive repertoire of magic tricks. Hannah and Lily are each sleeping with a slice of cake and their bouquets under their pillows." Unexpectedly, tears welled in her eyes. Lily bent her head quickly and dashed them away. She didn't know Roen had seen them until a crisp white handkerchief appeared in her line of vision. She murmured a thank-you and took it. "I'm sorry. I don't know what —"

Roen curled his fingers around her delicate wrist and drew Lily to her feet. It would have been difficult and uncomfortable for both of them if she had resisted. She didn't. She came out of her chair and stepped into the circle of his arms as if she belonged there, as if it were where she wanted to be. At that moment it was.

"Shh," he said. His chin moved back and forth across the crown of her head. "You're exhausted, too."

She was, but it didn't account for her

tears. She had started to tell him that she didn't know why she was crying, but his gesture of comfort had interrupted her lie. She did know, and she believed now that he deserved to know the same.

"It's your kindness that moved me," she said against his shoulder. The fabric of his jacket muffled her words, but they were intelligible. She knew that because his hands tightened at the small of her back, and for a moment his chin only rested against her hair.

"You deserve kindness, Lily," he whispered.

He said this with such quiet conviction that she almost believed it was true. She raised her head and put some space between them. He let her go. Just like that, he let her go. While she was marveling that he understood what she wanted, he turned back to the stove to get the kettle. They both returned to their chairs after he poured and the tea steeped.

"It won't be long before Miss Headley will be here," Lily said, tucking his damp handkerchief under her sleeve.

"If she wasn't lying. If she hasn't changed her mind. If her train wasn't delayed. If she didn't miss a connection."

"I suppose we'll know one way or another

within a week."

He shrugged. "I suppose."

Lily studied his face. His perfectly symmetrical features were set without expression. "Are you worried? I can't tell."

"More concerned that she won't show. I don't want the threat of her suspended over my head like John Henry's hammer. I want her here and I want her gone. If she insists on remaining, it will be to cause trouble. In that case, I'll return to that plot of land where I was shot and wait until someone tries it again."

"Wouldn't it be easier to invite Miss Headley to shoot you?"

Roen's jerky laugh shook the teapot as he was pouring. Hot tea splashed the table and would have caught the back of Lily's hand if she hadn't quickly withdrawn it. "Are you all right?"

"I'm fine. It was my fault. I caught you unawares." She got up to get a cloth to wipe the table and also pick up the sugar bowl. "Did you love her?" she asked when she sat down. "You never said."

"Didn't I? I wish I could tell you that I did love her and that I felt betrayed by her affair, but that wasn't the case. She's a beautiful woman, but perhaps you surmised that."

"I did."

"I was flattered by her attention in the beginning, and there was a curious sort of excitement having the daughter of my employer on my arm. Victor never voiced objections, but I also have no idea how much he knew about our relationship. I don't know, for instance, whether he realized Victorine and I were intimates."

"Oh."

"Am I speaking too plainly? You understood she and I were lovers, didn't you?"

"I, um, yes. I think I understood that." Had she? It was truer that she hadn't wanted to think about it.

"I believe I have poked at your gentle sensibilities."

"I am not naïve, Mr. Shep—" She caught herself. "Roen."

A faint smile lifted the corners of his mouth. "I never thought that."

"You did . . . you do. I'm well aware that you are outside my experience. You've seen things, done things, that I only know from books. My world is small compared to yours, but it doesn't mean I don't know what goes on in that wider world. I have progressive opinions that might surprise you."

Roen arched an eyebrow as he picked up

his teacup. "Tell me one."

"Women's suffrage. I'm in favor of it."

"Don't you already have the right to vote here?"

"Yes, but not nationally. I'm in favor of that."

"That was too easy. Tell me another."

Lily shook her head. "No, you asked for one and I gave it to you." She pressed the back of her hand to her mouth to stifle a yawn. Her eyes were apologetic as she pushed her cup away. "I need to retire before my head hits the table. It came over me all at once."

Roen nodded. "Give me a few minutes to get my nightshirt, robe, and slippers. I can wash here at the sink and you can have your bedroom to yourself."

"All right. I may as well go up with you. You'll need a towel and washcloth. Did you bring toiletries? I saw you with a small case earlier."

"I have what I need."

Lily stood. Roen didn't. She saw him tilt back his head and look at her from under dark lashes set at half-mast. Looking at her, she realized, not in a studying sort of way, just looking at her as though it pleased him to do it. She stayed where she was, not sure what she should do. Turning her back and leaving seemed somehow cowardly, though she wasn't sure why. Standing her ground made her feel as if she were challenging him, but she knew nothing else in her posture bore that out. She didn't know what to do with her hands so they remained at her sides, neither curling into fists nor twisting in the fabric of her skirt. She kept her chin down and her eyes on his face. She didn't blink.

Was this what he'd meant then when he had likened her to a poor creature in the wild and himself to a feral predator? She waited him out, uncertain if he meant to speak or pounce. It seemed that the wait lasted the near side of forever, but it couldn't have been more than seconds.

Roen said, "Have I told you how lovely you look? I don't think I did."

Lily's entire body twitched.

Seeing her reaction, one corner of Roen's mouth lifted. "It's difficult for you to accept a compliment."

"It's difficult to accept a lie."

His half smile vanished. "Don't do that. You *do* look lovely, and I don't care for your accusation that I'm lying." Suspecting that an apology was in the offing, Roen spoke before she could. "Did you fashion and make what you're wearing for yourself?"

Lily shook her head. "There wasn't time. I had a dress picked out, one I wear to church, but Ben showed up with this jacket, skirt, and shirtwaist that Mrs. Fish made for his wife. I don't think Ridley wore it even once. She wanted me to have it. I had to alter it a bit here and there, but Ben said she wouldn't mind. I'll remove the stitching before I return it to her."

"What color do you call the skirt and jacket?"

"Claret. It's a very rich color. I wouldn't have chosen it for myself, but it would have been churlish to refuse Ridley's offer. She meant well."

"Maybe she knows something about you that you don't know yourself. The color suits you. Ah, you're blushing. That suits you, too."

"Must you say everything that comes into your head?"

"Maybe I should say everything that comes into *your* head."

"Perish the thought."

He chuckled. "All right. Upstairs. It's time to make your escape." When she blinked, wide-eyed, his grin deepened. "Yes, Lily, I know when you're looking for a way out."

Chapter Sixteen

The sofa was about as comfortable as Roen thought it would be, which was to say it wouldn't do at all. He found a book and read in the armchair for over an hour after Lily stopped moving around upstairs. When he nodded off twice, he thought it was safe to try the sofa. He was wrong. He decided he would have to be drugged or dead to find any rest there. After tossing and turning for almost as long as he'd been reading, he stood up and moved the cushions to the floor. He added the one from the armchair to make his new bed the proper length and made it up with the sheets and quilts. Nesting wasn't hard after that, and when sleep came, it came deeply.

Lily also slept, but in contrast to Roen's, her sleep was restless. Her dreams were a series of disjointed images, some from the distant past, others more recent memories. Most troubling was her dead husband's presence in places he'd never been or couldn't be. Jeremiah appeared in place of Lizzie at the fountain bar in Mangold's drugstore while she was sitting with Roen at a table. She saw him sitting outside the sheriff's office in the chair Ben usually occupied while Ben was sitting in the jail cell most often occupied by her husband. She followed Roen and Clay out to the edge of the Double H, and when shots were fired, it was Jeremiah who was doing the shooting.

The most vivid image was of Jeremiah standing over her while she lay in bed, helpless in a tangle of blankets as he raised his fist. She promised herself she wouldn't make a sound because crying out only infuriated him, but as soon as he lowered his fist, she screamed.

"Ma!" Clay shook her shoulder. "Ma! Wake up!" Ham clung to his side and for once Clay didn't mind. It was more reassuring than annoying. "You're dreaming, Ma. Do you hear? Dreaming."

Lily shrugged off the hand on her shoulder as she bolted upright. She was breathing hard. Her pounding heart made the sound of thunder in her head. "Clay?"

"Yeah. It's me. Ham's here, too. You want I should light a lamp?"

"No." She didn't want her boys to see her

this way, disheveled and distressed. "I'm sorry that I woke you. I'm all right now. Go on back to bed."

Neither Clay nor Ham moved. "It was a bad one tonight," said Clay. "Where's Mr. Shepard?" It wasn't so dark in the room that he couldn't make out that his mother was alone in bed.

"Downstairs."

From the doorway, Roen said, "I'm right here now." He was carrying a lamp, but he thought he must look like an apparition in his long white nightshirt. Both boys retreated a step but did not leave Lily's side. He approached the foot of the bed and took it as a good sign that Lily didn't cower. Clay's eyes were darting back and forth, watching both of them for reactions.

"Please, Clay," said Lily. "It was good of you to come, but you can go to bed now. You, too, Ham."

Roen gave Clay full marks for not only listening to his mother but also for not asking the questions that were so clearly on his troubled mind. Roen touched Clay's shoulder in what he hoped was a reassuring manner as the boy passed him on the way to the door. Clay's only response was to put his own arm around Ham's shoulders and lead him off.

"Should I close the door?" Roen asked.

"Please."

He did, but when he turned around and saw Lily staring at him strangely, he realized she expected him to be on the other side of the door. "I'm not leaving yet, but I promise I will leave." He moved to the bed and set the lamp on the nightstand closest to her, then pulled up a straight-backed chair and sat. "That's quite a scream you have, Lily. I was lighting the lamp so I could find my way when I heard the boys running down the hall. I overheard Clay say it was a bad one tonight. From that I can infer it wasn't your first and probably not your second. How often do you have nightmares?"

Lily pushed herself back against the iron rail bedhead and wrestled with the blankets to untangle them.

"Lily?"

She slapped the mattress with the palm of her hand. "I need a moment. Can't you see that I need a moment? Move the chair back. You're too close."

Roen didn't so much as raise an eyebrow. He pushed his chair back far enough to stretch his legs toward the bed, crossed them at the ankles, and then folded his arms comfortably across his chest. He could wait out all the moments she needed.

Lily yanked at the quilt that had her legs in a vise and felt as if she'd won an important battle when she finally freed herself. Once she'd unwound all the blankets, she spread them out and smoothed them over her lap and legs. She nodded, satisfied with the arrangement, and took in her first easy breath. It was only after she'd released it that she addressed Roen's question.

"It's been months since I had a dream that woke one of my children."

"A dream? That's what you call it?"

"A bad dream."

Roen saw no benefit to debating semantics. "So you don't always wake up screaming."

"I don't always wake up in the moment, but in the morning there are often vague recollections that remind me that I dreamed."

"Will you tell me what you dreamed tonight?" She didn't answer immediately, and Roen was hopeful for as long as she was silent, but in the end she said no. He followed that question with another. "Will you ever tell me?"

"I don't know." Then, "I don't know if I can allow myself to be that vulnerable."

It seemed to Roen that her whispered words were not meant for his ears, but he heard them and wondered what meaning he could attach to them. He was mindful that she'd felt vulnerable when he closed the door and remained in the room and felt a deeper vulnerability when he sat at her bedside. But was she so unaware of the defenses she'd erected that she believed she couldn't protect herself? He was still struck by the passion she unleashed when she slapped the mattress and told him to move his chair away. He'd never considered arguing.

"For another time, then," he said with all the casualness he could muster. "Will you be able to sleep now?"

"Yes."

"I can stay until you fall asleep if you're afraid."

"I'm not afraid."

He uncrossed his ankles and drew back his legs, but he didn't rise.

Lily said, "Is that chair really more comfortable than the sofa? Is that why you're reluctant to leave?"

A chuckle rumbled at the back of his throat. "Not quite, although I did put the cushions on the floor and made my bed there. I'm still here because I'm trying to decide if I can take you at your word."

"Do you often wonder that?"

"No. Not at all."

Lily pointed to the door. "Go."

He went, taking the lamp and closing the door quietly behind him, and because it seemed like something he should do, he checked on Clay and Ham. Ham was curled on his side, every breath a soft snuffle, but Clay was lying on his back staring at the ceiling. He didn't even pretend to be asleep.

"Clay? Are you all right?"

"Yeah. Fine."

"Uh-huh. Are you worried about your mother?"

Clay lifted himself up on his elbows. "I'm worried about you."

"Me?"

"When I heard her screaming, I thought you hurt her, but then I got there and you weren't nowhere to be found. I reckon one is worse than the other, but I can't figure which one it is. I'm thinking you being Ma's husband isn't the good thing I hoped it would be."

"I happen to think you're wrong, and we'll leave it there. Tell me why you thought that I might have hurt your mother."

Clay shrugged and flopped on his back again.

"Has someone hurt her before?" asked Roen. Clay's silence was palpable. "Your father perhaps?"

Clay turned on his side away from Roen and pulled the covers over his bony shoulder.

Roen stood in the doorway a little longer, but when Clay gave him no indication that he intended to answer, he backed out of the room and went downstairs.

He woke when he heard the first footfalls across the ceiling. He assumed they were the first because no one had yet come down the steps. He yawned hard enough to make his jaw crack and then moved it side to side to be sure he still could. After stretching his arms, curling his toes, and rolling his shoulders, Roen rose up on his hands and knees and pushed aside the blankets. He tossed the cushions back on the sofa and chair, fit them snugly like pieces of puzzle, and eventually got to his feet. He folded and stacked the blankets and placed his pillow on top. Not knowing what to do with the linens, he pushed everything under the table beside Lily's rocker.

When he opened the back door and saw it had snowed at least another inch overnight, he kicked off his slippers and pulled on his boots. Like a courtier of old, Roen made an elegant leg in his nightshirt and robe when he returned from the privy and found everyone was seated at the kitchen table awaiting their turn.

"I'll get my things and get dressed," he told Lily as Ham jumped up and rushed past while Hannah looked him over and giggled.

"Not the worst idea you ever had," she said. "I put the few things you brought with you yesterday in the wardrobe. The items that couldn't be hung are in the top drawer of the chest."

"Thank you." He nodded at the remaining children and left the room only a little less speedily than Ham.

He didn't think he was gone long, but Clay was tending to the fire in the stove, Hannah had a pot of water on top and a bag of oats under one arm, and Ham was almost done setting the table. Lizzie was in Lily's lap at the table having her silky hair fashioned into a becoming French braid. Roen didn't ask what he could do. He located a coffeepot, pumped water into it, and set it on a burner beside the porridge pot.

"Coffee?" he asked hopefully. He could not drink another cup of tea. That would never start his day. He followed Lily's index finger to where she pointed out the canister. He opened it and breathed deeply. He must have sighed appreciatively because when he turned away from measuring, Lily was smiling in that quietly amused way he found so fascinating. "You'll have some?"

"Certainly. There will be milk in the cold box on the back porch if Mr. Sanford was able to make his rounds. Would you be good enough to pour a glass for each of the children? If you skim off the cream, we can use it in our coffee."

Clay stepped away from the stove and said, "I'll do it, Ma. Anyway, Mr. Shepard takes his coffee black."

Lily looked quizzically at Roen. She knew her son well enough to know that the offer was not made out of kindness. Clay was stewing. He was the only one who hadn't acknowledged Roen's presence.

Roen mouthed the words *I'll tell you later* and returned to making coffee. He was adding cream to Lily's cup at the same time Hannah was doling out large portions of hot oatmeal. Lily stopped her when she had half as much as Hannah had given everyone else. Roen wished he had known he could do the same, but it had seemed impolite. He looked at his bowl and smiled rather grimly at the contents before he tucked in. He thought he heard Lily chuckle, but when he glanced up, her lips were closed over her spoon in a way no sound could escape.

She was a witch, he thought, and not for the first time.

"When are you going to get the rest of your things and bring them here?" she asked.

"I thought I'd begin after breakfast. I'll stop at the sheriff's to see if Hitch is really going to help me." He looked to the end of the table where Clay was sitting. Roen had had no desire to take up that chair. It had been Jeremiah's and now it was Clay's. It was not his place to take it away. "You're going to help, aren't you?"

Clay only shrugged.

"Clay Salt," said Lily. "Don't make me use your middle name. That was rude. You answer with your voice, not a shrug."

"Clay Bryant Salt," said Lizzie in singsong tones. "Clay Bryant Salt."

Lily merely looked at her youngest and the little girl's mouth snapped shut. "Clay?"

"Yes, I'll help you." He didn't meet Roen's gaze directly but stared sullenly at his oatmeal instead.

Lily's lips parted as she intended to reprimand him again, but the almost infinitesimal shake of Roen's head stopped her. She did not know how she felt about him inserting his opinion. He was not exactly interfering, but he had a definite idea about the way she should deal with her son in this moment.

"Thank you, Clay," said Roen. "So I'm clear about the division of labor, are you still working for me?" Roen watched Clay's head snap up. This was obviously something the boy hadn't considered. "I'm not firing you, and I don't expect you to work for free because there's been a change in our connection, but there are family chores that you'll be expected to do for no remuneration, and there are business tasks for which you will continue to be compensated. I think helping me move my things here is a gray area. I'll give you half pay if you still want to be in my employ. Otherwise, you'll help and get nothing. Fair?"

Clay stared at him and didn't answer.

"That's all right. You think it over and let me know your decision when I'm ready to leave."

Clay's eyes swiveled to his mother. "May I be excused?"

"Please."

The remainder of the meal was eaten in silence. One by one the children asked to be excused, and when it was just Lily and Roen, she stood and began clearing the table.

Roen observed her nervous energy. "Will you sit, Lily?"

"I'd rather not." She carefully placed the glasses, bowls, and utensils in the sink and removed the oatmeal pot that was soaking there. "We can still talk."

"Not when I have to speak to your back. No, stay there. I'll come to you." He picked up a dishtowel while she pumped cold water into the sink and added soap flakes. When she turned her head to look at him in astonishment, he said, "What? Do you think I've never done this before? Once my mother had children old enough to fetch and carry, she didn't do housework. As the youngest, a lot of it eventually fell to me."

"You didn't have help?"

"A housekeeper twice a week and a cook when my parents remembered to pay her."

Lily was suspicious.

"Truly," said Roen. "My parents have ideas about money that don't lend themselves to acting responsibly." He took the clean glass she handed him, dried it, and put it up on the shelf. "Do you want to hear about Clay?"

"Do I? I don't know anymore. I thought I understood him. He's acting in ways that are foreign to me." She set two more glasses on the towel beside the sink.

"He's scared."

"Of what? Of you?"

"Not exactly. It's more like he's scared for you." He told her what transpired when he visited Clay's room after leaving hers. "He shut me out when I asked him about his father, but before then he already knew he'd said too much. When he heard you scream, why did he think I might have hurt you?"

Lily took a handful of spoons and washed each one individually before she set it aside.

"What secret are you harboring, Lily?" asked Roen. "I can guess, but I'd rather hear it from you. I think Clay wants to tell me, but he won't because he thinks he'd be betraying you. That's a lot of weight on a young man's shoulders."

"You should have stayed downstairs," she said quietly. He was a dangerous man, not in the manner her husband had been, but dangerous nonetheless. She pressed her lips together for a moment, holding in what she couldn't say. "We agreed you would stay downstairs."

"No, we didn't. We agreed I would sleep there. Your screaming woke me, and we had no agreement about where I could go when I was awake."

"Let it be, Roen. You already know the truth. Why must you hear it from me?"

"Because what I'm imagining must be worse than the reality."

"So I am supposed to humiliate myself so your imagination isn't troubled? Is that it?" She scrubbed out a bowl and set it down hard. "Have you struck a woman?"

"No."

"At the zenith of your frustration with Victorine Headley, did you ever once consider banging her head off a wall or wrapping your hands around her neck?"

Roen flinched. "No. Never."

Lily stopped scrubbing and looked sideways at him. "I believe you, and because I do, I'm telling you that it's you who are naïve. You don't have the capacity to imagine the worst." She tossed her dishcloth into the sink. "Be grateful that you don't." With that, she left the room.

Roen stared after her until she'd disappeared into the front room to be with her children. He dropped the dishtowel and picked up the cloth, then he stood at the sink and finished the work that she could not.

CHAPTER SEVENTEEN

Hitch was waiting for Roen outside the office when he caught sight of Fedora Chen coming out of Maxwell Wayne's bakery. He rarely saw her outside the hotel. Sometimes he caught a glimpse of her returning to her boardinghouse room after work. She always had an escort if it was dark. Usually it was Mr. Butterworth, and that was Ellie's doing. Fedora was under Ellie's protection almost from the first. Hitch thought it was a good idea since some folks had prejudices and suspicions about Fedora and weren't above taunting her, but all that protection sure was an impediment to striking up a conversation or just mooning after her.

Hitch looked down the boardwalk, and when he didn't see Roen coming, he decided he would cross the street and see what came of it. Fedora had a brisk walk so he had to cross on the diagonal to meet up with her. She also walked everywhere with her head slightly bent, something she did to avoid catching anyone's eyes. This morning there was the wind to consider so she dropped her head forward more than usual.

"Can I help you carry those?" he asked when he was beside her. "Those" were at least a dozen loaves of bread each wrapped in brown paper tied off with a string. The aroma of warm bread might have been tantalizing if it weren't for the fragrance that Hitch identified solely with Fedora. It was a fragrance unfamiliar to him. Something exotic, he was sure, like her.

Hitch stumbled a bit when Fedora stopped in her tracks. Momentum carried him ahead a couple of steps before he caught himself. He smiled a little crookedly as he backed up and held out his arms. She was looking at him now. He couldn't tell if she was smiling because the lower half of her face was hidden behind a thick woolen scarf. He saw she was undecided about taking him up on his offer, and he couldn't blame her. She'd just witnessed him stumble and then there was the time he pitched forward on his face in the hotel kitchen. Remembering that graceless fall made his face flush. He hoped she would think his cheeks were bitten by the wind.

"Really," he said. "I want to help." She

was difficult to understand behind that scarf, but he saw her head bob and took it as a yes. He began plucking the loaves from her arms and transferring them to his. When he had eight, she told him it was enough and began walking again. It seemed to him that she failed to reestablish the pace she had set before, and he interpreted that as her wanting to draw out the trek back to the hotel so she could spend more time in his company. It might have been a flight of fancy on his part, but it put a bounce in his step. He searched for something to say to her.

"I thought Mrs. Vandergrift made all her own bread," he said, nodding to Mrs. Palmer as she passed them going in the other direction. He noticed that Fedora gave no indication that she had seen the milliner.

Fedora tugged at her scarf until it was snug under her chin. "Mrs. Vandergrift complained of feeling poorly so Ellie sent her home. Louella Fuller is working in her place, but she can't manage all the baking."

Two full sentences, Hitch thought. It was the most she'd ever said to him. She had a sweet voice. She spoke words as if they were musical notes. He wondered if anyone else noticed or if narrow-mindedness made one person deaf to another. Mrs. Palmer hadn't acknowledged Fedora either.

"I suppose Louella will need help in the kitchen," he said. "Will that be you?" He asked because no one was occupying a cell, which meant he'd have no reason to visit the kitchen. He'd see Fedora again only if he took a meal in the dining room.

"No. Ellie asked Annie Fish not to wait tables so she could help Mrs. Fuller. Ellie and I will take care of the diners." She hesitated while she gave him a sidelong look. "I'm not permitted to prepare food. I only carry it out."

Surprise made Hitch's next step awkward, but he caught himself before he tripped over his own feet. "Ellie doesn't allow you to cook?"

"For myself, yes. Not for others."

"Why in the world not? Unless you don't want to cook, of course. That'd be different."

"Ellie would permit it if the customers wouldn't complain, but some people don't even like me serving them. If they knew I was cooking, they'd stay away altogether."

"Maybe they should. Who complains? Give me a name."

Fedora shook her head. "Ellie won't tell her son for the same reason I won't tell you."

"Now, see, that doesn't make sense. We're the law."

"That would be the reason."

"Oh. I guess you don't want interference."

"We don't want trouble. Ellie says you can't reason with stupid."

Hitch chuckled. "That sounds just like her." He tried to shorten his long-legged stride and slow his steps as they approached the hotel. It required only a few moments to realize that Fedora wasn't going to go slower than she already was. Surrendering to the inevitable parting of their ways, he said, "We should cross the street here. Watch your step." He managed to thrust an elbow toward her without dropping a single loaf. "Here. Take it."

Fedora shook her head with unmistakable vehemence.

"It probably seems ironic, me trying to help you, you bein' so full of grace that you put me in mind of an angel, and me fallin' all over myself when I'm around you." He pulled in his elbow and stepped off the boardwalk. When she didn't follow, he turned to see what was holding her back. Apparently it was because she was staring at him so hard that he flushed for the second time in her presence. "What?"

"Don't you know people are watching us?"

What was he supposed to say? That he *didn't* know because he was oblivious to everyone except her? He turned back to face the opposite side of the street. Dolly Mangold was standing by the large plate glass window at the front of her store, looking in his direction. Farther down the street, Buzz Winegarten was leaning on his broom at the entrance to the Songbird. He'd stopped sweeping to take measure of what was going on. There were folks going in and out of the butcher's and the mercantile who paused when they saw him and a few passersby who openly stared.

"They're looking this way because they know me." He made sure the bread was secure before he raised a hand to recognize Dolly Mangold. "See? She waved back." He watched Dolly turn away from the window and move out of his sight. "And she's gone. Folks are friendly here."

Fedora stepped down from the boardwalk. "These people have known you all your life. Of course they're friendly."

"And I'm a deputy," he said with mocking conceit.

She waited for a wagon carrying dry goods to pass and then started to cross to the hotel. "More importantly, you're Amanda Springer's son."

"Why do people say that? I'm my father's son, too." But he knew why and didn't expect an answer. His mother was practically a force of nature. Not only did she operate her own business, she had a leadership role in a half-dozen charitable, political, or social causes. She also had definite opinions and was not shy about sharing them. He wondered which of the people who had seen him offer help to Fedora would be the first to tell his mother and how long it would be before she showed up at the jail to confront him.

"We should go in the back," Fedora said when he started to take the stairs to the hotel's large porch.

"Right." Hitch backed down and followed her around the building to the trade entrance. She was at the point of juggling her loaves to open the door when he stopped her. There was a lump in his throat that made speaking difficult. He cleared it twice and pushed on. "I was thinking . . . wondering, actually . . . if you'd allow me to call on you."

She looked at him over her shoulder. For once, her dark eyes were not unfathomable. They hinted at sadness, at regret. Still, she did not say no outright. "I don't see how that's possible."

Hitch had given it some thought and now he didn't hesitate. "I can walk you from the hotel to the boardinghouse. Not every night because sometimes I'll be working, but there are plenty of nights when I'm not. I could talk to Ellie and Abe Butterworth about it. They'd give me their blessing."

"They'd give you their concerns. A list of them, I suspect."

"*Then* they'd give me their blessing."

Fedora regarded him doubtfully. "It will cause trouble for you."

"I only care if it causes trouble for you."

She nodded once before she opened the door and led him into the kitchen.

Roen and Clay arrived at the sheriff's office without having exchanged more than a score of words. Ben was cleaning his Colt at his desk when they went in. He paused long enough to tell them he'd seen Hitch dash across the street to lend assistance to Fedora Chen.

"He's sweet on her," said Clay. Aware that Ben and Roen were staring at him, he said, "Well, he is."

"Yes," said Ben, "but how do you know?"

"Before Mr. Shepard took me on, I used to do more odd jobs at the Butterworth, and I saw how it was with Deputy Springer.

Frankie's got the work there now. I bet if you ask him, he'll tell you the same."

"Huh." Ben put down his gun. "I wouldn't be at all surprised. Does Miss Chen reciprocate his feelings?"

"Reciprocate?"

Roen said, "It means share or return."

"Oh." Clay looked back at Ben. "You could've just said so, Sheriff."

"Now that you know what it means, I don't have to," said Ben. "Well, what's the answer?"

"Can't really say about Miss Chen. She's not one for showin' herself. I'd be real careful about inviting her to play poker. She's got the face for it."

"I'll keep that in mind."

"Did Hitch tell you when he'd be back?" asked Roen.

"He didn't tell me he was leaving. Hitch is still a little green behind the ears."

"How long has he been your deputy?"

"About two years now." He grinned. "Plenty of time yet to iron out the rough edges. You might like to know that I sent him out to the Double H yesterday while you and I were otherwise occupied. Thought it would be good for him to follow up our visit, and he knows the Hardy brothers better than I do. He went to school with three of them for a while. Harrison's oldest son was already working the ranch then."

"And?" asked Roen. He was aware of Clay leaning in to hear Ben's response. "Did he learn anything?"

"He did. It seems that Caleb, that's the third son and one closest in age to Hitch, has suspected for a long time that the strip of land you're questioning doesn't belong to the Double H."

"He said that?"

"Hitch said he did. There was a touch of hubris in the confession. Caleb wanted Hitch to know he was at least a half step smarter than his father and brothers."

"I don't suppose he confessed to shooting at us."

"No, and Hitch doesn't think he did. The most likely culprit is Judah."

"The oldest."

Ben nodded. "His father's heir. Harrison told his sons he's not dividing the land like it's some damn piece of pie. Caleb's words again, not mine." He glanced at Clay. "Sorry, Clay. I should mind my words even when they're not mine."

"It's all right," said Clay. "I won't tell my mother."

"Thank you."

"I won't tell his mother either," Roen said

solemnly.

"Yeah," he said shortly. "Thanks."

Roen returned to the subject of the property. "So you're telling me Judah would have the most to lose if the land went to the Frosts."

"Uh-huh. Unless his brothers take off for greener pastures when Old Harrison dies, they'll work for Judah. I still think someone was trying to scare you off, not kill you."

"Don't worry. I'm not asking Northeast for Pinkerton protection."

"Have you been back out there?"

"Not to that spot specifically."

"Good."

Roen didn't react or respond to that. "If Hitch shows up, tell him to meet us at the house."

Ben looked past Roen and Clay to the empty street beyond. "You don't have a wagon?"

"I don't have that much. I figured three of us would get it all in one trip. Maybe it'll take two now."

"All right. I'll send him along if you don't cross paths first."

They did cross paths. Hitch was coming around the corner of the Butterworth as Roen and Clay were walking along the hotel's front. "Glad I didn't miss you," said

Hitch, pivoting. "Where's your wagon?"

"Don't have one," said Clay. "Mr. Shepard thinks we're pack horses."

Hitch was in too fine a mood to be bothered by Clay's sulky announcement. "Then that's what we are," he said, grinning toothily.

Clay knew the origins of the deputy's abundance of good humor. He resented Hitch's happy disposition, not the reason for it, and he took some cheeky satisfaction in the aside he stage-whispered to Roen. "I told you he was sweet on Miss Chen."

Chapter Eighteen

Lily saw immediately upon Roen and Clay entering the house that the situation between them had not improved. In contrast, Hitch was as cheerful and as light on his feet as she had ever seen him. He set down the cases he was carrying inside the door, brushed snow off his boots, and tossed Lizzie in the air when she ran to him. He was like a puppy, Lily thought, nuzzling and tickling and laughing, all big feet and big hands. It was hard to say who was enjoying the attention more, Hitch or her daughter.

"Have a care there, Hitch," Lily said. "Lizzie just had a cup of ham and bean soup. You don't want to be wearing that if it comes up again."

"Sorry, Lizzie." Hitch set the little girl down and swatted her playfully to go back to the parlor. He tipped his hat to Lily. "How are you, Mrs. Salt?" He frowned. "Told myself I wouldn't make that mistake.

How are you, Mrs. Shepard?"

Lily blinked, startled a little to be addressed in this new way. She'd have to get used to the name herself. "I'm doing well, Hitch. You?"

"I don't know how I could be any better." He looked at the stairs. Clay and Roen were already at the top with their bags. He was in no hurry to follow. "So you got married yesterday. Congratulations."

"Thank you."

"Ben says it's not general knowledge yet, but you know it'll get around pretty quick. Now, just so we're clear, I'm not going to be the one to mention it to my mother. She can hear it from someone else."

"That's up to you. I'm not asking you to keep it to yourself. I imagine people saw you carrying off Roen's things. Didn't anyone ask you what you were doing?"

"Buzz. He was the only one. Thought it was strange myself."

"And what did Mr. Shepard tell him?"

"It wasn't Mr. Shepard. It was Clay. He jumped right in. Told Buzz Mr. Shepard was going to live here from now on. Never mentioned marriage, though. I thought Mr. Shepard would, but he just let Clay go. I didn't feel it was my place to explain. Don't worry. It'll straighten itself out."

"Oh, it will be straightened out," said Lily. "You can depend upon it." There was a thump abovestairs and Lily glanced at the ceiling. She reined in her scowl for Hitch's benefit. "Tell me about you and Miss Chen. Have you screwed your courage to the sticking place and spoken to her yet?"

If Hitch had had the cases in his hands, he would have dropped them now. His jaw went slack and he blinked several times. "How did . . . that is . . . where did you hear . . . what are you saying again?"

"Clay. He told me months ago that you admired Miss Chen. My son is my eyes and ears, Hitch. I might not get out much, but it doesn't mean I don't know things." She added meaningfully, "And your mother visits, too."

"Oh, Lord. Don't tell me that she —"

"Calm yourself. She's never breathed a word. I don't think she's aware, but I'm not sure she'd mention it to me if she was. I can't begin to fathom how she would take the news."

"Neither can I," he said, looking down at the floor.

Lily realized she had pricked his happy bubble and was sorry for that. "So? Have you spoken to her?"

Hitch's expression brightened marginally.

"Today. This morning actually. She was carrying an armload of bread from Maxwell's and I had two arms I wasn't using, so I offered my assistance."

"That was gallant of you."

"Good to know. I was only trying not to be clumsy."

"And you spoke to her."

He nodded. "And she spoke to me. That was the best. She's quiet, you know. Like you, I think. Keeps to herself."

"Also like me," said Lily.

"I suppose that's true. Hadn't thought of it."

Lily smiled graciously and pretended to believe him. She pointed to the stairs. "I think you should probably go up now. If Clay is sulking in a corner, send him down."

"Will do." He hefted the cases and started up. He was on the third step when he paused and looked back at Lily in the rocker. "It was real nice talking with you, Mrs. Shepard." Pleased that he'd got it right this time, he went on his way.

Lily cocked an ear toward the kitchen when she heard the back door open. The squeaky hinge announced that Hannah and Ham had returned from outdoor play in the snow. She heard them knock snow off their shoes and then begin arguing over who made the better snow angel. Snow angels. That meant the pair of them were covered in a dusting of snow. Ham would have clumps in his hair because it was likely he left his hat in a drift.

"Hang up your coats and scarves," she called to them. There was a brief pause while they did as instructed and then they were jostling for position in the hallway to see who could get to the parlor first. "Did you have a good time?"

Ham was more enthusiastic in his response than Hannah. Now that she had her mother as an audience, she pretended she only suffered her brother's presence. It always made Lily smile to see how her daughter played a scene as if she were onstage.

"Warm yourselves at the stove," she said. "Deputy Springer is here. He came back with your brother and Mr. Shepard."

Ham forgot all about warming up. He bolted for the stairs and took them as if he were being chased.

Lizzie abandoned her cross-legged position on the floor in favor of the sofa while Hannah stood at the stove. When her sister joined her, Lizzie snuggled. "You're toasty," she said. "Read to me."

Hannah reached for the book on the side

table, opened it, and began to tell Lizzie a story that had nothing to do with the words on the page.

Smiling to herself, Lily returned to her mending.

It was this tranquil tableau that halted Roen before he reached the bottom of the stairs. He took it all in — Lizzie curled against her sister's side, Hannah quietly reading aloud, and Lily in the rocker, head bent, the thimble on her middle finger flashing as she deftly plied her needle. This was not a scene familiar to him growing up, and the contrast to his own noisy, untidy family struck him anew. Moments like he was observing now simply didn't occur, and while he'd gotten accustomed to the creative chaos around him, he had harbored a longing for quiet that he had never expressed. This peace was a gift, and he was reluctant to disturb it.

Ham, though, had no such qualms. Roen heard the boy thundering behind him. He put his back against the wall to make room for Ham's speedy descent and then made the spur-of-the-moment decision to corral him. That decision almost cost him his balance as Ham ran full tilt into the arm he extended. They teetered on the precipice for several long seconds before Roen recovered, threw Ham over his shoulder, and took the last few steps to the bottom with something approaching dignity.

The reason for Ham's flight became apparent when Clay bounded down the stairs after him. Roen set Ham down and the boy ran for his mother. What sanctuary he expected to find there, Roen didn't know. Lily was already on her feet, and Roen suspected she had been there since he tossed Ham over his shoulder, but now she ignored him and had Ham in her sights instead.

"What did you do?" She put out a hand to stop him before he bowled her over. When Ham merely shook his head, she used her thimble finger to point him to one of the spindle-legged chairs. "Sit."

Clay slowed his steps as he reached Roen and ended the chase on the threshold of the parlor.

"What did he do?" Lily asked her older son.

Clay's answer was to look over his shoulder at Roen. His accusing glance was still there when he looked back at this mother.

Lily's eyes lifted to where Hitch was standing on the stairs. "Do you know what happened?"

Hitch put up his hands. "Don't think I

want to be in the middle of their dispute. Is that everything?" he asked Roen.

"Yes. Thank you."

"Then I'll see myself out." He nodded to Lily and the girls, shook Roen's hand, and then made his escape.

"All right," said Lily when the deputy was gone. "Clay. You sit, too. What's this about?"

Clay jerked his chin at Roen. "Him."

Frowning, Lily looked to Roen for some hint that would explain Clay's answer. His bewilderment matched her own. "Hannah. Lizzie. Upstairs, please."

Roen almost envied the girls as they fled. Lizzie gave him a particularly pitying look as she hurried past. He watched them until they reached their room and then he left the foyer for the parlor. He did not take a seat. Instead he stood behind the sofa and set his hands on the curved back.

"Hamilton?" Although Lily did not raise her voice, using her son's full Christian name was enough to prompt a response.

"I only said that we could call Mr. Shepard 'Da' like you told us. Clay opened one of Da's cases, the one with his fancy equipment, and he was showing them off to Deputy Hitch, telling him what they were for and how he was learning all about them. He was saying Mr. Shepard this and Mr.

Shepard that and so I told him we was to call him Da. That's what you said, isn't it? I wasn't lying."

"No," said Lily. "You weren't lying."

"Clay said I was. I said I wasn't. He said I was so I punched him." Ham raised his right hand and showed off the fist he had used. "I punched him before I remembered what you said about no hitting, and Clay, well, he musta forgot the same as me because he was goin' to punch me back if I hadn't run." Ham's fingers uncurled. He lowered his hand to his lap but not before he solemnly crossed his heart. "And that's what happened."

Lily listened to this on her feet, but when Ham had finished, she slowly sank back onto the rocker. She said nothing while she took gentle, even breaths until her racing heart quieted. Her boys were watching her closely, but then so was her husband, and while she saw wariness in her sons' eyes, she saw concern and something else, something she could not quite identify, in Roen's.

"Clay. What your brother told you is true. You were already gone from the house when Hannah asked me how she should address Mr. Shepard. Since this was something Roen and I had already discussed, I told her his preference. Ham and Lizzie were in the room so they heard it as well." She turned to Ham and pointed upstairs. "Make yourself scarce."

When Ham was gone, Roen stepped out from behind the sofa and sat in the armchair. Leaning forward, he rested his forearms above his knees, and folded his hands. He regarded Clay with respectful frankness and waited for the boy — no, the young man — to return his attention. When he did, Roen was ready for him.

"It's entirely up to you if you call me Da, Mr. Shepard, or that son of a bitch who married your mother." He ignored Lily's sharp intake of air. "I prefer Da, but I will answer to the others." Roen did not miss the slip of a smile that briefly changed the shape of Clay's mouth. "I did not anticipate that marrying your mother, indeed, marrying into this family, would be without challenges. I *did* think they would come at me more slowly, and I did not expect that you would be my first hurdle. I've always recognized your desire to protect your mother and found it admirable. Again, I was not prepared for you to feel a need to protect her from me."

Clay shifted uncomfortably in his chair. His dark eyes darted in his mother's direction but quickly returned to Roen. He thrust his chin forward. "You weren't there," he said. "You don't know."

Out of the corner of his eye he saw Lily was preparing to intervene. He spoke before she could. "I wasn't there last night, not at the beginning, but I don't think that's what you meant. It's all the other times you're talking about."

Clay shrugged.

"I know that your father hurt your mother, Clay, but you're right that I don't know what it must have been like for all of you. I don't know how often it happened or for how long. I don't know the extent of your mother's injuries, and I don't know if you or your sisters and brother were harmed. You can tell me or not. Your mother can tell me or not. What I want *you* to know is that I won't raise my hand against any of you. Ever. That's my solemn promise, but I'll understand if it takes weeks or months or even years of proving myself before you believe me."

Clay didn't respond immediately, and when he finally did, it was only to nod.

Lily said, "We can talk about it, Clay." She pretended she didn't see that Roen was now looking in her direction and that one of his eyebrows was lifted in surprise or skepticism. She couldn't be certain without study.

Perhaps it was both. "It will be two years to the day your father died come New Year's Eve. Not too long ago, Lizzie said we never talk about the fire. She's right. We don't talk about it, we don't talk about your father, we don't talk about what you saw or heard or thought. That's my fault, Clay. Maybe we should talk sometimes so what we think we're tucking deep down doesn't keep escaping sideways."

Clay looked down, raised his arms slightly so he could examine himself on both sides. "Nothin's escaping now, Ma. I had a touch of gas earlier, but I reckon it was the oatmeal that caused that."

Roen gave a short shout of laughter that had both Clay and Lily staring at him. He cleared his throat, smiled a shade guiltily, and said, "Sorry, Clay." To Lily, he said, "The literal interpretation was unexpected."

Lily set her mouth in a disapproving line, but it was all in aid of suppressing her own laughter. When she had herself in hand, she addressed Clay again. "I was speaking of the secrets we keep, Clay. Sometimes keeping things to myself twists my stomach."

"Nothing twists my stomach."

"That's because you have what's called an iron constitution, but it doesn't mean that keeping things to yourself doesn't show in other ways. You've been nothing short of hateful to Mr. Shepard today."

Clay ducked his head and mumbled a reply under his breath.

"How's that again, Clay? I couldn't make out what you said."

He repeated himself, this time looking Roen in the eye. "Yes, ma'am. I've been purely hateful."

"And what are you going to do about it?" she asked.

"Change my ways, I reckon."

"How will you do that?"

"Say better what's on my mind when I'm thinking it." He turned to his mother. "Not like Lizzie. Not the way she blurts things out. I mean I could talk about what you said. The fire. Pa. What it was like when he was drinking and looking for a fight. How it was kinda peaceful when Sheriff Ben locked him up. It's hard to say that, him being dead and all. Sometimes I forget and think he's just in jail. I dream about him getting out and coming back."

"Oh, Clay." Lily's heart lodged in her throat. "Did you have that dream last night?"

"No. Well, sort of. It's muddled in my mind. It came to me and then I heard you scream so it was hard to tell the actual from the dream. Truth, it all seemed real."

Lily said, "Truth. When I saw you standing at my bedside, I thought you were your father."

Clay's eyes, those eyes that were so like his father's, opened owl-like in wonder. "You did?"

"I did."

"Musta scared you."

"It did."

"You scared me, too, when you screamed that way."

"And you've heard it before," she said. "Imagine how it must have frightened Roen."

"Did it?" Clay asked Roen. "Did it frighten you?"

"Made the hair on my arms stand at attention."

Clay nodded. "Mine, too. I guess we got that in common."

"A lot more than that, I suspect."

"You think so?"

"We both care about your mother."

"Yeah, but I love her."

Lily held her breath.

Roen didn't miss a beat. "What makes you think I don't?"

"You didn't kiss her after. Hannah and me talked about it. There should have been kissing. There was when Sheriff Ben married the doc. We were there."

"Ah. So you have experience to draw on."

"Uh-huh."

"Well, the truth is I wanted to kiss your mother. She wasn't comfortable with it."

"Probably because she's skittish. I told you about that."

"You what?" Lily said. It was as if she hadn't spoken.

"I remember," said Roen. "I figured that was it so I went along with her."

"Guess it's good that you didn't argue." Clay's eyes drifted to the stack of blankets under the table beside the rocker. "You gonna sleep down here again tonight?"

"Clay!" Lily was mortified. "It is not your place to ask questions about where anyone chooses to sleep."

As deep red roses bloomed in Lily's cheeks, Roen said, "It was my choice to sleep down here. I saw logs. You know what that means."

"You snore."

"I didn't want to disturb your mother."

"You couldn't. My pa snored so loud I could hear him when I got up to go to the privy. Ma slept right through it."

Roen gave Lily an arch look but spoke to Clay. "Oh, well, she didn't mention that."

"He's going to sleep upstairs tonight," said Lily.

Roen knew what that meant. He would get the bed, but his wife of about twenty-four hours was going to be sleeping on the sofa. Was that irony or just a cruel joke? Sometimes he couldn't tell the difference.

"Is that right, Da? You'll be upstairs?"

Hearing Clay call him Da, Roen decided then that he'd sleep on a bed of nails if that was what Lily set out for him.

Chapter Nineteen

Roen sat at the kitchen table with his maps and notebook and drawings spread out in front of him. Lily was standing at the stove with her back to him as he'd first seen her in this kitchen. His maps, which usually fascinated him, were less interesting than the exposed nape of her neck as she bent her head forward to peer into the stockpot. Her rust-colored hair was fixed in a loose coil at the top of her head, and sometimes the untethered strands gleamed dark orange in the lamplight or curled damply from the heat of the simmering soup.

"You need a better place to work," she said without turning around. "Dinner will be ready soon, and you'll have to move so Hannah can set the table."

"That's not a problem. I don't mind moving."

"You will when you have to do it for three meals a day."

"You have a point." He pushed away from the table and stretched his back and arms. He extended his legs and rolled his neck. He'd been working as long on his project as she had been preparing the soup, and while he sat the entire time, she never sat once. He worked quietly. She hummed. He did calculations on paper. She chopped winter vegetables on a hardwood board. He checked measurements with a protractor and a compass. She checked portions with a scale.

Lily put the lid back on the pot before she opened the oven door to look at her bread. Satisfied that the bread's crust was browning nicely, she quickly closed the door and pressed a hand against her midriff when her stomach growled. Leaning back against the sink, she gave Roen a surreptitious glance to see if he noticed. He had. There was the remnant of a smile still on his lips.

Vaguely embarrassed, Lily murmured an apology.

"You were chopping vegetables," he said, "when my stomach started growling. That was an hour ago. I would have had a cup of your beef stock if I hadn't thought you'd take a cleaver to my hand."

"You should have told me you were that hungry. You saw the children come in and take jelly bread to tide them over."

"Hmm." He pointed to the corner of one of the maps. "Fort Grape Jelly."

"Oh! Are those Lizzie's fingerprints? Of course they are. You can't let her near anything."

Roen put out a hand to stop her before she came at the map with a damp dishcloth. "Give it to me. I'll do it." He wrung out a few more drops of water before he touched it to the paper and gently wiped the purple stain. "There. Not so bad."

Lily took the cloth back and tossed it in the sink before she sighed heavily and sagged into a chair. "This is never going to work, Roen. You're going to hate it here. Lizzie's fingers are always sticky. Ham will get under your feet and bowl you over. I saw him on the stairs. He almost did. Hannah has the most ridiculous romantic notions. You said so your —"

"I never said they were ridiculous."

"Well, they are, and you'll tire of them. And Clay . . . he needs you too much, I think. This arrangement isn't fair to either of you."

"Lily." Roen reached for her hand. When she didn't pull away, he wrapped his fingers around hers and squeezed only enough to let her know he had her. "You were making soup. Now you're making a mountain out of Fort Grape Jelly. It's hard to keep up."

"This is who I am," she said mournfully.

"I like who you are."

"You've said that before."

"Do you think I'm lying?"

"No, but I give you leave to change your mind when you know me better."

"If that eases your conscience."

"It does."

"All right." He released her hand and began collecting his work materials. "I told you that train wouldn't arrive on schedule, didn't I?"

She nodded. "This is the third time you told me. Did you think I wasn't paying attention?"

Roen answered but with a great deal of hesitation. "I might have thought that."

"You probably shouldn't admit it."

"So I'm learning." He glimpsed her faint smile. It was all right, then. She was amused. "It occurred to me that Victorine's imminent arrival might account for your apprehension."

"Well, it doesn't because I heard you."

"Mm."

Lily got up and checked the bread again. This time she pulled the loaf pan out of the oven and set it on a cooling rack. "What are we going to do about a place for you to work?"

"What's in the room between here and the parlor? I've never seen inside. The door's always closed."

"It's where I do the ironing and cut out patterns. I keep the fabric that Mrs. Fish gives me in there along with items to mend and remnants for quilting. The door's not locked; the children know better than to go in there. Look for yourself and see if it will do. I can rearrange my things, clear the table, and put the ironing board against the wall. You'll need a chair, though. You could take one from the parlor."

"Let me look," he said before Lily went on reorganizing in her head. If he let her — and he wasn't sure he could stop her — she would have the room ready for him before it was time for bed. "If you don't mind, I'll put these materials in there now." He rolled up the maps; slipped his compass, protractor, and pencils into a leather case; and closed the sketch pad and notebook. Carrying all of it under one arm, he went halfway down the hall and stopped at the closed door.

"You might have to push your way in," Lily called to him from the kitchen.

She was right. The door met resistance

before it was two-thirds of the way open. He shouldered his way in but stopped when he heard something fall. Whatever it was had a soft landing, and he hoped that meant no permanent damage had been done.

A light suddenly appeared over his shoulder, illuminating the space, and he realized Lily had come up behind him with an oil lamp.

"I forgot that you would need this," she said, wiggling past him to get into the room. "You can see now that there's a window. I keep the curtains closed when I'm not in here." She skirted the table, the ironing board, and a hip-high stack of neatly folded material so she could reach the window. She drew back the curtains. Since it was already well after dusk, the moonlight was of marginal value at best. "Well, at least you can see the window is here. It might make sense to move the table here so you can take advantage of the sunlight when you're here during the day."

Roen indicated the things under his arm and then pointed to the table. "May I?"

"Yes, of course. Here. Let me move these patterns out of your way." Lily cleared half the table for him by using one arm to sweep the muslin cutouts aside. "There. And here's the lamp that stays in this room," she said, removing it from the ironing board and setting on the table. She opened a drawer under the table, took out a matchbox, and handed it to Roen. "I have to go back to the soup, but you look around and decide if this will suit." Lily waited until Roen struck the match and lighted the lamp before she returned to the kitchen.

Roen watched her go. After a moment, he realized he was shaking his head and grinning rather stupidly at the same time. He sobered immediately, grateful she hadn't been witness to it, and wondered if he was well on his way to becoming besotted.

"Does Ma know you're in here?"

Roen gave a start at Hannah's sudden appearance in the doorway. His hip bumped the table and the lamp's flame flickered wildly. He steadied the table and the lamp and then moved a step away from both. "Does your mother know you sneak up on people?"

"You jumped."

"You scared me."

As if that had been her intent all along, her response was a short burst of laughter. "What are you doing in here?"

"Trying to decide if this will be a suitable place for me to work when I'm not out in the field."

Hannah set her hands on either side of the door frame and leaned in. She looked around with a critical eye. "I suppose if you move the material and notions to one side, there's enough space for you on the other. Still, there's a lot that's particularly female about this room."

"Uh-huh. I noticed that right off."

She shrugged. "I like it."

"That doesn't surprise me." Aware that Hannah hadn't moved from the doorway, Roen began a slow turn to examine every corner of the room. When he completed the circle, she was still there and still watching him closely. He wasn't sure he wanted to hear what she was thinking, but he prompted her with an arched eyebrow anyway and she snapped at the bait.

"Clay says that it was Ma who didn't want to kiss after the ceremony."

Roen was deeply regretting encouraging her. "That's right."

"But have you kissed her since?"

"You need to stop reading Felicity Ravenwood adventures."

"So you haven't."

"I'm thinking you are rather more inquisitive than is proper for a girl your age. Any age, actually."

"You *really* haven't."

"Ask your mother."
"She won't tell me."
"Neither will I."

Hannah screwed her mouth to one side as she considered this. "Ma says you're sleeping upstairs tonight."

"Your mother didn't tell you that. Clay did."

"Yes, but it's true, isn't it?" When Roen nodded, she went on. "I didn't know you stayed down here until I saw the blankets in the morning and Clay told me about Ma's nightmare. Lizzie and I slept through it. Sometimes we do that. It's better for Lizzie that way. She doesn't remember a lot of what was before."

"What *was* before?"

Hannah dropped her braced arms to her sides and took a step backward into the hallway. There was nothing saucy about her reply. On the contrary, her expression was grave. "Ask my mother."

After dinner Roen went upstairs to help Lily put Lizzie and Ham to bed while Hannah and Clay washed dishes and tidied the kitchen. He read to Ham from *Treasure Island.* Sometimes he could hear Lizzie giggling from her room across the hall, but he was more attuned to Lily's lilting voice than that of her daughter's. Ham drifted off before Lizzie, but Roen waited until he heard Lily back out of the room and shut the door before he left Ham's bedside. He met up with her in the hall.

"You know, I've never read *Treasure Island.* I enjoyed it."

"This is the third time Clay's taken it out of the library for him."

"Ah. That explains why he knew so much about the story. I think he could have read some of it to me. What did you read to Lizzie?"

"Tales of Mother Goose."

"Yes. The classics."

She chuckled. "Why? Were you afraid it was Felicity Ravenwood?"

"Mm, no. I'm fairly sure that's what Hannah reads to her."

There was still a bubble of laughter on her lips as she indicated he should follow her to her bedroom. "I'll help you move your instruments down to the workroom now that you've said it will do for you." She pointed to where his tripod leaned unobtrusively in a corner. The black case with his surveying tools was beside it. "What would be better for me to carry?"

"Neither. This is why I have an assistant."

She was skeptical. "Really?"

He sighed. "No. You can take the case. The tripod is an ungainly armful." Roen started toward it but stopped when he felt Lily tug on the sleeve of his jacket. He looked down at where she held him back with only the tips of her fingers. It only required him to give attention to her hold for her to jerk her hand away as if scalded. "You've changed your mind?"

Lily shook her head. "I want to talk to you about tonight while two pair of ears are sleeping and the other two pair are downstairs."

"Of course. Should we sit?"

"If you like, but this won't take long."

"Then I'll stand." With his back to the wall. Preferably wearing a blindfold. He gave himself good marks for not inviting her to see through his expression to his thoughts.

Lily folded her hands in front of her and took a deep breath. "I've been thinking about our conversation with Clay, specifically what I told him about you sleeping here tonight."

"You've changed your mind. I understand."

"No," she said quickly. "That's just it. I fully intend that you'll sleep here."

"And you'll take the sofa."

A vertical crease appeared between her eyebrows. "No. That won't do; I realize that now."

"Then we'll both be here." Roen tilted his head toward the bed. "There."

"Not exactly," she said. "I was thinking we would flip a coin for the bed. The loser gets the floor. There are plenty of blankets. It won't be uncomfortable for whoever that is."

"Hmm." His eyes darted warily toward the floor. "Have you spent a night there?"

"No."

"Then we should forgo the coin toss. I'll take the floor. I have experience sleeping on the ground. This will be an improvement over doing it out of doors."

Lily's eyes were apologetic. "I know it's not an ideal arrangement."

Ideal? It was barely satisfactory. Again, Roen did not allow her to guess at what he was thinking. "It will work," is what he said.

"Thank you. I had no idea that Clay and Hannah had notions that would complicate the terms of our agreement."

"Truly? I seem to recollect mentioning that Hannah at least would expect there to be kissing."

"You did, and reminding me you told me so is not an attractive feature."

"So my sisters tell me."

"It's not really possible to stay angry with you."

"So my sisters tell me."

Lily rolled her lips inward to keep her amusement in check. Roen Shepard required no encouragement.

"It's probably only a matter of time," he said, "before someone mentions the absence of a ring."

"Perhaps. Let us just agree for now that it will present another opportunity for you to say you told me so."

He smiled a trifle crookedly. "So there is a silver lining."

Lily turned to go.

"Aren't you forgetting something?" he asked.

"We are *not* going to discuss the marital bed."

"I was thinking about the instrument case. You offered to take it."

"Oh." Her cheeks warmed. "Yes, of course."

"But since you brought it up, it's not unreasonable for your children to expect us to share a bed."

"You simply can't help yourself, can you?"

"Evidently not."

Lily picked up his case. "Shall we go?"

He gestured to her to precede him. It was his assurance that she wouldn't clobber him when his back was turned, and her smug smile seemed to indicate that she knew it.

Chapter Twenty

Hannah and Clay were playing cards on the floor of the parlor when Lily and Roen passed them on their way to the workroom. Neither of the children looked up when they passed, but Roen didn't believe for a moment that they weren't keenly interested in their mother's activities as well as his own.

After Lily moved her mending and muslin and returned her basket of notions to a shelf, Roen had enough table space to unfold his maps. He set the tripod beside the folded ironing board and his instrument case on top of the maps. There was more work to be done, and Lily would have kept at it if Roen had not insisted it was enough for tonight.

"We have to go to bed sometime," he said, catching her eye as she began to fold yet another arm's length of fabric. "Lily?"

She stopped but didn't put the material down. Instead, she held up the red-and-white-striped cotton remnant in front of her. Roen simply regarded her and her flimsy shield from under a sardonically raised eyebrow and waited her out. She required a few moments to steady her breathing and then mocked herself with a short soft laugh. "I'll do better," she said. "I suppose I am skittish."

"A little. May I?" he asked, pointing to the fabric she was still clutching.

"Oh. Yes." She passed it to him.

Roen made short work of folding it and added it to the stack leaning somewhat precariously to the left of the door. "You need more shelves."

"Mm."

Roen fully intended to leave then, to extinguish the lamp and follow Lily out, but she stayed his hand simply because she was standing beside the table looking heart-breakingly lovely in the flickering light. Her blue-green eyes were luminous, her sweet mouth gently parted. Her topknot tilted slightly to the right and loose, curling threads of hair trapped the lamplight and glowed like a Madonna's halo in a Renaissance painting. Her porcelain-smooth complexion was tinged with pink color, and the way the light played against her neck emphasized the delicate hollow of her throat.

"Lily?"
"Hmm?"
"I want to kiss you."
Those luminous eyes widened a fraction.
"Very much. May I?" He was encouraged when she remained where she was, though every line of her body was pulled taut. "I'm wondering if you might want it, too."
"I, um, I . . ."
"That's not permission," he said. "But neither is it a refusal. May I take your hands?"
She hesitated a long moment before she nodded.
Roen thought she would hold out her hands and thus maintain some distance between them, but she didn't do that. Whether she didn't think of it or was too stunned yet to manage it, he didn't know, but her hands remained at her sides and he had to breach that firm but invisible boundary she kept around her. His fingers circled her wrists and then slid down to cup her palms. His thumbs brushed the backs of her hands. He held her loosely so that she was not in any way his captive. It was Lily who kept herself there.
"Will you look at me?" he asked. "I mean my face. You're staring at my vest. That's only acceptable if I have a soup stain."

She looked up. In contrast to his steady gaze, her smile was tremulous.

"Better," he said. He slowly bent his head. "Much better." Roen wasn't sure that Lily wouldn't turn away. He would have been disappointed, but he wouldn't have been surprised. She didn't, though. He heard her quiet intake of air when his mouth was a mere hairsbreadth from hers. It made sense to him, that sound, because it was his breath that she took away.

His mouth touched hers. The shape of her mouth did not change under his. Her lips remained firm, not pliant. She did not return the pressure he applied, though the pressure he applied was a light touch. She was unresponsive, untouchable, unfathomable. Roen drew back and his eyes grazed her face. She was pale; whatever color the lamplight had infused into her complexion was gone now. Her eyes were open and he suspected she had never closed them.

Lily had suffered his kiss. Roen thought he might be sick that this was her reaction. When his stomach quieted, he said, "I didn't mean for it to be a punishment."

"And I didn't mean for you to realize it feels that way."

"You were holding your breath, weren't you?"

She nodded and pressed her lips together.

"Your hands are cold," he said, squeezing them lightly.

"Mm-hmm."

He started to release her, but she slipped her hands under his and held on.

"No," she said. "It's good like this."

Roen folded his hands around hers a second time and then he raised them and pressed them to his chest. She'd be able to feel his heartbeat, feel the furnace that was his skin through his clothes. A sound escaped her lips; a hum of pleasure, he thought, and because she did not appear embarrassed, he decided she hadn't heard or hadn't realized it had come from her.

When she closed her eyes, he bent his head and placed his mouth against hers again. She stirred, surprised, but stayed exactly as she was. Her lips parted on the same sweet breath she had taken before, only this time she breathed out as well. Roen stole that breath.

He took care to see that the kiss was brief, that it remained chaste, and that she wasn't merely suffering his touch. When he lifted his head, her eyes were still closed, her face stayed tilted toward him, and the imprint of his kiss lingered in the shape of her mouth.

A small shudder shook Lily's slender

frame. She tipped forward and rested her forehead against Roen's shoulder. "I wish you hadn't done that," she whispered. "You didn't ask if you could."

His chin rested against her hair. "Was it against your will?"

She was a long time in answering. Finally, "No."

"But you would have liked a moment to prepare, is that it?"

"Yes."

"To steel yourself."

"Yes."

"Why?"

Lily ducked out from under his chin and tugged on her hands to free them from his grasp. He let her go easily, but she didn't go far. Her back was to the table. She curled her fingers around the edge. "Must you have a reason? Isn't it enough that I don't want to be surprised?"

Roen considered this. It was a half-truth at best. "It's enough," he said at length. "For now."

Lily stared after him as he left the room and continued to stare at the vacant doorway. It felt like a long time later that she extinguished the lamp and followed in Roen's wake. She had provided him with an explanation, hadn't she? It had to be enough. For always.

Hannah and Clay eventually tired of their waiting game. Playing cards had only ever been an excuse to stay up as long as possible and keep Lily and Roen in their sights. Some of the pleasure they derived from that was taken away when Lily suggested that they play cards as a foursome, and after she and Roen won the first three games, they surrendered to their yawns and trudged off to bed.

"You cheated," Roen said, gathering the cards.

"Shh. They'll hear you."

"You cheated," he whispered. He got up from the floor and held out a hand to Lily. "I haven't played cards on the floor since I was eight. The next time you have this idea, we move the game to a table."

"Agreed." She put her hand in his and let him assist her to her feet. "Why do you say I cheated?"

"Because I watched you deal from the bottom of the deck and tuck cards you didn't like up your sleeve."

"Oh."

"Don't try that if we're on opposite teams. I'll call you out and your children will learn how they've been duped."

She tried to judge how serious he was, but his features were inscrutable. "Oh, very well," she said uncharitably.

Roen chuckled. He squared off the cards, set them on the mantel, and glanced in the direction of the stairs. "Do you want to get ready for bed first or shall I?"

"I'll go. I'm only a little less tired than my children. Will you bring the blankets when you come up? I'll take the pillow." She and Roen stooped at the same time to retrieve the items under the side table. Their hands brushed. Lily pretended not to notice and imagined it was the same for him.

Once she was in her room, Lily quickly readied for bed, brushing out her hair and securing it with a ribbon, washing her face at the basin, and brushing her teeth. She removed two thick comforters from the trunk under the windowsill and laid them on the floor between the wardrobe and the bed. She added a quilt and tossed the pillow Roen had used the night before on top. It landed in the middle, which she thought was just as well. He could decide which end he wanted to claim as the head. When she was satisfied that she had done enough for him, Lily lifted the covers on her bed and slid in under them. She left the lamp burning because he would need the light to navigate but it made her feel somehow vulnerable. It helped when she turned away from the lamp and burrowed her head more deeply into her pillow. Still, she couldn't help listening for him.

It was not possible to know how much time passed before she heard him on the stairs. More than a few minutes, certainly. Less than an hour, probably. Contrary to what she thought was possible, she'd actually fallen asleep. It was his quiet footfalls that roused her. She remained as she was, turned on her side away from the door with her eyes closed.

Roen paused upon entering the room. "You're awake," he said. "I thought I'd left it long enough that you'd be sleeping."

Lily rolled onto her back. Her cheeks puffed as she expelled a long draught of air. Until then, she hadn't realized she'd been holding her breath. "How did you know?"

"You weren't breathing. I didn't figure you for dead so it meant you were playing possum."

"Oh."

"Mm-hmm." His eyes drifted to the neatly laid out comforters and quilt on the floor. He hefted the blankets in his arms. "Where do you want me to put these? I didn't expect you'd have a bed made for me."

"Put them on the floor beside your bed for now. You might find that you need them. When the fire in the stove dies, it will get cold in here."

Roen dropped the stack and nudged the pillow with the toe of his shoe to the far end of the blankets. When he lay down, he would be lying in the same direction as Lily. "Do you want me to turn back the lamp?"

"I left it burning so you wouldn't stumble around." She turned her head a fraction in Roen's direction. He was surveying the room, memorizing the placement of the furniture, she supposed. "You can extinguish it when you like," she said. "I don't need it."

Nodding, Roen opened the wardrobe and removed his nightshirt. He flung it over his shoulder before he turned back the wick in the lamp. Darkness was not absolute. Coals in the corner stove burned hot with a red and orange glow. The light flickered dimly through the grate, throwing objects in the room into dark relief.

Roen sat down on the vacant side of Lily's bed.

"What are you doing?" she asked when she felt the depression he made in the mattress.

"Taking off my shoes."

"There are other places you can sit. The chair, for instance."

"This is more comfortable."

For you. Lily thought it but refrained from saying it aloud. She rolled on her side again so her back was to him. She flinched as one shoe thumped to the floor, and again as the second one fell. Lily was relieved to know that the rest of his clothing would be removed silently until her imagination provided her with a picture of what she couldn't hear.

She saw him removing his jacket and laying it over the back of the chair because she suspected he was fastidious that way. He used only one hand to deftly unfasten the buttons on his black wool vest. He would fold it, she thought, and place it on top of the jacket. She fancied him tugging on his stiff collar and then pulling the shirt over his head. It would join his other belongings. She felt the bed shift as he got to his feet and dropped his suspenders and trousers. She wondered if he would kick the trousers into the air and try to catch them before they fell to the floor. Clay did that sometimes; Ham did it less successfully.

In her mind, Roen was wearing a flannel undergarment. She squeezed her eyes tight as if that could prevent her from seeing if he removed it. It didn't. And he did. She stared at his naked back, the movement of his shoulders and the taut curve of his buttocks as his nightshift fell into place, covering all of his best parts, at least the best parts she was willing to imagine. If she had been able to conceive of him turning around, she decided she would spontaneously combust.

"Are you done yet?" she asked when he sat down on the bed again. She thought he might have chuckled at what she considered a reasonable question.

"Socks," he said. "I take them off last when the floor's cold."

"Are you folding them?"

"Rolling them. Is that a problem?"

"Not if you can teach Clay and Ham to do the same."

"Done."

Lily didn't know if he meant he was finished with his socks or agreeing to teach her boys how to take better care of their clothes. When she felt him move off the bed, she supposed it was the former. She heard the blankets being moved around. He lightly punched the pillow to make it a comfortable place to lay his head. She waited until he was quiet before she said good night.

She expected him to return the sentiment. Instead he posed a question.

"What do I do if one of your children comes in?"

Lily sighed. "You'll think of something. I can't right now."

"I'll probably say I fell out of bed."

"See? You're very good."

"Or that you kick me in your sleep and I had to move down here."

"Say whatever you like." She yawned widely. "G'night."

Laughter rumbled quietly at the back of his throat. "G'night, Lily."

Roen was aware of heads turning as he and Lily arrived at church with the children in tow. Hannah and Ham slid into the pew first. Lily and he followed with Lizzie and Clay coming in behind. Roen knew that strangers would find nothing remarkable about their family, except perhaps that the children were so well behaved, but Roen also knew there were no strangers in Frost Falls and he and Lily were attracting more than their fair share of attention.

Someone let the cat out of the bag. It might have been Maxwell Wayne, who had suspicions because of Lily's cake order, or Mrs. Mangold, on account of the little bouquets that Roen bought for Hannah and Lizzie, or even Hitch, who'd sworn he wouldn't breathe a word to his mother but hadn't actually promised not to tell anyone else. If he'd mentioned it to Fedora, it was likely she had mentioned it to Ellie, and Ellie would have confirmed it with Ben and Ridley, and from there it would have spread like butter on a warm biscuit.

Roen made it his business to smile politely at members of the congregation who tried to surreptitiously glance his way. Lily had a different approach. She pretended she didn't see them. Roen nudged her with an elbow. She poked him back. When it was time to rise for the first song, Roen held his hymnal high and grinned diabolically at Lily from behind it. She trod hard on his foot.

There was no escaping the genuine well-wishers and the merely curious who lined up to greet them following the service. Roen slipped his arm through Lily's to keep her steady, but after accepting the first few congratulations, he realized it was unnecessary. Lily rose to the occasion and stood on her own, smiling as people she'd known all her life took her hand and shook it, folded her in a happy embrace, or bussed her on the cheek. There were exceptions, of course. Amanda Springer spoke all the right words.

It was her delivery that was cool, distant, and vaguely skeptical, and based on the disapproving looks she gave her son, Roen believed she resented not being one of the first to learn about the marriage. Her husband, on the other hand, offered warm compliments and invited Lily, Roen, and the children to join him at the Songbird the following evening for a congratulatory toast. Ginger beer or sarsaparilla for the children, he promised when Lily hesitated and Amanda looked at him as if he'd lost his mind. Jim Springer was so sincere in his offer, so hopeful for agreement, that Lily graciously gave in.

The children cheered her decision, but Roen was suspicious of it. When they were on their way home and the children were walking ahead chattering among themselves, Roen asked her why she had accepted Jim's invitation.

"Amanda's nose was already out of joint," she said. "I couldn't see the harm in tweaking it."

Chuckling, Roen offered his elbow as they prepared to cross the street. "I'm beginning to realize there is a side of you that is just a little twisted."

Lily looked up at him sharply as she took his arm.

Roen grinned and the sometimes dimple on the left side of his mouth appeared. "I like it."

CHAPTER TWENTY-ONE

When Monday evening came, Lily had doubts about her decision to go to the saloon. "You won't drink, will you?" she asked Roen as he was helping her on with her coat.

"I'll toast you with ginger beer, if you like."

"You would do that?"

"I said I would. You have to learn to take me at my word."

"I've heard words before. Promises. They're hard to keep."

The front door opened from the outside, and Clay ducked in his head. "C'mon. It's cold out here."

"We have our marching orders," said Roen, tucking Lily's scarf around her neck. "It will be fine." When Clay opened the door a little wider, Roen turned Lily and nudged her forward. Her shoulders were stiff, braced as if for battle. He bent his head and whispered in her ear, "Amanda Springer's nose."

Behind her scarf, Lily smiled.

The Songbird had been a fixture in Frost Falls almost from the time the town was founded. In the early days, it was nothing more than a large tent where ranchers and their itinerant cowboys came to drink and carry on after a cattle drive. The railroad made long drives a thing of the past, and the Songbird changed with the times. Some folks with long memories said the town grew up around the saloon, though it was true that Frost Falls came into its own when it had a stop and a station on the rail line.

Buzz Winegarten hadn't always operated the Songbird, but he'd been the owner for more years than not. He was a gregarious individual when he wasn't suffering with gout, friendly, if sometimes on the loud side, expansive in his gestures, and stubbornly set in his ways. People pointed to the canted sign above the saloon as proof that Buzz could not be moved to change his mind. The sign had slipped fifteen degrees below level years earlier, coincidentally at the same time his wife ran off with a cardsharp. Buzz said he kept it that way as a reminder of the perfidy of the female sex, but since his behavior toward woman suggested that was a lie, there were folks who thought he simply lacked motivation to make the repair.

Lily stopped short before entering the saloon and stared up at the sign.

"It's not going to fall on your head," said Roen. "No matter how much you wish it would. Go on. We've made it this far." He hefted little Lizzie in his arm. Beside him, Ham was dancing with excitement. Clay and Hannah were only marginally more successful at containing their eagerness. They were standing on tiptoes trying to see past the doors to the interior.

Lily had expected to see customers when she stepped inside. The Songbird was open for business, after all, but the number of people crowding the bar and tables overwhelmed her. If Roen and the children hadn't been pressing at her back, she would have turned and run.

It was an ambush. She said as much to Roen, but her voice was drowned out by the cheers and clinking glasses that accompanied her entrance. Jim Springer was rushing forward, holding out both his hands to take hers, and insisting at the same time that he wasn't responsible for the reception.

"It grew like Topsy," he told her. "I told Buzz that you accepted my invitation, and he took it from there. You'll stay, won't you? Folks who weren't at church yesterday want to wish you well."

Aware that the children were looking at her as expectantly as Jim Springer, Lily said that of course they would stay. A second round of cheers followed when Jim gave the crowd a thumbs-up. He led the children to the only vacant table in the saloon. Lizzie refused to leave the cradle of Roen's arm, but the other three sat down. Ridley Madison squeezed through the gathering around the table and took Lizzie's place. She smiled innocently when Lily turned a mildly accusing look in her direction but had no illusions that it released her from culpability.

Lily flinched as her arm was taken. It was only when she saw it was Ben that she relaxed. He provided an escort for her, taking her from one person to the next to receive their best wishes, and was careful not to allow her to be passed around. She could admit to herself that Roen's following presence helped to calm her. Lizzie's giggling raised her smile. She doubted that she appeared as nervous as she felt, though she imagined that Ben felt the light tremor in her arm.

Jim had a glass of sweet red wine waiting for her when she and Ben reached the bar.

There was a shot of whiskey beside it for Roen and a little glass of sarsaparilla for Lizzie. True to his promise, Roen asked for a ginger beer and passed the shot to the sheriff.

"Look up," Roen said, raising his glass. "There, in the mirror."

Lily lifted her eyes to her reflection and then let her vision encompass all that was behind her. Everyone present was raising a glass, even if it was empty. Her vision blurred so that she had to blink rapidly to stay her tears. This was not the first these dear people had gathered on her behalf. They had fought the fire that destroyed her home and built a new one in its place. They had helped her bury her husband. The bank had found a buyer for the forge, and there were offers of employment from a number of shop owners before she accepted the position with Mrs. Fish. And all of that was the very least of what they had done.

Lily sought out her children. They were sitting at attention, beaming their approval almost as widely as the doctor. Her heart swelled. The town had adopted them as well, so much so that Hannah had once remarked that it was as if she had dozens of parents to mind instead of just one, and although Lily had been relieved to hear it, she appreciated Hannah's frustration.

She turned to face everyone when Roen did and simultaneously lifted her glass. She had thought it would be Jim Springer who made the toast, but it was Buzz Winegarten from where he was seated with his gouty foot supported by a padded stool whose voice boomed encouraging words and happy thoughts. It was all very nice until he called for a kiss before they drank.

Lily couldn't hide her panic from Roen, but he used Lizzie to hide it from everyone else. He angled his body and Lizzie to protect Lily. What the crowd could observe was the back of her head in the mirror. He bent his head, bussed the corner of her mouth, and then gave Lizzie a smacking good kiss on her proffered cheek. Everyone roared, the moment passed, and Lily had her features composed by the time Roen moved away.

There were other moments, some of the ribald, more of them respectful, when people called for Lily and Roen to demonstrate affection. Lily grew more easy with each kiss. And while she thought her confidence might be proportional to the wine she was imbibing, she was only peripherally aware that Jim Springer never allowed her to empty her glass.

The impact of all that wine didn't hit her until she stepped outside. Had she thanked everyone for coming? Lord, she hoped so. She was in no condition to walk back inside and make amends.

Roen held out Lizzie to Clay. "Can you carry her? She's almost asleep."

Nodding, Clay put out his arms and took his sister in. Her head dropped to his shoulder. "Ma's drunk," he said, looking Lily over. "I've never seen her drunk before."

"Tipsy," Roen corrected.

"No," said Lily. "Clay's right. I'm drunk." She leaned heavily against Roen. "Do I sound sorry about it? I don't think I am."

Roen straightened Lily and gripped her arm. "All right, troops. Home." Lily started out on a stumble, apologized, and then took every step after that with considerable care. The children were already in the house, coats, scarves, and hats off and draped over the banister by the time Roen and Lily arrived. Roen helped Lily remove her outerwear before he led her to the rocker. She was compliant, smiling a little giddily as she dropped like a stone. It was only when the rocker shifted that her smile vanished, replaced by a sickly look common to new passengers at sea.

"Hannah," Roen said. "Fetch a pail for your mother."

Lily pressed her hands to her midriff as she leaned forward. "I'm fine."

"All evidence to the contrary. Hannah. The pail." When she ran off, Roen tossed Lily's coat and scarf on the sofa and put his own things there as well. "Will you put Lizzie to bed, Clay? I'll look after your mother. Ham, go with your brother."

"Will she be all right?" asked Clay, frowning as he resettled Lizzie in his arms. "She doesn't drink. We don't have liquor in the house anymore."

"She'll be fine. Promise." He was curious about Clay's "anymore" comment, but it was not the time to inquire. "Go on. Hannah will be up shortly."

Roen was on his knees beside the rocker when Hannah reappeared with a pail. She handed it over but waited on tenterhooks to see whether it would be needed.

"Fine," Lily insisted, holding the pail between her knees.

"Go on, Hannah," said Roen. He turned his head to watch Hannah slowly back out of the room. When she was out of sight on the staircase, he spoke to Lily. "It's safe. You can purge now." The lethal, narrowed-eye stare she gave him set him back on his haunches. He thought she might sit up, but she remained leaning over the pail.

"I'm not going to be sick," she said.

"If you say so."

"I do." Then she promptly threw up.

Roen winced but remained at her side, steadying the pail when her hands shook and her body shuddered. He rubbed her back until the purge ended and she moaned softly, then he took the pail away and handed her a handkerchief. He left to empty and clean out the pail and pour a glass of cold water. He returned with the water and a small bowl. He gave her the glass and held the bowl. "Rinse and spit."

Lily was beyond embarrassment. She did as he instructed. When she was done, he removed the glass from her hand and went back to the kitchen. She was on her feet by the time he reappeared.

"Maybe you should sit a little longer." It surprised him that she took his suggestion. Less surprising was the fact that she chose the armchair instead of the rocker. Roen moved their coats and sat on the end of the sofa closest to her.

Lily tilted her head and touched three fingers to her temple. She knew better than to close her eyes. She'd done it once while Roen was in the kitchen and the parlor began to spin alarmingly. "I want to blame you," she said. "I just don't know how to make it sound as if I believe it. Did you know how much I was drinking?"

"You sipped," he said. "It was deceiving."

"I think Jim kept refilling my glass."

"Just a little at a time."

"Fiendish." When Roen didn't disagree, she looked sideways at him. "Did you know there was going to be a reception there tonight?"

"An ambush, I think you called it."

"So you did hear me."

"I heard you, but it didn't seem prudent to agree. You warmed to it after a bit, and yes, I had my suspicions that there'd be folks there to wish us happy. I didn't anticipate there would be so many. Buzz wasn't even offering free drinks. There are a lot of good people in this town, and most of them care about you."

"I know. Sometimes their kindness is crushing."

"Crushing?"

"Because I've done nothing to earn it except survive." The hand that was massaging her temple dropped quickly to her mouth. Drink had loosened her tongue. Made her stupid. She lowered her hand and dared to infinitesimally shake her head. "I didn't mean that."

"What *did* you mean?"

Lily didn't answer.

"Perhaps another time," he said.

He wouldn't forget, so Lily didn't ask him to. "I'm ready to go to bed."

"Do you need help?"

"No."

"All right. I'll come up in a bit." He stayed where he was as she rose and remained there until she climbed the stairs without mishap, then he hung up everyone's outerwear and went to his workroom to study.

It was hours before he joined Lily in the bedroom. He anticipated that she would be asleep, and she was, but it was a restless, troubled sleep. In spite of the chill in the room, she had thrown off the blankets where they should have covered her feet. One bare calf was also exposed. Before he undressed, he added coals to the stove from the scuttle and prodded the meager fire with a poker.

He scrubbed his face at the basin, brushed his teeth, all the while watching out of the corner of his eye as Lily tossed and turned. He didn't know if this was a precursor to a nightmare, but he thought he should be prepared. He carried the chair to her side of the bed and sat while he removed his shoes.

Leaning back as comfortably as he was able, Roen propped his heels on the bed frame. Every time his eyes drooped, Lily would stir again and he would remain alert for a little while longer.

"Roen?"

He jerked, almost toppling the chair, unaware until he heard his name that he had fallen asleep. His feet landed solidly on the floor as he sat up. The room was dark. The lamp that he had left dimly lit had gone out. He had to squint to make out Lily's figure. She was also sitting up, covers pulled as high as her shoulders. "What is it? Are you all right?"

"Why are you sleeping in the chair?"

Roen rubbed his face with this palms. "You were moving about so much when I came in that I thought you might be having a nightmare. It seemed wise to stay close."

"If I was dreaming, I don't recall it."

"What woke you?"

"Call of nature," she whispered. "Do you mind stepping out? The chamber pot's under the chair you're sitting in."

Roen jumped to his feet, jostling the commode's lid. It was the first time he realized the chair had a dual purpose. "Leaving now," he said, eliciting a quiet laugh from Lily. "Good to know about the pot, though.

Last night I went all the way to the outhouse." Actually he hadn't walked that far. He relieved himself off the back porch after Clay confided that sometimes it was what he did. He also cautioned Roen not to tell.

It wasn't long before Lily called to him. She'd moved the chair close to the window and had returned to bed. What was different than their previous two nights together was she was not lying on her back or facing away from him. She was on her side, her head propped on an elbow, and Roen could feel, but not see, her eyes following him.

"Don't you want to turn around?" he asked.

"No."

"I'm going to put on my nightshirt."

"Yes, I know."

"You're drunk."

She said nothing for a long moment, evaluating. "No. Only a little tipsy now."

"It's a fine line where you're concerned."

"Probably. It's not a line I've ever crossed before." She patted the empty side of the bed. "Go on. You can sit here."

"Definitely feeling no pain." He removed his nightshirt from the wardrobe and sat down in the same spot he had claimed on earlier nights. The invitation to do so did not exactly ease his mind. Not only did he wonder what she was up to, he wondered what he would do about it.

Roen removed his jacket, vest, and shirt with his usual care. He pulled on the sleeves of his flannel undershirt, rolled his shoulders, and stripped to his waist. He was preparing to raise the nightshirt over his head when he felt Lily set her hand squarely between his shoulder blades. Her palm was warm. There were points of heat at the ends of her splayed fingers. He didn't draw a breath until his heart slammed hard in his chest.

"What are you doing, Lily?"

"You know. Can't you feel my hand?"

"I can. I do. I don't know what it means." He shivered slightly as she drew her index finger down the length of his spine. "I don't think you should do that." She immediately ran the same finger back up the ladder.

"You don't like it?"

"It doesn't matter if I like or it not, our agreement has conditions."

"I know. I made them."

"Are you testing me, Lily? Is that it?"

Her hand moved again, this time to the base of his neck. She slipped her fingers under his hair, fiddled with the ends, winding them around a finger and then tugging gently. "You need a haircut."

Roen reached behind him and laid a hand over hers, stopping her play.

"It's nice, though," she said, "the way your hair brushes your collar."

"When I'm wearing one," he said dryly.

"Yes, of course. When you're wearing one." Lily slid her hand out from under Roen's. She walked her fingers across his left shoulder, paused, then lightly grazed his skin on the way back to his neck. "Now, about the barber. When you see Sam Love, ask him to give you a trim, not a scalping."

Roen circled Lily's wrist and removed her hand from his neck. He laid her hand beside his hip and then quickly stood up. He did not have to look down to know that his erection was filling out the front of his trousers. "I think it would be better if I slept downstairs tonight." It was not his intention to alarm her, but her movement behind him suggested he had done precisely that. He looked over his shoulder in time to see her wrestling with the covers as she tried to scramble to her knees.

He put his arms in the sleeves of his nightshirt and pulled it over his head. When it fell into place, he took a step away from the bed and began gathering the blankets laid out on the floor. Holding them in front of him, he finally turned toward Lily. She hadn't left the bed, but she had moved across it on her knees. If she extended an arm now, she would be able to reach him. He inched backward, but not far enough, fast enough, and when Lily struck, it was not with the clumsy, loose-limbed effort of a drunk. She grasped a fistful of his nightshirt and pulled. Hard. There was nothing playful in the gesture.

Lily was not able to topple him, but to save his shirt from being rent, Roen had to step up to the edge of the bed. He thrust the blankets at her chest, and when she was off balance, he pried her fingers loose and backed away so that he was out of her reach.

"What the hell, Lily?" He stared at the vague silhouette that she made. She was no longer on her knees, but she was still sitting up, her legs curled to one side and a shoulder resting against the iron rail head. "What's wrong?" He managed not to add the two words he was thinking. "What's wrong *with you*?" If he thought it would sound like an accusation, there was no chance that she would hear it as concern.

"Don't go," she whispered. "I don't want you to go."

"I understand what you *don't* want," he said quietly, matching her tone. "I don't understand what you *do*."

Lily drew one of the blankets he'd shoved at her across her legs. The rest she pushed aside. "I don't know."

"You don't know or you don't want to say?" When she didn't respond, Roen decided it was time to light the lamp. It wasn't as if he was still aroused. That erection was at best a memory. "Shield your eyes."

"What?"

Roen opened the drawer in the side table and felt around for the box of matches. Fire flared as he struck a match. He raised the glass globe on the lamp, set the match to the wick, and replaced the globe. He shook out the match and returned the box to the drawer. When he looked over at Lily, she still had a hand over her eyes but was slowly separating her fingers. He waited until her hand fell away from her face before he pointed to a vacant portion of bed near her feet. "May I?"

She nodded but didn't look at him.

Roen eased himself onto the bed. "Is it the drink, Lily? Is that what explains this?"

"That can't be an excuse," she said. "That can never be an excuse."

It was tempting to pose another question, but Roen decided to allow silence to run its course and see what came of that.

Lily bent her head, stared at her hands.

The quiet felt heavy. At last, she said, "I'm afraid."

Roen stared at her troubled profile. Clearly the admission had cost her, but it wasn't enough. Not yet. He didn't speak.

"I didn't know. That is, I didn't know how deeply afraid I was or that I wore my fear like a hair shirt for so many years that I no longer felt it chafe. It's not that meeting you made me unafraid, in fact, the opposite was true, but our situation is different now, and there is something like relief in my heart, an easiness when I breathe that is as unexpected as it is welcome."

Roen was struck by her confession, for almost certainly that is what it was. None of it was drunken sentiment. Lily's declaration was as sober as she was. He opened his mouth to speak and closed it again when she went on.

"I understand why you wanted to go," she said. "You were saving me from myself. What I did . . . it's embarrassing when I think about it. I've never . . . well, I couldn't . . ." Unable to find the right words, she shrugged. "I don't know."

"That *was* the drink, Lily. Not an excuse, an explanation. It was definitely out of character."

She looked at him then, straightforward

and grave. "How do you know?"

Roen was momentarily taken aback. "You just said you never, that you couldn't . . ." He didn't finish the sentence because neither had she.

"Yes, but what if that has nothing to do with my character? What if it's merely discipline?"

Roen didn't answer. He reached under his nightshirt for the watch in his pants pocket and opened it. "It's ten minutes after two," he said, holding the face out for her to see. He closed the cover and returned the watch to his pocket. "If you still have these questions in the morning, perhaps we could discuss them then."

"Coward. I heard you tell Clay you're going out in the field tomorrow morning."

"Then another time," he said, not snapping at the word "coward." He started to rise and stopped when she took his hand. He sat again and studied her from under arched eyebrows.

"You said earlier that you didn't understand what I wanted," she told him. "I want you to stay. I haven't explained it well enough, I suppose, but having you here, in this room, makes my mind easy. My sleep was fitful at best before you came in. I saw the state of my covers when I woke, but I knew such a sense of peace when I realized it was you sitting in the chair."

"Who else would it be?"

"You know."

"Tell me anyway, Lily. You've said almost nothing about him."

"Jeremiah," she said. "I had a moment's panic when I thought it was Jeremiah."

"Because you thought you were seeing a ghost?"

She laughed without humor. "Because I thought I was seeing *him.*"

Roen considered that. "I understand now."

"Ghosts, if there are such things, don't frighten me."

"All right. I'll stay. Hand me the blankets you tossed behind you. The one that's covering you, too. That was mine."

"I have a better idea," she said, plucking the blanket off her lap and legs. Instead of handing it to him, she began to roll it.

"What are you doing?" he asked.

"You'll be more comfortable in bed."

"I'm not letting you sleep on the floor."

"I won't. This is what is called a bundling blanket. Surely you've heard of the practice."

"Yes, but we are not living in colonial times. You know what they call people who practice bundling? Parents. I'll sleep on the floor."

Lily threw the half-rolled blanket at him. "If you must."

"Oh," he said. "I must."

Something about the way he said it forced a flush under Lily's skin. She quickly turned away, gathered the rest of the blankets, and dropped them over the side of the bed. Before she returned to her place, she reached for the lamp and extinguished it, plunging the room into darkness that seemed more impenetrable than it had been earlier.

Lily took some small satisfaction that once Roen was down for the night, he was the one tossing and turning. She, on the other hand, slept without stirring, as quietly as a babe.

Chapter Twenty-Two

Roen followed the smell of fresh coffee and bacon all the way to the kitchen. In spite of the schedule he had set for himself, he was the last one at the table. He should have already been halfway to his work site. Bleary-eyed, he sat gingerly, feeling stiff in his lower back and neck. He smiled weakly as the children greeted him, and for some reason that made them giggle.

"They think you're hungover," said Lily, pouring coffee into his cup.

"I'm not," he said, looking each child in the eye. "I'm cursed. Your mother cursed me."

"Did you, Ma?" asked Ham, much taken by this information. "What curse did you use? Damn? Hell? Maybe dammit to hell."

Roen put a hand across Ham's mouth. "That's enough." When he felt Ham clamp his mouth closed, he removed his hand. "It wasn't that kind of curse."

"I know others," said Ham.

"I don't doubt it. Clay, pass the bacon, please."

"Sure." He pushed the plate in front of him toward Roen. "I remembered what you said about going out this morning. I went to the livery and got your horses. They're waiting outside for you. Yours is saddled. I just need to pack the other. Didn't want to do that in case you changed your mind."

"Late start," said Roen, "but I haven't changed my mind. Thank you for doing that." He forked two slices of bacon and put them on his plate. "Shouldn't three of you be on your way to school?"

"Mr. Stanton hasn't rung the bell," said Hannah. She mopped up her dippy egg with a triangle of toast. "Maybe he won't today on account of being at the Songbird last night and refilling his glass more times than either you or Ma."

"I was drinking ginger beer last night, so it doesn't matter how many times my glass was filled. I told you, your mother cursed me."

"Jumpin' Jesus on a griddle," said Ham, snapping off a piece of bacon. "That's another good one." He smiled as innocently as one of the devil's minions when everyone stared at him. "What? Ben says that sometimes. He told me he knew a deputy who liked to say it."

Lily waggled her fork at Ham. "Well, I don't like you saying it, so stop."

He looked down at his plate but his smile didn't disappear. "Yes, ma'am."

"Hmm," Lily murmured, watching him. She shook her head, somewhere between amused and distressed, and then spoke to Hannah. "I didn't see Mr. Stanton last night. I wonder why he didn't make himself known."

"Probably because we were there," she said. "And he wasn't walking so well from what I could see. It was better that he held his end of the bar up."

Clay nodded. "He thinks no one at school knows he is a regular at the Songbird, but we all do. I reckon he thinks it doesn't set a good example, but if he thinks that, he should drink at home like Pa did."

A hush fell over the table. Even Ham was staring at him. Alarmed by what he'd said, Clay's head snapped in his mother's direction.

Lily said calmly, "It's all right, Clay. Remember? We said we could talk about things. This is one of them. Your father did drink at home, but you know that he did some of his hardest drinking when he was at the Songbird. He liked being around other people, liked swapping stories, and making folks laugh. It was always fine until it wasn't. He didn't know when he'd had enough. When he was done, it was because he'd had more than enough. Maybe it's the same for Mr. Stanton. Your father worked every day."

"Except when he was in jail," said Hannah. "I don't think Mr. Stanton's ever been in jail."

"No," said Lily. "We'd all know if he'd been there."

Just then they all heard the school bell ring and echo. Clay almost tipped his chair over as he pushed back from the table. Ham went sideways over his chair. Hannah politely excused herself before she dashed off.

Lily called after them, "No stories at school about anything you saw last night."

"Or thought you saw," Roen said.

There was a chorus of "yes, sir" and "yes, ma'am" that indicated they'd heard and understood. Whether they would listen was an entirely different matter.

Sighing, Lily wet the corner of her napkin and wiped Lizzie's mouth. She examined her daughter's plate. More than half of everything was gone. "Are you finished?"

"Uh-huh."

"Go play in the front room." Once Lizzie was gone, Lily said, "None of what you heard surprised you, did it?"

"Only the part about jail. I didn't know that. I suspected the rest."

"I thought Ben might have said something."

Roen shook his head. "A regular Sphinx, our sheriff."

"I suppose he is. You know, last night I couldn't help but think that guilt is what prompted Buzz Winegarten to give the toast. Ben tried more than once to encourage Buzz to cut Jeremiah off after a few drinks. I don't blame Buzz for not being able to do it, but I think he blames himself." Her smile was a bleak curve. "I heard that Buzz was one of those who came to put the fire out. Gouty foot and all. That's impressive."

"You heard?" asked Roen. "You didn't see?" Something about that struck him as odd, and he knew he was right to think so when Lily changed the subject.

"Do you want an egg? It will only take a moment."

Roen shook his head and reached for Lizzie's plate. "I'll eat what she didn't."

Lily tried to stop him, but he hugged the plate and she had to give up. She stood and began to clear the table. "About last night," she said. "Thank you."

He nodded but said nothing.

"I told the children before you came down that you weren't sleeping in because you'd been drinking, but then you came to the table looking the way you did and that's why they laughed. They're comfortable with you. When Jeremiah came to breakfast looking much as you did, no one laughed. No one would have dared. You have a bit of a cowlick, you know."

Roen put a hand on top of his head and smoothed his hair. "I thought I'd taken care of it. Is it gone?"

"Almost." She freed up a hand to tamp it down. "There. Now it's gone."

He glanced up, suspicious. "Did you spit on your fingers?"

"No. I only do that when I need to tame Ham's hair. Relieved?"

"Yes."

She laughed and continued removing items from the table and setting them in the sink. "Where are you going today? Clay didn't tell me."

"I didn't tell him. I'm more comfortable if he doesn't know. There's less chance of him following. I told Ben and Hitch last night. Are you familiar with a place called

Thunder Point?"

"Familiar with the name. I've never been there."

"The way I understand it, it used to belong to someone named McCauley. He was an early prospector and later just a hermit."

"Mm. Old Man McCauley. I've never heard him called anything else."

"That's right. Remington Frost owns the property now. Purchased it from the government after no proper deed for the place could be found. Ben got permission from his brother for me to look around out there. There's a cabin and that parcel is off limits, but Ben thinks there's more property that might be of interest to the railroad. I've looked at the maps, and I think there's good reason to believe he's right."

Lily pumped water into the sink. "Will you be here for dinner?"

"Back before dark."

She nodded. "Then good luck. I hope you find what you're looking for."

"Lily?"

She looked over her shoulder. "Hmm?"

"I was thinking . . . Do you want to come with me?"

Lily stopped pumping and turned around. She wiped her hands on her apron. "Come with you? Do you mean it?"

"I did when I asked. Why? Do you think it's reckless?"

"No. No, I don't. Apart from getting shot at, that is."

"No one's going to shoot at us."

"I know, but I thought it should be mentioned."

"Well?"

"What about Lizzie? I can't leave her behind."

"You can leave her with Mrs. Rushton."

"Your housekeeper?"

"My former housekeeper. She really works for Ben and Ridley. They shared her with me. I feel certain she would enjoy looking after Lizzie."

Lily hesitated. "There's one more thing."

"And that is?"

"I don't ride. Or at least it's been years since I sat on a horse. The last time was easily before I was married. I'd slow you down."

Roen started to speak, but Lily held up a hand. He nodded and waited to hear what obstacle she would present next.

Lily lowered her hand. "I don't have the clothes I'd need to ride in this weather. And no, I can't simply stitch them up this morning. Also, I don't own a proper pair of riding boots or gloves suitable for holding the reins."

"All of those things can be purchased. It's what I had to do when I arrived in Frost Falls."

"I suppose, but not before you need to leave."

"So I'll go out today on my own, and you will come with me tomorrow after you've been to the shops." He pushed his plate away and stood. "I've heard enough."

"But not everything," she said.

"What further complication can there possibly be? You still want to do this, don't you?"

"Yes. Yes, I do, but I can't afford what you're suggesting."

"I see. I apologize. It didn't occur to me that you'd think you would be paying out of your pocket. I have credit in all the shops you'll need to visit, even Mrs. Fish's because you did the alterations to my shirts and trousers. Does that satisfy?"

Lily bit her lower lip and nodded.

Roen regarded her doubtfully. Hers was not the face of satisfaction. "I'm going to pretend that you mean it because I have to leave, but we will discuss it this evening. If you don't change your mind about accompanying me, you'll be able to make arrangements with Mrs. Rushton." He stepped around the table and crossed to her at the sink. "It was a serious invitation, Lily. I hope you'll be joining me." He bent, kissed her cheek, and left before she was able to find words so she could have the last one.

Lizzie was excited to be going out. Lily was much less so. Her stomach turned over the moment she stepped out of the house, and a bead of sweat trickled between her shoulder blades. For her daughter's sake as much as her own, she put on a brave face. It was not that she never went out but that her destinations were limited to the church, Mrs. Fish's dress shop, the sheriff's, and less frequently, the doctor's and the drugstore. Mr. Hennepin at the mercantile was visibly taken aback when she walked in the store. He tried to hide his astonishment by fussing over Lizzie, and Lily smiled because it was really very sweet of him. If he had questions about her purchases, he was too polite to inquire. He wrapped everything neatly in brown paper and tied it off with a string before he took the pencil from behind his ear to add up the cost. He applied it to Roen Shepard's credit and gave Lily a receipt, which she tucked into her reticule.

At the leather goods store, Lily tried on

several pairs of boots. She was disappointed but not surprised that none of them fit well. Mr. Addison suggested taking her measurements to have a pair made specifically for her. She declined and chose the pair that was the least ill fitting. Extra thick socks and some crushed newspaper in the toes would fill out the boots. She reasoned she would be doing more riding than walking and they would suit for that purpose.

Lily had better luck with gloves, and when that package was boxed, she gave it to Lizzie to carry. Her daughter swung it back and forth like a pendulum as they crossed the street to the sheriff's.

Lizzie made herself at home on Ben's lap once he dropped his chair from its angled position behind his desk to rest on all four legs. She carefully set her package down so Ben could help her off with her coat and scarf.

"What's in there?" he asked. "Is it for me?"

She giggled. "No. They're Mama's new gloves. She's going riding."

Ben's dark red eyebrows climbed his forehead as he looked up at Lily. "Riding? Does she mean that?"

"She does. Roen asked me if I wanted to go out on a survey with him. I said yes." Lily took the coat and scarf that Ben was dangling at the end of his arm and hung them up. She added her own outerwear to the next empty peg. She pointed to the packages she had dropped on the bench when she walked in. "Boots and a belt. Woolen undergarments. Pants. I still have to visit Mrs. Fish and see if she has something that will serve as a shirt. Flannel would be best, I think. I might have to make it myself, but I should be able to find the time."

Lily sat in one of the chairs for visitors that Ben kept opposite his desk. "Have I sprouted an extra head?" she asked. "Grown a third eye? You're looking at me as if I have."

Ben's eyebrows settled back in place, although the small vertical crease between them remained. "No additional head. No third eye. I'm stunned, is all."

"But not alarmed?"

"No. Is that why you're here? To find out if I would be?"

She nodded. "I've been questioning my judgment of late."

"It's hard to know what to say to that, Lily. Probably nothing I can say with Miss I-hear-everything sitting on my lap." He tapped Lizzie's nose when she beamed at him. "Yes, I'm talking about you."

Lily sighed, nodded again. "Have you heard anything about train arrivals? Seems it's been a while since one came in."

"Are you expecting something?"

She thought quickly. "I ordered a set of kitchen knives from Sears and Roebuck."

"Well, I checked this morning because folks have been asking. The word the stationmaster has is that the 462 is moving again but that only happened late last night. Hope your knives are on it."

She nodded.

"So where is Roen now?"

"On his way to Thunder Point. He said you spoke to Remington about it."

"I did. There won't be any trouble."

"I didn't think there would be. Roen wouldn't have asked me to go with him if he thought differently."

"Well, you're right about that. He didn't let you stray far last night."

"No, but he didn't stop Jim from refilling my wineglass. Now that I think about it, neither did you."

Ben chuckled. "Had too much, did you?"

Before Lily could comment, Lizzie said, "Mama was sick. She had her head in a pail."

"How do you know?" asked Lily. "You

were sleeping when Clay carried you upstairs."

"I was a possum."

"And too proud of it," said Lily. She looked at Ben. "Nothing gets past her."

"I'm aware."

"I also stopped by to hear what you think about me asking Mrs. Rushton to mind Lizzie tomorrow while I'm gone."

Ben gave Lizzie a bounce on his knee. "Why don't we just put this one in a cell? Even Hitch can mind her there."

Lizzie's distress was immediate. "Like Pa?"

"He's teasing, Lizzie. No one is going to put you in a cell." To Ben, she said, "She's heard stories. Don't tease, not about that."

Ben's cheeks warmed with color. "Sometimes I think I know better and then I learn that I don't." He kissed Lizzie on the forehead. "Sorry." His reward was that Lizzie settled more comfortably against him, once again perfectly at ease. He looked at Lily over the top of her daughter's head. "I'll arrange it with Mrs. Rushton. If there's a problem, I'll let you know. Otherwise she'll be at your house by the time the other children leave for school. Will that suit?"

"Very well. Will you ask her to stay after school in the event that Roen and I are late returning?"

He nodded. "She's going to thank me for this, you know. It's not a secret that she's hoping for Ridley to announce there's a baby coming."

Lily's gaze dropped to Lizzie and then returned to Ben. "What about you?"

"I reckon it's the same for me." He shrugged philosophically. "In the meantime, I've got this little one to keep me occupied." He gave Lizzie another bounce and groaned softly when she giggled. "Though not so little any longer."

"School next year. Right now she's playing teacher to her doll. You don't want to know what things that doll is learning."

Ben laughed. "Coffee? It's fresh."

"No, but I'll get you a cup." She stood, picked up Ben's empty mug, and went to the stove to refill it. "Where's your deputy this morning? I didn't see him out."

"You're going to find this difficult to believe, but he's with my mother and Fedora Chen. They're target shooting a couple of miles south of the station. Ellie asked me to accompany her and Fedora, but I knew —"

Lily finished for him. "But you knew how Hitch feels about Fedora and gave him the assignment."

"Yes, but how did you know about Hitch

and Fedora?" Before she could answer, he responded to his own question. "Oh, Clay. Of course."

"And Hitch confirmed it when he was at my house helping Roen move." She set Ben's mug in front of him and cautioned him not to burn his tongue or spill coffee on her daughter, then she sat down. "Why target shooting? And for whose benefit?"

Ben chuckled. "Probably Hitch's. Ellie used to be a crack shot when she worked at Twin Star so I imagine the skill will return relatively quickly. It's because of Fedora that Ellie wanted to do this. She thinks Fedora needs to be able to protect herself, and when Fedora mentioned that her father taught her how to shoot game, Ellie hit upon this notion. Hitch might be the least experienced with a weapon. He hasn't had cause to draw his Colt once except for practice."

Curious, Lily asked, "Do you think Fedora needs protection?"

"I do. But she has my mother's. She has Hitch's and mine. I don't know what kind of gun my mother has in mind for her, but if it's bigger than a derringer, it's not a good idea."

"Maybe you can talk her out of it."

Ben's eyebrows rose again. "My mother?"

"Oh, well, maybe not, but Fedora might listen to you."

"We'll see."

Lily didn't think he sounded hopeful. "Fedora's had threats?"

"Invitations to leave town, I'd call them. Menacing looks almost daily."

"Is there something I can do? Would it help to invite her to dinner, for instance? Make it known that we accept her."

"I doubt that she'd come. She, um, she keeps her distance from Roen when she can."

"Why? Has he done something to her?"

"No. No, nothing like that. It's his job with the railroad. There's a history there, not with Roen, not even with Northeast, it's just that it's the railroad. Your husband is guilty by association."

Lily found it odd to hear Roen referred to as her husband. She hadn't heard it before, not even last night at the Songbird. He was Roen or Mr. Shepard to everyone. She wondered if people avoided it, thinking of Jeremiah. "I'd still like to think about it," she said. "I'll discuss it with Roen."

She stood and went to get her coat. "I still have to go to the dress shop. Lizzie, come here."

Ben lifted Lizzie off his lap and gave her a

gentle push toward her mother. "I like your idea about inviting Fedora to dinner, but I'm thinking we can make a larger gesture if Ridley and I host the dinner. You and Roen and the children will come, of course, my mother and Mr. Butterworth, Fedora and Hitch."

Lily stared at him. "I don't know, Ben. Ridley might have objections to hosting a dinner party of that size."

"She won't," he said confidently. "She's said before that we should entertain, and I was the one who objected. Ridley will be pleased that I've changed my mind."

Chapter Twenty-Three

Ridley appeared on Lily's doorstep two hours later when Lily was working on her shirt. Lizzie answered the door and invited Ridley inside. "It's the doctor," she announced importantly, ushering Ridley into the parlor.

"Don't get up," said Ridley. "I see you're working." She set her medical bag on the end table beside the sofa and took off her coat. "I hear you're going out to Roen's work site tomorrow. I didn't know you rode."

"I don't. Not well. And I haven't for years. He doesn't seem to think it's a problem. We'll see." Lily invited Ridley to sit. "Since none of us is ill, I imagine you're here to ask me about Ben's dinner party plans."

"Oh, Lord, that man. He keeps things interesting."

"Did he say it was my idea?"

"He said you had the germ of the idea."

"Well, that's true. The scale of what I planned was considerably smaller. I thought I would invite Fedora to dinner. Ben expanded on that theme. If it helps, don't feel obligated to ask us to attend. I would not be hurt in the least."

"Not invite you? I'm here to make sure you know you're wanted. You wrangle four children. I need you."

"Nonsense. You'll have Mrs. Rushton. And Ellie. She manages an entire hotel."

"Ellie respects me as a competent physician, but I'm not certain she respects me as competent wife."

"Oh, I don't believe that." She caught Ridley's stricken expression. "I'm sorry. It only matters if you believe it. I know that. What do you want from me that Mrs. Rushton can't provide?"

"Your presence," said Ridley. "Your calm. You can't imagine what dinner parties were like in my home in Boston. My mother would invite upwards of thirty people and then not attend the dinner herself. My father made excuses, but the responsibility to play hostess fell to me. It was an agony. I know this isn't the same, but it *feels* as if it could be the same. I was prepared to host two or three people, but this idea of Ben's is considerably more daunting than what I had in mind. You handled yourself so beautifully last night that I think you can help me manage this."

Lily's smile was wry. "I was drunk."

"So? I can keep your glass filled as well as Jim Springer. And with better wine."

Amused, Lily laughed. "I don't think that will be necessary, or at least I hope it won't be."

"You'll come, though, won't you? It will ease my mind considerably if I know you'll be there. Fedora's, too, I imagine."

"I don't know Fedora except to see her. Oh, you mean because I'll be there with Roen. Ben told me she is wary of him."

"Say you'll be there. All of you."

Lily glanced over at Lizzie, who was sitting quietly on the floor pulling yarn through a sewing card. "What do you think, Lizzie?"

"We should go. I heard Fedora eats with chopsticks. I want to see that."

Lily groaned. "We'll be there," she told Ridley. "And the wine needs to be very fine indeed."

Roen arrived home before Lily had to make a decision about whether to hold the meal for him. He washed up and came to the table, surprised to find Clay no longer sitting at the end opposite Lily. "You're in my seat," he told Clay.

"No, Da. You take that one now. This is my place here beside Ham."

"It was his idea," Lily said much later as Roen prepared for bed. "I never would have suggested it."

"I wouldn't have either." It had been a noisy dinner this evening, reminding Roen of his family dinners growing up. Everyone had something to report about his or her day. Hannah received a star and had her name put on the board for a perfect spelling score. Ham had to pound erasers after school because he spoke out of turn. It wasn't his fault, of course. Janie Wilmot, the prettiest girl in the class, talked to him first, but if that was true, she had mastered the ability to whisper, whereas Ham had not. Clay was called on to solve equations at the board, which he did easily, but he also wrote over Hannah's name. There was lingering resentment about that, and Hannah dealt with it by poking Clay with her foot under the table. Roen reported on his ride out to Thunder Point, which was not particularly eventful except that he didn't tell it that way. He held them captive with a tale about spotting Old Man McCauley slipping in and out of the rocky terrain, prospecting for gold with a pickaxe and a canvas bag full of dynamite. It hardly mattered that Clay and Hannah were skeptical. Ham and Lizzie were rapt.

"You were the only one who didn't share anything at dinner," he said, opening the wardrobe for his nightshirt. "Ah-hah! I see a new shirt in here. And pants." He took them off the peg and held them up against his waist. "Definitely not for me. Did you get these at Hennepin's?"

"I did."

"Did he ask why you wanted them?"

"No. And I didn't offer. Mr. Addison didn't inquire about the boots either. They're on the floor beside the wardrobe."

Roen put away the pants and picked up the brown leather boots. He examined them with the critical eye of someone used to calculating measurements, then compared them to Lily's left foot, which was outside the covers while she rolled her ankle and alternately curled and pointed her toes. "An observation," he said, setting the boots down, "and a question. These boots are too big for you, and what in the world are you doing?"

"I know about the boots," she said, continuing to exercise her foot. "I already crumpled newspaper in the toe of each and

I'm going to wear two pair of socks. They'll be fine. I walked around in them when I got home."

"And the other?"

"It's something Ridley showed me. I hurt my knee a few years ago, and this is one of the exercises I do to strengthen my leg. All done." She slipped her foot back under the covers.

"How did you hurt your knee?"

"Tumbled down the stairs. It swelled to half again the size it is now."

Roen didn't point out that he had never seen her knees. It seemed like the safer option. He reached for the lamp and turned back the wick. He stopped short of extinguishing it, choosing to keep the room dimly lit. After performing the bedtime rituals, he began to undress. He looked over his shoulder once to see if Lily had turned to watch him, but she was still lying on her back, her attention fixed on the play of light and shadow across the ceiling.

"Did you speak to Mrs. Rushton about Lizzie?" he asked.

"Ben did that for me. She'll be here before the other children go to school, and she'll stay until we return, even if we're late. I spoke to Clay about getting the horses from the livery."

"So he knows you're going with me?"

"He does. He's disappointed, of course, that he's not the one going, but after he thought about it, he declared it was an excellent thing I was doing and that I shouldn't be afraid that you won't take good care of me. He brought up last night and the pail as proof that you were capable of handling emergencies."

"Huh. You'd think he'd have mentioned that I pushed him out of the way when someone shot at us."

"I had that thought, too, but my condition last night was fresh in his mind, and I think he derived some satisfaction bringing it up again."

Roen chuckled. "Then it's all taken care of. Are you looking forward to going?" He slipped his nightshirt over his head and then stood to let it fall to his knees before he removed his trousers and drawers.

Lily said, "I'm looking forward to catching a glimpse of Old Man McCauley."

"Hah! So you were listening at dinner. You had your head bent over your plate and you didn't comment so I wasn't sure."

"All of that was in aid of not laughing, but I will say that if the two younger ones have nightmares about that prospector, they are your responsibility."

"Oh. Well, I guess I can manage that."

"You'll have to. I'm snug."

"Hmm." Roen straightened the comforters on the floor. "I notice that you put the bundling blanket in the middle of the bed again."

"I wondered if you'd seen it."

"Well, I have. It belongs on the floor with me."

Lily finally turned on her side to look at him. She propped her head on an elbow. "Sleeping on the other side of the bundle doesn't make this a marital bed. If I don't think it's a violation of our agreement, then I'm not sure why you do. You'll be more comfortable sleeping here."

Roen was not as certain, but he said nothing.

"You can't sleep on the floor indefinitely. Is it that you don't think you can trust me to stay on my side? I can understand why you'd think that after last night, but I promise it won't happen again."

"Lily, have you considered that I might not trust myself?" Roen thought her silence was telling. "So you haven't."

"But . . . last night . . . you didn't . . ."

"That's right. I didn't but not because I didn't want to." He leaned over the bed and yanked the bundling blanket toward him.

"It's going to happen sometime, Lily. You. Me. We will make this our marital bed. I'm giving you time to get used to the idea that the terms you set and the ones I agreed to were mostly nonsense. It doesn't seem that way to you now, but it will, and you'll know it and then I'll know you're ready." Roen punctuated this last by snapping the bundling blanket open. He laid it over the others. "Nothing?" he asked Lily when she remained quiet.

"Not yet," she whispered, falling onto her back. "Maybe never."

"I doubt that. Good night, Lily." Roen did not miss the forlorn note in her voice as she murmured the same to him.

Lily didn't have a lot to say on the ride to Thunder Point. Roen supposed that her silence was a combination of the concentration she needed to stay in the saddle and thoughts from last night that she was still mulling over. The progress they made together was slower than what he'd made alone, but that suited him. He was in no hurry, and it was more important to him that Lily had this opportunity to see past the boundary that defined Frost Falls.

He pointed out the cabin that had been Old Man McCauley's home. "Ben said it was in a sad state before Remington bought this land and made repairs. He also said Remington and his wife still use the place from time to time. Apparently there is some sentiment attached to it."

Lily nodded but didn't comment.

Roen said, "We only have a couple of miles to go. Are you still all right?"

"Yes."

"The animal Mr. Ketchum and Clay chose for you is sure-footed."

"She's dainty."

"I suppose that's one way of describing how she picks her way around and between the rocks."

"She also respects her rider's lack of experience. I have to do very little to guide her."

"Did Clay tell you her name?"

"Dancer. It's perfect."

It was, Roen thought. He smiled to himself and gradually picked up the pace. Dancer had no difficulty keeping up, and Lily managed herself competently. When they reached the site he had marked with a stake and a strip of red fabric, he dismounted and then went around to help Lily. Her legs were wobbly when she touched down and she fell against him.

"Sorry," she said, placing her palms on

his chest and pushing away.

"Don't try walking until you feel steady."

It was good advice, and Lily took it while Roen unloaded the packhorse. She had regained her balance and confidence by the time he'd finished, and she led the horses away to tether them. She joined him as he was setting up the tripod.

Looking around at the rocky incline ahead of her and the shallow stream they had crossed to reach this site, she asked, "What makes this place of interest to you?"

"If you'd like to look at a map, you can. You'll see that it's one point on a fairly straight line connecting Frost Falls to Stonechurch. The tracks would have to deviate from their current route in several locations, so it's not ideal, but without clearly establishing who owns the panhandle that I really want, this is a good second choice."

Lily unrolled the map that Roen presented to her and studied it. She saw Lizzie's grape jelly smudge in the corner and recognized this was the map Roen had been poring over at the kitchen table. "I can't tell where we are."

Roen pointed to the place that identified their location. "This map shows the elevation of those rocks and ridges in front of us.

I've made some notes and drawings to show topographical features that hadn't been described before. Today, we're going to review the work and my calculations."

"You want this to work," she said.

"I want this to be right. That panhandle is ideal, but I have no desire to invoke eminent domain. Northeast Rail would lobby for it and they'd get it. They're about eighteen hundred miles to the east. I'm here. I've had to supervise laying track on land seized by the government before. It's dangerous for everyone. I'd have to create my own security force or hire Pinkertons. There'd be hazard pay for the crew. The supply route would have to be guarded. No town welcomes that kind of conflict, and there'd be folks on both sides of it. So yes, I'd like this to work, but it's more important that I get it right."

Lily rolled up the map and tapped it lightly against her leg. "How can I help?"

Roen held out his hand for the map. "First things first." He slid the map into its leather case and laid it on the ground a few feet from the tripod. "I'll show you how to use the chains." He repeated the chain demonstration he'd done for Clay. Lily had no difficulty following directions and she was better at following his calculations than Clay had been. Except for comments by teacher and questions by student, they worked in relative silence. Roen acknowledged to himself that they were more efficient as a pair than he ever was alone, and in spite of the fact that he had to teach her as they went along, she was a better assistant than the one he had fired and left behind in New York and infinitely less talkative than her son.

It was well into the afternoon when they stopped to unpack the lunch Ellie Madison had provided. Roen's rumbling stomach provided the prompt. Lily hadn't said a word about being hungry, but she bit into the ham sandwich with such relish that Roen knew she had been.

"You should have told me you were hungry," he said.

She shrugged, took another bite almost before she'd swallowed the first. "We're working on your schedule. Not mine."

"Say something the next time." He gave her a pointed look. "And don't choke."

She smiled guiltily, swallowed, and addressed what was most important. "There will be a next time?"

"Certainly, unless you don't want there to be."

"No, I'd like that." She stared down at

her sandwich, not at him. "I like this."

"So do I."

She simply nodded and took another bite. "Why didn't you ask me to make our lunch? You didn't yesterday either."

"Northeast provides me with an allowance. It's part of my contract. I made arrangements with Abe and Ellie Butterworth early on. I suppose I need to write a draft to you now that I'm taking most of my meals at your table. I should have thought of that on my own."

"It seems to me that preparing meals for you is one of my responsibilities."

He sighed. "You know, we might have rushed to come to terms. I'm concluding there are things we didn't think through."

Lily chuckled. "You're only now concluding that?"

"Mm."

"Bit of a slow top, aren't you?"

"You're not the first to say so."

"Miss Headley, eh?"

Roen shook his head, grinning. "How did you know?"

"I'm not sure. Maybe intuition. You realize I wasn't being serious. You're *not* a slow top. Just the opposite."

"Well, Victorine meant it, and she wasn't wrong. Not where she was concerned. I was slow to realize certain things." He searched the canvas bag for the hard-boiled eggs Ellie usually packed and passed one to Lily. "Let's not talk about her." He cracked his egg against his knee and began to peel it, flicking the shell away from the blanket they were sitting on. "I'm going to write you that draft when we get back, but it will be for household expenses as well as meals. How did it work when you were married before? Should we do it the same way?"

Lily's response was immediate and emphatic. "No!"

Roen blinked. "All right," he said slowly. "How did you do it so we *don't* do it that way?"

"I've managed well enough without your money. I don't want to come to depend on it. Having one extra at the table is no hardship, and you just paid for everything I'm wearing except my coat and scarf, so there's that. I've already cost you considerably more than you've cost me."

Roen blew out a long breath. "Another condition we should have worked out."

Lily finished peeling her egg. "We will work it out, just not right now. It'll be fine. Pass me the canteen." When he did, she tipped it and drank deeply before she passed it back. "Do you have experience with a gun?"

"What brought that on?"

"Thinking about Old Man McCauley taking aim from among the rocks."

"Then we're goners because I don't have a weapon with me."

"But you have one?"

"Two. A rifle and a piece that fits a shoulder harness."

"You didn't bring them with you to the house."

"With four children around, it seemed like a good idea to leave them. Actually, they're with Ben at his office."

"Are you a good shot?"

"Better than adequate. No sharpshooter, that's for certain. Eminent domain, remember? I had to learn to shoot back." He frowned slightly as he turned to examine her profile. "Do you not feel safe?"

"Oh, no, it isn't that. You have permission to be here. No, I was wondering if you'd teach me to shoot. I don't expect that I'll ever own a gun or even have cause to use one, but I'd like to learn. Ben said his mother is a crack shot, or she was when she worked at Twin Star. I had no idea. And Fedora Chen's father taught her to hunt. Hitch escorted them south of town yesterday to target shoot. I thought about it and decided it's something I'd like to do."

"Did you mention *that* to Ben?"

"No. Why would I? I figured I should tell you first."

"Thank you for that, but I'm wondering if Ben really wants a vigilante band of women taking to the boardwalk. From what I can tell, he has his hands full with Mrs. Springer's temperance league."

"Vigilante? It's nothing like that."

"If Ellie Butterworth is honing her shooting skills, it's because Fedora has been threatened. Tell me I'm wrong." When she didn't, he said, "I'm thinking this interest of yours has something to do with that."

"Did you hear me say I don't expect to own a gun or ever use one? Really, Roen, I don't know Fedora Chen except to see her in passing. That certainly hasn't happened often. I have sympathies for her, but I don't intend to take up cudgels on her behalf. Why would I when you're one of the people she feels threatened by?"

"What? Where did you hear that?"

"Ridley told me. And perhaps 'threatened' is too harsh a word. It would be better said that she mistrusts you."

"I haven't done anything to earn her mistrust."

"Of course you haven't. I know it's not personal. Ridley says it's who you represent. As to what Ellie is thinking, I don't know because I'm not party to it. All I want to do is learn to handle a gun like women used to do when this was unsettled territory."

Roen fell quiet, thinking it over. "I'm not opposed to it, Lily. You need to keep in mind that I have experience with a woman and a gun and it wasn't a good one."

"Oh. I hadn't forgotten. I just hadn't thought of it. Maybe I should ask Ben to teach me."

"No. I'll do it."

"You don't think I'd shoot you, do you?"

"I'm not sure I'm a good judge. I didn't think Victorine would do it either." He felt Lily's eyes on him. When he turned, she was studying him narrowly, trying to evaluate how serious he was. He kept a straight face and let her wonder for all of a ten count before he allowed his grin to give him away.

"Beast," she said, not unkindly.

For some reason, he didn't mind that at all.

Chapter Twenty-Four

Roen left some of his calculations for later so they could leave while there was still a chance of arriving home before school was done for the day. Lily knew what he was doing by setting a quicker pace, and she appreciated the effort, but her thighs and bottom ached from holding her own and she finally had to ask him to slow down.

"Unless you want to go ahead," she told him. "I think Dancer can find her way back without my help."

"Not leaving you," he said. He tugged on the reins and waited for her to come abreast.

Lily used the remainder of their ride to tell Roen about the dinner party she almost hosted and the dinner party they were going to be attending. "I don't know when it will be, but Ridley is anxious for it to happen so I suspect it will be sooner rather than later."

"And this is for Fedora's benefit?"

"Well, it was when I thought we would invite her to dinner, and Ben's intention was the same when he took over my idea, but Ridley has a slightly different motive. She wants to impress her mother-in-law."

"I don't know how Ridley could be any more impressive. Ellie has a high regard for her. She speaks of her often and in terms that can blind with their glow."

"That's what I thought, but Ridley thinks differently. Hazarding a guess, I would say it's because she hasn't yet had a child."

"No dinner party is going to fix that."

"She knows, but it's something she can do and she believes she needs to do something."

"So Fedora is the catalyst for a much larger experiment."

Lily laughed. "I reckon that's true."

"And you said Hitch will be there?"

"He'll be invited. I think it would take a town brawl to keep him away."

"It seems the doctor is also matchmaking."

"She's rounding out the number of guests."

"Uh-huh."

"Well, she is." Lily paused and then reluctantly admitted, "And also playing Cupid."

"Playing with fire is more like it. Hitch's mother will get wind of this, and I don't imagine she will approve."

"Maybe not, but she doesn't have a say."

Roen had not known Amanda Springer long, but he couldn't think of a situation where she didn't have something to say. He let it go. "What prompted your interest in Fedora Chen? You said yourself you've only exchanged a few words in passing."

"I suppose Hitch got me thinking about her when he was at the house. I knew from Clay that he liked her, and when he came in carrying your things, I don't think his feet touched the ground. And I thought, her being Chinese and Amanda being, well, being Amanda, that courting her was going to be difficult for Hitch. That was probably the seed. Then Ben watered it some when he told me about the way Fedora is treated, or maybe I should say mistreated. My mind wandered back to the reception at the Songbird and how encouraging and kind everyone was to us, and I was reminded that folks in Frost Falls have been good to me — very good — and I decided right then that I should return that goodwill. Fedora Chen seemed the best place to start."

Roen said nothing for a time, taking all of it in. "You know, Lily, some of the people at the reception are among those who have no use for Fedora."

"I know."

"They might not be so encouraging and kind when they learn you've taken up with her. They might even see it as some sort of betrayal of their goodwill."

"No one thinks worse of Ellie for standing by Fedora."

"You don't know that. There are subtle ways people make their disapproval known. Maybe they don't visit the hotel dining room as frequently. Maybe they don't visit at all. They might make themselves more of an annoyance to Ben just because he's her son. He usually has a busy Saturday night pulling people apart. It wouldn't surprise me if Ellie receives the occasional cold shoulder when she's with Fedora. She'd notice and she'd pretend she hadn't, but Ellie Butterworth impresses me as someone who keeps score. That's what she would do."

Lily sighed. "You're thinking about her shooting targets again, aren't you?"

"I kind of came around to that."

"You're like the railroad," she said. "One track."

Roen grinned. It wasn't a compliment, but from Lily's perspective, he thought it was probably true.

■ ■ ■ ■

Mrs. Rushton had dinner started by the time Lily and Roen returned home. Roen tried to pay her, but she would only accept his thanks. Once she was gone, Lily washed up and took over. Roen said hello to the children before he secluded himself in the workroom to finish his drawings and calculations. Lily stirred the stewpot while imagining Roen hunched over the table with one pencil in his hand and a spare tucked behind his ear.

"I would have rather been with you," Lily told him much later. She was lying on the side of the bed closest to where Roen's blankets were spread. After he once again refused her invitation to join her in the bed, she shifted her position so that she occupied the usually vacant space. She dipped her head over the side. The room was only dimly lit, but she could make out Roen's rather stoic features. She supposed that stoicism went hand in hand with that noble profile. "After spending the day with you doing important work, stirring a stewpot was not particularly satisfying."

"I submit it was more important in the moment than what I was doing, and I know four hungry mouths who would agree with me."

"I suppose," she said, unconvinced.

"You could have joined me, Lily. I would have welcomed it."

"And you would have had no dinner. I need another me. That's a thought I've never had before. It used to be that I was up to every task."

"You have expanding interests. If you're going to accompany me into the field, we should have a housekeeper. Someone like Mrs. Rushton who can cook as well."

The idea appalled Lily. "I would never. I couldn't."

"Why not?"

"Keeping the house in order and preparing meals are my responsibilities."

"You're adamant about this?"

"I am."

"Odd, that. I'm recalling someone who spoke rather heatedly about women not having opportunities. She looked like you, but I must be thinking of someone else."

"I suppose you think you're being amusing."

"I think I'm being ironic. Ridley and Ben employ a housekeeper. So does Amanda Springer. What's her name?"

"Mary Cherry."

"That's right. Ellie worked for the Frosts in that capacity for years. From what I can tell, it afforded her a good life and prepared her for managing the Butterworth. Mrs. Cherry and Mrs. Rushton also benefit from their employment. If you can see that hiring a housekeeper is not shirking your responsibilities but shifting them, maybe you can see your way clear to partnering with me."

"Partnering?"

"Junior partner. Like a New York law firm."

"What about Clay?"

"Still my assistant. Yours, too, if you agree."

"I would require compensation."

"Naturally."

"It would have to be at least as much as Mrs. Fish is paying me." Lamplight glanced off Roen's teeth as he smiled up at her. Clearly, she thought, he was enjoying himself.

"Ah, the negotiation begins. How much is that?"

When she told him, his grin vanished. "What?" she asked. "Is it too steep? She pays me by the piece, so it's difficult to calculate the salary on a weekly or monthly basis. I've given you my best estimate."

"I trust your numbers, but now I am wary

of Mrs. Fish's goodwill. She can afford to do better by you. I certainly will." He named a figure that was two-and-one-half times what she was earning from the dressmaker.

"Can you truly offer so much? You already have an arrangement with Clay, and earlier you wrote a draft to me for the household. In light of this, I should give it back to you."

"If you do, I will have Mr. Washburn at the bank deposit it directly into your account. Northeast Rail pays me very well, Lily. When it comes to money and knowing my value, I am a better negotiator than you."

Lily had no argument for that. He was right. Unaccountably, she felt a lump forming in her throat and tears blur her vision. She blinked back the tears before they dripped on Roen. The lump, though, would not be swallowed. She wanted to tell him that there was still so much she had to learn, but then she suspected it was something he already knew.

Abe Butterworth was a genial innkeeper, perpetually pink-cheeked and kindly featured. He owned the hotel, and Ellie was indispensable as its manager, but the registration desk was his personal fiefdom. He welcomed everyone with equal enthusiasm, made the weary traveler feel at home, and greeted the return guests as if they were family. Folks in Frost Falls couldn't have named a situation in which Abe's temper was tested, but then they were unfamiliar with Victorine Headley.

"I reserved the suite," Victorine said, tapping her gloved fingers on the desktop. She did not allow herself to be distracted by her reflection in the polished wood. A boy, whose name she could not recall, had carried her bags into the hotel, and now he was pressed against the wainscoting waiting further instructions. "How often do I need to remind you that I reserved the suite before I'm permitted to go there? And my trunk is still on the bed of that contraption standing outside your establishment. The boy says he can't carry it in. I believe him because he barely managed to get it on the wagon."

"I'll see to your trunk, Miss Headley, but there is nothing I can do about the suite."

"How is that possible? You own the hotel, don't you? It's called the Butterworth. Your name is Butterworth. That would make them connected in any guest's mind."

"Yes," he said, drawing a breath and releasing it slowly through a forced smile. "I own the hotel, but my guests — all of my guests — deserve consideration. I've explained that your reservation for the suite was to have begun several days ago. When you did not arrive and sent no word that you were delayed, I gave the suite to a family of five who found their accommodations uncomfortably crowded. They would have made do, if you had arrived as planned, but they didn't have to since you are only arriving now."

"You're giving me their room?"

"No, but there's another one available. I assure you it's clean and comfortable."

"I've been traveling in a private car that was clean and comfortable."

"Well, perhaps you'd like Frankie to take you back to the station. Your car is still there, isn't it?"

"On a side track."

"Then . . . ?"

"If I'd wanted to stay there, Mr. Butterworth, that's what I would have done, but it's the middle of the night, I was looking forward to a bath — your suite does have a bath, I hope — and sleeping in a bed bigger than a coffin."

"The suite does indeed have a bath, but since you won't be able to use it until the Mastersons leave, I can arrange for a tub and hot water to be carried up to your room."

"Wooden tub? I've seen pictures."

"Copper with a muslin liner. I believe you've seen old photographs. The Butterworth is a modern hotel."

Victorine offered a bland smile. "If modern means quaint, then it certainly is."

Abe Butterworth opened the registration book and pushed it toward Victorine. He held out a pen. "If you intend to stay, I need you to sign the book."

"When is that family leaving?"

"The day after tomorrow. In the morning if the trains are running on schedule."

Huffing softly, she took the pen. "Then it could be a week or more." She signed her name. "I expect to have that suite as soon as it becomes available."

"You will, Miss Headley. You have my word."

"I thought I already had that," she said, trading the pen for the key he held out. "I'll expect my trunk shortly."

Mr. Butterworth nodded and watched her go. Behind her back, he gave Frankie Fuller a significant look meant to convey equal parts sympathy and dismay. Frankie grinned and clasped his hands, holding them about six inches forward of his belly, then he picked up Victorine Headley's cases and followed in her haughty wake.

Abe's good humor returned. He supposed that the boy had a good point. Miss Headley's ill temper was likely related to her condition.

Victorine slept until noon. That was why Roen didn't see her in the dining room when he went to collect his lunch at the Butterworth. He left alone for the location he had mapped out. It was out of the question that Lily could join him when she'd ticked off all the things she had to do that day. Roen noted that once again none of the seven things included finding a housekeeper. He had considered asking Ellie for a recommendation but bit back the question in the event that Lily changed her mind. The decision had to be hers, and what seemed so logical, even natural, when they first struck the deal might be giving her second thoughts as time passed.

He missed her, though, and had every day since their initial excursion. She was a restful and conscientious companion. She asked thoughtful questions, followed directions, and listened. If he could have glimpsed into her mind, he was sure he would have seen an elaborate arrangement of cogwheels turning furiously. She was a quick study, and it was further confirmation that Clay took after her.

Roen's chuckle made his horse nicker. He leaned forward and patted the animal's neck. "That's right, boy. She's a fast learner. Cautious, too. But neither of those is helping her see that she's standing on the tracks and this train is barreling down on her."

Martin Cabot also slept late. Victorine had been stubbornly opposed to him taking a room at the Butterworth; therefore, he showed up at Mrs. Brady's boardinghouse in the middle of the night and considered himself fortunate to share a bed with only one other occupant. The man woke long enough to introduce himself as Clark Bennett, laid claim to the left side of the bed, and promptly returned to sleep. Martin never heard him leave in the morning, so there was no time to learn anything about Mr. Bennett. Martin did that after he woke, going through the man's possessions to determine the man's trade, the depth of his pockets, and whether or not he carried weapons. Martin Cabot's own pistol fit neatly in a leather holster strapped to his chest and was virtually invisible under his jacket. If Bennett had something similar, he was certainly wearing it. Martin wasn't worried. He could sniff that out. He was also able to conclude that his bedmate was a salesman, in this instance a hawker of medicines. There was no case to examine, but plenty of sample bottles lined the top of the dresser. The man's clothes were modest but of decent quality, leading Martin to the opinion that Bennett was moderately successful at what he did.

It could be worse, Martin concluded. These drummers moved on and then he would have the room to himself. It would cost Victorine, and she would fuss about it, but she would pay in the end. She'd have to; otherwise he would be moving into the Butterworth. Her edict that he keep his distance be damned. It did nothing but make his job more difficult anyway.

Because he rose late, Mrs. Brady was no longer serving breakfast. She never served a meal in the afternoon and told him if he wanted dinner, it arrived at the table promptly at six. There were currently seven other boarders, five of whom regularly appeared at dinnertime. Mrs. Brady was tall, angular, and carried herself with military bearing. Without saying as much, she managed to communicate that she expected to know his intentions. Martin's response was polite but noncommittal, and he left without making a distinct impression, which was always his goal.

Martin arrived at the Butterworth thirty minutes later after he'd taken a brisk walk around the town. He stopped in several shops and looked around but never introduced himself and bought nothing except a newspaper. He smiled pleasantly at those who looked in his direction. He even ran into Clark Bennett trying to sell his wares at the druggist's. Mr. Bennett didn't recognize him, which pleased Martin.

The Butterworth's wraparound porch was an appealing feature. He counted ten rockers across the front and imagined there were more along the side. Snow dusted all of them. It was too cold to sit outside, but he could picture people using them in every other season. If he wasn't tortured by boredom first, he could see himself settling in Frost Falls.

Victorine was not in the dining room. Either she had risen early and already been, which was unlikely, or she would appear sometime while he was enjoying his meal, which would ruin it. A third possibility was that she would have breakfast in her room, but the Butterworth did not strike him as an establishment that would offer that amenity. He hoped he was wrong.

He was told he could sit anywhere, and he chose a table for two where he had an angled view of the town's wide thoroughfare. He ordered steak and eggs and black coffee from a comely woman who introduced herself as Ellie Butterworth and welcomed him to Frost Falls. She tried to engage him in conversation, but he was a practiced deflector, and she left without knowing his name or where he was from.

He did not make firm eye contact with any of the other five diners, although he did observe them from time to time over the top of his newspaper. The Frost Falls *Ledger* was only a weekly broadsheet, but it contained articles reprinted from Denver's *Rocky Mountain News* and those tidbits common to small-town papers. There were three birth notices and one death reported. The death was a native of Frost Falls but no longer a resident. The town's population remained on the plus side.

Martin folded the paper and put away his spectacles when his food was brought to the table. He looked down at the plate as it was placed in front of him, but the hand that delivered it was so delicately beautiful that he allowed himself to follow the curve of those fingers all the way to their owner's face.

He could not stare, of course, but he saw enough to know she was a rare flower in a place like Frost Falls. He'd not seen a single Chinaman on his tour around town, and it was his experience that they came together in protective clusters wherever they lived. There was no such ethnic enclave in Frost Falls or he would have discovered it. She was alone, then, or mostly so. That was interesting.

Her dark, almond-shaped eyes were downcast. He had no fear that she was studying him. Her smile could hardly be called that since it was so tentative, and it seemed to him that she remained at his side by sheer force of will. He would have liked to see her coal black hair unbound and brushing against her slim neck and shoulders, preferably with a pillow supporting her head. She was that lovely.

He returned his attention to this plate, but now he had the vision of her small breasts and slender waist at the back of his mind and could reach for it anytime he chose. He thanked her when she finished pouring his coffee. She hurried away without acknowledging that he'd spoken. That surprised him a little. He was used to the deference her kind showed.

In other circumstances, he'd have enjoyed teaching her how to show respect, but the fact that he was working and required to be discreet meant that he could look but not touch. That pained him. She was an unexpected complication, and the fact that she was young, easily less than half his age, only made her more desirable. He had always liked his women young.

Pride in his greatest assets, the nondescript appearance and unremarkable manner, was all that kept him from opening his fly and relieving himself under the table. Wondering how it would be reported in the *Ledger,* Martin Cabot smiled to himself as he cut into his steak.

Chapter Twenty-Five

Hannah stabbed a dumpling with her fork and waggled it while she spoke. "And then Frankie Fuller fell dead asleep right there at his desk." She dropped her head in imitation of her classmate and Clay's best friend. "He tipped forward and cracked his slate when his head hit it, but the part that made us all laugh was that he didn't wake up right then."

Lily was watching her daughter more than listening to the account. "Eat that dumpling, Hannah, before it flies off your fork and hits your brother."

Hannah plopped it into her mouth and spoke around it. "Yes, ma'am."

Roen speared a piece of chicken. "So when did he wake?"

"When Mr. Stanton hit him with the pointer."

Clay frowned. "He whaled on him. Could have just given him a shake, but no, he had the pointer in his hand so he used it."

"No one laughed after that," said Hannah. "We felt terrible for Frankie."

"As well you should," Lily said. "Does he often fall asleep like that?"

Clay shook his head. "Never happened before. It was on account of the train coming in so late. Frankie got himself a sometimes job taking passengers and bags to the hotel. It was his turn yesterday so he had to wait until the train arrived. He slept on a bench in the station, but he told me it wasn't restful. That's why he nodded off."

"That's too bad," said Lily. "Perhaps Mr. Butterworth should find someone else to help when there's a late arrival."

"Now that would make Frankie real sad," said Hannah, waggling another dumpling. "I'm serious, Ma. He's always jingling coins in his pocket and not cause he's showin' off. He's kind of musical that way."

"Oh, musical. Well, in that case —" Lily stopped because the dumpling on the end of Hannah's fork catapulted across the table. It would have landed on Clay's plate if Roen hadn't intervened. He caught it neatly in his palm, returned it to Hannah's plate, and then went to the sink to wash chicken gravy off his hand. Lily stared at him right along with her children when he came back to the table.

"What?" he asked, picking up his fork.

Lily shook her head, hardly knowing if she should be admiring or admonishing. "You're just so . . . *unexpected.*"

"Huh. I suppose that's something."

And that was that. Lily watched Roen's attention return to his meal. It was a cue that everyone else should do the same. There was no commotion, no chastisement; nothing was upended except Lily's heart, and that, she realized, was the other thing that Roen caught neatly in his palm.

Clay helped himself to a warm biscuit and slathered it with butter. He gave half to Ham. "Frankie told me that Mr. Butterworth gave him something extra for his trouble last night, but not because it was late. I guess the woman he delivered to the hotel was a —" He stopped, searching for a more appropriate word than "bitch." "A real unpleasant person."

"Good for you," said Roen, tapping Clay's plate with the tines of his fork. "Your mother approves."

Clay nodded, grinning. "I had another word in mind."

"We know," Lily said dryly. "And I feel certain fatigue accounts for this woman's unpleasantness."

"I don't know. Maybe. Frankie mostly talked about her private car. I guess he got to step inside to help the porter take her bags. He said it was something like he's never seen. Not even in a book."

"Private car?" asked Lily, looking at Roen and not at her son. Roen had the same stillness of expression as she did. "And she's here? In Frost Falls."

"Uh-huh. At the Butterworth. Made a fuss, Frankie says, about not getting the suite, but Mr. Butterworth gave it to a family when she didn't show up to claim it. Guess she's staying for a while. Frankie thinks so anyway."

Roen asked, "Did she give Frankie something for his trouble?"

"Yeah, she did. Frankie said you could have knocked him over, she was that generous."

"Keeping him on a leash," Roen said under his breath.

"What?" asked Clay.

"Nothing. A stray thought."

"Oh, yeah. I have those all the time."

"You know what's good for that? Cod liver oil."

Clay made a face that brought laughter back to the table, and they finished the meal with pleasant banter and no more flying dumplings.

Lily joined Roen in the workroom after she and Hannah had finished clearing the table and washing the dishes. It was curious not to find him hunched over his maps or his notebook or even cleaning the lens on the telescope. He had a pencil behind his ear, but she couldn't see one in his hand. His arms were folded across chest, and he was leaning back in the chair with his legs stretched under the table. It could have been the posture of a relaxed man, but Lily knew better now. She was able to observe the fine thread of tension pulling his body taut.

He opened his eyes when she closed the door behind her, but he didn't force a smile. Instead, he blew out a breath. "So," he said. "She's here."

"Yes." Lily walked to where he was sitting and lifted herself onto the edge of the table and braced her arms. Her feet dangled inches above the floor. "Will you see her?"

"Not tonight, but eventually, yes."

"Don't leave it until too late. I'd rather she didn't arrive here first looking for you. Now that she's in Frost Falls, she only has to pose a single question to find you."

"Tomorrow morning," he said. "I'll call on her tomorrow morning."

"Good."

Roen unfolded his arms and laid a hand on her knee. He squeezed it reassuringly. "No, it's not good, but it has to be done."

Lily looked down at his hand. He had long fingers, beautifully crafted to hold a paint-brush, wield a chisel, or run scales on a grand piano, none of which he said he could do with better than a mediocre result. She'd assumed he was being modest, but then she came to know him better and realized he was merely being truthful. He was not particularly humble about his aptitude for calculation, his skill for capturing detail in pencil, or visualizing the lay of the land in three dimensions where it existed on a map in only two. He was merely honest about the talents he didn't possess.

Lily lifted her eyes to his and was glad when he didn't take it as an indication he was supposed to remove his hand. "Did your family approve of Miss Headley?" If he found the question an odd leap, he didn't say so.

Instead, he asked, "Before or after she shot me?"

Lily gave him a withering look.

"All right," he said, chuckling. "My parents thought she was an uninspiring choice. My mother had no interest in painting her, and my father told me he could not be induced to sculpt her in wet sand, let alone in marble. Artemis made all the proper noises about how perfect she was for me, but I believe I told you that Victorine supports the opera and that Artemis relishes harassing me, so her judgment is suspect. Apollonia was in Europe and never met her. Rand was the most complimentary. He thought I didn't deserve her, which I later came to believe was true, though not in the way he meant it."

"Do you think they know she's here?"

"I have no idea. I didn't tell them about her telegram."

"Have you told them you're married?"

"No, not yet. It would not be out of character for them to rally and descend on us. I thought we should give ourselves time."

Lily's nod was barely perceptible.

He raised one dark eyebrow. "Do you think I should have already told them?"

"I, um, no. I suppose not. We married with an end in mind."

"Hmm. About that, Lily, there's been —" He stopped and the hand on her knee dropped to his lap as the door opened and Ham poked in his head.

"Da?"

Lily's lips parted in surprise when her son

asked for Roen and not her.

"What is it, Ham?" Roen asked. "What do you need?"

"Bed and a story."

"Ah, yes. *Treasure Island.* Go on up and I'll be there in a few minutes to help you." When he was gone, Roen said, "Lizzie is either already asleep or ready to drop. I'll take her. You can stay with Clay and Hannah."

"You don't want to work?"

"No. I don't think so. Long John Silver and Jim Hawkins beckon."

Lily sat up, thumped her pillow, and tried lying down again with one arm hanging over the edge. She was back to sleeping on her side of the bed, but there was nothing comfortable about the familiar depression. She may as well have been sleeping on stones. Huffing softly, she turned again, this time flinging her arm sideways toward the middle of the bed.

"Lily?" Roen flipped back his blankets and got to his knees. He rested his forearms on the edge of the mattress and peered over the side of the bed. "Have you slept at all?"

"Hardly a wink." She turned toward him and drew her arm under the pillow. "I'm sorry I woke you."

"I wasn't sleeping well myself. Only quieter about it." He picked up a blanket from the floor, stood, and began to roll it. "May I?" he asked, using his chin to point to the middle.

Lily nodded, realized he could only dimly make her out, and then said she was fine with the bundling blanket. When Roen tossed it on the bed, she straightened it. "Perhaps it should be thicker," she said. "Taller."

"It's the middle of the night. I'm not building the Great Wall." Still, he yanked on one of the comforters and began to roll it on the edge of the bed. When he was done, he pushed it toward the middle. "Good?" he asked.

"Better."

Roen lifted the covers and slipped under them. He turned onto his back and cradled his head in his hands. "Infinitely better."

"I don't think we're talking about the same thing."

"Oh, I know we're not."

Lily chuckled quietly. "Good night." She edged toward the barrier blankets and curled on her side so that her knees were close to her chest. She folded her arms around them and shut her eyes.

"According to you, those blankets are

there so you keep your distance."

"You're wrong. They are there so you keep yours."

He sighed. "G'night, Lily."

They were a complicated tangle of arms and legs and twisted blankets when they woke. Lizzie was standing at the foot of the bed, watching them as raptly as she had listened to Roen's tale about Old Man McCauley.

Lily was flushed pink with sleep and a fair amount of embarrassment as she tried to disentangle herself. Roen, she noticed, looked perfectly at ease as if this were a situation he managed every morning. He sat up while she was only able to raise herself on her elbows. His feet were uncovered and he wiggled his bare toes at Lizzie.

Giggling, she pointed to his feet. "I wear my socks to bed."

"Mine are on the floor. Would you get them for me?"

She nodded and went to the side of the bed closest to him. She put them on her hands like mittens and held out her arms to show him that his socks came nearly to her elbows.

Roen plucked them off one at a time and pulled them on his feet. "Thank you."

Lily's efforts to kick away the blankets

covering her were stymied when Roen threw off the last of his and dropped them on her. Sometime during the night he had removed all evidence of his bed on the floor and it was now lying heavily on top of her. Also, one of the bundling blankets, the smaller one, was suspiciously no longer bundled. Had she done that? Had he?

"Where is Hannah, Lizzie?" she asked. "And why hasn't she put a brush through your hair? It looks as if you're wearing a tumbleweed on your head."

Lizzie's lower lip trembled slightly as she patted her tangled mat of baby-fine hair. "I don't want a tumbleweed head."

"Get my brush and crawl up here."

Lizzie ran around the bed to take the brush from her mother's dressing table and climbed onto the bed.

Roen helped Lily free herself and lifted Lizzie into place so the brush could be applied. "You haven't told us where Hannah is," he reminded her.

"School. She left with Ham and Clay."

Lily and Roen spoke in unison, their voices similarly pitched but with different inflections. Roen framed the single word as a question. "School?" Lily's said it with an exclamation. "School!"

They traded slightly wide-eyed looks. "We

overslept," she said, dismayed. He said the same thing at the same time, but the difference was that Roen was hardly distressed. He had already begun to grin crookedly.

Lily lightly tapped him on the shoulder with the back of her hairbrush. "This is your fault."

"How is that?"

"I don't know, but it'll come to me in time."

He laughed, tweaked Lizzie on the nose, and got out of bed.

"You have a tumbleweed head, too," said Lizzie, wincing as her mother tugged at her hair.

Roen plowed his fingers through his crosshatch of hair. "Right. I'll take care of that."

"C'mon, Lizzie. We'll finish this in your room. Your da needs to wash and dress." Lily looked at Roen over the top of Lizzie's head. "I suppose you'll have breakfast at the hotel now."

He nodded. "It's better that I meet her in a public place."

"Witnesses," she said matter-of-factly. Out of Lizzie's sight, Lily made the shape of a pistol with her hand and used her thumb to pull back the hammer. She aimed at the ceiling. "Always a good idea to have witnesses."

"You frighten me, Mrs. Shepard." But he leaned across the bed and dared to kiss her on the mouth anyway.

Roen sat down at what had been his usual table when he regularly took his meals at the hotel. Abe Butterworth left the front desk to chat with him for a few minutes, mainly about the progress he was making establishing a new route. Roen brought him up to date, explained the weather was hampering his progress but that he expected to submit a proposal to Northeast by the end of January. Abe was encouraged by this, imagining his hotel filled to bursting with Roen's out-of-town hires.

Abe excused himself when Fedora stepped up to Roen's table. She was considerably less apprehensive about approaching him and stood patiently at his side as she took his order. When she looked him in the eye, he smiled and she actually returned it.

"Busy morning?" he asked, looking around. As long as Victorine showed up, Roen considered that his timing was good. There were just two empty tables, and he was the only single diner.

"Yes, sir," Fedora said, nodding at the same time.

"So all the rooms are taken."

She nodded again. “We have two families.”

“I see one of them over there.” He lifted his chin to indicate the table with three children, all of them under ten, and two harried adults who were busy cutting pancakes into manageable triangles.

“Yes. The Mastersons.”

“New arrivals?”

“Not so new. A week, I think. They’re leaving this afternoon.”

“No, I meant have you had new arrivals?”

“Oh, yes. Certainly we have.”

“That’s good, isn’t it?” Fedora surprised him by frowning ever so slightly. She was usually so careful to remain unreadable. It was also her custom to be agreeable. Excepting the occasion of their first meeting, she was as disturbed as he had ever seen her. “Isn’t it?” he prompted.

She bobbed her head quickly, too quickly, and then hurried off.

Roen didn’t watch her go. He was used to her hasty departures. He did wonder, however, at what had disturbed her enough to cause her to lower her guard. It was on the heels of that thought that one possible answer occurred to him. The lovely Victorine Headley had come to stand at the entrance to the dining room.

Heads turned, though she did nothing to

call attention to herself. Roen was used to that reaction. At one time, he had enjoyed seeing it, knowing that he was her escort and that she would be leaving with him. Now he wished she would simply leave. She didn't. Her remote gaze moved from one table to the next until her eyes rested on his face. Although neither of them moved, the distance between them fell away. In Roen's mind she stood just feet away, and her posture was the same as it had been when she showed him her palm pistol moments before she fired. He wanted to throw himself sideways, avoid the shot by feinting left or right, but he remained riveted to his chair. He couldn't even get to his feet.

Roen thought it might have been better if it had been that memory that pressed to keep him in his seat. He would have eventually come to his senses. The reality of what he was seeing now was as cruel as the first ball she'd fired, except this one was a shot to the gut. He felt the pain as if it were a fact.

Victorine Headley was pregnant.

Roen recovered his equilibrium by the time Victorine reached his table. He stood. Ellie had stepped out of the kitchen and was making her way to Victorine's side for the purpose of seating her. Roen stopped her with a glance in her direction and a subtle shake of his head.

"Victorine," he said when she was upon him. She leaned toward him with the attitude of one expecting a warmer greeting, perhaps a kiss. He held out the companion chair for her and left her in no doubt that he wanted her to sit.

"Roen," she said politely, sweeping the skirt of her ruched day dress to one side as she gracefully folded into her chair. "It's good to see you at last. I was so hoping I would find you here this morning."

He joined her. Her dress was aquamarine silk, chosen purposely, he was sure, to match her rather remarkable eyes. He admired her calculation. Was every garment she brought similarly colored, or had she seen him approaching the hotel and dressed accordingly? She wore a loose-fitting overblouse of the same color with large mother-of-pearl buttons. It was a tasteful accommodation for her condition.

"You'll understand if I don't return the sentiment," he said.

"No, I don't. Not really. Are you carrying a grudge?" She glanced down at her belly, which was touching the edge of the table. "That's too bad of you because I'm carrying your child."

"So you win? Is that it?" he asked. "Never mind." His gaze swiveled from Victorine and her feigned disappointment to Fedora Chen, who was standing unobtrusively at Victorine's side. He had little doubt that Fedora had heard Victorine's last words, but her expression remained neutral. "Miss Chen would like to know what you want for breakfast. I can recommend the pancakes."

Victorine smiled wanly. "Miss Chen, is it?"

"Yes, ma'am."

"I'll have two pancakes, one strip of bacon, and one egg. Tea, please, not coffee." When the girl had left, Victorine said, "You're friendly with the help."

"I've been here long enough to get to know people."

"She's Chinese, Roen."

"And?"

"And?" she asked. "You know what they're like. Dirty creatures. I don't believe she should be working where there is food. I could barely eat my dinner yesterday for thinking she might have touched it." She shivered delicately. "I asked that woman to send another waitress to my table from now on, but she's obviously ignoring me."

"That woman is Ellie Butterworth," said Roen. "And if she sent Miss Chen here in spite of your wishes, then she had a reason for it. Mrs. Butterworth works hard to accommodate all her guests."

"Hmm." Victorine was skeptical. "Oh, let's not talk about them. Were you surprised to hear from me?"

"Very little that you do surprises me."

"Liar. You looked as if you were poleaxed when you saw my condition."

"I said very little surprises me. Your current state is an exception."

Victorine placed one hand lightly against her belly and smiled. "I think it's going to be a boy. Would you like a boy, Roen?"

He ignored her question. "How did you find me?"

She shrugged. "I hired a private investigator. He's an inconspicuous sort, but apparently that is an advantage in his profession."

"I imagine it is."

Victorine huffed softly. "Why are you being like this?"

"Like what?"

"I don't know. Cold. Distant."

"Sitting with you is not pleasant for me. Would you prefer that I pretend that it is?"

"I would prefer that you make an effort to be agreeable. For the sake of our child."

The effort that Roen made just then was not to recoil. "Why are you here?"

"Has living here dulled your mind? You have always been accounted to be a sharp wit. What's happened?"

Roen leaned toward her and repeated his question, this time in a whisper. "Why are you here?"

She frowned at him. Thin horizontal creases marred her normally smooth brow. "How can you not know I'm here because of our baby?"

"Writing would have been an acceptable method of communication. Less expensive than a telegram. Much less costly than your trip here."

She waved this last aside. "Father insisted that I take one of his private cars. It's cost him nothing at all."

Of course she would think that. "Writing?" he asked. "A telegram?"

"Haven't you always told me you trust facts? Evidence? What proof could I offer in a letter? Am I wrong that you wouldn't have believed me?"

"You're not wrong," he said after a long moment. "I don't believe you now."

Victorine reared back in her chair as though struck. She opened her mouth to speak but clamped her jaw shut again when Ellie appeared with their food and a pot of tea.

Roen sat back so Fedora, who'd followed on Ellie's heels, could pour his coffee. He noticed her hand trembled slightly and doubted it was the weight of the pot that was responsible. She remained at his side until Ellie put down the plates and the teapot and wished them well, then she led the way back to the kitchen.

"Do you think she touched this?" Victorine stared at her plate. "The China girl, I mean. Do you think this is safe?"

"I can introduce you to the cook, if you like. Her name is Mrs. Vandergrift. She's a harridan of a similar mind as yours."

"Oh. You could have simply said the food was safe."

Roen applied himself to his meal, not at all surprised that he had no real taste for the scrambled eggs or the grits. The crispy bacon was like gravel in his mouth.

"You look well, Roen," said Victorine. "I confess I was hoping I'd find proof in your appearance that you missed me."

"Dark circles under my eyes?" he asked. "Sunken cheeks? My heart on my sleeve?"

"All of that, I suppose. You must think me the worst sort of person to wish that on you."

"I think you are the worst sort of person no matter what your wishes are."

"Roen! Really, you are impossible. Your appearance may not have changed, but you have hardened your heart. If you were truly wearing it on your sleeve, it would be a lump of coal the size of your fist."

Roen shrugged, unperturbed. Everything she said was true so there was no point to argue.

"This," she said. "*This* is why I broke it off with you. Your little cruelties. The manner in which you close yourself off. It's unconscionable the way you treat me."

Roen was in the process of lifting a forkful of eggs to his mouth. He stopped, lowered the fork to his plate, and regarded Victorine as though she were a point on one of his maps, something to be studied but, in the end, of no particular interest or importance.

"To clarify," he said, "I ended our relationship, such as it was, when I learned that your interests had wandered. You didn't deny your involvement with other men, and out of respect for where we are, I am using the word 'involvement' most euphemistically. If it seems to you that I am closed, look to yourself for the reason, and if you believe I have treated you unconscionably, you have but to recall that you tried to kill me."

He chose coffee over his eggs and picked

up his cup. He narrowly observed Victorine over the rim. "Are we done?"

"I don't see how we can be," she said airily, taking a dainty bite of bacon. "You haven't said what you intend to do about our child."

"Did you not hear me mention your involvement with other men? That should be a clear indication of my intentions. To be perfectly forthright, I have none."

"None? But this child is yours. I swear it. You have obligations."

Roen lowered his voice. "You can't possibly know that the baby you conceived is mine, and your admission that you slept with other men, while honest, is also damning."

"But I wasn't honest. I said it because your accusation stung and I wanted to get a little of my own back. I was never unfaithful to you."

"I have always admired how quickly you think on your feet, but I don't believe you, Victorine. I didn't question you without cause. I was told what you were doing."

"Gossipmongers," she said. "There are always people who want to make trouble."

"Yes." His stare was pointed. "I know."

"You *don't* know," she protested. "You *don't.*"

Roen set his cup down. "I assume I am not the first man you've applied to for help, so the others must have turned you down as well. Your father will support you and your child."

"He will insist I give our baby to a home. You know what those places are like. I won't be able to do it when the time comes, and he will put me out and cut me off."

Roen frowned. "Am I hearing you correctly? Your father doesn't yet know about the baby?"

"No. I haven't told him. On the few occasions I've spent time with him, I've been able to hide my condition. He would never look too closely, Roen. He wouldn't want to know. There is only one way he will accept our child."

Roen knew what was coming, had suspected this end all along. He removed his napkin from his lap and set it beside his plate. "Then we *are* done, Victorine. I am already married." It gave him a rather shameful satisfaction to stand while her mouth was still agape. "I'll take care of the bill," he said. He walked away without looking back.

Chapter Twenty-Six

Lizzie pointed Roen in the direction of the backyard when he finally arrived home. It was hours after he'd spoken to Victorine, and for most of that time he'd been wandering aimlessly. It was out of character. He never ambled. His stride had direction and purpose and, most often, a sense of urgency. It was when he found himself standing in the cemetery on the outskirts of town that he made the deliberate decision to return home.

Lily looked up anxiously when she heard the back door close. Lizzie knew better than to come out, so it had to be Roen. It was. He was standing on the lip of the porch, his shoulders hunched inside his heavy coat. She refastened the stiff shirt she had been taking down from the clothesline and started toward him. He shook his head and ignored the steps in favor of jumping to the snow-covered ground. With no encouragement from her, Roen began to unpin clothes and toss them in the wicker basket. He was wearing gloves, but Lily wasn't, and her hands were red and chafed. Her fingers were nearly as stiff as the clothes.

Once they were inside, he dropped the basket on the kitchen table and removed his gloves. He took Lily's hands in his and warmed them. She would have tucked them under her arms, but this was better. So much better.

"You were gone a long time," she said, tipping her head back to examine his face. His complexion was ruddy; wind had beaten color into his cheeks. There was a tiny crease between his eyebrows, and a muscle jumped in his jaw. The expression he cast in her direction was not merely interested. It was intense. "There was a great deal to discuss, I imagine." Lily followed this with a quick, negating shake of her head. "No. I promised myself I wouldn't ask. You can tell me all of it or none of it or something in between. Whatever you like."

Roen's smile was faint but it touched his eyes. His features softened but not his intentions. "I'm going to kiss you, Lily." He swooped before she could duck or mount a protest. Her lips were cool, but her mouth was warm. He touched the tip of his tongue to her upper lip, nudged it, and then he was inside. She stiffened but didn't pull away. Her hands remained in his. He thought she might have sighed and wanted to believe that she had, that far from being offended by the liberty he had taken, she had decided it wasn't a liberty at all.

Her response was tentative, but it was most definitely a response. She mirrored the movement of his mouth on hers, touched his tongue with her own, teased and taunted in a carnal dance. She stepped into him, and when he released her hands to open his coat, she understood he was inviting her inside. Lily slipped her arms around him. He clasped his hands at the small of her back.

She was as warm as she ever had been. It was usual for that warmth to be accompanied by a lovely lethargy, but this was different. She felt a rising excitement that made her anxious to stop and want more at the same time. Some part of her confusion must have asserted itself because it was Roen who lifted his head first. His dark eyes grazed her face and he brushed his lips one, twice, against the tiny crease between her eyebrows.

"Poor Lily," he said gently. "You have no idea of your appeal."

She removed her arms but not before she placed her hands against his chest and gave him a light push. "Take your coat off and sit down. Would you like something hot to drink? There is cider that I can warm."

"Save the cider for the children. I'll have tea." He removed his coat and gloves and hung them up. He placed his hat on the seat of an empty chair and pushed the clothes-basket to the end of the table closest to the stove, where the garments could thaw. "Why did you hang those clothes outside?"

"Necessity. I usually put up a line in the workroom, but I was reluctant to take damp things in there."

Roen sighed heavily. "I have complicated your life, haven't I?"

She turned away from the stove. "I agreed to it."

"With considerable reservation."

"Don't make our agreement be anything less than my decision, Roen. It diminishes me if you think that you being here is in some way against my will."

"Then I stand corrected." He took out cups and saucers. "Should I check on Lizzie? She was reading to her doll when I came in but she's awfully quiet now."

"You sit," she told him again. "I'll go."

Roen sat. He thought about the kiss and

wondered if Lily knew the bundling blankets were going to be permanently unbundled. She might feel differently about that when she heard what he had to say. "What's she doing?" he asked when Lily returned.

"Napping. She had a busy morning helping me with the laundry. She scrubbed the socks. Apparently she likes the sound they make against the washboard." She expected Roen would smile at that. He often did when it came to Lizzie. What he did, though, was pick up one of the empty cups and turn it around in his hands. She knew something was coming. She just didn't know what that something was.

"Victorine is pregnant." His eyes lifted to Lily. To her credit, she didn't gasp, although there was no color in her face when she finally breathed again. "She says I'm the father. I don't believe her, and I told her that. Our conversation didn't last all that long. I left most of my eggs and grits on the plate. I was late getting here because I went for a walk after I left the hotel, not with any destination in mind, just to turn down the slow boil to a simmer."

"What are you going to do?" she asked.

"Do? Nothing."

"But there's a child."

"Not mine."

She frowned. "But could it be?" His hesitation gave her the answer. "I see. You can't do nothing, Roen. That's not a choice. If you think it is, then you need to walk some more."

"What is it that you think she wants, Lily?"

"I'm not sure. Money?"

"Her father is one of the robber barons. She claims he will cut her off if she doesn't give up the baby, but I know her grandmother settled a fortune on her that is no longer in trust. She will hardly be destitute no matter what she decides."

"Then?"

"She wants marriage."

Now Lily gasped.

"Right," he said. "I told her I was married and left. I don't know what she'll do now."

"So this marriage of ours has served its purpose."

"I wouldn't put that in the past tense."

"Serving its purpose, then."

"Yes. You're saving me."

"Hmm." Lily removed the kettle from the stove and poured hot water into the teapot. She put the kettle back but did not sit. "I don't know how I feel about that. If I'd known there was a child, I wouldn't have agreed."

"If I'd known about the child, I wouldn't

have asked, but child or no, I would never agree to marry Victorine."

Lily stared at the floor, nodded slowly. "The child will be a bastard. That won't be easy for her."

"Him," said Roen. "Victorine thinks it will be a boy."

"Please. Don't say foolish things. You know that's the least of it."

"I apologize. You're right. I'm still simmering."

She surprised herself by saying, "Jeremiah used to simmer."

Roen looked up from pouring his tea to see if she would say more. It took some time for her to go on, but his patience was eventually rewarded.

"Looking back," she said, "it seems as if he was always that way, which isn't true, naturally. My point is that I knew what it looked like. I don't recognize it in you."

"I walked for a very long time."

"Mm. Perhaps that's it. Jeremiah drank."

He nodded. "So I've come to understand."

"He never had a slow boil. Only a rapid, raging one." Lily fell quiet again then made a visible effort to shake herself off. "I don't know why I told you that. We were talking about Victorine." She pulled out a chair and sat at a right angle to Roen. He poured tea into her cup and she reached for the sugar. "When is the baby due?"

"I didn't ask and she didn't offer."

"Well, then, how far along is she?"

In response, he cupped his hands in front of him to indicate the swell of Victorine's belly.

Lily shook her head. "That's the best you can do? You make your living calculating things."

"All right." He flung his mind back to the last time he had been intimate with Victorine and worked from there. "My best estimate is that she's at least six months. If it's less, I cannot be the baby's father."

"Perhaps you can insist that she have an examination. Ridley might be able to accurately determine the length of time."

"Lily, it doesn't matter when she conceived or when she gives birth. I am done with her. I had to remind her that she *shot* me. I didn't think I'd have to remind you as well."

"I hadn't forgotten. She must be foolishly desperate if she's turning to you."

"Foolishly desperate? She's lost her mind."

"I know it must seem that way."

Roen's low growl came from the back of his throat.

Lily paused in stirring sugar into her tea

and looked at him askance. "Oh, I recognize that simmering sound. Do you need to go outside to clear your head?"

Roen rubbed the back of his neck, rolled his shoulders, and finally stretched his legs under the table. "No," he said. "I'm fine. But if you feel safer in the front room with Lizzie, I'll understand."

"I feel safe here." And it was true. She was not afraid he would hurt her physically, but she was also not unaware that she was vulnerable to other kinds of hurt. She sipped her tea. "What do you suppose she will do next?"

"I thought a lot about that while I was walking. I don't know. If she had sense, she would leave, but I don't imagine that will happen anytime soon. Did I tell you she hired a private investigator? That's how she was able to find me."

"Were you hiding from her?"

"No, but only because I didn't expect this." He laughed humorously. "I would have made a better job of it if I'd known she'd come for me."

"She could have surprised you and shown up unannounced. It's curious that she sent you that telegram. Why do you suppose she did that?"

"I don't like pretending that I know how

she thinks. It's uncomfortable and, if I'm honest, a little frightening."

"Guess."

"All right," he said, resigned. "She sent it to needle me. It gives her pleasure to take a poke at me. I told you at the outset I wasn't sure she would even come. She'd derive some satisfaction knowing I was looking over my shoulder. I know it's an exaggeration to say Victorine's lost her mind, but you have to believe me when I say she isn't well."

Lily nodded slowly. "I believe you."

He went on as if she hadn't spoken. "Her recounting of the end of our relationship was a fantasy. She said she was the one who broke it off. She changed her story about being with other men, denying it totally, saying my accusation stung and that she admitted the affairs in retaliation." He snapped his fingers. "That quick she was to explain it all away."

"Or perhaps not so quick," said Lily. "She's had a lot of time to practice her lines. She's shrewd, Roen."

"And unwell."

"A woman that scheming probably is. Lady Macbeth comes to mind." She rubbed her hands together as if washing them. " 'Out damn spot! Out, I say!' "

That made Roen groan and laugh at the same time. "Finish your tea and then we'll wake up Lizzie. She won't sleep tonight otherwise, and I have plans." He set his empty cup down and picked up the wicker laundry basket. She was still searching for words when he left with it.

Martin Cabot reported to the lobby of the Butterworth ten minutes before the appointed time. It gave him an opportunity to observe the China girl going about her work. She moved with infinite grace. In the noisy dining room, she was a silent breath. It gave him pleasure to watch her. He was delighted to discover that she boarded at the same house he did. He'd nearly made a fool of himself stumbling on the stairs when he caught sight of her leaving this morning for the Butterworth. He learned in passing from diners who were not as discreet as he was that her name was Fedora Chen. A lilting name, he thought. Beautiful.

He turned when he heard someone descending the staircase. It was two someones, in fact. Victorine's progress was marked by her rustling skirt. The heavy tread that caught his attention belonged to Abe Butterworth.

He wasn't certain what she expected of

him, but when she held out the fur-lined cape she was holding over her arm, he dutifully draped it around her shoulders. She thanked Mr. Butterworth for making her transition to the suite an easy one and then dismissed him as if he were one of her father's servants and not the owner of the hotel. Martin had seen it before. She had a similar disregard for him.

"Where are we going?" he asked. He'd thought when she sent that Frankie boy around with a message for him that they would be meeting in her room or in the dining room. His disappointment that it wasn't the latter was keen, but there was no reason she should know that. He opened the front door for her and followed her onto the porch. He hoped to God she wasn't going to insist they sit in one of the rocking chairs. He had many insignificant features, but he did have balls and they were already shrinking with the cold.

"Mr. Butterworth told me there is a soda fountain in the drugstore. No egg cream, I'm sure, but it will be a satisfactory place to talk."

He offered an elbow to assist her down the steps, but she pulled back, making her preference to go it alone quite clear. "What did I misunderstand?" he asked when they reached the boardwalk. “I was under the impression you wanted me to keep my distance, and yet here we are. I don’t attract notice on my own, but with you beside me, I might occasion second glances, if only because people will ask themselves what I am doing with this beautiful woman.”

“That’s a pretty compliment, Mr. Cabot.” Victorine pulled the hood of her cape up over her hair and bent her head against the wind. “Thank God it’s a short walk.”

“I know. I bought a paper there yesterday.” He pointed out the sign several storefronts ahead of them. She didn’t answer his question until they were inside and seated at one of the small tables out of sight of the large front window. He asked for a root beer. She asked the druggist’s wife for one of her specialty teas.

Waiting for the arrival of their drinks, she said, “I’ve changed my mind about not being seen with you. It doesn’t matter any longer.”

“So quickly? You only met with him this morning.”

“You know?”

“That’s why you’re paying me. Of course I know.”

“Don’t be smug, Mr. Cabot. It doesn’t suit you. You didn’t know he was married.”

She leaned toward him across the table. “How did you not know that?”

“Probably because it’s a recent occurrence. That newspaper I bought? I read it. Birth and death notices. No marriage announcements.”

“What about in today’s paper?”

“It’s not the *Times.* It’s a weekly. It comes out on Mondays. You’ll have to wait.”

“No. I don’t. You will learn to whom he’s married before then. I am depending on it.”

“Are you sure he’s telling you the truth? Mr. Shepard would not be the first man to try to dodge the responsibility of fatherhood.”

“Then you’ll find that out, too.”

It would not be a difficult assignment. He’d overheard enough during his walkabout to know people talked easily and knew most things before they were reported in the *Ledger.* He negotiated a bonus for himself anyway. She owed him at least that much.

They fell quiet when their drinks arrived. Victorine looked pointedly at the woman who brought them when she appeared to hover nearby. “Busybody,” she said when the woman moved out of earshot. “I despise them.”

“Really? I’ve always liked them. They’re

valuable in my line of work."

Victorine sniffed contemptuously. "I thought you were going to demand a room at the Butterworth."

"It occurred to me, but I find Mrs. Brady's boardinghouse has its charms, and as I will take my meals at the hotel from now on, I have the best of both worlds."

Roen purposely left the lamp burning as he prepared for bed, though he turned back the wick before he slipped under the covers. The bundling blankets were still dividing the mattress in two, and he noticed as soon as he entered the room that a third blanket had been added to the roll. The bundle was now higher and thicker than it had been the previous night. It made him chuckle when he turned on his side toward Lily and his bent knees bumped into it.

"What can you possibly find amusing?" she asked.

Roen propped his head on his elbow. He could easily see over the bundle. Lily was lying stiffly on her back. Her hands were folded outside the blankets and rested rather corpse-like on her midriff. He grinned when she turned her head to look at him and patted the top of the bundle.

"This," he said. "You've added a blanket."

"Yes, but I don't see how that is amusing."

"You added it because I said I had plans."

"I added it because we made short work of it last night in our sleep."

He ignored her explanation. "What sort of plans did you imagine I had? That interests me."

"I'm sure I don't know," she said crisply. "You didn't explain yourself."

He chuckled again. This one rumbled at the back of his throat. "Liar," he said.

"I'm not. And you shouldn't say that as if it's an endearment."

"Huh. I didn't realize."

"Liar," she said, not without affection.

"Oh, I see what you mean." He patted the bundle again. "I propose we make short work of this now. What do you think?"

"I think that's a bad idea."

"Really? Because I had the impression earlier that you might be open to dispensing with it."

"Your impression was incorrect."

"I don't think so. That kiss in the kitchen was powerfully persuasive."

"You took advantage. We'd just come inside and I was cold."

"That explains why you let me hold your hands."

"Yes, well, the rest just happened."

"Are you blushing? I can't tell if you're blushing and it seems as if you might be."

Lily's cheeks puffed as she blew out a breath. She turned her head away and stared at the ceiling. After a moment, she closed her eyes. "Good night, Roen."

Roen's head collapsed onto the pillow as he unfolded his elbow. She couldn't see it, but he was smiling to himself. "Good night, Lily."

Chapter Twenty-Seven

The bundle did not come unrolled as much as it was pushed out of the way. Lily might have done it when she burrowed deeper into the mattress and sought out Roen's warmth in her sleep, or it could have been Roen who shoved it toward the foot of the bed because he did, in fact, have plans that dreams did not deny.

Lily's soft murmur had the sound of satisfaction as she fit her bottom against the cradle of Roen's thighs. His arm slipped around her waist, holding her in place. She laid a hand over it, keeping him there.

A warm breath stirred her hair. Individual silken threads tickled her temple and brushed her cheek. She moved her head slightly to dislodge them. Something rested against the crown of her head. It was pleasantly abrasive against her scalp. She didn't think about what it was. She wasn't thinking at all.

Roen's nostrils flared slightly as he breathed in a fragrance he identified only as Lily. His chin rubbed her hair; the nighttime stubble moved strands of it and released more of its freshly washed scent.

It happened naturally, not by design, that their mouths found each other. Her lips parted under his, mirroring his touch until the balance shifted and he was mirroring hers. She was no longer nested in his thighs but instead was lying on her back with his weight pressing comfortably against her side. Perhaps if she had felt restrained, she would have woken then, but having him so close felt the opposite of that. She felt as if she'd chosen this and there was freedom in choice.

Roen's lips found the gentle hollow behind her ear. He kissed her there. He kissed her again on the corner of her mouth, her jaw, and where the pulse beat in her neck. He wound the ribbon that closed the neckline of her nightgown around his index finger and tugged. The gown parted. His mouth found her collarbone and traveled the length of it before he returned to the base of her throat.

Lily lifted her chin and gave herself up to the warmth of his mouth, and when he moved lower and left a damp trail of kisses on his way to her breasts, she gave herself up to that, too. His mouth closed over her aureole. The thin fabric of her nightgown was much less of a barrier than the bundling blankets had ever been. A barely formed thought flitted through her mind: She should have worn flannel.

Beneath the quilt and comforter, Roen's fingers scrabbled at the hem of Lily's gown. The heel of his hand brushed her bare leg as he lifted the shift. He laid his hand on the curve of her thigh. He used one of his legs to part hers.

Lily's hands were equally busy. One of them moved across his shoulder blades while the other slipped under his nightshirt and palmed a buttock and squeezed. His hips jerked involuntarily. She shifted to accommodate him, and when his mouth found hers again, she met him eagerly, measure for full measure.

He was already aroused, but now his erection swelled and throbbed and demanded his attention. The rush of blood to his groin made him groan, and the sound was deep and rough and loud enough to wake them both.

Lily stared into Roen's heavily lidded eyes. The look was slumberous, but there was no doubt in her mind that he was alert. She could feel that in every tense line of his body, just as she was sure he could feel the same in hers.

"Oh," she whispered. "So here we are."

He nodded, breathed shallowly and carefully, but didn't move away. The light in the room was dimmer than it had been when he'd crawled into bed but sufficient for him to make out the contours of her face and the faint smile that shaped her lovely mouth.

"Where is the bundle?"

Roen didn't look around for it. "I don't know. It's wherever you pushed it."

"I didn't move it. I think you kicked it out of the way."

"Does it matter? You said it yourself. Here we are."

"I did say that, didn't I?" Lily was not so much breathing shallowly as she was not breathing at all. It had to end, and when it did, her chest heaved and her breasts momentarily flattened against him. There was an unfamiliar ache between her thighs that was more disconcerting than the one that swelled and tightened her breasts. "What do we do now?"

"That's up to you. It's encouraging that you haven't pushed me away like you did the bundle."

"I did not —" Lily stopped because one

corner of his mouth was a fraction higher than the other. She returned his uneven smile. "I'm encouraged, too."

"Are you?"

She nodded. "I want this, Roen. I'm ready."

He did not ask if she was certain. He took her at her word and lowered his mouth to hers. She welcomed him with damp kisses and the sweet sound of satisfaction. He felt her fingers graze his back, and the hand that rested on his ass slid sideways to his hip. He slipped his hand between their bodies and laid his palm against her abdomen. She sucked in a breath and her midriff dipped. His fingertips drew lower until they reached her mons. She grew very still and then he slipped two fingers inside her. Her head lifted off the pillow but dropped back almost immediately.

"What are you doing?" she asked. She despised the edge of panic in her voice and was glad when he didn't answer. She squeezed her eyes closed as he moved his fingers back and forth, added a third. His thumb parted her lips and brushed her clitoris. Her hips rose and fell just as her head had done. She whimpered.

"It's all right," he whispered against her mouth. "Just feel."

And she did. The movements were familiar but the consequences were not. There was pleasure here and none of it was because she was trying to please him. He wanted her to experience this, expected it actually, and knew infinitely more than she did about how to bring it about.

"Please," she said. It struck her then that she had never uttered that word in bed except when commanded to say it. She offered it freely now and hoped he understood what should follow. She didn't have any other words.

Roen removed his hand and parted her thighs. He slipped between them and told her to raise her knees. She complied without hesitation. He took her loosely by the wrist, dragged her hand toward his groin, and folded her fingers around his cock. "Show me," he said. His voice grated at the back of his throat like sandpaper. He softened to a whisper that was only half as harsh. "Show me what you want."

Lily lifted her hips and opened to him like the flower she was. She guided him inside her and they collapsed together when he made his first deep thrust. Lily's hands went to his shoulders as he rose on his elbows. She knew her body would accommodate him, but the fit was tight and she was glad he gave her time to catch her breath. "Just feel," he had said. She was doing that now. "Wonderful" was too insipid a word to describe what she felt. "Brilliant" was better. She felt brilliant, luminous, sparkling with flashes of heat and light.

Roen began to move and she was struck by how easily she moved with him, matching his rhythm without conscious thought. It simply came to her, and she knew it was right, just as she knew the man was right. She opened her mouth to tell him that, but he bent his head and kissed her and the words disappeared as she tasted him on her tongue. She savored his kiss, the heat and firmness, the edge of hunger and urgency, and she recognized herself as his equal and returned what she received.

The sparks she felt as tiny explosions skittered across her skin and down her spine. She flung her pillow aside and pressed her head and shoulders into the mattress. She dug in her heels. There was a quickening in her blood; something hot and purely pleasurable was lifting her. She was flooded with a tide of new sensation, sometimes delicately balanced on the crest for so long that she began to fear it would not break, and then fear it would.

She breathed in air as though she were

sipping a fizzy through a straw. The sounds she made were little bubbles bursting in her throat. She wanted to laugh, to cry, to do them at the same time. What she did, though, was fly over the crest and shudder all the way to her toes.

Lily learned about restraint then. His. He began to move differently. His thrusts were rapid and shallow and she understood how much he had held back, how careful he had been. She cupped the back of his head, threaded her fingers in his hair, and said his name over and over on a thread of sound so insubstantial that she couldn't hear herself above the rattle of the bed and, finally, his guttural cry when he released his seed.

She expected him to collapse against her, might even have welcomed it, but she didn't have to find out. He withdrew and heaved himself onto his side, still close enough that she could feel his heat and hear his breathing as it steadied. Her heart was still thrumming. She pressed three fingers above it.

"You're a quiet lover," he said eventually.

"Mm."

"And just as quiet after."

"Jeremiah didn't like me to talk after."

Roen knew her husband's name would come up sometime. He regretted opening the door to it so soon. "I'm not Jeremiah."

"I know," she said, slanting a sideways look at him. "I *know.*" Still, she fell silent.

"Do you have regrets?"

Did she? "I regret my fears. I wish I had confronted them sooner."

"How much sooner?"

"When you approached me with your outrageous proposal."

"It was outrageous, wasn't it?"

"You sound pleased with yourself."

"Never doubt it." He leaned over and laid his lips against her temple. The kiss had the shape of a smile. "What would you have done differently if you had confronted your fears?"

"I would have asked for flowers for myself."

"Mm-hmm."

"And I wouldn't have objected to a kiss at the end of the ceremony."

"Ah, yes. That would have been brave of you."

"Maybe I would have said yes to a ring. I'm not sure."

"All right. Anything else?"

"You know."

"Say it anyway."

"You'll be so full of yourself, your hat won't fit."

"So? I'll buy a new hat."

She blew out a breath and spoke quickly in a rush of air. "I would have demanded my marital rights."

Roen found her hand under the covers, threaded his fingers through hers, and tightened his grip. "May I tell you something, Lily?"

There was such gravity in his tone that she hesitated a moment, uncertain if she wanted to hear. Confronting her fears again, she said, "Yes."

"The way you did it was better. Waiting was better. The flowers, the kiss, even the ring was theater. This, tonight, was real, and it couldn't have happened before it did. You weren't ready, and I couldn't be if you weren't."

Lily was quiet, thoughtful. "It *was* real, wasn't it?"

"Yes."

"You were waiting for me."

"All my life."

She disengaged her hand from his and sat up so suddenly, the bed rocked. Leaning over him, she reached for the lamp and turned up the wick, then she sat back and stared down at him. After he blinked a few times to adjust to the light, he stared right back.

"You heard me," he said.

"Say it anyway."

He raised his hand, touched her cheek with his fingertips. "I've been waiting for you all my life."

She put a hand against his and held it there. "I think you mean it."

"I do. Do you believe there is another woman I would have approached with my wildly absurd proposal? Not just in Frost Falls. I mean *anywhere.*"

"Didn't you come to me because you thought I was needy?"

"Needy? You?"

"Vulnerable, then."

"You disabused me of that when we spoke about Clay."

"But before then, when you sat for supper that first time, you knew I was nervous."

"Skittish, is how Clay described it. I think that's accurate."

She removed her hand and his slid away. "So you came to me because . . ."

"Because I wanted to be with you."

"Just like that."

"Mm-hmm. Just like that."

"But —"

"Listen to me, Lily. For now. For later. For always."

She blinked. "Oh, my."

"Indeed," he said. His mouth twisted

wryly. "It seemed the right thing to say when it was only in my head. Now I'm not so sure. How did it sound?"

"Perfect."

Roen chuckled and sat up. "And now for the prosaic, I need to wash." He lifted the covers, got out of bed, and padded to the basin on the other side. He raised his nightshirt and started to wash. When he glanced toward the bed, he saw Lily was watching him with interest. She didn't look away even when he kicked up a questioning eyebrow.

"Something you would like to ask?" Roen dropped his shirt and laid the washcloth over the lip of the basin. "Would you like me to wash you?"

"Um, no." Suddenly shy with thoughts better kept to herself, Lily looked elsewhere, getting out of bed as he climbed back in. She picked up a cloth and dampened it before stealing a glance at Roen. He was watching her, and she turned her back on him. "I should have put out the lamp," she said, more to herself than to him, but a moment later he further endeared himself to her by extinguishing the light. She cleaned herself and then returned to bed. "Thank you for that," she whispered. "For the lamp, I mean. I'm not so comfortable yet."

"May I point out that you seemed comfortable watching me?"

"It's different when the shoe is on the other foot. And besides, you didn't mind or you would have turned around."

"You have me there."

"For now," she said, and left it at that.

Roen waited for her to say more, and when she didn't, he reached for her and hauled her in. Her low laughter stirred him to action. She fought off his tickling fingers, surrendered to his kisses, and finally between breaths, she said the words he wanted to hear. "For later," she whispered. "For always."

"Huh," he said, letting her go. "It does sound perfect."

"Well, the next time I'm only going to say uncle."

Laughter rumbled in his chest. "That will sound perfect, too." He waited for her to settle. When she backed up against him, he made a cradle for her bottom with his thighs and slid an arm around her waist. "Good night, Lily."

She laid an arm over his, murmured something that might have been good night, and then fell deeply asleep.

Chapter Twenty-Eight

Martin Cabot had the information that his employer wanted less than twenty-four hours after she'd demanded it. He waited three days to tell her. It was a petty triumph but hardly unethical, and he was the only one aware of it anyway. He bought a newspaper at the drugstore and carried it to the hotel to read while he ate his breakfast. His landlady voiced no objections when he announced he would be taking all of his meals at the Butterworth. And why should she? It was one less at her table. He was also paying — or rather Victorine was — more than double for his room so Mrs. Brady did not foist another itinerant salesman on him. Martin was very much enjoying the peace and privacy his contract with Victorine afforded him.

Martin waited at the entrance to the dining room for Mrs. Butterworth to show him to his table. He'd learned quickly that she liked to do that, considered it important to the hospitality of the hotel. She greeted him warmly when she came upon him and apologized that the table he preferred was already occupied.

"That's Judge Miner. He's waiting for my son. Criminal business, I expect."

"Of course," Martin said graciously. "You could not very well ask him to find another seat." He looked around the dining room. It was crowded this morning. He recalled there had been a train arrival late in the day, so that explained so many unfamiliar faces. He would have to join a table that was already populated. It was not his preference. "May I wait in the lobby for a table to become available?"

"Certainly, if you wish it."

"I do." He indicated the paper under his arm. "I can read while I wait." Ellie took his coat and hat and showed him to the padded bench below the staircase. Martin thanked her and sat, opening his paper immediately to avoid conversation with her husband at the desk. He glanced up when the front door opened. He recognized Sheriff Madison. The lawman did not look in his direction, which Martin accepted as a good sign. It meant he had not attracted unwelcome attention.

The next time he looked above the broadsheet was because he heard Victorine. She'd been silent coming down the stairs but was now making her presence felt complaining to Mrs. Butterworth. Martin hid his satisfaction behind the paper. It seemed there were still no empty tables in the dining room.

Ellie invited her to sit at a table with an empty chair but otherwise occupied or return to her room and be notified when a table became available. Victorine clenched her jaw and chose the latter simply by walking away.

Martin lowered the paper. He knew the moment she spied him because she stopped so suddenly that she practically vibrated. Her skirt fluttered before it settled in place. There could be no meaningful conversation while Abe Butterworth stood behind the desk fiddling with the room keys and pretending to be oblivious. The man was aware that Victorine was at least an acquaintance because of their previous meeting in the lobby, but Butterworth couldn't begin to know the facts of their association. He wanted to keep it that way.

"Are you waiting for a table?" asked Victorine.

"I am, but you are welcome to take mine when it becomes available. I don't mind waiting."

"Perhaps we could share. Would that be acceptable to you?"

"It would." He watched Victorine look over her shoulder at Ellie Butterworth, who was also pretending not to observe their exchange.

"I will share a table with this man," she said. "You'll let me know." With that, she turned toward the stairs and began the climb.

Martin judged that Victorine could have only reached her room when Ellie sent one of her girls to announce that a table was ready. He wondered if the sheriff's mother had done it on purpose, but if she had, she did not give herself away, even when her husband regarded her with a raised eyebrow.

Martin stood when Victorine joined him at the table and politely held out a chair for her. She was slightly out of breath but he refrained from commenting. He sat opposite her with the paper opened beside him. He was wearing his spectacles now so he could read the broadsheet and not simply make a pretense of it.

"You are an awful man," she said. "I would not suffer you if there were a choice."

He looked at her over the top of his spectacles. "Oh?"

"I sent that boy around on two separate occasions because I wanted to know what you learned. You've given me nothing. Not so much as the satisfaction of a reply."

"The boy's name is Frankie."

She ignored that as of no account. "Where have you been? I thought you were going to take your meals here. I've never seen you once."

"Then it's because we simply take our meals at different hours."

"No, it's not. I've come down at different times and waited for you. I know you must be watching me."

"Must I?"

"You're purposely avoiding me."

"How do you explain that I'm here with you now?"

"You've learned something. Tell me."

"In time. Food first." Martin watched Fedora as she listened to Victorine. She kept more than a respectful distance from their table. He thought she was becoming accustomed to him, so perhaps it was Victorine who made her wary. It showed good sense on her part, and he liked her all the more for it. He gave her his order, and when she was gone, he shook his head at his breakfast companion. "I don't think she's an admirer."

"If that's true, it's mutual. I've asked Mrs. Butterworth several times to send someone else to my table, but she is either deaf to my concerns or finds it ridiculously satisfying to frustrate me."

"Either is possible, I suppose."

Victorine's pale blue eyes narrowed. "Stop delaying. Tell me what you know about Roen."

Martin tapped the newspaper. "It's in here. They were married Friday two weeks past. Too late for it to be announced in the previous edition." His eyes swiveled to the table near the front window. "Do you see that man there? The one with the heavy mustache and talking to the sheriff?"

Victorine turned her head slightly. "That man with him is the sheriff? I didn't know. So who is he?"

"Judge Miner. He performed the civil ceremony for Mr. Shepard and his bride."

"Not a church wedding?"

"You can read it for yourself." He pushed the paper toward her.

She pushed it back. "So he wasn't lying as you suspected. He's truly married."

"Yes, I was wrong, but if you will note the date, you will understand the wedding occurred shortly after your telegram arrived. It may be of small comfort to you, but even if our train hadn't been delayed by that snowstorm, you would not have arrived in time to stop it. The ceremony would seem to have been hastily arranged."

"What are you implying? That he hurried the wedding in anticipation of my arrival?"

Martin held up his hands with the thought of warding her off in the event she pounced. She was already leaning in.

"That's your not-so-subtle way of reminding me you tried to stop me from sending that telegram. I didn't appreciate it then, and I don't appreciate what you're saying now. You will kindly keep your suppositions to yourself."

"As you wish." Martin lowered his hands, unfolded his napkin, and spread it across his lap. He cast his eyes toward the paper and began to read. "Lower your voice," he said without lifting his head. "It's pitched in a way that will attract attention."

Straightening, Victorine laughed lightly as if he had said something witty. "What is the rest?" she asked after taking a few moments to calm down. "Who did he marry?"

"Lily Salt."

"That's it? That's all you know?"

"That's all the paper announces." It was true. He didn't tell her that he knew a great deal more, owing to his conversation with

Amanda Springer in the butcher shop and Frankie Fuller on one of his errands to the boardinghouse. He liked the irony of Victorine sending Frankie with messages for him when she could have learned almost everything from the boy if she had considered him the least consequential.

"I could have read that for myself."

"But you didn't. You haven't."

"Didn't you talk to anyone?"

"I will. You'll know everything I know tomorrow. Shall we say two o'clock? I've observed you take a walk around that time."

Victorine frowned but nodded. Their food arrived, and they ate without another word passing between them.

Roen was up before Lily and cracking eggs into the skillet when she came upon him. He held out one arm and pulled her to his side. He bussed her on the cheek while expertly opening an egg with his free hand and stacking the shell with the others. He would have liked to kiss her long and hard and deep but was aware of four pairs of eyes at the table watching him closely. Roen knew better than to think they were interested in him kissing their mother. They'd grown accustomed to it over these last few days. It did not arouse comment; although sometimes he caught them exchanging knowing looks.

No, they had no curiosity about the kissing. They were hungry. Ham had already announced it twice and patted his growling stomach as evidence. They cared very much that he didn't burn the eggs or the toast or the bacon. He released Lily and put her in charge of turning the bacon.

"You're wearing your outside-the-town clothes, Da," Clay said. "I reckon that means you'll be riding out today. I didn't get your horses. I didn't know you were going anywhere."

"I only decided last night after you'd gone to bed. It's all right. I can manage it this once. You can take them back when I return." He slipped a turner under one of the frying eggs to make sure it was hardening on the bottom. "You recall that problem I was helping you with last night?"

"I sure do. Did you show it to Ma like I told you?"

"I did, and you were right. She figured it out. She's going to explain it to you later because she'll make a better job of it than I did."

"Aw, you're not so bad."

"Thank you for that," Roen said dryly.

Lily continued to turn the bacon while

she looked over her shoulder at Clay. "It comes so easily to him that it's hard for him to imagine it's challenging for the rest of us."

"Yeah," said Clay. "But he's real patient. That's different than Pa was."

Lily stole a glance at Roen, but he was plating eggs and at least acting as if he hadn't heard. "Yes," she said. "He's different that way." She poked him gently in the side with her elbow and pointed to the plate. He handed it over, and she added the bacon to it. "I love that you're different that way," she whispered.

This time when he kissed her, it was on the mouth, and it lingered just a little.

"Eggs, Ma!" Ham shouted from the table. "You're going to lose our eggs!"

The plate was indeed tipped sideways. Lily stepped back and righted it so nothing was lost. She pushed it at Roen and told him to take it to the ravenous horde. "I'll get the toast," she said.

Once the children were off to school and Lizzie was playing in the parlor, Roen asked Lily if she'd done anything about looking for a housekeeper. He was fairly certain the answer was no, but he thought he should give her the benefit of the doubt.

"Nothing except think about it," she told

him, dropping dishes and utensils into a tub of soapy water. "I don't have a candidate in mind, and if I do this, I'd like it to be someone I know."

"If?" he asked. "There's still a question in your mind? I thought this was settled."

"It's extravagant, Roen."

"There will be two incomes," he said. "Yours and mine, and if Clay wants to add a little something, there will be three."

She smirked. "Sometimes your calculations are suspect. No matter how many times you slice it, the pie is still yours."

"Then allow me to do as I wish with it. I'll speak to Ellie. She'll be able to recommend someone. That's how Ridley found Mrs. Rushton."

Lily recognized she was on the losing end of the argument. "Oh, very well. Ask Ellie when you pick up your pack."

He sidled up to her at the sink. "You know, I'd rather get rid of the outside-the-town clothes and take you back to bed."

She flushed and flicked water at him. It should have sizzled when it touched him. His dark eyes were that hot. "Last night was quite enough," she said before the heat overtook her.

Roen moved behind her and nuzzled her neck. "You don't mean that."

She didn't. "Well, you shouldn't make me say what I don't mean." She felt his laughter bubble against her skin. He'd marked her in almost the same spot last night. A love bite, he called it, and she thought it was a proper name for what he'd done because it had been deliciously erotic. When she saw it this morning in the mirror, she called it what it was: a bruise. She batted him away. "No more of your branding," she said, tapping the side of her neck.

He squinted at where she was pointing. "That? That's nothing."

"Nothing you have to cover up. Go on. Get out of here."

Roen reluctantly stepped away. "Think about what I'm going to do to you tonight," he said, and then he was heading down the hallway.

"You can't leave like that," she called after him. "Roen!" But he didn't turn and he didn't come back. She heard him talking to Lizzie and then saw him collect his things at the front door and walk out. She was wet by then, and damn him, he knew she would be.

Hannah and Clay were squabbling in the kitchen when Roen got back. He scraped snow off his boots and beat his hat against his thigh before he walked in. Icy clumps clung to the lamb's wool collar of his coat. The children stopped to look him over.

"Escaped an avalanche, Da?" asked Clay. "You're a sight."

"Mm." He was wet and tired and took no pains to hide it. "Forget about taking the horses to the livery," he told Clay. "It's done."

Clay nodded. He looked past Roen to the window. Snow was coming down sideways. "I reckon the storm's just getting started here."

"Well, it started a lot earlier in the higher elevations."

Hannah had a stack of dinner plates in her hands. "Did you ask Mr. Wayne about the weather before you left?"

"No, I didn't, but I most assuredly will seek him out the next time I go out Thunder Point way." He plucked his damp collar away from his neck. Melting snow trickled down his spine. "What's for dinner?"

"It's bean soup," said Hannah. "Ma started it and I'm keeping watch. Clay's in here to annoy me."

"That's more or less Ham's job. Where's your mother?"

"In the sewing room."

Roen nodded. Hannah had decided that

the space formerly known as the workroom was now the sewing room when Lily occupied it and the study when he was in there. "Carry on." He was opening the door to the sewing room when he heard them return to squabbling.

Lily looked over when Roen walked in. She was standing at the dress form, pinning a lace collar on the neckline of an ice blue satin bodice. "Why are you smiling?"

"Hannah and Clay are poking at each other."

She sniffed the air. "Is anything burning?"

"No. At least not yet."

Lily stepped away from the dress form and placed her pincushion on the table. There was more scrutiny in the way she looked Roen over this time. "You look awful. You're wet through and through."

"Damp."

"Get out of those clothes and Clay can draw you a hot bath."

"Dinner's happening in the kitchen. The bath will have to wait." He stopped her when she started to argue. "But I will get out of these clothes." He kissed her on the cheek before he left. "Are you still thinking about what I said to you this morning?" Then he laughed as she drove him out of the room with the skill of a wrangler.

■ ■ ■ ■

Roen was the third person to get the benefit of a hot bath, but since Lizzie and Hannah were the first two, the water was soapy but still relatively clean. Lily added hot water from the kettle moments before he folded himself into the large galvanized tub, so it was warm enough to suit him. She was already refilling the kettle while he was still trying to find the soap.

"I thought it floated," he said.

"It does." Lily looked down at him, shook her head, and directed him to lean forward. She plucked the bar from where it was hiding behind his back and put it in his hand then she sat at the table. "Warm enough?"

"Just." The tub was close to the stove, and Clay had stuffed the firebox so heat emanated toward him in waves.

"You were quiet at dinner," she said.

"Thinking." He saw her blush in a way that could not be explained by the heat from the stove, and she shifted in her chair. "I wasn't thinking about *that,*" he said, "although I like it that you are." He wiggled his eyebrows at her in a parody of wickedness.

"Stop that. You're horrible." When he offered her a contrite expression that she knew he didn't mean, she gave up. "So what were you thinking about?"

Roen rubbed soap into the washcloth that Lily had set out for him and began to scrub. "I saw Ben this morning when I stopped by the hotel. He told me he'd seen an odd duck around town this past week and wondered if I'd seen him or maybe knew him. I told him I wasn't expecting anyone from Northeast. Ben described the man as having no remarkable features, so it was entirely possible that I'd seen but hadn't noticed him."

"Why is Ben interested in him? Has he done something?"

"No. Ben says not. That's what troubles him. He has no discernable occupation, and he isn't looking for work. He's not a salesman or a gambler or a reporter. He hasn't inquired about property at the land office or shown an inclination to put out a shingle that would announce his business. He's been a regular diner at the Butterworth, but he's rooming at Mrs. Brady's. Ben says he's been to the bank several times that he knows of, but the manager and tellers weren't particularly helpful because they don't really remember him. He doesn't have an account so there's no record of transactions."

"So our sheriff thinks this person is visiting the bank with the intention to rob it?"

"It's a thought." Roen bent his head and washed the back of his neck.

"It's natural that Ben's mind would veer in that direction. There was a robbery a few years back. He was in the bank when it happened and fortunate to walk out of it. Has he asked if the man has kin nearby?" Lily left the chair and knelt beside the tub. "Duck your head in the water. I'll wash your hair."

Roen complied. It was a tight fit, and when he came up, he shook his head like a puppy, spraying water droplets. The ones that hit the stove sizzled.

"You didn't have to do that," she said. "I expect it from Ham." Lily pushed his head down and began applying the soap. "So what about kin?"

"None that he knows of. The man doesn't leave town."

"Maybe he's waiting for someone."

"Ben thought of that, but he thinks that person is already here."

"Oh?"

"Victorine Headley. It seems that he's had occasion to converse with her."

Lily stopped soaping his hair. "Did you tell Ben who she is to you?"

Roen corrected her. "Who she was to me." He took the soap from her and told her he would finish. Lily stayed where she was, her hands resting on the rim of the tub. "I told him all of it. The whole sordid melodrama. I think that's what you called it, and you were right to name it that. Ben shook his head so often, it began to rattle." He looked sideways at Lily. She wasn't smiling. "I'm sorry, Lily. I realize you didn't want him to know."

She shook her head. "No. You had to tell him. He'll question whether he and Ridley should have stood up for us, but he'll eventually conclude that it was the right thing to do." She stood. "The water in the kettle is warm, not hot. Let me rinse your hair." When he agreed, she retrieved the kettle, tested it on her wrist to be certain she was right about the temperature, and then poured it over his head. He finger-combed his hair to remove the soap as she poured. She stepped away from the tub before he shook off the water and tossed him a towel.

Roen rubbed the towel over his head then stood and wrapped it around his waist. "Martin Cabot," he said, stepping out of the tub. He used a damp towel left by the girls to finish drying himself.

"Pardon?" Lily held out his nightshirt.

"The man's name. Martin Cabot."

"Not an alias."

"No. Ben doesn't think so." Roen poked his head out from under his shirt and let it fall into place before he removed the towel. He handed it back to Lily and sat down to put on his socks. "Cabot doesn't appear in any of the wanted notices. Ben couldn't find anything in the Denver papers, and he spent hours in the library reading the arrest records in the *Rocky* going back as far as Miss Fletcher kept them."

"Ben is thorough."

"He is, and he wished he'd asked me sooner because after we'd concluded discussing Victorine, I told him who I thought Mr. Cabot was."

"And? Don't leave it there."

"Her private investigator."

Lily considered that, her expression troubled and curious at the same time. "Why do you suppose he's here?"

"I have no idea, but it's a certainty that she asked him to come. She didn't arrive with a companion. Perhaps he's performing that role."

She nodded, thoughtful but unconvinced. "Perhaps. Did you notice the gown I was working on earlier?"

"I did. Very nice ice blue silk."

"Satin. But you're right about the color. I collected the material from Mrs. Fish this morning. She had the pattern cut and some of it basted. Wrote down all the measurements for me so I would be sure to get the correct fitting. Mrs. Fish has a machine, you know, that could have been used to put the gown together, but the person who ordered it wanted every part of it hand stitched. Mrs. Fish gave it to me to finish because I'm better at handwork and this customer is particular about what she wants."

Roen was in the process of moving his chair closer to the stove. He stopped. "Did Mrs. Fish tell you name of this customer?"

"Uh-huh."

"And?" he asked, mimicking her. "Don't leave it there."

"Victorine Headley."

"Jesus," he said under his breath.

Lily frowned at him. "There are children who might hear you."

"Jumpin' Jesus on a griddle."

In spite of herself, Lily laughed. "Ham is a terrible influence."

Roen set the chair down and put himself in it. "You only got the dress today?"

"Yes, but according to Mrs. Fish, Miss Headley has been in the shop several times to look over the fashion magazines. She decided on this yesterday. Mrs. Fish didn't tell her that she wasn't going to make the gown herself, so there was no intent on Victorine's part that her dress would end up in my hands."

"Maybe. Maybe not."

"Then we'll see, won't we? I'm not going to sabotage my work. What would I do? Fashion the dress so a single pulled thread unravels all of it?"

Roen's expression brightened. "Could you do that?"

She threw a towel at him. "No. I couldn't. And I wouldn't if I could."

"It was only a thought."

"Yes, and you've had your wicked share of them today."

"I know." He draped the towel around his neck. "Here's one I believe you will approve. I spoke to Ellie about a housekeeper and cook for us. She thought it was a splendid idea, by the way. Splendid. That was her word for it. She also used it to describe my idea about you working alongside me."

"Mm-hmm. So she has a recommendation?"

"She does. What do you think of Fedora for the position?"

"Fedora? She'd never agree."

"Because of me, you mean."

Lily nodded. "I only think that because of what you and Ben have told me."

"What if she did agree? Would you accept her?"

"She has Ellie's recommendation; naturally I would accept her."

"Then it's done."

Lily's eyes widened. "Done?"

"Uh-huh. Out of concern for Fedora's comfort, Ellie sat with me when I proposed the position. I thought that leaving Ellie and the familiarity of the hotel would be a sticking point, but after briefly consulting with Ellie in private, she came back to me with her answer. That left the final decision with you, and you've agreed. Done."

"You engineer everything, don't you?"

Roen shrugged modestly. "It's a gift."

"It is," she said, serious. "It truly is."

Chapter Twenty-Nine

Lily lay naked under the blankets. Roen had told her to take off her nightgown but had neglected to say specifically how she should do it. When he refused to turn back the lamp, she slipped into bed and wriggled out of the garment while he stood beside the bed and chuckled at her modest performance.

"Not what I had in mind," he said, grinning, "but the end result is still the same." He reached for the lamp, but instead of extinguishing the flame, he turned the wick up so the light was marginally brighter.

"Roen!"

"Well, if I'm going to do things to you, you should be able to see them."

"You are a dreadful man." She paused, looked at him askance, and asked, "What sort of things?"

"I'm not sure yet. I haven't been thinking it about all day. I left that up to you. Suggestions?"

"Oooh! I think I might actually loathe you."

"You don't mean that."

"I don't," she said. "But that doesn't mean I shouldn't."

"Noted." He stripped off his nightshirt and joined her naked in bed. He rolled toward her, placed the flat of one hand on her abdomen, and cradled his head with the other. Her flesh was smooth and warm, and there was a gentle rise and fall as she breathed. "Anything coming to you?" he whispered.

She huffed softly. "I suppose you could begin by kissing me."

"Always a good start." Roen flipped back the blankets and uncovered Lily's breasts. Before she could do anything save inhale sharply, his mouth was at the hollow of her throat and blazing a trail south.

Lily looked down at herself the moment she could and saw that her nipples were already standing at attention. Honesty prevented her from blaming the chill because there wasn't any. She *wanted* him to put his mouth there. It was nothing other than anticipation and excitement that made her breasts swell and her nipples harden.

He had kissed her there before, laved her

aureole through her nightshift, but this was different. This was her naked breast and the damp, rough pad of his tongue, gently abrasive, and because this was Roen, gently persuasive. Her fingers threaded in his hair when he began to suck. The pleasure was exquisite. She hummed.

Roen lifted his head. "Like that, do you?"

In answer, she nudged his head toward the neglected breast and sighed contentedly when he found it. He lifted his head again, this time to stretch over her and cover her mouth with his. The kiss was tender at first, but that was only meant to tease. His lips darted to the corner of her mouth. He nibbled at her lower lip. His tongue swept the ridge of her teeth. It was when she moved restlessly under him that he deepened the kiss. He pressed his advantage by tilting his head and giving her the hard slant of his mouth.

His tongue darted and swirled around hers. There was hunger here and need and it touched her at her core, firing her senses, making them snap smartly. The kiss was humid; it tasted faintly of peppermint tea. He smelled of soap and, in her mind at least, improbably of snow. The scent of him lingered in her nostrils even after he moved away. It was the same with his touch; she felt it as warmth flickering on her skin after his fingertips had moved on.

His fingers circled her wrists and lifted her hands so they rested on either side of her head. His grip was firm, not tight. She didn't fight him overtly, but he felt resistance and he released her. His thumbs brushed the delicate undersides of her wrists, and after a few moments she opened her eyes and looked into his.

"It's all right," she whispered. "It's you."

"It's me," he said. Dipping his head, he kissed her again, sweet and soft and straightforward, and then he started a second trail with his lips that began at her chin and ended when his mouth was between her thighs. He glanced up to make certain she was all right. Far from resisting, she had propped herself up on her elbows and was watching. The centers of her eyes were dark and wide and more than a little curious. His roguish grin answered the question she hadn't asked. "Bend your knees," he told her, and when she did, he lifted them so they rested against his shoulders. He lowered his head and parted her lips. His tongue darted across her clitoris, lightly at first, like his kiss, and then more firmly, also like his kiss.

Lily didn't hum her pleasure this time;

she gave a little cry that she tried to choke off. If he had asked for more suggestions, she wouldn't have told him this. She didn't know what it was except that the heat was intense and the pleasure was so fine, it was almost painful.

She rose on that swell of need and wanting until she was riding the crest again. Her fingers curled in the blankets under her as she pressed her shoulders back. She was almost there, wherever there was, and she could feel herself being urged toward the very edge of the plunge she wanted, needed, to take. Lily held her breath and dove. Her body shuddered in release, and for those few moments, she was rocked by sensations powerful enough to shatter her every thought, so when it was over, she knew nothing as much as her own contentment.

She stretched, smiled, when Roen moved from between her thighs to hover over her. Then he was inside her, and she welcomed that. He moved slowly at first, deeply, and when she contracted around him in a snug fist, he closed his eyes and held himself still. "Breathe," she whispered, setting her hands on his shoulders. He did and began moving again. She waited for him to open his eyes, and when he did, she didn't avert her gaze. "Beautiful man," she whispered.

He shook his head. That made her smile again, this time indulgently because he just didn't know. She touched his cheek, brushed it with her fingertips. She traced the hard line of his jaw. Something, perhaps it was the sudden, purposeful lift of her hips, or the way she softly spoke his name, drove his next hard thrust. His rhythm changed. His movements were urgent now, as if they not merely needed, but also necessary. She went with him, glad that she could, glad once again that she was free to choose this, and when he climaxed and spilled his seed, it was joyous.

Roen made to roll on his side, but Lily stopped him, wrapping her arms and legs so he was temporarily her captive. "Not just yet," she said, and then more softly, "Not just yet." So he stayed. She felt his breathing calm and his heartbeat slow and was comforted by both. She slowly unfolded and he moved away but didn't go far. They lay naked on their backs on top of the covers, staring at the ceiling and smiling stupidly with satisfaction. They traded glances once, and the timbre of their shared laughter was in excellent harmony.

"God," Roen said feelingly.

"Mm," Lily murmured. "Me first." She rolled out of bed and went to the basin to wash. Her nightgown lay on the floor at her feet, and she left it there until she was ready to return to bed.

"Reckless, brazen woman," Roen said, trading places with her at the nightstand.

Lily gave him a cheeky, over-the-shoulder grin and shimmied into her shift before she dove under the covers. She was already nesting, huddled on her side with her knees drawn up by the time he extinguished the lamp and slipped in beside her.

Roen bumped her knees with his when he also drew them up. He found her hand in the dark, but he didn't thread his fingers through hers. Instead, he took her wrist, and as he had done earlier, his thumb brushed back and forth across the underside. His hand moved higher and did the same over her forearm.

"Tell me about these scars," Roen said. He felt Lily grow very still. "I can hardly feel them, they're so faint, but I saw them." When she remained silent, he asked, "Did he do this to you?" This time he waited her out.

"No," she said at last. "I did."

The scars were horizontal and spaced closely together. They rose like the rungs on a ladder from the base of her wrist halfway to her elbow. There was a similar pattern of scars on her other arm. "You wanted to kill yourself?"

"No!" She drew in a breath. "No," she said more quietly. "I did it because it made me feel better. I have no other explanation."

He thought about that, tried to imagine how it could possibly be true and couldn't. "I don't understand."

"Neither do I, but it's what I did and how I felt." Her voice rose slightly. "You shouldn't have left the lamp burning. You shouldn't have wanted to see me naked. I have scars on my belly, too. Do you want to know about them?"

"Lily," he said gently. "You haven't hidden your children from me. I know what those marks are, and they're not scars." He let her break free of his loose grip. She didn't turn away or even turn on her back. She remained on her side facing him and tucked her arms together. "Do you still cut yourself?"

"Let it be, Roen."

"No. I won't do that. Do you still cut yourself?"

"No."

Roen had another question, but he held on to it a little longer to see if she would say more without prompting. When she did, he knew that waiting her out would always be the right thing to do. She needed time to collect her thoughts. He could give her that.

"Sometimes I want to," she whispered. "I don't, though. I haven't since shortly after Jeremiah died. The urge to do it hasn't passed entirely; I simply have more reasons to resist it."

"What prompts the urge?"

Lily didn't hesitate. "Loathing."

"Of him?"

"Of myself."

Roen wished he could make out her features, but she was turned away from the meager light from the stove, and her face was hidden in deep shadows. "Help me understand, Lily." He found her cheek, brushed it with his fingertips. He was encouraged when she didn't try to avoid his touch. "I want to understand."

"Hmm. I believe you. You would be served better by speaking to Ridley. She helped me to see the truth of what I was doing. She told me that she'd seen women in my situation do similar things. You can't imagine what it was like to know I wasn't alone. Sometimes I thought I was going mad or even that I was already there. I would cut on myself and be mesmerized by the tiny beads of blood, and I would know relief. That's what you need to understand, Roen.

Pain, the kind I brought on myself, gave me relief. The bloodletting gave me relief."

Roen nodded even though she couldn't see him, even though he couldn't grasp the totality of what she'd told him. She seemed to understand the reason for his silence because she unfolded her arms and reached for him. She took his hand in hers and squeezed gently.

"It's all right," she said. "I barely comprehend it myself."

"Don't excuse me, Lily."

"I didn't mean —"

"Tell me this," he said, interrupting. "You said that sometimes you still feel the urge to harm yourself. Was the day I took you and Lizzie to the soda fountain one of those times?"

It pained her to say so, but she knew he would see through the darkness to the lie. "Yes," she said. "Yes, it was one of those times."

Roen removed his hand from hers and dropped onto his back. He laid his forearm across his eyes. "God. That I forced your hand that day. It was unconscionable."

"No, it wasn't like that. You didn't know, and in the end it was better for me that I went with you. Yes, it was difficult to do something outside my routine, and more difficult because it was with you — a man — someone who was hardly more than a stranger. I despised myself for being ill afterward. That feeling of weakness and inadequacy is paralyzing. Worst of all, Clay and Hannah suspected what had happened and why. So yes, I thought about using my scissors, my pins, my seam ripper, anything sharp, to find relief in the pain, but I didn't do it, Roen. That is what is important. That is why it's better that I went with you. I'm stronger for the experience. I'm learning that."

Roen uncovered his eyes. "Give me your hand." She did, and he drew it to his heart and covered it with both his hands. "Do you feel that?"

"Your heart? Yes."

"It's yours, Lily. Nothing you say will change that. Now, do you feel strong enough to tell me what he did to you?"

Her laugh was short, humorless, and just a little watery. She sniffed.

"Are you crying?" Roen didn't know why he asked. She'd deny it and he wouldn't believe her. "Never mind. Come here." She came willingly when he tugged, rolling against his side. He brought her head to rest in the cradle of his shoulder.

"I don't know what made me weepy."

"It's all right. It doesn't matter. You're safe here."

Lily drew up the neckline of her nightgown to dab at her eyes and then pushed it back into place. She took a steadying breath. "I want to tell you. You might be the only person in Frost Falls who doesn't know at least some version of what went on during my marriage."

"You're exaggerating."

"Some. Not as much as you might think. There was a time when I would have answered your question differently. I would have told you why Jeremiah did the things he did to me. I was an inadequate, miserable wife. I couldn't satisfy him in the kitchen, in public, or in the bedroom. He was the hard worker. I was lazy. He didn't like to see me sitting because he was on his feet all day. He said I coddled his children, that I was turning Clay into a mama's boy. I couldn't fix my hair the way he liked it. I didn't dress his children properly. Dinner was late. Dinner was early. Dinner was cold. I burnt the coffee. The floor wasn't clean. I used too many lamps. I spent too much at the butcher. There were so many things I did wrong, but when he was drinking, everything could be exactly as he wished and it still wouldn't be right.

"Ben wanted me to press charges or take the children and leave. I wouldn't. Jeremiah loved us, I told him, and I believed it. He provided for us, and we were dependent on him. I was his wife and it was my duty to stay with him. For better or worse. It didn't matter that it was almost always worse. I never once thought that I could raise the children without him."

Roen took in every word, glad for the dark that kept her from seeing him wince. He had asked, so he was duty bound to listen. "And how do you answer my question now?"

"He punched me, threw me to the ground, and kicked me. He dislocated my shoulder so often I mostly could put it back on my own. I had black eyes, a swollen jaw. He broke my fingers. He liked to put his hands around my neck until I almost passed out, and when I was as limp as a ragdoll, he'd release me. I fell down the stairs trying to get away from him. I still have a slight limp when I'm tired because of the time I hurt my knee. Jeremiah had fists as big as hams, or it seemed that way. He could drive the breath from my lungs with a single blow. I lost a child that he didn't know about because he punched me in the belly. For a long time I thought there was a possibility that I somehow encouraged him to hit me there. Perhaps you'll think it was wrong of me, but I didn't want the child.

"The law doesn't account for a husband raping his wife, and I didn't either back then, but I know now that's what it was to be in bed with him. He raped me."

"Jesus," Roen said under his breath. Lily fell quiet for a time and Roen did nothing to coax more from her. If she hadn't exhausted herself, she was nearing that end.

"I loved him," said Lily. "Or I convinced myself I did. You might think that I married young, but I was almost twenty-one. I knew he liked his drink before I married him, but I was naïve enough to believe I could change that. He never struck me while he was courting me, although it was a brief courtship. I am primarily responsible for that. I wanted to leave home. I spent years caring for my mother, who complained of one malady after another and insisted she needed me close. Doc Dunlop saw her regularly back then and he told me that she was a malingerer, and that if I let her, she'd make me her life-long captive. My father left years earlier. My brother married and moved away. I believed I was doing my daughter's duty by her. It was Doc who made me wonder if that were true."

Roen squeezed her hand. "Frying pan into the fire."

"Exactly," she said. "I left my mother for Jeremiah, traded one cage for another. Mother, by the way, moved to Denver shortly before my wedding. She lives with her sister and is doing very well according to my aunt, so Doc wasn't wrong in his estimation of her illnesses."

Roen nodded. "When did the abuse begin?"

"The denigration began within weeks of marrying. There were so many things I couldn't do to meet his expectations. You probably know how I responded to that."

"You tried harder."

"Yes. I wanted to please him." She sighed. "I couldn't. It's another thing I know now that I didn't understand then. For years, I truly believed I was at a fault. If he hit me, I thought I must deserve it. If he berated me, it was because it was justified. I can give you dozens of examples of how I disappointed him, and you will shake your head because you'll see right through to the truth and know no one could have satisfied him. Violence was in his nature. Drinking unleashed it, but so did I, or I believed I did."

It was difficult for Roen to reconcile the strength he saw in Lily now with the subjugated woman she had been, but he trusted every word of her account. "Did he hurt the children?"

"No. Not intentionally. Sometimes Clay would put himself in harm's way trying to protect me and get swatted or fall, but Jeremiah never turned on them. I've often wondered if he had struck them whether I would have left him. I think I would have, and I think he knew it. He never crossed that line."

"You would have left," said Roen. "I know it as well as your husband knew it. Believe it, Lily. You would have gone."

Lily slipped her hand out from under his. She lifted one of his hands in hers, bent his fingers, and pressed her mouth to his knuckles. "Thank you for that. Thank you for trusting me to do it."

"You said that people knew what was happening inside your marriage. Did anyone try to help you?"

"Doc did. Doc Dunlop at first, and when he left, it was Ridley who treated me."

"I understand, but they took an oath to do that. What about other folks?"

"Ben. Once he became sheriff, he more or less made it his mission to get me out of my situation."

"And when was that?"

She thought back. "About four months before Jeremiah died."

"Lily. You were married at least ten years when he died, and you're telling me Ben intervened only in the last four months?"

"I will not tolerate you being critical of him," she said firmly. "He was a deputy for five years before and he did what he could, mostly at Sheriff Brewer's direction. You need to understand, Roen, that I didn't want their interference. I discouraged it. It was worse for me when they'd lock Jeremiah up and then release him a day or so later. I didn't acknowledge that my husband hurt me, and even if people suspected or knew for a fact it was happening, I was grateful for them pretending it was otherwise. I had my children and I had my pride. Folks obliged me. I was gratified that they spared me the humiliation."

"So you were alone."

"For a lot of years that was true, and I accept that it was by my choice. What I didn't know was that people had never stopped being concerned. Behind my back, Ben presented the draft of a law to the town council that would make it a crime for a husband to beat his wife. Before that, if I'd pressed charges, enforcement of the existing law would have been difficult because

Jeremiah and I were married."

"The law passed?" he asked.

"It did. Unanimously. They barely had time to record it in the books when Jeremiah was killed."

"Then it never helped you."

"On the contrary. It helped me to know that there were people who cared deeply. The thinking had turned against men like Jeremiah. I thought because I blamed myself for how he treated me that folks also blamed me. That wasn't true, at least not in the main. Amanda Springer supported the law. So did Ridley Madison. They were important voices on my behalf because I no longer had one."

"And this all took place before Jeremiah died?"

"Mm-hmm. He felt as if the entire town had him in its sights. He knew the law targeted him."

"How's that?"

"They called it Lily's Law."

CHAPTER THIRTY

Martin Cabot did not acknowledge Victorine's presence when she joined him in the dining room. He stared morosely at the meal he had only picked at. The roast was still hot. The aroma teased him but he had no appetite for it or the potatoes. He pushed the carrots around before he finally stabbed one and carried it to his mouth.

"For God's sake," said Victorine. "What is wrong with you?" She swept her skirt aside, sat opposite him, and spread a napkin across what passed for her lap. She might have glowered at her swollen belly if other diners weren't glancing in her direction. Raising a hand, she gestured to the waitress who was setting down beer at another table. When the young woman finally attended her, Victorine ordered the special and curtly waved her away. "Well?" she asked. Her pointed, impatient expression was lost on Martin because he still didn't look up. She picked up her fork and tapped the tines against the edge of his plate.

Martin looked up, annoyed and not pretending that he wasn't. "I didn't invite you to sit here."

"As I'm ultimately paying for your meal, I'll sit here if I like, and I like knowing that sitting here is an aggravation to you. There is so little in Frost Falls that gives me pleasure, I take it where I can." She withdrew her fork. "Now, what is it? Something to do with Roen Shepard?"

Rather than answering, Martin posed a question of his own. "Why are you still here, Miss Headley? It's been every bit of ten days since I told you all there is to know about Shepard and his wife, and you've not spoken to him since. You've made no overture to Mrs. Shepard either. What is your purpose for staying here?"

"That's my business, isn't it? Do you have somewhere to be? Another job waiting for you back in New York?"

He shook his head.

"I'm paying you well enough, am I not?" She didn't wait for him to respond this time. "Your questions are of no account. Mine, however, are."

Martin was saved from answering by the delivery of Victorine's dinner.

Victorine watched the departure of the plump brunette and then turned her attention to her meal. "Mrs. Butterworth has finally seen fit to respond to my concerns about that little China girl. She hasn't served me once all week, and I can say I am most appreciative. My digestive system is similarly grateful."

"She's gone," Martin said flatly.

Victorine found her roast beef was fork tender. She lifted a piece to her mouth. "Who's gone?"

Martin watched her take a bite and chew with a clear expression of enjoyment. She was oblivious to anything save her own needs and pleasures. He didn't have the liberty of scowling at her so he relied on his perfectly dull features to keep her at a distance. It had been a mistake to allow her to see that he didn't want her company.

"The China girl," he said. "She's been gone a week."

"Hmm." Victorine speared a trio of carrot medallions. "I hadn't realized that was the case. Let go, I presume."

"No. She left for another position."

Victorine raised an eyebrow. "Really? Why do you know so much about it?"

"I was curious. I asked." He'd actually followed Fedora the day after she didn't show up at the hotel, but that was not something Victorine needed to know.

"Good riddance, I say. The hotel is much improved by her absence. She's gone from Frost Falls, then?"

"Actually, no."

"Not that I care in the least, but I can see that you want to tell me. I'll bite. Where is she now?"

Martin didn't believe for a moment that his countenance was communicating a desire to tell Victorine anything. She wanted to know what had become of Fedora to indulge her penchant for prying. "A family here in town hired her as their housekeeper."

Victorine's features were distorted by her revulsion. "Someone *wants* her in their home? That is beyond my understanding."

"You're making that abundantly clear."

Victorine replaced repugnance with a bland smile and continued eating. When Martin offered no other information, she had little choice but to ask for it. "So? You seem to know so much, where is she now?"

"Does it matter?"

"No. It doesn't."

Martin shrugged. "Do you anticipate remaining here long enough to give birth? What is that? Three months from now?"

"I thought I was clear that your probing is unwelcome."

"It occurred to me that you will want to see the doctor, and I wondered if you knew who she is."

"I could hardly *not* be aware. Mrs. Butterworth has recommended her daughter-in-law to me on more than one occasion."

"Ah. Of course. I should have guessed that. I confess that I'm surprised that Mr. Shepard hasn't approached you since your first meeting. He must be very certain the child isn't his."

"He's not certain at all. He can't be. Roen is simply waiting. He's very good at that."

"Have you considered that he doesn't know you're still here?"

"No." Taken aback by this possibility, Victorine's fork hovered halfway between her plate and her mouth as she gave it real thought. "No," she said again after a few moments. "He knows. You told me yourself that he stops here to pick up food when he's going out on survey. I am sure he asks after me."

"You'd think so, wouldn't you? From my vantage point, Mr. Shepard seems supremely uninterested in your whereabouts."

"I don't believe that."

"You could always rise early and be here

when he arrives. That would assure that he knows you're present."

"Perhaps I will," she said airily. "But it begs the question why are you so eager to provoke a confrontation?"

"I am not eager to provoke anything. I am merely being thorough."

Victorine regarded him skeptically. "I am unconvinced, Mr. Cabot."

Martin did not reply. He nudged his plate away, set his napkin beside it, and then rose, checking his pocket watch as he did so. Fedora would be leaving the Shepard house soon. He wanted to observe her walking to the boardinghouse. Since she'd left the hotel, he'd made it his responsibility to see that she arrived safely. She didn't know she had a guardian angel and he wanted to keep it that way. Now that Victorine had confirmed she had no intention of leaving anytime soon, he needed to rethink his plans for Fedora. He always knew that he would not be returning to New York with Victorine but had hoped it wouldn't be long before she departed. She was his Achilles' heel, the person who knew who he was and what he did and, most important, how to find him.

Martin bowed his head slightly before departing. She took no notice of it, and he left without a word. If there was a benevolent God, he thought, Victorine would not seat herself at his table anytime soon.

Hitch waited for Fedora in the kitchen as she finished cleaning after the family had left the table. Lily came in on two occasions and tried to shoo Fedora out the door, but Fedora would have none of it. Hitch knew Lily had good intentions, and yet he was satisfied to sit in the warm kitchen and pass the time watching Fedora go about her duties. He offered to help every time he came to walk her home, but that was another thing she would have none of, and so he sat back and allowed himself the pleasure of seeing her move from one task to another. It was not only her grace that captivated him. She had an economy of motion that kept him entertained with its efficiency.

Hitch suspected Fedora never gave her movements a thought. Unlike him, they came naturally to her. He still had uncoordinated moments where his feet tripped over each other and his hands knocked things aside when he was only trying to reach them. That's why he never took a cup of anything when Fedora offered it to him and why, when she was finished, he rose carefully to his feet.

He was helping Fedora into her coat when

Roen came into the kitchen. Hitch nodded at him. "Hey, Mr. Shepard."

"Good to see you, Hitch. I was afraid I missed you. I was working on a new map." He reached in his pocket and withdrew some bills and counted them out. "This is for you, Fedora," he said, handing over her week's pay. "Don't ever be afraid to ask in the event I forget."

She nodded, taking the money and folding it half so it fit neatly in her palm. "Thank you, Mr. Shepard."

"Thank *you.*" His gaze returned to Hitch. "Any news for me?"

"Ben says I'm supposed to tell you that she's still there. No bags packed either."

Roen nodded. Nothing had changed since this morning when he had stopped to pick up his pack.

"Oh." Hitch's face brightened suddenly. He held up an index finger. "That man you and Ben were wondering about? He had dinner with her this evening. Or maybe she had dinner with him. Leastways Ellie said they shared a table for a time. Ben got me curious about him but hasn't told me much except to keep an eye out. Who is he?"

"Don't know. I think he might be employed by a rival railroad." Roen had no remorse about lying. "You can see why I want to know what he's doing."

"Sure. That makes sense. And him being with her, well, that makes sense, too. She's Victor Headley's daughter, ain't she?"

"Yes, she is."

"And he owns a rail company."

"That's right. One of Northeast's largest competitors." That was true.

"Huh. It's still a head scratcher, her being here and all, especially in her condition. She doesn't look like a spy. I guess maybe that's the point."

"It probably is."

"Well, I'll keep my eye out like the sheriff asked." He grinned. "Both eyes."

"One eye is sufficient. Keep the other on Fedora." Roen smiled at her but continued speaking to Hitch. "We are very happy she's here with us."

"Reckon that's good night, then," said Hitch, tapping the brim of his hat.

Roen waved them off, and when the door closed behind them, he went to find Lily. She was sitting on the sofa beside Clay looking over his answers to a series of problems Roen had given him earlier. Roen walked behind the sofa and looked over their shoulders. There was no help that he could offer that Lily hadn't so he moved to the rocking chair and sat. He had the odd thought that he had just usurped Lily's throne, and apparently he wasn't alone in that. Hannah, Lizzie, and Ham stopped what they were doing and stared at him.

He shrugged a shade guiltily and that appeared to be enough for them. Ham and Lizzie resumed playing cards, and Hannah put her nose back in her book.

"Did you catch Fedora and pay her before she left?" asked Lily without looking up.

"I did. Hitch was loitering in the kitchen. Did you know that?"

"Uh-huh. And so would you if you hadn't gone straightaway to your study after dinner." She smiled a little at the word "study." It was pretentious to call that cubbyhole a study, but they were all following Hannah's insistence that it be so.

"I'm working on a new map."

"Yes, I know. I peeked in on you once."

He frowned. "You did?"

"It's all right, Roen. You were deep in thought."

Roen realized he must have been because it wasn't like him not to be aware of Lily's presence, even if it was only brief. "I apologize. Did you need something?"

"I wanted to remind you that Fedora was due her wages, but you took care of that on your own." Lily pointed out an error to

Clay. He used the side of his hand to rub the slate clean and started again. Lily said to Roen, "He's been working hard at this since he left the table."

"It appears you have, too."

She shrugged as if it was of no account. "Did Hitch have anything new to tell you?"

"No. The same."

"Hmm. What do you suppose she's waiting for?"

Roen looked to see if they had an interested audience for this conversation. No one's ears pricked. "I don't know, but if this delay is because there's hope I'm going to change my mind, I'm not."

"Do you think you should have another talk? Perhaps make that clear?"

"No. I couldn't have been clearer the first time." Roen changed the subject. "I'm planning on going out tomorrow. I could use your help."

"Take Clay," said Lily. "He can miss a day of school. He's worked hard enough this evening."

"But we agreed I wouldn't take —"

Lily waved aside his objection. "You're not going to the disputed property, are you?" Roen shook his head. "Well, then, he can go. I know you'll look after him."

Clay looked up from his slate. "Thanks,

Ma, but no one's going anywhere tomorrow. Maxwell Wayne says a storm's heading our way. It'll come down hard from the mountains and drop ten inches on us by the afternoon."

"He can't possibly know that," said Roen.

Clay screwed his mouth to one side as he considered this. "Maybe he doesn't know. But do you want to risk him being wrong?"

"Ten inches?" Roen asked skeptically. "He actually said ten inches?"

"Hannah?"

Hannah laid her book in her lap. "He said either side of ten inches."

"That's right," said Clay. "Either side of ten inches."

Roen dropped his head against the rocker's back rail and groaned softly. "That's that, then."

"You could start interviewing local men for the jobs you're going to have," said Lily.

"Won't the storm keep them away?"

"Not if you conduct the interviews at the Songbird. Word will get out and a blizzard wouldn't keep them away."

"This storm that's coming isn't a blizzard?" No one responded to his question directly. What they did was share laughter at his expense, which Roen decided was its own kind of answer and one that he appreciated more as soon as he joined in.

Martin Cabot knew what he was going to do when he saw Deputy Springer was once again accompanying Fedora to the boardinghouse. The opportunity presented itself the following morning when his daily visit to the drugstore to purchase a copy of the *Rocky* coincided with Amanda Springer's weekly visit to purchase her particular blend of teas. He doubted the steadily falling snow would prevent her from getting out, and he was gratified to see that he was right. The only other place she visited with predictable regularity was the butcher shop, which Martin had learned she owned. The difficulty there was that he had no reason to be in the shop and his presence would have been met with suspicion, if not immediately, then soon afterward.

He waited until she had finished paying for her tea before he approached the counter to pay for the newspaper. When she turned away, she bumped into him.

"Pardon me," she said and made to sidestep him.

Martin sidestepped in the same direction. "Pardon me," he said. They lurched toward each other once more and then Martin stood his ground so she could proceed. His smile was a tad embarrassed. "I *do* apologize."

"No need. I believe I began this dance."

He tipped his bowler. "It's Mrs. Springer, isn't it?"

"Why, yes." She regarded him more keenly. She was a dark-haired angular woman with a sharp chin and sharper eyes. Her brown eyes softened marginally as she continued to stare. "Oh, we've met before, haven't we? I'm sorry, I don't recall your name."

"Cabot. Martin Cabot."

"Of course, Mr. Cabot. It's been a while. I had no idea you were still in town."

"I had not expected to be in residence this long. My business, well, it continues to have its challenges."

"Just so."

"Yes, you would know, wouldn't you? The butcher shop. That's yours."

"It is indeed." As little as two years ago, there would have been a measure of pride in her voice. She was still proud of her ownership, but she could say it matter-of-factly. "And what is your business? I don't believe you ever said."

"I didn't because I can't say. I suppose that's the very nature of my business."

"Then it must have something to do with the railroad. Every rail man who's come through Frost Falls keeps his own counsel." She paused, considering what she'd just said. "Every man except Mr. Shepard. He called for a town meeting and laid out Northeast Rail's plans for everyone in attendance."

"Clever that. You must wonder what he's keeping up his sleeve." He gave her a moment to think about that and then moved the conversation to where he wanted it to go. "Deputy Springer is your son, isn't he?" When she nodded, he went on. "I've observed that he is diligent in the performance of his duties. That has not often been my experience with the law in towns like Frost Falls. There is a lot of swagger and very little attention to duty. I imagine you're proud of him."

"I am. Some days, though, I am more worried than proud."

Martin nodded empathetically. "Understandable. The fact that he escorts the China girl home every night must give you pause. He puts himself between her and the vicious threats against her. All very brave of him."

"He is brave," she said. "But you're mistaken. Mr. Butterworth accompanies her from the hotel to Mrs. Brady's."

Martin lifted his eyebrows. "Oh, I thought you surely would have known."

"Known?"

"The girl. Miss Chen, I believe she is called, no longer works at the hotel. The Shepards employ her now. She's their housekeeper."

"The Shepards," she repeated softly. "Hitch never said. I suppose you know this because of your interest in Roen Shepard."

"I never said I had an interest in Mr. Shepard."

"No, but your business is the railroad, and he is working for Northeast. I'm not a fool, Mr. Cabot. It simply stands to reason."

"I am happy to allow you to draw your own conclusions, Mrs. Springer, as long as you don't say you heard it from me."

Amanda looked around for Dolly Mangold. The druggist's wife had stepped away from the counter and could not have overheard their conversation. "Your business is your own. I'm afraid I must be going, but not before I thank you for your kind words about Hitchcock."

"You're very welcome. It's been a pleasure." He walked her to the door and opened it for her and then returned to pay for his newspaper. If Mrs. Mangold wondered why he was smiling following an encounter with Amanda Springer, she didn't ask.

Hitch walked into the Songbird and found Roen where Ben said he would be — set up at a table in the back with men lined up to take their turn in the chair opposite him. Hitch excused himself and stepped in front of George Hotchkiss, the next in line.

"Hey," said George. "You looking for another job? Maybe you should go to the end of the line, and maybe I should apply to the sheriff to take yours."

"You do that, George, and you'll lose your place."

"Humph. Seems I already done that." He clapped Hitch hard on the back. "You're up. You want that seat or not?"

Hitch turned to see that Lincoln Jordan had vacated the chair and was on his way back to tend bar. He wasn't surprised that Buzz Winegarten's nephew was hopeful for a job that would get him out from under his uncle's thumb. He took the seat.

"Name?" Roen asked without looking up.

"Hitchcock Springer."

That got Roen's attention. "What are you doing here?"

"Not looking for a job. My mother just

cornered me at the jail for a rather ugly conversation. I couldn't lock her up so I had to take it on the chin until Ben walked in and saved me. Actually, calling it a conversation is inaccurate. It was a diatribe."

"Miss Chen?"

"How did you know?"

"I didn't. It was a guess. I thought she would have had her feathers ruffled a while back. When I never heard a word about it, it occurred to me that she knew about your affection for Fedora and was fine with it."

"Well, she didn't and she wasn't." He stared glumly across the table. "She wants you to walk Fedora home. She says since you employ her, it's your responsibility same as it was Mr. Butterworth's."

"I can do that."

"No. My mother's wrong. It's my responsibility to look out for her. And it's Ben's if I can't do it."

"That's why you're doing it? Because you're looking out for her?"

Hitch's expression was a tad sheepish. "Mostly."

"Right."

"I only came here because Mother asked me to. Now I can tell her I spoke to you and not lie about it."

"Uh-huh. It's hard to lie to our mothers.

Just to make it a little easier for you, you tell her I said I wouldn't do it because it would make Fedora uncomfortable. That's true, too." Roen set down his pen and squared off the short stack of papers in front of him. "Why now?" he asked.

"Hmm?"

"Why is Amanda bringing this to your attention now? If she didn't know that you've been Fedora's regular escort since before she left the Butterworth, what's happened that she knows about it now?"

"I asked her that. She was vague. She wouldn't say more than that someone told her."

"I suppose that's a long list of suspects."

"You have no idea."

"Odd that no one said anything to her earlier. Is that something they would purposely keep from her?"

Hitch frowned, struck by the question. "No. No, it's not."

"So perhaps the list isn't that long after all."

"That's something to think about."

"You do that and let me know what you come up with. No special reason, just that I'm interested. Are you going to tell Fedora?"

"No. It will make her unhappy. She might

refuse to allow me to walk with her. She's already conscious of people watching her."

"Anyone in particular?"

"She's never said. I think it's a general sense of being watched because there are people who don't want her here. I don't get it myself. She's never hurt anyone."

"You took her out to shoot."

"With Ellie. And it was Ellie's idea for Fedora to be comfortable managing her own protection. Fedora's real sharp with a rifle, but she couldn't hit a barn door with a six-shooter if her life depended on it. It's too heavy for her small hands, even with a double grip. She pulls her shot every time. Goes up. Goes down. Goes wide. Ellie gave up so you know it was bad. I haven't taken them out but that once."

"What about a derringer?"

"The thing is," said Hitch, "she's firm about not wanting to shoot anyone. She won't agree to carry one. Ellie offered Fedora hers, but she turned it down. My opinion? I don't think anyone wants to hurt her, but if someone could scare her off, there'd be folks satisfied with that."

"She still gets threats?"

Hitch nodded. "One or two every week. She got one yesterday. Someone slid it under her door. She showed it to me. Big block letters with a simple message: GO HOME. She was born in California, for God's sake, but no one seems to care about that. Some of the other messages refer to the yellow peril or the yellow terror. They're all disturbing."

"It's hard to believe Mrs. Brady doesn't know who put the last note under Fedora's door."

"She's not saying. I asked. I think she's fears the consequences of speaking up."

"Really? Who would dare retaliate? That woman could frighten the devil with her gimlet eye."

Hitch chuckled, his humor returning at last. "Right you are." He stood. "I'll let you get back to your interviewing. Good day for it. Better to be in than out. Must be half a foot of new snow by now. Dang me if Maxwell didn't say so."

Roen merely sighed.

Chapter Thirty-One

Lily was sitting up in bed with a book in her lap when Roen finally joined her. She continued to read while he stripped down to his drawers and washed at the basin. He replenished the coals in the stove and padded to his side of the bed, where he removed his socks. He did this last more slowly than usual and was equally unhurried about turning back the covers and dimming the lamp. Lily closed her book with rather more force than was necessary. She saw Roen's head snap up when he heard the sound.

"Oh, you're still reading," he said. "I hadn't realized."

Lily put the book aside. "That's because you're preoccupied with your own thoughts, and you have been since you came home. I noticed you smiling at the children when they told you about what they'd been doing, but I don't think you heard a word they said."

"I heard."

Lily didn't press. There was a hint of defensiveness in Roen's tone that told her she was right. "I looked over the list of applicants you signed up today like you asked, but you haven't wanted to know what I think. Do you want to know now?"

"Hmm?"

"You're still not listening." She put her hand on his shoulder to get his attention. "Look at me, Roen." His eyes shifted to hers. "I'm not angry. I'm concerned. What happened today while you were out?"

"Does Fedora talk to you much while she's here?"

It wasn't an answer to her question, but Lily decided to go where Roen led her. "Not a lot. She stays busy, mostly in the kitchen. I'm usually working in the parlor or the sewing room. She and Lizzie chatter quite a bit."

"She wouldn't be chatting with Lizzie about this."

"About what?"

"About the anonymous messages she receives. Hitch calls them threats, but I'm not sure they reach that level. They tell her to go home or mention the yellow peril, as if her presence is a danger to all of us. Hitch told me today that she gets at least one each week. Sometimes more than one."

Lily frowned. "No, she's never said a word. What a terrible burden to carry."

"You would know something about that."

His dry retort stung a little. "I do," she said stiffly. "And we are not talking about me."

"Oh, God," he murmured. "Lily, I'm sorry. I shouldn't have said that."

"Not the way you said it."

Roen rubbed his face. "Let's leave this until morning."

"If you like, but will you sleep?"

"Probably not."

"Then tell me the rest."

He drew in a breath and released it slowly. "Hitch says that Fedora is conscious of being watched. I asked if there was a specific person, but she's never said as much. He dismissed it as a general awareness of being observed because she's different. I accepted that explanation at the time, but I've been wondering ever since if Hitch is right."

"Then you should ask her."

"I want to but not alone. It would go better, I think, if you were with me."

"I will, of course, but perhaps you should ask Ellie."

"No. I prefer not to alarm Ellie. She's been Fedora's champion and takes all these smears and slights personally. She'll want to take Fedora target shooting again."

"Perhaps she should."

"Fedora will hang if she shoots someone," he said bluntly. "Self-defense, if it is that, won't matter much. She will have no jury of her peers. No women. No one of Chinese heritage. It will be the yellow terror that some folks in Frost Falls are already imagining."

Lily pressed her lips together, afraid just then that if she spoke, she would say too much. The secret that she kept locked inside needed to remain there. She knew that. Ben and Ridley and Hitch had insisted that she accept their version of what happened the night Jeremiah died. And she had. She loved her children too much to do otherwise, and now it was the same with Roen. The truth would not set her free.

"Are you asleep?" he asked.

"No," she said softly. "Just thinking."

"Hmm."

Lily moved closer and rested her head against his shoulder. She found his wrist and drew his arm across her waist. "When will you want to speak to her?"

"Tomorrow. There is no advantage to waiting."

"Do you suspect there is a particular

person watching her?"

"Yes. A gut feeling. Nothing more. I have no evidence to suggest who it might be. It's up to Fedora to help there."

"Why do you care?" asked Lily. "I'm glad you do, but why?"

"I've been asking myself the same thing. Maybe it's because I was the odd one out growing up. I told you they called me the black sheep. It was meant in jest, and I didn't think I minded, but I'm coming to realize I must have because Fedora is the odd one out here, and I mind it very much."

"So Ellie is not alone in taking the slights against Fedora personally."

"No. I don't suppose she is."

Lily lifted her head and kissed Roen on the cheek. "You're a good man, Mr. Shepard."

"Not so good," he said. "Fedora certainly doesn't think so."

"Does that matter?"

"It does if she's tempted to shoot at me again."

Fedora left the boardinghouse with a warm roll snuggled between her mittens. She nibbled on it as she walked. As was her habit these last few weeks, she no longer kept her head down and her eyes lowered. Now she looked around, mostly over her shoulder, to see if she was being followed. Mr. Cabot had offered to escort her when Hitch did not arrive in time to do the same, but she politely refused him. They left Mrs. Brady's together and then went their separate ways. His progress toward the hotel was slower than hers in the other direction, and sometimes when she looked back, she caught him looking after her, presumably because he was concerned for her safety. She wondered, though, if that were true. He knew about the messages that were being slipped under her door. Everyone in the boardinghouse knew because he found one of them in the hall outside her room and proceeded to castigate all the boarders seated for breakfast that morning. Her humiliation was complete, but he did not either notice or take it into account. In any event, he did her no favor, so his offer to walk with her left her colder than the biting wind.

She brushed snow off her shoulders, shook out her scarf, and stamped her feet on the porch. Even before she opened the door to the kitchen, she heard Hannah announce, "Miss Chen is here!"

The children were all seated around the table. Lily had already started breakfast. "Am I late?" asked Fedora as she hung up her coat and scarf.

"Not at all," said Lily. "My heathens are hungrier than usual this morning. All that playing in the snow yesterday. I thought I'd better begin."

Fedora sidled up to Lily at the stove and Lily gave way, handing over the fork she was using to turn bacon. "Are you going to Mrs. Fish's today?"

"I have to. I suspect she has patterns and piecework for me, and I didn't go out yesterday. Mr. Shepard won't be leaving the house today. He'll be in his study. Will you be all right with that while I'm gone?"

Fedora nodded and turned the bacon. Water in the pot was at a rolling boil. She added a little salt and then oatmeal. "Please, sit," she said when Lily continued to hover nearby.

Lily did, taking her usual place. Roen walked into the kitchen a few minutes later. He kissed Lily on the crown of her head as he passed by. Lizzie lifted her head for similar attention and Hannah proffered her cheek. The boys examined their plates lest they be targets of affection. Roen leaned across the table and knuckle-rubbed their heads before he sat.

Lily saw nothing that made her think Roen's easy mood was forced, although the shadows under his eyes would have excused it. If she hadn't known about the confrontation that was coming, she couldn't have suspected that one was in the offing. "Confrontation" was, perhaps, too strong a word. Roen would be gentle with Fedora, as gentle as he was with her when he wanted to draw her out. She would not have agreed to sit with him if she thought otherwise.

After Clay, Hannah, and Ham were bundled and booted out the door, Lily sent Lizzie to play in the front room. She exchanged glances with Roen and nodded. "Fedora, will you leave the dishes for now and come and join us?"

Fedora turned away from the sink. Worry lines creased her forehead. "Have I done something to displease you?"

"No. Not at all. This is about another matter entirely. Please, sit."

Fedora took Lizzie's seat, placing her closer to Lily than Roen. She sat stiffly, shoulders braced as though for a blow, and folded her hands in her lap. She met no one's eyes, casting her own at the tabletop.

"I think we've alarmed you," said Lily. "That is not at all what we meant to do." When Fedora said nothing, Lily went on. "Very well, then we shall do this quickly."

Roen said, "Hitch mentioned that you've

been receiving threatening messages. I heard the same from the sheriff not long after I came to Frost Falls, but the frequency of them was something I only learned yesterday. Did you receive one this morning?"

Fedora shook her head.

"And yesterday?"

"Yes."

Roen knew that she had, but it was important to know if she was going to be truthful. It seemed that she was. "We're concerned, Lily and I."

Fedora's head swiveled in Roen's direction. "Oh, but the children are in no danger. I wouldn't have taken the position if I thought they were. Ellie wouldn't have allowed it either. You mustn't worry about them on my account."

"We worry about them on account of them being children, and that has nothing to do with you. You are our concern here, Fedora. We can't stop the messages unless you know who's sending them. Do you know?"

"No."

"All right, but we do want to know when you receive one."

"Why?"

"It will assist in identifying the sender."

"It hasn't thus far. I used to tell Ellie."

"I understand. And she told Ben. We employ you now, and we will let him know."

"I've been telling Hitch."

When Roen looked across the table at Lily, she gently spoke up. "I'll wager you don't always tell him. I'd say it was also the same with Ellie. You're fond of them both and you don't want to distress them. I know something about that, Fedora. A lot about it actually. There are people who want to help. You only need to let us."

Fedora shifted her dark gaze to Lily then lowered her eyes again. "Then, yes. I received a message this morning."

"Did you tell Hitch?" asked Roen.

She shook her head. "He didn't come by Mrs. Brady's today. I walked here on my own."

"Have you been accosted on the street before?"

"Once by a group of children on their way to school. They were hurtful but meant no harm. And on two other occasions."

"By the same person?"

"No. Mr. Stanton one time."

Lily's jaw went slack. "My children's teacher?"

"I shouldn't have said. I knew I shouldn't have said." Miserable, Fedora bent her head.

"You certainly should have. Who else

knows?"

"No one. He said no one would believe me and I believed him."

"He was wrong," said Lily. "I believe you."

With Lily supporting Fedora, Roen could return to his original question. "You said two occasions, Fedora. Mr. Stanton was one. Who was the other?"

"He works at the Songbird. I don't know his name."

"The owner?" asked Roen. "Buzz Winegarten?"

"No. I know who that is. I think he must tend bar."

Lily's eyebrows climbed her forehead. "You don't mean Jim Springer."

Fedora shook her head. "No. Mr. Springer is kind, like Hitch."

"Then it must be Buzz's nephew," said Roen. "Lincoln Jordan."

"If you say so," said Fedora. "I told you I don't know his name."

"How do you know he works at the Songbird?"

"Because he asked me if yellow girls are allowed to serve drinks. He fancied I could help him behind the bar."

Lily blanched. "Did he touch you, Fedora?"

"I wouldn't let him. He tried. I ducked

and ran. He was drunk and fell over himself running after me."

"Good." She looked at Roen. "That's one person on your list you will not be hiring."

"Already made a note of it." Roen turned to Fedora. "I suppose it's possible that either of these men are leaving you the messages, but judging by their behavior, I would say they'd prefer to harass you than see you gone. Is there anyone at Mrs. Brady's that you suspect?"

Fedora hesitated. "No."

Lily said, "I'm not convinced, Fedora."

"I'm telling the truth," she said. "It's just that . . ."

"Yes?"

"I don't suspect him of anything. It's me. It's just that I'm uncomfortable when he's present."

"Who is he?" asked Roen.

"Mr. Cabot." Fedora removed her hands from her lap and folded her arms in front of her as if suddenly taken by a chill. The hair on her arms stood up and she rubbed them to get warm again. "He found a message someone left outside my door and made such a fuss about it to the other boarders. He said if anyone knew who had left it, it was a moral obligation to come forward, and if the person who did it was actually sitting at the table, then it was a certainty that hell was waiting. He meant well, I suppose, but you don't know how I wished that a hole would have opened up and hell had taken me right there."

"Oh, I think I do know," said Lily. "Sometimes the devil seems preferable to well-meaning angels."

"Yes," she said quietly. "Yes, exactly."

Roen gave Fedora some time to collect herself. She was dry-eyed but blinking rapidly. When he thought she was ready to hear more, he said, "Hitch told me that you have a sense of being watched." Roen saw her frown, obviously unhappy that Hitch had shared so much. "It's true, isn't it?"

She nodded.

"Is there anyone in particular who watches you?"

Fedora shrugged.

"That's no answer."

"Anytime I'm out, there are always people looking on from the shop windows. Maybe they'd be there under any circumstances. I don't know. Mostly I try not to look, but sometimes I see them out of the corner of my eye as I pass, stepping up to the window as if they want to make sure I move on."

"So you haven't identified a single person observing you."

She hesitated again but spoke up before Roen prompted her. "Mr. Cabot."

"Your well-meaning angel," said Roen.

"Yes."

"He doesn't take his meals at Mrs. Brady's, does he? I seem to recall Ellie commenting that he's a regular at the hotel. You must have served him there."

"Almost exclusively. He asked for me."

"That's different than some diners."

"Yes. There are people who don't want me near their table, let alone their food."

"Were you flattered?"

"No. Not at all. I told you, he makes me ill at ease."

"Why do you suppose that is?"

"Roen." Lily interrupted him. "It doesn't matter. Accept that it is."

Roen nodded and switched tacks. "Do you know what business brings him to Frost Falls?"

"No. There's speculation that it has to do with the railroad. Not the one you work for. A different one."

"Victor Headley's railroad company."

"I suppose so. Ellie thinks he's here to spy on you."

"Maybe he is. The rail lines are rivals."

"I don't know anything about that."

"What if I tell that I know for a fact he's

working for Mr. Headley's railroad? Would you shoot at him, too?"

Except for the slight tremor that moved through her from head to toe, Fedora didn't stir. She stared straight ahead, unblinking. Lily began to extend a hand toward her, but Roen warned her off with a look.

"Is that why I'm here?" Fedora asked. "Is the sheriff coming to arrest me?"

"No. No one is going to arrest you. Unless you told someone, no one but Lily and I know the truth."

"How long have you known?"

"For certain, only now, but I've had an inkling ever since you went target shooting with Ellie and Hitch."

"I told her I didn't want to go."

"You could have made a poor job of sighting your targets."

"Pride. I couldn't do it."

"Hitch says you're terrible with a gun."

"I am."

"How did it happen, Fedora, that you were out there on Double H land?"

So she told him how she had done it, sparing herself nothing in the retelling. She explained that when Roen told her he was doing a survey near Double H land, she decided right then that she was going to follow him. She didn't know it was Clay he was taking with him. There was an incident with Hitch in the kitchen that morning but it worked in her favor. Ellie could see she was upset about it and allowed her to leave for the day. She couldn't attract notice by taking the train to Liberty Junction, so she walked. She was familiar with the route, having worked briefly in one of the pleasure houses before escaping to Frost Falls. It was hard to say this last and she had to stop, inhale, and begin again.

She went on to describe how she stayed clear of Roen, and since his progress was slow — on account of Clay, she knew now — she was able to get out in front of them and find a protected place in the crags and crooks of the mountainside.

Lily's eyes widened fractionally as she listened. "Where did you get the rifle, Fedora?"

"From the hotel. It was Ellie's. I hid it under my coat until I was out of town."

"You went to great lengths to shoot Mr. Shepard. It's a little frightening."

Fedora nodded. She set her hands on the table, folded them. "Yes. I understand why you think that, but it was never my intention to shoot him. I meant to scare him away. These railroad men frighten easily when they're on their own. Without thugs to protect them, they scatter like roaches."

Roen cleared his throat to remind Fedora he was still sitting at the table. Sometime during her recitation she seemed to have forgotten that. It was Lily's faint smile of amusement that made him get over himself. She would remind him about the roaches remark later; he was sure of it.

Lily asked, "What if one of the Hardy brothers had been arrested for the shooting? Had you considered that?"

"Yes. I would have turned myself in."

Lily had no reason to doubt her. "My son was there."

Fedora swallowed hard. Tears came to her eyes, but she made no move to dash them away. When Lily pushed a handkerchief toward her, she crumbled it in her fist. "I didn't know it was Clay. I didn't know it was a child. I thought Mr. Shepard had George Hotchkiss with him."

Roen sputtered and then caught himself. "I can see why you could have thought it was George. He's wiry and about Clay's height."

"You pushed him aside. That's why my shot caught you. If you hadn't moved . . ."

"No," said Roen. "I have no fault in what you did."

"I know," she said, sniffing. "The fault is

mine." Fedora pressed the handkerchief to her nose. "Are you sure you don't want to take me to jail?"

"I am not even tempted, Fedora, so put it out of your mind. Why didn't you try again?"

Fedora stared at him, astonished by the question. "I *shot* you. I will never try that again."

"Good to know," he said wryly. "I take it this means that Mr. Cabot is also safe."

"Don't tease her," said Lily.

"I don't know that I was teasing exactly."

Fedora looked from Lily to Roen and back to Lily again. "Ellie said I could have my job back at the hotel if I wanted it. I'll tell her you weren't satisfied with my work. Will that be all right?"

"No," said Lily. "If you leave, it will be because you want to, not because we're asking you to. Roen and I discussed this last night. We decided that if you took responsibility, we would want you to stay. You have and we do."

Fedora looked down at her hands. "I am ashamed."

There was nothing either Lily or Roen could say to that. They sat with silence for a while. Roen eventually excused himself and went to his study. Lily got up and began washing the dishes that were still in the sink. Fedora stayed where she was, head bowed, occasionally pressing Lily's handkerchief to her eyes. It was only after Lily had left the room, touching her lightly on the shoulder as she passed, that Fedora finally wept in earnest.

Victorine was annoyed. That Roen continued to avoid her was like a splinter in her thumb. She could ignore it for only so long before she had to pick at it again. It occurred to her that she should force a second confrontation but was uncertain where she should do it. Would he accept an invitation to her suite, where they would have privacy, or would he agree to see her only in public? Perhaps a location where there would be only a few witnesses would be better. He might be agreeable to that, and she required but a single person to overhear their conversation.

She considered the proper venue. Her familiarity with the town was sufficient for her to have choices. The majority of the shops, as she ticked them off on her fingers, were not right for her purposes, although the drugstore with its soda fountain bar was a possibility. She kept that in mind as she considered other places that might work.

Her face brightened considerably when she hit upon the perfect setting.

Victorine gestured to Ellie Butterworth to attend to her at her table. She smiled warmly, with no hint of guile, when the older woman came over with a teapot in hand.

"More tea?" asked Ellie, raising the pot to pouring height.

"No, thank you. A favor if you will. Could you send that child around? The one I see here from time to time?"

"You mean Frankie Fuller?"

"If he's the one who has performed small tasks for me before, then yes."

"He's not here at the moment. He's in school, but he'll stop by afterward. It won't be long now. The school day is about over. Shall I send him up to your suite?"

"Yes. Do that."

"Is there anything else?"

"No. That will be sufficient." Victorine was aware that the teapot was still hovering above her cup. "Is there something you wish to ask, Mrs. Butterworth?"

"As a matter of fact," said Ellie, withdrawing the teapot, "my husband and I were wondering if you intend to extend your stay for another week. We've had requests for the suite and need to know how to respond to them. We thought you might want to return to New York for Christmas."

"Yes. Christmas. I'd forgotten. When is it? Three weeks away?"

"A bit less than that."

Victorine nodded, pretending to consider. "I'm afraid I can't give you a firm answer. I simply don't know. I will pay for at least one more week, and I will let you know if I require another after that. Will that be all right?"

"Yes. Thank you."

Victorine watched Ellie wend her way between the tables and return to the kitchen. For all that the old busybody was polite about it, Victorine was aware that she wanted her gone. It was too bad, really. Victorine was developing a certain fondness for the hotel, enough affection, at any rate, that she no longer entertained thoughts of burning it to the ground.

Chapter Thirty-Two

"Hey, Frankie," Clay said, opening the front door to his friend. "You need some help with an odd job?"

Frankie shook his head. Only his brown eyes were visible above his woolen scarf and below his hat. He pulled down the scarf to reveal a seriously set mouth and a cluster of freckles across his nose and cheeks. "I'm here on an odd job. Got a letter for your da from that lady at the hotel." He pulled an envelope from inside his coat and held it out to Clay. "Go on," he said. "Smell it. That's her scent there. Hounds could follow it all the way to San Francisco."

Clay sniffed, wrinkled his nose. "Huh. Hounds could probably follow it farther than that. C'mon in before Ma tells me I'm letting the cold in or the heat out. It's always something." He closed the door behind Frankie. "Wait here. I'll get Da."

Frankie waved to Hannah, who was curled

in one corner of the sofa in the parlor. She returned his wave shyly and went back to reading. Lizzie and Ham didn't pay him any mind, but Mrs. Shepard looked up from her sewing and smiled at him. He shuffled his feet a little and smiled back. She was looking awfully pretty these days. Frankie thought a fellow might hurt his eyes if he stared too long so he looked at his feet instead. Besides, she was his best friend's mother, and it gave him a queer feeling when he thought about her being pretty. There was a time he just thought of her as old and sad. He should go back to that.

Approaching footsteps made Frankie look up. Clay and Mr. Shepard were coming toward him. He held out the envelope. "Miss Headley said I was to give this to you and wait for your reply."

Roen sighed heavily, but he took the envelope and turned his back on Frankie and Clay while he opened it. He wrinkled his nose at the scent that was released as he unfolded Victorine's letter. It required only a single glance to take in the totality of her message. He refolded it and slid it back into the envelope. Aware that he was clenching his jaw, Roen forced himself to adopt a pleasant mien when he faced Frankie and Clay again.

"Tell her that will be fine," he said to Frankie.

Frankie repeated the words and then asked if there was anything else.

"Not a thing," said Roen. "You tell her what I said. It will be enough." He found a coin in his pocket and held it out to Frankie. "For your trouble."

"No trouble, sir." But he took the coin from Roen's hand as deftly as the Artful Dodger. "See you in the morning," he said to Clay.

Clay nodded and opened the door for him. Once Frankie was gone, Clay turned his suspicious expression on Roen. "I never heard you say you know that lady."

"I don't suppose I thought it was any of your business." His tone was both pleasant and serious.

Clay took the reprimand on the chin, but he also cast a wary look over his shoulder at his mother. Her head was bent toward her work. He couldn't tell if she'd heard any part of the conversation in the entranceway, and if she had, whether she was disturbed by it.

"Clay." Roen drew the boy's attention back to him. "Your mother is aware that I know Miss Headley. Nothing about the letter that Frankie delivered will surprise her."

Roen was met by Clay's dubious expression. "You can't stop yourself from worrying about her, can you?"

"No, sir."

Roen put a hand on Clay's shoulder. "All right. I understand. But may I advise you on one point?" Clay nodded and Roen continued. "Don't be so obvious about it. For myself, I don't mind, but your mother does not want you to be concerned for her welfare. She is doing splendidly on her own."

"Do you think so?"

"I do."

Clay nodded, his shoulders relaxed. "That's good, then." He pivoted and returned to the kitchen, where he had been refilling lamps.

Roen caught Lily's eye when she looked up as soon as Clay disappeared. He tilted his head toward the workroom. She set her sewing aside and followed him.

"What was that about?" she asked, closing the door and leaning against it to bar interruptions.

Roen handed her the envelope. "From Victorine. It's why Frankie was here."

"Oh. I was trying not to show too much interest." She opened the envelope and read the letter. "Tomorrow? She wants to meet with you tomorrow? But you and I planned to finish your last survey."

"I hadn't forgotten, but I told Frankie to let her know that I was fine with this."

Lily did not take pains to conceal her disappointment. "I wish you had consulted me. I would have suggested that keeping her waiting at least one more day would be a better strategy than appearing to be at her beck and call."

"I have no intention of meeting her tomorrow. You and I have plans and we're going to see them through."

"You lied? You don't lie."

Roen chuckled. "I am climbing down from that pedestal now. I'll meet with Victorine at a time of my choosing and preferably with little advance notice. It will be better if she doesn't have time to plan."

"If you think she is going to arrive with a derringer in her reticule, then I forbid you to go."

He blinked. "Forbid?"

"Yes." Lily was unapologetic. She tossed the letter and envelope on the table. "I forbid it."

"All right," he said easily. "But I don't think that. She has something other than a pistol up her sleeve . . . or in her reticule."

"Not amusing, Roen."

"She's not going to shoot the man she claims is the father of her baby."

Lily shuddered. She had been largely successful at ignoring the fact of Victorine's pregnancy.

Roen closed the distance to Lily and took her by the elbows. "I promise it will be fine." He bent his head and kissed her lightly on the mouth. "Promise." When he pulled back, Lily was still frowning. "What do I need to do to convince you?"

"Take me with you."

Roen arched one eyebrow then the other. "Why?"

"Because if you're lying to me and it is dangerous, you won't allow me to accompany you."

"I liked it better when you thought I didn't lie."

She ignored that. "Well? I think it's time we met, Victorine and I."

He winced. "That's not something that's generally done in polite society, introducing one's wife to one's former mistress."

"What gave you the idea that Frost Falls cares two bits for polite society? Our wedding reception was in a saloon. Buzz Winegarten used to court Amanda Springer and now her husband tends bar for him. Our doctor stopped a bank robbery with a soup bone. The sheriff, who may or may not be the bastard child of Thaddeus Frost, was responsible for burning a barn to the ground out at Twin Star, and his deputy is head over heels in love with a China girl who could have killed you if she'd had a mind to."

Roen said the only thing that occurred to him. "A soup bone?"

"Some other time. What do you say?"

"The library's open to everyone. I guess that means you can be there, too."

Pleased with herself, Lily put her arms around Roen's neck and planted kisses on his mouth, his jaw, his cheeks, and bit him gently on his neck just above his collar. She laughed when he pressed her hard against the door.

"What?" he whispered at her ear. "I like it when you're full of yourself. You're a lively handful."

"Is that your idea of a compliment?"

"Yes."

"All right, then." Lily turned her head so he could nuzzle more of her neck. Her breasts swelled above the edge of her corset when he passed a hand over them. Even through the fabric of her gown and shift, she could feel the heat of his palm. Lily didn't know when he put his hands on her waist that he intended to lift her, but that's what he did. She wrapped her legs around him as he carried her to the table and she only lowered her legs once he set her down. He pushed up her skirt and palmed her bare knees above her stockings. He stepped into the space she made for him and he slid his hands under her shift and up her inner thighs.

Lily was a captive of his dark chocolate eyes. She imagined falling into them and liking it so much that she would stay there, joined to him in some fantastical manner, and know nothing but the pleasure of a hedonistic existence.

He touched his forehead to hers. "I don't want you to wear drawers. In fact, I forbid it."

"Forbid?" Her breath brushed his lips.

"Yes."

She drew back and studied his face. "You're serious."

"I am."

"I couldn't."

"You could." Roen caught her mouth again in a kiss that teased and tempted. Her lips were a feast for his senses, warm and tender and pliant. She placed her hands on either side of his face and held him. What he began, she encouraged. Her mouth was damp. The kiss was humid. He found the drawstring to her drawers and pulled at it.

Lily came up for air and gripped the edge of the table. "What are you doing?"

"Getting rid of these. They're in the way."

"Roen!"

He lowered them as far as her hips. When she didn't help him, he pinched her lightly on her bottom. "Lift."

Laughing under her breath, Lily slapped at his arm. "I will not."

"You won't?"

She shook her head. "There are four children in the next room, any one of whom could walk in here."

"That's it?" he asked. "That's your reason? I'm putting a lock on the door."

"No. No locks."

Roen righted her drawers but left his palms cupping her bottom. "You mean that."

"I'm afraid so. This is a poor time to tell you, but there was a lock on my bedroom door in the old house. Jeremiah installed it when Clay and Hannah were older. He used it mostly when he beat me because he could not abide their interference. I promised them there would no locked doors in this house. Ever. It's a promise I aim to keep. They trust you. *I* trust you, but a locked door would provoke unhappy memories."

Roen closed his eyes. The scene that played out in his mind was too horrible to contemplate for long, but he did because she had lived it. He could imagine Hannah and Clay on the other side of the door, listening to their father using his fists against their mother, helpless to stop it. He opened his eyes and stared into hers. "Oh, Jesus, Lily."

She laid a hand against his cheek. "It's done," she said quietly. "I'm sorry to tell you now. Sorry you had to know."

"Don't apologize for him."

She blinked. "I wasn't."

"You wouldn't have to say any of it if he hadn't used his fists on you. I swear to God, Lily, if he were here . . ." He stopped, letting his voice trail off, because it was an empty threat. There *was* nothing he could do. The feeling of helplessness overwhelmed him as it had overwhelmed her children. "I hate that this happened to you."

"I know," she said.

"I hate that I can't make it right."

"Don't you understand, Roen? You already have." She leaned into him, dropped her hand from his cheek to his shoulder, and placed her mouth over his. It was a tender kiss, the kind of kiss that made all things better, a kiss that healed scrapes and bruises and made hearts right again.

When she drew back, he was smiling. "What?" she asked. "Why are you looking at me like that?"

"You don't know?"

She shook her head.

"Listen," he said. Three quick raps on the door broke the silence. "The barbarians are at the gate."

Chapter Thirty-Three

Victorine quickly grew bored with waiting. At ten minutes past two, she closed the book she was pretending to read and did not return it to the shelf where she'd found it. She thought the librarian looked at her disapprovingly, but the reproach of such a person was of no account. Victorine had already been scolded once for speaking too loudly when she asked another patron to point her to the histories. It was more amusing than distressing to be spoken to in such a manner, but Victorine still felt compelled to drop one of the large tomes on the floor so the thud startled the librarian enough to make her jump.

It was clear to Victorine that Roen was not going to appear. He was nothing if not punctual, considered it an obligation in his business and in his personal life. Unless that little Frankie fellow had got Roen's message wrong, she was being stood up. It would be a comfort to blame the boy, but as he had been reliable on every other occasion that she'd used him, it seemed unlikely he'd misunderstood Roen's reply. No, this was Roen's doing. He had lied.

Victorine wished now that she'd asked Martin Cabot to accompany her to the library. He could have made himself unobtrusive among the periodicals while she spoke to Roen. But she hadn't invited him, hadn't told him that she intended to meet Roen. He was skulking somewhere nearby — that was his job after all — but he hadn't followed her into the library. The termagant at the front desk would have fussed over him, and Victorine was certain she would have noticed that.

Victorine turned up the collar on her coat before she stepped outside. Her kid leather gloves were stylish, but they did not offer the warmth of woolen mittens that many of the local women wore. She considered purchasing a pair as she walked past the mercantile. It remained only a consideration. Perhaps she would buy them on her way back to the hotel. For now, she wanted to reach her destination as quickly as possible. What was the maxim she was relying upon? If the mountain will not come to Mohammed, then Mohammed must go to the mountain? That sounded right, although she questioned the wisdom of depending on a Muslim axiom to guide her. Muslims. Chinese. Irish Catholics. Jews. Negroes. It was intolerable, this merging of peoples that New York had come to embrace. To Victorine's way of thinking, with only a single China girl in residence, Frost Falls had a distinct advantage over the city.

That single China girl, though, was the one who answered Victorine's summons at the door. Her initial thought was that she must have arrived at the wrong residence even though there were no houses on either side of this one and it was situated some thirty yards behind the forge just as Mr. Cabot had described to her. Still, she looked to her right and left and then behind her to get her bearings.

Because Cabot had told her of its proximity to the forge and the livery, she had imagined the house as a gray, washed-out, dreary dwelling with a sagging roof and smoky windows. She hadn't asked her investigator for more than the location of the house. Clearly that was an oversight. This was not the home she had been inspired to create, and she would have noticed that earlier if she had been walking with her head up instead of watching her step on the icy flagstone path.

Upon inspection, Victorine saw the house was a relatively new structure, newer certainly that the storefronts along the main thoroughfare. It gleamed almost as white as the snow around it. The bright yellow shutters did not evoke dreariness. There were curtains in the windows, none of which were smoky or smudged, and the door, the one that was opened to her now, was also painted yellow. It would be like walking into sunshine, and Victorine's mood was not improved by the thought of it.

"You," she said, staring at the China girl.

"May I help you?"

It was cold standing on the small front porch, but Victorine was prepared to suffer that until she had answers. First, she required confirmation she was in the right place. "Is this the Shepard residence?"

"Yes."

"Then what are you doing here?"

"I work here."

Victorine had a vague recollection of Mr. Cabot telling her this young woman had been hired away from the hotel. She also recalled her response. *Someone* wants *her in their home? That is beyond my understanding.* Damn the man. He'd known where she'd gone and he'd purposely kept that to himself. It shouldn't have mattered that she hadn't asked. He was obliged to tell her. She was paying him for answers whether or not she posed the questions.

"Is he here?" she demanded. "Don't look at me as if you don't know to whom I am referring. Is he here?" Victorine was trying to look past the girl's shoulder or over the top of her head when a child thrust her way to the forefront and stared so openly as to be rude. The child presented a distraction, and Victorine used that to her advantage, pushing the door open wider so she could step inside. She closed the door behind her. The child was no longer out in front of the China girl; she was clinging to her skirts.

"What *is* your name?" Victorine asked, frustrated and impatient. "Lee? Wong? Chang?"

"Fedora Chen."

"Chen. Of course. I would have come to it eventually. You know who I am?"

"Yes, ma'am."

"Good. Let us begin again," said Victorine. "Is he here, Miss Chen?"

Fedora put a comforting arm around Lizzie's shoulders and kept her close.

Victorine saw the gesture and it annoyed her. "For God's sake, I am not going to bite the child. I *like* children."

"All evidence to the contrary."

"What? What did you say?" She shook her head. "Never mind. I heard you. I merely required a moment to collect myself." Victorine raised a gloved hand and slapped Fedora.

The blow was swift and stinging, and it moved Fedora off her feet. Beside her, Lizzie also stumbled. Tears welled in her eyes.

"Oh, for heaven's sake, I didn't touch *you,*" said Victorine. "Where is your father?"

"Dead," Lizzie said.

Victorine huffed a pent-up breath. "Your stepfather, then. Where is he?"

"Stepfather?" She looked up at Fedora for an explanation.

"She doesn't understand," said Fedora. "She calls him Da. And she doesn't know where he is. Neither do I. Not precisely. He and Mrs. Shepard left at first light to complete a survey. The important thing you need to know is that he is not here."

Victorine examined Fedora through narrowed eyes. The truth eluded so many of these Chinese that it was quite possible the girl was lying. Victorine could still make out the print of her hand on the girl's cheek. For no particular reason, she was tempted to slap her again. "I want to look for myself," she said. She took a step forward on her way to brushing past Fedora but found her path immediately blocked.

"Mr. Shepard isn't hiding from you," Fedora said. "He wouldn't. Neither would Mrs. Shepard. They're not here."

Victorine stayed where she was. Fedora held her stare, which she found faintly unnerving because it was not the shy, servile demeanor she had come to expect. "Very well," she said. "I wonder if you will give Mr. Shepard a message from me."

"Of course. What is it?"

"This." Victorine gave in once more to the impulse that had tempted her earlier and raised her hand. It was only later that she wondered if she should be troubled by the fact that Fedora hadn't tried to dodge the blow.

Roen and Lily were stupid with laughter as they entered the kitchen at the end of their workday. If anyone at the table had looked outside minutes earlier, they would have witnessed their parents throwing snowballs at each other and their mother getting the best of their da as he pitched forward into a drift. None of them saw it, though. Fedora held their attention. She didn't know they were watching her because she was at the stove with her back to them. They were uncommonly quiet, but each time she glanced over her shoulder to see what they were up to, they were always staring at their cards or trading them.

Roen was still chuckling as he helped Lily out of her coat. He shook it out, spraying snow toward the table. That should have elicited some laughter, some objections, but it did neither. He noticed that Lily had gone quiet as well. He hung up her outerwear and then removed his own.

"You ask," he said, nodding toward the solemnly set faces at the table. "They're not playing cards. They can't be. No one's arguing."

"Fedora?" Lily said. "Who are these children, and where are ours?"

"I couldn't say, ma'am." Fedora kept slowly stirring the winter vegetable stew and didn't turn away from the stove. "I've been wondering the same thing myself."

Lily sought out her older son. "Clay?"

He shrugged and put down his cards. Everyone followed his lead. "Ask Lizzie. She'll tell you."

Lily looked sideways at Roen and saw her confusion mirrored there. "All right," she said. "Lizzie? Clay says you'll tell me."

"Everyone asks Clay first, but this time

it's me that knows."

"Just say it," said Clay. "You told us as soon as we got home from school."

At the stove, Fedora sucked in a breath.

Lizzie sat up straight. "This lady came and she slapped Miss Chen." She held up two fingers. "Two times. Miss Chen didn't cry, but I did. She said it didn't hurt, but I think it did. I said she should lie down like you used to do and I would brush her hair. That made you better. I remember that."

Lily felt as if her heart were being squeezed. Her memory was identical to her daughter's. If she stopped too long to think about it, she would be able to feel the brush being pulled through her hair. Lizzie's manner of healing was very real.

Lily studied Fedora's ramrod spine, her stiff shoulders. "Fedora? Turn around, please."

Fedora did as she was asked. There was no question of not complying. She kept her hands at her sides. She had not examined herself in the mirror after Victorine left. Whatever evidence existed immediately after the blow would certainly not be in evidence now. She would not give herself away by trying to hide something that was no longer there.

Lily's sharp intake of air told her how

wrong she was. Now Fedora's hand flew to her cheek.

Roen stepped forward and touched Hannah on the shoulder. "Get the ice bag. I assume we have one." Hannah nodded, shoved away from the table, and was off. "Ham, get your coat on. When Hannah comes back, you take the bag and pack it with snow. Clay, your coat, too. You're going to go to Dr. Madison's and ask her to come here." They jumped to their feet simultaneously and went to get their coats.

"What can I do?" Lizzie asked plaintively.

Roen scooped her up and hefted her against his chest, supporting her with one arm. "You've already done the most important job. You told your brothers and sister what happened, and then you told us."

"No one said I shouldn't this time." She looked at her mother for confirmation.

"That's right, Lizzie," said Lily. "No one said you shouldn't."

Lizzie slid an arm around Roen's neck. "That lady, she had a message for you."

"She did?" Roen looked at Fedora questioningly but spoke to Lizzie. "What was it?"

"This." She tapped Roen on the cheek with the flat of her hand. "Except hard. That was the second time she hit Miss Chen."

"Is that right, Fedora?"

Fedora cast her eyes everywhere but at Roen and eventually nodded.

Hannah returned then with the ice bag. Ham took it and bolted out the door. Roen passed Lizzie to her sister and asked her to go to the front room. "Sit down, Fedora."

"The soup will —"

"I'll take over at the stove," said Lily. She took the long-handled wooden spoon from Fedora's unresisting fingers. "Go on. Please sit."

Roen pushed out Lizzie's chair for her and she sat. Ham came back in, triumphantly holding the ice bag over his head. Roen sent him to the front room to join his sisters and then wrapped the bag in a kitchen towel. He gave it to Fedora before he chose the chair beside her and sat. Because he was watching her, he saw her nearly imperceptible flinch. "Was it Miss Headley?" he asked without preamble.

She nodded again.

"And if Lizzie hadn't spilled the beans and you weren't wearing the marks from Miss Headley's visit, did you intend to tell us she was here?"

"Yes."

"The ice bag is for your cheek, not to hold in your hands. Here. Like this." He cupped his cheek as if holding the ice bag to it, and she slowly mirrored his action. "That's better. You haven't looked at yourself, have you?"

"No."

"Probably just as well. Are you certain it was a slap? It looks as if she delivered a haymaker." When Fedora regarded him blankly, he explained. "That's a swinging punch. A powerful one."

"She slapped me."

"Twice, according to Lizzie. Is that right?"

"Yes."

"And you were supposed to convey that slap to me?"

"Yes, but I would have never —"

Roen stopped her. "I know that." So did Victorine, he thought. She had slapped Fedora because she wanted to, not because it served a purpose. "Why did she hit you the first time?"

Fedora looked away. "That was my fault. I was impertinent."

Lily was listening to every part of their exchange, and now she made a three-quarter turn toward the table and spoke up. "You're going to have to explain that. It stretches my belief to imagine you were rude."

For a few moments, Fedora said nothing

as she worried her lower lip. "Lizzie came to the door while Miss Headley was demanding to know where Mr. Shepard was and attached herself to me."

Lily nodded. "She does that when she's feeling shy or afraid. I'm thinking it was the latter this time."

"Yes, that's what I thought. I'm not certain what I did to annoy Miss Headley, but she snapped at me. I think she said something about not biting the child, but I know she said she liked children." Fedora's attention swung to Roen when he sputtered a laugh. "That's when I said, 'All evidence to the contrary.' And that's when she slapped me."

Roen sobered. "So you spoke your mind. It seems to me you did it in defense of Lizzie."

"Yes, sir, but in my defense as well."

"And Miss Headley objected to that."

Fedora lifted the ice bag a few inches from her cheek. "Strongly." She gently settled the bag back in place.

Roen was encouraged to see a glimmer of a smile touch Fedora's lips. It seemed to him that she did not regret speaking out, and perhaps did not even regret the consequences of it. "I hope you will accept my apology," he said.

"But you —"

Roen shook his head, interrupting. "Miss Headley was here because of me, and she made you suffer for the fact that I was gone from home. Did she ask after Mrs. Shepard?"

"No, but I told her that Mrs. Shepard was with you." She frowned. "Was I wrong to do that?"

Roen and Lily spoke at the same time. "No."

Fedora's glance darted between them. "What should I do if she returns tomorrow?"

"She won't. Not tomorrow. Not the day after. Don't concern yourself with her coming back. She won't. Not ever."

Now Lily frowned, looking at Roen over the top of Fedora's head. She opened her mouth to speak and closed it again as the front door opened. She looked down the hallway and saw Clay ushering in Ridley. Ben was right behind them both.

"Doc's here!" Clay announced rather more loudly then he had to.

Lily called out, "We're in the kitchen. Clay, you take their coats and stay there." She moved the soup pot to a warming spot on the stove and set the spoon aside.

Roen got to his feet when Ridley and Ben walked into the kitchen. He vacated his chair for Ridley to use to examine her patient. "Thank you for coming." He summarized what had taken place earlier in the day while Ridley removed Fedora's ice bag and looked over her bruised and swollen cheek and checked her left eye.

"Move your jaw back and forth for me," Ridley told her. "Good. You have full movement. There are broken capillaries in your eye, which is why the area around the iris is red."

Fedora drew her head back in surprise.

"She doesn't know," explained Roen. "She hasn't looked at the damage Miss Headley inflicted."

"Do you want to see?" asked Ridley. "I have a small mirror in my medical bag."

"No. If it's all the same, I'd rather not. I've been struck before." When the room fell silent, she pressed her lips together and did not meet anyone's eye.

Ridley gently placed the ice bag against Fedora's cheek. Without prompting, Fedora laid her hand over it. Ridley nodded to her husband.

"You should press charges, Fedora," said Ben. "Do you want to?"

She looked at him, patently horrified.

"No, I reckon not," he said.

"She works for me," said Roen. "Can I do it?"

"It's a bit of a stretch, but it's a start."

"Please. No." Distressed by the prospect, Fedora white-knuckled the ice bag. "I'll be run out of town."

"You won't," said Roen. "We have laws here."

"They don't apply to me."

Ben said, "They do if I say they do."

Ridley reached for her husband's hand and squeezed it. "Give her time and recognize that she's not entirely wrong. I know how it pains you to sit on your hands, but this is one of those situations where doing nothing may be the best you can do."

Lily said, "You, too, Roen."

Ben and Roen exchanged glances but said nothing.

"We saw that," said Ridley, removing her hand from Ben's. "I don't pretend to know what it means, but I'm suspicious."

"I don't know why," said Ben. "Don't I always take your advice?"

Ridley snorted. "If your tongue were not so firmly in your cheek, I might believe you."

"I certainly intend to speak to her," Ben said. "I imagine Roen will want to do the same, and if it will ease everyone's mind, we'll go together. Do you object, Roen?"

"No. A witness is always valuable in any conversation with Miss Headley."

Lily remained dubious that anything would come out of speaking to Victorine but was relieved to know Roen and Ben would be doing it together. "You'll be careful, won't you? Not for her sake. I don't care about that. I'm thinking about her child."

Roen said, "As careful as we can be and still get our point across. She needs to leave town, Lily. I won't let her use her pregnancy to keep from doing what needs to be done." He turned to Ben. "She'll tell you that her child is mine."

One of Ben's dark red eyebrows kicked up. "Is it?"

Ridley tapped the table to get her husband's attention. "None of our business, Ben." Her eyes darted right to remind him of Fedora's presence.

"Oh. Right. Sorry."

Roen plowed his hand through his hair. "Does Hitch know what happened?"

"No. He's at the office. I chose not to stop on our way here. I didn't think telling him was a good idea right now."

No one missed that Fedora was comforted by this news.

Roen checked his pocket watch. "He'll be

here soon to walk Fedora to Mrs. Brady's. Except for this, we'd be finishing dinner about now."

"I'll head him off if you'll provide Fedora with an escort. Ridley, are you about done here?"

Nodding, she opened her medical bag and withdrew a packet of four aspirin tablets. "Take two now and two more in six hours. You can get more from the drugstore in the morning."

"I'll do that for her," said Roen.

"Good. Fedora, do you have an ice bag? Or access to one at the boardinghouse?"

"No," said Fedora. "I don't want to ask Mrs. Brady. If I can avoid seeing her, I'd prefer it."

"She can take that one," said Lily, handing Fedora a small glass of water. "Roen will pack it with more snow."

Ridley closed her bag and stood. She took Ben by the hand. "Then we're going. There's no permanent damage, Fedora, but healing will take time. That was a vicious slap. If I hadn't been told differently, I'd have said it was a haymaker. Do you know what that is?"

"Mr. Shepard explained it to me, but it was only a slap."

"Only," Ridley said under her breath.

"Leaving now." Her tone was a shade too bright. She pulled Ben along before anyone asked her if she was all right.

Lily followed them to the front door, thanked them again, and saw them out. She asked the children to be patient a little while longer before she returned to the kitchen. "The only thing preventing Ridley from choking the life out of Miss Headley is the oath she took. I believe she's regretting it."

Roen chuckled. "So Ben's not the only one pained to be sitting on his hands."

The truth of that made Lily smile. "I don't think you can ever know how much it bothers her."

"But you do?"

"I have experience." She left it there and went to the stove to move the soup pot to the hot burner plate. "The children are hungry. Fedora, stay where you are. You're eating with us and then Roen's going to walk you back to the boardinghouse." She held up a finger. "Not a word. Roen, would you kindly get another chair?"

Chapter Thirty-Four

The hotel's dining room was closed when Martin Cabot returned to the Butterworth. He tapped the bell at the registration desk but no one came to attend him. The kitchen was quiet. He walked back, peeked in, and saw it was empty. Everyone was gone for the night. Apparently no late arrivals were expected. He returned to the front desk and looked at the slotted box that held room keys and mail. Martin knew that Victorine had a suite, but he wasn't familiar with the Butterworth's upper floors and didn't know the location of her room. He thought it was at the front of the hotel because she had once commented about having a view of the library and the bakery and not particularly caring for it.

All of the slots had only one key, which meant the hotel was full up and the other keys were with the occupants. He turned the registration book so he could read the names. He found Victorine's signature beside room 212 and was prepared to go there, but then he remembered she hadn't remained in the room she was first given. He examined the book again and found her name — not her signature — beside room 301. He removed the key from its slot and began to climb the stairs.

Standing outside the door to Victorine's suite, Martin considered knocking and then decided against it. Surprising her was a better strategy and precisely what she deserved. He slipped the key in the lock and turned it. The main room with its large four-poster bed and sitting area by the fireplace was empty. It had not occurred to Martin that she might not be in residence. He had always felt comfortable returning to the boardinghouse once Victorine headed to her room. What amusements were there for her in Frost Falls? It wasn't Manhattan. He had observed that her status as pregnant and unmarried made her the subject of speculation and sometimes derision. She appeared not to notice, or if she did, she appeared not to care. To him it was further proof that the people she had dealings with were supremely unimportant to her. She craved only the attention of Roen Shepard. Martin Cabot found that unfathomable. Shepard had made it clear that he wanted nothing to do with her. Instead of accepting her comeuppance and leaving, she was waiting him out as though she expected him to change his mind.

That hadn't happened, and Martin did not believe it would. As much as he wanted her gone, there was a part of him that admired her forbearance. It was unexpected, and the unexpected was always a good tactic. He did not know what had provoked her loss of patience or when exactly it had happened, but sometime today she had clearly lost her mind.

Martin cocked his head, directing his hearing toward an adjoining room. He heard the trickle of water, some splashing, and then humming that sounded a lot like "The Band Played On," only a little flatter.

So this suite at the Butterworth had a bathing room. Martin was impressed that the amenity existed in a cattle community but not surprised that Victorine Headley had seized it for herself. The door was already open a few inches. He walked toward it and used a fingertip to push it open the rest of the way. He stood framed on the threshold for almost a minute before she realized she was not alone. Her startled mien was comical as she rose a few inches above the water and then immediately dropped again so only her head, neck, and the slope of her shoulders were visible.

"What in God's name are you doing here?"

The disadvantage of her position did not soften her tone, he thought, or make her the least vulnerable. If he asked her to raise her hands, he was sure he'd see that her claws were out. "Did you hit her?" he asked. It pleased him that he was able to pose the question calmly. That was a demonstration of his control.

"Get out, Mr. Cabot. Back out of the doorway and close the door behind you. Say or do anything else and I will bring this hotel down around your head."

He didn't move. "It's your head, too, Miss Headley. Pray, remember that." But he knew Victorine well enough to know she did not make idle threats. When she opened her mouth to scream, he was on her, pushing her head underwater. He had a look at all of her while he held her down and had the thought *Isn't that interesting* before he removed his hand. She came up spitting and gasping and, as he suspected, tried to claw him.

Martin sat back on his haunches and easily batted her hands away. She had every reason to stay in the tub and he had every reason to keep her there. They shared the same goals. He doubted it was any more comforting to her than it was to him.

"Are you done?" he asked calmly.

She growled at him, choked on water, and lost what remained of her dignity in a fit of coughing.

There were some folded towels on a nearby stool. Martin handed her one. He watched her pat her face dry. Her hair, which had been perfectly arranged to keep it dry while she bathed, was a bedraggled coil hanging limply to one side. She angrily plucked the loose pins, threw them at him one at a time, and then wrapped the towel around her head. He thought she looked vaguely regal, although he would have his tongue cut out rather than tell her. If she kept lying to him, maybe he would cut out hers. The thought excited him, but not as much as it would have excited him to do the same to Fedora Chen. Victorine Headley had robbed him of that opportunity. The China girl was damaged goods now.

"Why did you go to the library this afternoon?" he asked. "And don't say you had an itch to read. You were there possibly ten minutes, and you left without a book."

"I made arrangements with Roen to meet

him there."

"Did you?" Martin moved the towels remaining on the stool to the floor. He sat down. The stool wasn't high, but it lifted him enough that he was no longer at eye level with Victorine. "He left this morning with his wife and all his equipment. You were still asleep, I suspect, when he came into the hotel to collect his pack. If you'd shared your plans with me, I would have told you he was gone. What was the purpose of meeting him? And why the library?"

"The purpose doesn't concern you in any way. I chose the library because it wouldn't be crowded but there would be witnesses."

"Ah," he said. "So you intended to make a scene but with a small audience. I agree with you that sometimes a more intimate venue is better. It contains the drama. Were you concerned you'd overact?"

"Get out."

Ignoring her, he said, "I suppose you were. You're not working from a script any longer. That changed when you learned he was married. I don't know what your play is about now. It occurred to me that you were going to ask me to kill the wife. I wasn't sure what I would do if it came to that. It would have been an interesting exercise because she's never alone. I would have had to kill the child, too. Mrs. Shepard is either with her younger daughter or with her husband. I don't think you would want me to murder Mr. Shepard, so it would have to be the child. I admit that gave me pause."

Victorine stared at him. "I didn't ask you to kill anyone."

"I know. I said it was only a thought that occurred to me. Why did you show so little interest in his new family?"

"Can we not have this conversation in the sitting room? The water is getting cold."

"Oh? How can you tell?" He gave her a moment to let the insult sink in. Sitting there in the tub with her pale skin and the white towel on her head, she did indeed put him in mind of an iceberg. "No, here is fine for conversation, but we can quickly move it along if you answer my question."

"I simply had no interest in her or her brats. Is that so difficult to understand?"

"It is actually. Do you recall the gown you purchased from Mrs. Fish? Ice blue. It's probably hanging in your wardrobe now."

"What about it?"

"She did most of the work on it. Not Mrs. Fish. Mrs. Shepard. She's a seamstress. Highly regarded for her hand stitching. I've wondered whether she knew she was making it for you. Have you checked it for pins?"

"It is long past the point where you've forgotten yourself, Mr. Cabot. You should leave."

"I am deaf to that tune. Hum 'The Band Played On' again. I like that one." He chuckled under his breath when she splashed water at him. He didn't bother to pick up a towel and dry his face. "Haven't you asked yourself if Mr. Shepard told her about you? Perhaps you are such a minor annoyance to him that you weren't worth mentioning. Shall I tell you why I think you finally decided you wanted to meet him again?"

In bored accents, she said, "If you must."

Martin smiled but it did not reach his eyes. "I think you were prepared to announce in a manner that would be overheard that Mr. Shepard is the father of your child. Perhaps it would humiliate him, although I'm not so sure, but it would have humiliated her. By all accounts, she has tender sensibilities, which you would know if you had asked me about her. I made it my responsibility to find out. Regardless of what you knew or didn't know, her humiliation was what you wanted. You desired a state of mind that you hoped would cause a rift. He would leave her and return to you. If it worked, you could count yourself as very clever, but the odds that it *would* work are not in your favor. Time, for one thing, is not on your side. For another, I've heard it said that Mr. Shepard is persuasive. I believe it was his minister who told me he could sing the birds out of their nests. Did you know that within days of his arrival, he organized a town meeting to discuss the rail project and had everyone eating out of his hand?"

"What are you saying?"

"I'm sorry. I thought it obvious. He has the ability to explain you away. He can dismiss you. His wife, who loves him according to the wags, will forgive him. You will be out in the cold, no worse off than when you arrived except that you will know you've failed. I shouldn't think that would set well with you."

"You don't know anything about me, or him for that matter. The wags that you cozy up to for your information like to hear themselves talk, so you have that in common."

Martin went on as if she hadn't spoken. He could see her skin was prickling with the cold. "You were angry when he didn't appear at the library. You decided, rather impulsively I imagine, to walk to his home. I followed and was impressed that you found it. Apparently you did pay attention to some things I told you. You had to know there was a chance that he would not be there, but you had no reason to suspect that his wife would also be gone."

Victorine's ice blue eyes narrowed on Martin's unexceptional face. "Why didn't you tell me that *she* was working there?"

"You didn't ask," he said simply. "I gave you every opportunity."

"So it was a game to you."

"In a manner, I suppose. In a town like this, I am forced to craft my own amusements. I never opposed you or raised an obstacle. The information I gave you depended upon your interest. You are remarkably lacking in curiosity, even when it would behoove you to have a better understanding."

"I know enough," she said. "I know *him.*"

"Yes, well, informing you that Miss Chen left the hotel specifically to work for the Shepards had no relevance to you. I don't know why you're troubled by it now."

"I am not at all troubled by it. I was not prepared to find her there. It would have been better if I'd known."

"Better for whom? You or her?"

Victorine sighed, exasperated. "Oh, do shut up."

He went on. "Did you strike her?" Martin gave her full marks for not flinching. She was going to brazen it out. His fingers curled into loose fists that he used to smooth his trousers over his thighs.

"You asked me that when you came in here. What are you going on about?"

"Did you strike her?"

"Are you saying I did?"

"It's a question, Miss Headley. Not an accusation."

"I don't understand why you're asking me."

"You stepped into the house. Pushed your way in, I thought. I did not have the best vantage point, so I could be mistaken there."

Victorine offered no information that would have cleared that up. "And?"

"And you came out minutes later. I followed you back to the hotel to make sure you arrived safely and then I went to the drugstore to buy a paper. I read it while I waited for the hotel's dining room to open for —"

Victorine waved a hand dismissively, although she was careful not to splash him. "I'm sure you find your comings and goings to be of significance, but I assure you, they are not."

Once again, Martin continued as if her

words were merely noise in the background, like the ticking of a clock that no one noticed until it struck the hour. "— to open for dinner. I had a superior steak, done rare, and mashed turnips and candied carrots. I drank a beer with dinner and another after at my leisure, then I returned to Mrs. Brady's. Sometimes I observe Miss Chen leaving the Shepard home. I like to make certain she arrives safely. There have been threats, you know, against her person."

"I didn't know, but it stands to reason that people would object to her presence."

"Why?" he asked. "Why does it stand to reason?"

"She's different," said Victorine. "And not in a way that makes her superior to others."

"As you are."

"If I must say so, then yes, as I am. You read the papers. You must know about the yellow peril. Even I know that such a thing exists. We invited them to this county and now they present a danger."

"That is a gross distortion, but I will not ask you to elucidate on what you think you know about it. It will make my head hurt, and frankly, it is throbbing already."

"Poor man," she said without sympathy. "There are headache tablets in my reticule. It's in the other room. You may take as many as you like, only you will have to get them."

Martin shook his head, but he did it carefully. He was not lying about the throbbing. He felt it all over and the worst was behind his eyes. "I did not observe Miss Chen's walk home this evening. I surmised I was too late to do that. The second beer was a mistake, I thought, but then my path crossed with hers as I was making the turn to Mrs. Brady's. Roen Shepard was Miss Chen's escort this evening. That is a change. Usually she is accompanied by the deputy."

"I know who you mean. Loose-limbed sort of young man. I've seen him here."

"Yes. Hitchcock Springer."

"That's all very well but immaterial. You said Roen was with her."

"Not only with her. He was protective *of* her."

"What does that mean?"

"He tried to shield her from me. She turned her face away and he stepped between us. Naturally I was curious. I greeted her as I typically do. I have learned not to expect a reply because she is both shy and wary. Tonight was no different. Mr. Shepard did not exchange introductions. He was occupied helping Miss Chen. I held the door open for them when we reached it. It was then that the light from inside the house allowed me a glimpse of Miss Chen's face. Her features were distorted. The simple explanation is that it was a trick of the light, but that would be incorrect. The left side of her face was clearly swollen. Her eye on that same side was only partially open."

"Did you express concern? Ask her what happened?"

"No. That would have been inappropriate. I'm asking you."

"And that's appropriate?"

"I believe it is. Did you strike her?"

"That's a ridiculous notion."

"But not an answer to my question."

"She probably tripped over that child who was clinging to her skirts. Or perhaps she walked into something."

"She is the definition of grace."

Victorine's eyebrows rose. "Why, Mr. Cabot, I believe you have found something to admire about her. I find that repugnant and a betrayal of your Christian upbringing but will not endeavor to make you see reason."

"She was mine," he said quietly.

Victorine's head tilted to the side. She regarded him oddly. "What?"

Martin could not help it. He teared up. "She was mine."

Victorine shivered. The cold water had

nothing to do with it. "What do you mean, she was yours?"

As quickly as his eyes had watered, they dried. "I had plans for her and you ruined them. You ruined her."

"I did nothing. Nothing."

"You're lying."

"If you believe that, then why even ask me if I struck her?"

"I thought you deserved an opportunity to defend yourself."

"Defend myself? That assumes I did something requiring a defense. I didn't. There. That is my defense. I am not guilty of whatever it is that you think I've done."

Martin sighed. "An opportunity squandered. You really shouldn't have touched her face. It was perfect. Perfect."

Victorine had nowhere to go. She tilted her head backward to watch Mr. Cabot rise from his stool, and she flinched when he kicked it out of the way. It was impossible not to shrink from him as he bent over the tub. She felt his hands on her shoulders before he actually set them there. All that remained for her to do was confess.

"Yes," she said hastily. "I slapped her."

Martin did not remove his hands. His thumbs were very near the hollow of her throat. "You must have struck her very hard.

Perhaps you did it more than once."

"Twice."

"Not more?"

She shook her head. It was both a negation and an attempt to loosen his grip.

"All right. Tell me why."

"She was insolent."

"A perceived slight, no doubt. Miss Chen does not possess the wherewithal to be insolent."

"You're wrong, but I will admit that her impudence was unexpected."

"So that's all of it."

"Yes. The truth. I swear it."

"I believe you. Do you want to take a breath?"

"What?"

"It will take longer if you do. I'd like that. You owe me that after spoiling her beautiful face."

"I did not —"

"Breathe," he said, and pushed her under.

Chapter Thirty-Five

It was early when Roen and Ben arrived at the Butterworth. Circumstances dictated that Roen tell the sheriff that Victorine was not at her finest in the morning. That bit of intelligence decided Ben that the better course was to wake her.

There was no one in the dining room, but Abe Butterworth was at his post behind the registration desk. He welcomed both men warmly. "If you're looking for your mother, Ben, she's already gone to the butcher's. Best cuts are always at the start of the day, she says."

"Not looking for her actually. We don't expect to be long, so give her my best if I miss her."

"Certainly." He looked from Ben to Roen and then took them both in. "So what is your pleasure?"

"We'd like to visit Miss Headley," said Ben. "What room is hers?"

"She has a suite, but she's a late riser, and with no companion to help her dress and do whatever she does to her hair, Miss Headley doesn't come down for breakfast until after ten."

"We assumed she would still be sleeping, Abe."

"Oh, well, I don't know. The privacy of our guests is —"

Ben stopped him. It was not often that he had to point out that he was the law, but he did so now, opening his coat and tapping the star on his jacket.

"Right," said Abe. "She's in 301."

"The key?" said Roen, holding out his hand.

"Yes, um, the key." Abe gave them his back while he retrieved the key. "Odd," he said, staring at it.

"What's odd?" asked Roen.

Abe turned around and dropped it in Roen's palm. "It was in its cubby backwards. Ellie and I always put the keys away in the same direction, with the head out and the working end in. No particular reason for it; I've just always done it that way and Ellie followed suit. I guess one of us could have put it in differently. It's just that it's not the usual thing."

Roen closed his hand around the skeleton

key. He wasn't particularly interested in Abe's story but he listened politely and suspected Ben was a tad more impatient as he had experience with Abe rambling.

"Thanks, Abe," said Ben. He nudged Roen toward the stairs. "We'll bring it back."

Abe didn't respond. He was still mumbling to himself when they reached the first landing.

"He's particular," Ben told Roen by way of explanation. "That's why he and my mother suit so well."

"They're both going to be unhappy when they find out that Fedora was hurt. Will they ask Victorine to leave?"

"Probably." Ben pointed to another stairwell at the end of the hall. "This way. Maybe they won't have to. Maybe she'll leave on her own."

"Doubtful, if she's not ready. Can't you send her packing?"

"You'd think I'd be able to, wouldn't you? There are limits to my authority. You heard Fedora. She doesn't want to press charges. She doesn't want any fuss at all. If she knew we were here, she'd be trying to stop us."

They reached the third floor and came to Victorine's room almost immediately. Roen wasted no time inserting the key. He turned it and turned the knob. The door opened soundlessly.

There was sufficient light in the room thanks to the parted curtains to see that Victorine was indeed in bed. She was lying on her back with a heavy quilt pulled up to her shoulders. Her flaxen hair was like a halo around her head, arranged there as if by an artist who wanted to capture her purity.

Roen shook his head. It was an illusion.

Ben shook his head for a different reason. Something was wrong. He nudged Roen with an elbow. "Light a lamp."

Roen found matches in a side table in the sitting area and lit the oil lamp on top of it. He held it up to throw more light on the bed. Victorine didn't stir. He carried it over to where Ben was standing beside the bed and looked down at her. He saw her differently now, probably the way Ben had seen her from the first. The request for a lamp made sense to him.

Roen thought he should feel something, and maybe he would later, but at the moment what he was, was empty. "She's dead."

"Yes," said Ben. "Here. Let me take the lamp. I'll stay with her while you get my wife. I want Ridley to examine her. It's better if you go. That way I know there's been no tampering of evidence."

"I would not —"

"It's a precaution, not an accusation."

Roen nodded and handed over the lamp.

"And don't say anything to Abe or my mother if you see her. One or both of them will have questions when you return with Ridley. Just ignore them."

Roen's dark humor asserted itself. "You've met your mother, haven't you?"

Ben answered with a faintly appreciative smile. "Well, do the best that you can."

Roen left, and Ben looked around to see if he could see any obvious clues that would explain Victorine Headley's death. His gut told him natural causes were not to blame. All appearances had indicated a healthy woman. Ridley's only remark regarding the pregnancy was that Victorine was likely to have a difficult delivery. Ben had stopped her from giving him more information so he didn't know what prompted her to say it. After being present at the birth of his niece, there were things he simply didn't want to know.

He put that out of his mind as he walked around the bed and then moved to the sitting area. The suite was tidy. There was a neat stack of women's fashion magazines on the settee. He wondered if she had brought them with her or got them from Mrs. Fish. There were pots of creams and scented oils on the vanity. The highboy had nothing on top. He walked into the bathing room. Except for tiny pools of water in the grout between the black and white floor tiles, there was no other evidence that she had taken a bath before lying down. The porcelain tub was dry. A bar of soap lay in a tray beside the tub. He touched it. It was dry on top but a little spongy on the underside.

What had she done with the towels, then? Rang for someone to take them away? That didn't seem likely. In fact, he would have guessed that Victorine was used to having someone pick up after her. The towels should have been on the bathroom floor and perhaps a washcloth as well. He looked in the cupboard under the sink and in the narrow closet beside it. There were none there.

He returned to the bedroom area. He wanted to pull back the quilt on Victorine's body, and if his wife had not been so readily available, he would have, but he had been reading lately about new forensic techniques in criminal investigation. Ridley's medical journals were a surprising source of information in that regard. He did not want to be clumsy about this. Victorine was, after all, the daughter of Victor Headley. The man's name was as well known to him as were the names "Jay MacWorth" and "Cornelius Vanderbilt," both of them early founders of railroad empires. Jay Mac and the Commodore were gone now but their legacy remained. Victor Headley inherited his kingdom and then grew it ten times over. The fact that he'd started with a leg up did not win him respect. He had had to earn that.

Ben wondered how Victor Headley would take the news of his daughter's death. And if it was murder, what then? Would he send Pinkertons to scour Frost Falls? He stopped. He was getting ahead of himself. First, he needed to find the goddamn towels.

Never expecting to find them in the wardrobe, it was the only place left after he'd eliminated under the bed and the trunk at the foot of it. He found the towels bunched together at the bottom, partially hidden by two pairs of shoes and a folded blanket that he could assume came from the bed. He pulled them out — there were three, and one washcloth — and dropped everything on the floor. The towels had been wrung out but they were still damp and heavy. It wasn't long before a water stain appeared around them.

Ben had just seated himself in the chair beside the cold fireplace when he heard footsteps in the hallway. No one was speaking, which meant that neither his mother nor Abe was with his wife and Roen.

"Ridley showed me the back stairs," said Roen, closing the door and locking it. "We avoided the kitchen help and everyone else."

Ben stood. Ridley was already at the bedside. She placed her medical bag on the nightstand.

"Have you touched her?" she asked.

"Waiting for you."

She nodded and placed two fingers against Victorine's neck. "I'm getting a sense of temperature, not looking for a pulse," she told them.

Roen stood at the foot of the bed. "Does her death have something to do with the baby?"

"I don't know yet. I would think if she had a miscarriage, there would still be evidence of blood on the blankets, on the floor . . ." Ridley folded back the quilt to uncover Victorine's shoulders. She reached beneath and drew out a limp, lifeless hand and examined it. "And under her nails. They're clean, at least to my naked eye." She opened her bag and took out a pair of small surgical scissors and clipped her nails. Ben passed her one of the envelopes she had placed in her bag for just this purpose.

"This is largely to satisfy my curiosity," she said to Roen. "There is not a great deal to be learned from it yet. I read an article in a German journal about blood typing in goats that piqued my interest. It may have applications for improved success with transfusions, but someday it might also have applications for narrowing a field of suspects."

"Ridley." Ben said her name quietly with a hint of admonishment. He pointed to Roen standing at the end of the bed.

"Oh, of course." She regarded Roen over the top of her wire-rimmed spectacles and offered an apologetic smile. "Ben is used to me waxing on. Sometimes I forget myself around others."

Roen nodded but didn't speak. Victorine might have been anyone lying there and Ridley's detached, clinical interest had no impact on him. He still felt nothing.

Ridley handed Ben the envelope. He returned it to her bag while she made several more folds in the quilt. It now lay just below Victorine's breasts. Ridley used the scissors to make a cut in the neckline of Victorine's nightgown and then parted the material to reveal the neck and shoulders. "Well," she said, "that tells a story."

Rather than crowd Ridley and Ben, Roen moved to the side of the bed opposite them and bent forward to see what they were seeing. The bruises on Victorine's shoulders did indeed tell a story.

"She wasn't strangled," said Ben. "There'd be some bruising around her neck if that were the case."

Roen looked up at him. "So she was what? Held down?"

"Yes, I think so." Ben asked Ridley to step aside. When she did, he bent over the body and placed his hands just above the marks on Victorine's shoulders. "The thumbs would have been about here. The fingers placed more to the back. Like so." He straightened and pointed to the towels lying on the floor beside the wardrobe. "I found those inside. The killer made an attempt to hide them. He took considerably more care dressing and posing her than he did getting rid of the evidence of his cleanup."

Ridley waved Ben back. She fingered Victorine's hair at the ends, the scalp, and finally at the back of the head. "Damp," she said. "Only here at the back and only faintly. The pillow has absorbed some of the wet."

Ben nodded. He asked them to follow him into the bathing room, where he pointed out the small puddles in the grout and the spongy underside of the bar of soap. "The tub's bone dry. I think the killer used the towels to wipe it clean. He missed a few spots on the floor. He didn't anticipate that she would be found this soon or there'd be nothing here to suggest that she'd been bathing when he came upon her."

"He?" asked Roen. "You're certain of that?"

"My hands were a good match for the bruises and it would have taken considerable strength to hold her under water. Nothing is certain yet, but I am confident enough at this juncture to say a man did this."

Ridley concurred. She returned to the bedside while the men remained in the bathing room speaking quietly. Without Roen present, she was more comfortable throwing back the quilt to reveal all of Victorine. The body still held surprises.

"Ben. Roen. Come here. You need to see this for yourselves." When they were standing on either side of her, she did not explain herself. There was no need. The outline of Victorine's distended abdomen beneath her nightgown told its own tale.

Ben frowned deeply. "What happened to her? Why is her belly poking sideways?"

Roen stared at the curious contour of Victorine's belly and answered Ben's question before his wife poked him with her scissors, as surely she was tempted to do. "She's not pregnant." He looked at Ridley. "May I?" When she nodded, he lifted the hem of Victorine's gown high enough to reveal the roundly shaped cushion loosely strapped to her abdomen.

Ridley undid the ties and pulled off the cushion. She thrust it at Ben, who made a small oofing sound and clutched it to his stomach. "You really need to read that book on childbirth I gave you."

"Remington advised against it," he said. In an aside to Roen, he added, "The illustrations scared my brother."

Ridley ignored him. She asked Roen, "Are you surprised?"

"That she deceived me? Deceived all of us? No, that doesn't surprise. I believed her, though. Not her claim that the child was mine, only that she was carrying a child. I cannot fathom how her mind worked."

Ben said, "I hope you're grateful for that."

"I am."

Ridley lifted the hem of the nightgown and drew it down to Victorine's knees, preserving her modesty for the time being. There would be no modesty when she performed the autopsy. She asked, "If you had not married Lily and were free to make other choices, would the knowledge of the child have been enough for you to marry

Miss Headley?"

Roen did not have to think about it. "No. A gun to my head couldn't have prompted me to propose."

"I thought she aimed lower," said Ben.

Roen gave him a wry sideways glance and was in time to see Ridley poke him in the side with her elbow. At least she had refrained from using the scissors.

"I don't think she understood that," said Ridley, addressing Roen. "She didn't know you were married until you told her. She expected a pregnancy would produce a different outcome."

"I imagine you're right. Did you suspect something about her pregnancy wasn't right?"

"No. I would have told you if I'd thought that. It's obvious now why she wouldn't schedule an appointment with me. You know, Roen, she couldn't have remained in Frost Falls much longer, not without an elaborate plan for a miscarriage. And that cushion would not accommodate a growing belly. She had to know I'd discover her deception one way or the other."

"The fly in the ointment," said Ben with considerable pride. "That's my wife."

Roen noticed that Ridley did not take offense. "What's to be done now?" he asked.

Ben tossed the cushion on the far side of the bed. "Her body needs to be moved to Ridley's surgery. She'll be able to confirm that Miss Headley was drowned. I'll get Hitch and Abe to help. There's a stretcher in the surgery. Do you want to inform her father or shall I?"

"I will do it. You should send a telegram later. He will want to hear from the law."

"Were they close?" asked Ridley.

"No, not according to Victorine. Victor never spoke to me about her so I don't know what he thought about their relationship. I don't believe he'll come here, although he could surprise me. Regardless, he'll want to bury her in New York whether he accompanies her casket or not."

"We are skirting the obvious question," said Ridley.

Ben said, "I suppose you mean who did this. Roen? Suspects?"

"If I were in your shoes, I'd be at the top of that list."

"Yeah. You are." He looked at Ridley. "This is why I don't speculate before I have all the facts."

"Point taken," she said, mildly contrite.

"I'll want to speak to Abe and Ellie to learn if they heard or saw anyone last night."

"The backward key," said Roen.

Ben nodded. "Yes, there's that." He explained to Ridley what Abe had told them about the key that morning. "It suggests that someone used it to gain entry to this suite and put it back in the wrong direction. Perhaps the person was concerned about not being admitted if he knocked and announced himself, or perhaps he valued the element of surprise. There are only three other rooms on this floor. One is the apartment where Abe and Ellie live. The other two are rooms similar to those on the floor below. Hitch and I will speak to all the guests later today."

Roen said, "To answer the question you haven't asked, after you and Ridley left last night, I saw Fedora safely to Mrs. Brady's and then went straight home. I was there the rest of the evening, most of it in bed with my wife. Lizzie had a bad dream that closely mirrored the events of the afternoon and came looking for her mother. She can vouch that I was in the room."

Ben rubbed behind his ear and strained to tamp down his smile. "I think I can spare little Lizzie an interrogation. Lily's word will be enough."

"Thank you. I didn't expect that you'd rely on mine alone."

Ben nodded. "Can't say I'm not glad you

understand. If a man in my job isn't suspicious, he's dead."

Chapter Thirty-Six

Fedora was standing outside in front of the boardinghouse when Hitch arrived. She wore a scarf wrapped over her head instead of a hat and pulled it forward so that it covered most of the bruised side of her face. She kept her head down and spoke very little. None of that was unusual. No one who saw her leaving the boardinghouse gave her more than a single glance, and the absence of comments told her that her bruised cheek and red eye hadn't been noticed or no one cared enough to inquire about them.

Hitch didn't notice either. Fedora was content to listen to him prattle on about settling an argument at the Songbird between a ranch hand from Twin Star and Buzz Winegarten's nephew before it became a physical altercation.

"Folks were placing bets and Buzz was taking them," said Hitch. "He doesn't much care for his sister's son. Keeps him on 'cause he's family, but watches him like a bird of prey every time Lincoln's hand gets near the till. Hey, here we are already. It doesn't take long enough to walk you here. I liked the walk to the Butterworth better on account of it taking more time."

Fedora nodded and thanked Hitch for his escort. She opened the back door and out of habit began removing her scarf as she made to step inside. Hitch's sharp intake of breath stopped her. Her hand hovered near her face for several moments before she dropped it to her side.

Hitch grasped Fedora by the shoulders and turned her to face him. His eyes widened. Above them, his eyebrows rose. "What happened to you?"

"Ask the sheriff. Please, I'd rather not talk about it." She saw that he was disappointed in her answer but accepting of it.

"Then I'll be going. Put some ice on that cheek."

She reached into a coat pocket and pulled out the empty ice bag to show it to him. "I will."

Hitch left her, but not before he surprised them both by placing his lips against her bruised cheek and then the uninjured corner of her mouth. "I love you," he said.

Fedora stared after his retreating figure, and when she finally stepped inside the kitchen, she thought her feet did not quite touch the ground.

Martin Cabot saw Deputy Springer striding toward the jail. The young man was obviously in a hurry. Martin suspected he knew the reason for the deputy's haste, but the state of Fedora Chen's lovely countenance was no longer his concern, and as he was on his way to the train station to purchase a ticket, he didn't have time to dwell on it. There was always an early train heading somewhere, and he intended to be on it. The destination was of no importance to him. Eventually he would make his way back to Manhattan, but he could take his time about it. He had money of his own as well as cash he removed from Victorine's suite. He found her reserves in a black lacquered jewelry box at the bottom of her wardrobe when he stashed the damp towels. It struck him as ironic that the box was a Chinese work of art with gold hand-painted characters gracing the lid and sides. There was also jewelry with the cash, but because the rings and necklaces could be identified with Victorine, he moved the jewelry to a drawer, where it could be found. He kept the box for himself as a memento.

Martin had always liked mementos.

Smiling, he walked into the station house and rang the bell to bring the agent out from the back. "A ticket for your next train, please," he said.

"Going east or west? North or south?"

"Yes," said Martin. "All of those."

The agent, who had been working for the railroad since some of the first track had been laid, had heard it all. He did not even bother to ask for the answer to be repeated, nor did he take much notice of the man making the request. People came. People went. He stayed. That was just the way it was.

He adjusted his spectacles and studied the schedule lying on the counter. "Huh." Turning away, he took a piece of chalk from the slate board tray on the wall and changed the arrival and departure times of No. 462. "There," he said, returning the chalk to the tray. "That's the one you want. Forgot to change the times last night. She's going to north to Cheyenne. That'll do you?"

"Where's her end point?"

"That'd be Sacramento. 'Course, once you're in Cheyenne, you can change trains and go anywhere you have a mind to."

"All right. A ticket to Cheyenne." Martin

paid the agent, took the ticket, and headed back to the boardinghouse. It was early yet, and there were a couple of hours left before he would be leaving. He could still have breakfast at the Butterworth. The idea amused him, but then he dismissed it as a needless risk. It would have to be under-cooked eggs and overcooked bacon at Mrs. Brady's before he packed.

Roen intercepted Hitch as he was heading home from the hotel. Once Victorine's body had been moved to Ridley's surgery, his presence was irrelevant. He still had to send a telegram to Victor, but he wanted to see Lily first. He put out his hand to stop Hitch from stepping into the office. Hitch was determined to blow right past him so Roen said, "You've seen Fedora this morning?" That stopped the deputy dead in his tracks. "I thought so," he said. "Ben wants you to meet him at the hotel. I left him with Rid-ley in her surgery, but he might already be waiting for you at the Butterworth."

"What the hell is going on?"

Roen summarized what had occurred yesterday afternoon between Fedora and Victorine and then the events of last night. "Ben will give you details. I only wanted you to be headed in the right direction. I'm going home now." Roen saw it was useless telling Hitch not to call attention to himself. As soon as he'd finished speaking, the deputy took off running.

Lily was applying the ice bag to Fedora's cheek when Roen arrived home. "Ham was good enough to knock down some icicles so we have ice chips as well," she told him.

"He probably enjoyed doing it." Roen hung up his coat and hat. "Where are the children? I didn't hear the bell."

"In the front room. We are just getting breakfast under way."

"Hmm. Fedora, would you be able to start that on your own? I'd like to speak to my wife in private."

"Of course," she said, jumping to her feet. She laid the ice bag on the table.

Lily looked at it and sighed. "Well, keep it on your cheek as much as you're able. I won't be long."

Roen nudged Lily down the hall. She slowed outside the door to their workroom but he pressed her on. "Upstairs. Our bedroom."

She glanced back over her shoulder, a question clearly communicated in the look.

"Privacy only," he said.

Nodding, she led the way to their bedroom with no more prodding from him. "Are her bags packed?" Lily asked when they were alone. "I hope she felt the weight of her offense. She's a hateful woman, Roen."

"Was," he said. "She was a hateful woman. She's dead."

Lily blinked several times and then lowered herself onto the bed. "Dead?"

"Yes." He leaned back against the door. "We found her in bed."

"But — but how? Was it the child? Did she give birth prematurely?"

"No. She was murdered."

Lily's mouth opened and then snapped shut.

"There was no child, Lily. Victorine wasn't pregnant."

"But you saw her. She didn't hide it. Roen, I made a gown for her that had to make allowances for her pregnancy."

"Perhaps if you had done the fitting, and not Mrs. Fish, you would have known. The baby was a cushion, perfectly shaped and fitted to make the presence of a developing child look real. Even Ridley did not suspect. Death made the discovery easy."

"So it was all a lie to get you back."

"Seems that way."

"She must have truly loved you."

"Lily, a little while ago, you called her a hateful woman. Keep that thought. She never loved me. Maybe she allowed herself to believe it, but she played herself false. I don't know if she was capable of loving anyone but herself."

"That's a cruel thing to say, Roen."

"Is it?"

Lily stood and went to him, took his hands, and held them in hers. "If it's true, then she was horribly, utterly alone. That's sad. Terribly sad." She raised Roen's hands to her heart. Tears glistened in her eyes and made her lashes damp.

"You have a tender heart, Lily. If you didn't, you wouldn't have said yes to my mad proposal."

Her smile was watery as she blinked back tears. "I thought I made a rational, well-conceived decision. What are you saying?"

"I'm saying that you felt sorry for me. It was pity that allowed me to get a foot in the door."

She snorted softly and bent her head to his shoulder.

"It's all right," he whispered against her hair. "It's good of you to grieve for her. Someone should, and I can't. Not yet. Maybe never."

Lily nodded. Her tears dampened the lapel of his jacket. He gave her his handkerchief and she pressed it to her eyes and then crumpled it in one fist as she stepped back. She breathed in, settled herself, and released the breath slowly. She met Roen's dark eyes.

"Are there suspects?" she asked. The answer was in the shadow that crossed his face. "Oh, no. *You're* a suspect, aren't you? Ben's lost his mind if he thinks you killed Victorine."

Roen placed a finger over her lips. "Hush. He doesn't think I've done anything of the kind, but that doesn't mean he doesn't have to eliminate me. You're my alibi, by the way."

She pushed his finger away. "I should hope so. Where else would you have been?"

"Well, there was a time I would have been on the sofa."

"One night."

"See? That's your tender heart at play again."

"It wasn't that tender. You spent time on the floor after that." Now she put a finger to his lips when he would have spoken. "I suppose Ben will want to speak to me."

"I don't know when, but yes."

"He won't want to question Lizzie, will he?"

"No. I told him she got into bed with us."

"Lizzie hasn't had a bad dream for almost a year. What Victorine did to Fedora was awful but to do it while Lizzie was standing right there was unconscionable."

"You're right. It was."

The space between Lily's eyebrows narrowed as she pulled a thoughtful frown. "Am *I* a suspect?"

"No. Anyway, we share the same alibi."

She challenged that. "How do you know I didn't leave the house after you fell asleep?"

Roen used his fingers to make furrows in his hair. "Jesus, do you *want* to be considered a suspect?"

"No. I only thought that Ben might ask."

"If he does, it will be about me, not you. Victorine was drowned, Lily. She was held under the water in the tub until she had to take a breath and then she drowned."

Lily's frown vanished; her face paled. "Oh," she said on a thread of sound. "That would have required considerable strength."

"Yes. There is also other evidence that suggests a man did this." He regretted the words as soon as they left his lips. She would want to know, not because she was ghoulish, but because curiosity came as natural to her as breathing. He could hardly fault her for that since he possessed the same inclination. "There were bruises on her shoulder that more closely match a man's hands than a woman's."

Lily reached up and touched one of her

shoulders and drew her fingers across the collarbone to her neck. "I know about bruises like that. So does Ridley. She's seen them on me."

Roen took the hand at her neck and drew it toward him. "I wish you had never known that suffering. Not just the bruises. All of it."

She nodded. "I draw comfort from knowing that in some way it's led me to you. Or you to me. I don't excuse Jeremiah for what he did. I don't have forgiveness for him in that tender heart you think I have, but the pain he inflicted fades when I am with you. I can't imagine that I would be with you if I hadn't been with him first."

"And I like to think we would have found each other regardless."

The corners of Lily's mouth turned up. "Yes, well, you keep thinking that." She stepped into him and raised her lips to his. The kiss was as sweet as it was brief. A knock at the door put an end to it.

The back of Roen's head thumped softly against the door as he expelled an audible, put-upon sigh. "What is it?"

"The sheriff is downstairs," said Fedora. "He's asking to see you and Mrs. Shepard. Clay, Hannah, and Ham all left for school. I'm almost done cleaning up in the kitchen."

Roen squeezed Lily's hand. "Leave it for now. Stay with Lizzie and we'll be right down. Thank you, Fedora." He regarded Lily below raised eyebrows. "Are you ready?" When she nodded, he released her hand and turned to open the door. He let her go first and followed her to the parlor, where Ben was sitting on the floor engaged in doll play with Lizzie. It was a sight.

Ben shrugged a trifle helplessly as he got to his feet. "She's the only one who will play dolls with me."

"Growing up with a sister or two would have cured you of that," said Roen. "Shall we go in the kitchen?"

Nodding, Ben brushed himself off and let them lead the way. Lily offered him something to drink but he declined. She sat without fussing with the kettle for either Roen or herself. "Does Fedora know?" he asked when Roen took his usual seat at the table.

"No. That is, I haven't told her. I was just speaking to Lily about it. Why do you ask?"

"I need to question her. I couldn't ask Hitch to do it. He's already beside himself that I want to talk with her."

"You don't think . . ." He didn't finish the sentence as Ben was already shaking his head.

"Just being thorough," said Ben. He looked at Lily. "You understand?" When she nodded, he asked, "So where were you last night?"

She pointed above her. "I went to bed not long after Roen returned from escorting Fedora to the boardinghouse. I was there all night, as was Roen. Lizzie was there for the better part of it, but I swear, Ben, if you ask her about it, I'll —"

"Let's leave it there. You really oughtn't to threaten the law, Lily." Ben merely chuckled when she muttered the remainder of her threat under her breath. "So we're done with alibis. Roen, have you notified Miss Headley's father?"

"There hasn't been time. I was going to do that after I spoke to Lily. Is it that urgent? I thought you'd still be at the hotel."

"I gave Hitch the task of interviewing the guests. It will keep him busy and out of trouble. Ridley finished her preliminary work. There was water in Victorine's lungs. No question that she drowned."

Both men looked at Lily when she sucked in a breath. Ben said, "Forgive me. I thought Roen would have told you."

She indicated she was all right. "He did. More reluctantly than you, as it happens. It's only that it is as difficult to hear the second time as it was the first."

Roen asked, "Did Abe or your mother know anything that would improve your ability to find Victorine's killer?"

"No. They retired after the dining room was cleared and the kitchen was cleaned. Mrs. Vandergrift left before they went upstairs. Every room was occupied so there were no rooms to let. There's a bell on the front desk for an unexpected arrival to use, but they can only hear it if they're on the main floor, say, in Abe's office, and sometimes if they're in the hallway on the second. To the best of their knowledge, no one rang the bell."

Lily said, "Don't you think it's unlikely the murderer would have announced himself?"

Ben shrugged. "He might have if he didn't go to the hotel with the intention of harming Miss Headley. Something may have occurred while he was there that provoked him."

"He found her room," said Roen. "Doesn't that suggest that he knew her well enough to know where she was staying?"

"Perhaps. Abe and Ellie both said she never entertained visitors. Of course, that doesn't preclude her from extending an invitation to someone for last night or simply giving out her room number. There's also the register, which Abe keeps on the front desk. There were two entries for her because she moved from a room to a suite. Still, I had no difficulty locating her. I suspect her killer didn't either."

Lily wondered aloud, "Do you think Victorine might have known her life was in danger?"

Roen's expression was puzzled. "Why do you ask?"

"I suppose because she hired that man. The private investigator she told you about. Perhaps he was as much her guard dog as he was an investigator."

"She's talking about Martin Cabot," Roen told Ben.

"I gathered that. He's on my list to interview. Lily, don't you agree that if he were also given the responsibility of protecting her, he would have been staying at the Butterworth?"

"Hmm. I reckon so."

"And where was the threat? Did she think Roen was going to exact some sort of revenge?"

"It wouldn't have been out of the question. I'm sorry, Roen, but she did shoot you. You would have been well within your rights to retaliate. And if you were a man of different character, you would have."

"Um, thank you?"

"That was a compliment."

"Oh, then thank you," he said, more certainly this time.

She smiled at him and then addressed Ben. "I'm trying to point out that in her mind she had reason to be afraid of Roen."

"Lily's not wrong," said Roen. "Victorine was vengeful. It would have been difficult for her to accept that the same isn't true of everyone."

"All right. That adds to the questions I have for Mr. Cabot. He certainly failed her."

Lily asked, "Do you think Mr. Cabot knew she wasn't pregnant?"

"I intend to find out," said Ben. "The killer might have known beforehand, but he definitely knew when he killed her. She certainly wasn't wearing the cushion in the bath. He put it on her after he carried her to bed. He dressed her then and arranged her hair so that it spilled over the pillow in a manner pleasing to him."

"Who? Who would do something like this? *Why* would he do it?"

"I aim to learn." He leaned back in his chair to look down the hallway. "Would you mind asking Fedora to come back here? I need to speak to her alone."

Lily rose to get Fedora. Roen stood and announced he was going to the station to send the telegram. Fedora was entering the kitchen as he was preparing to leave. He touched his face. It was enough to remind her to place the ice bag she was carrying against her cheek. He nodded, smiled encouragingly, and left.

Roen used the time it took to walk to the station to compose the message he wanted to relay in the telegram. Of necessity the news had to be delivered bluntly. He followed this with a question regarding Victor's wishes and told the station agent that he wanted to receive the reply as soon as it arrived. When he returned home, Ben was gone. Fedora was tidying the kitchen and he breathed deeply of the aroma of rising bread. The ice bag lay on the table. He looked at it and sighed.

"Was it a difficult interview for you?" he asked.

Fedora stopped sweeping. "No. Sheriff Madison was kind. He wanted to know what I did after you left me at Mrs. Brady's. I told him I went to my room and stayed there. There was no one who could support my story. I explained that Mr. Cabot saw me go into my room but could not possibly know that I remained inside it."

"Huh. I should have mentioned running into Mr. Cabot to Ben. It didn't seem important. I imagine it was not the same for you. You didn't want anyone to see your injury. I recall you tried to avoid him."

She nodded. "It is always the same with him."

Then Roen recalled an earlier conversation with Fedora. "That's right. You told Lily and me that you were ill at ease around him."

"He watches me the way a cat watches a mouse."

It was an image that he would have remembered if she had been so direct before. "It begs the question as to whether running into him was serendipitous or orchestrated."

"I don't know, but he'll be leaving soon, won't he? Now that Miss Headley is dead. The sheriff did not explain the particulars of their association to me, but he hinted there was one. I told him that his mother suspected Mr. Cabot was a spy for Mr. Headley's railroad, and he didn't deny it."

"It's as good a reason as any for his presence in Frost Falls." Roen realized it would be a relief to both him and Lily for it to remain the prevailing explanation. "Is Lily in the front room?"

"Yes, with Lizzie."

Roen stamped his feet once more and then walked through the kitchen. Fedora swept behind him anyway.

Chapter Thirty-Seven

Martin Cabot was sitting alone in Mrs. Brady's parlor used exclusively by her guests when Ben Madison and Roen Shepard arrived. He had expected the sheriff. Mr. Shepard was an unwelcome surprise. It was indeed unfortunate that the earliest train leaving Frost Falls would not arrive for another two hours. His bags were already packed. There was nothing left for him to do but wait.

"Mr. Cabot." Ben touched his index finger to the brim of his hat then he pointed to Roen. "You know Mr. Shepard?"

Martin folded his paper, put it aside, and got to his feet. He held out a hand to Roen. "A pleasure, sir. I know your name, of course. Martin Cabot here."

Roen shook his hand and smiled politely but without enthusiasm. "Mr. Cabot."

"Martin, please. I saw you last night. You were with Miss Chen. Unfortunate what befell her."

"She told you?"

"Yes," he said. "I asked. Ill-mannered of me, but she would have never volunteered. Close-mouthed, she is. To take such a spectacular fall as she did, it defied my imagination. She has always struck me as graceful and light on her feet. I've seen acclaimed ballet dancers tread more heavily on the stage than she does."

Roen was momentarily at a loss. Fedora had not mentioned a conversation with Cabot or that she had offered an explanation for her injury. Ben spared him from replying.

"Yes," said Ben. "Unfortunate." He looked around the sitting room. It had space enough to accommodate them but it lacked privacy. "Is there somewhere we can go where no one will intrude? Your room, perhaps?"

Martin shook his head. The packed bags would present a problem for him. "Give me a moment to tell Mrs. Brady you would prefer not to be disturbed. She'll guard the room with the vigilance of Cerberus."

His reference to the three-headed dog at the gates of hell made Ben smile. When Cabot left the room, Ben nudged Roen. "I'll never be able to look at Mrs. Brady without

seeing the hounds of Hades."
"Hmm."
Ben said, "Are you sure you want to be here? You can leave, you know."
"I understand, but I asked to come along, mostly because of Fedora. For her sake, I'd like to know that he's leaving town. I want to hear it from him. I promise I won't interfere."
"All right. I won't hold you to it because you are *not* close-mouthed." Ben chose an armchair and sat.
Roen followed suit, taking the gently worn damask-covered seat of a cherrywood chair.
Martin returned. "We will not be disturbed, gentlemen." He sat and regarded them expectantly. "I hope you mean to explain the purpose of your visit."
Ben said, "You are in the employ of Miss Victorine Headley, is that correct?"
Martin did not answer immediately. He removed his spectacles, carefully folded the stems, and put them in the inside pocket of his jacket. "Is it correct?" he asked. "What makes you think so?"
Ben's mouth flattened. He shook his head and turned over his hand to indicate that Roen should speak up.
"She told me she hired a private investigator. It did not require a great deal of work

to identify you." And because he believed that Cabot intended to string them along, he added the lie. "And she confirmed it."

"I see. Then, yes, I am Miss Headley's employee."

Ben took over again. "And the reason you were hired?"

Martin shifted uncomfortably. "I think she should answer that. We have an agreement, she and I, that I keep her business confidential. Unless she tells me differently, I cannot in good conscience answer your questions. Moreover, I am still not clear on the point of your visit."

"We'll get to that," said Ben. "Right now, we are looking for confirmation of what Miss Headley told us."

"Do you have reason to suspect she's lying?"

"Always," said Roen. He shot Ben an apologetic glance. It was one thing to be invited to speak, quite another to insert himself into the interview.

"So." Ben gave weight to the word and went on. "The reason she hired you?"

"I was hired to locate Mr. Shepard for Miss Headley."

"Did she explain why she wanted to know where he was?"

"No, but I assumed it had something to

do with her, um, condition."

"Her pregnancy, you mean."

"Yes."

"Did she tell you she was carrying a child?"

"She didn't have to. It was obvious."

"So she never told you that Mr. Shepard was the father."

"No. Not then. Not in New York. She told me after we arrived and she had spoken to Mr. Shepard. She was disappointed that he refused to accept he was the father." Martin's eyes turned to Roen. "She was in expectation of a marriage proposal."

Roen merely nodded.

Ben said, "When Miss Headley hired you, was it your understanding that you'd be accompanying her to wherever you found Mr. Shepard?"

"Not at all. I was unaware that she planned to go to him. I thought she would insist on Mr. Shepard coming to her. It seemed to me that it was unwise for her to travel."

"Did you say that to her?"

Martin gave a start. "It was not my place. Miss Headley has definite opinions. I do not cross her."

"I understand. Was it your idea to accompany her?"

"No. It was hers."

"Did she explain why she wanted you with her?"

"What did she tell you?" asked Martin.

Ben followed the script that he and Roen discussed beforehand. "She said she believed Mr. Shepard might attempt to harm her. Is that what she told you?"

"Yes."

"Did she say why she thought that?"

"No. Not directly. She hinted at some incident between the two of them that still troubled her. I didn't need to know more."

"Your duties, then, while you are here involve seeing that nothing happens to Miss Headley."

"Yes. My sole purpose at the outset."

"Has she asked you to do other things since you arrived?"

"When Mr. Shepard told her he was married, she naturally wanted to know if it were true. She wanted me to find out. I did that for her."

"What was her reaction when you told her Mr. Shepard was indeed married?"

"Hmm. Frustrated, I would have to say. I told her the name of the woman he married and she wanted to know more."

"And you gave her that information as well?"

"I gave her as much as she wanted to know. Her curiosity had waned in the intervening days. She showed remarkable patience as she waited for Mr. Shepard to come to her. I believe she thought it was inevitable."

Roen pressed his lips together to refrain from commenting.

Ben said, "Miss Headley arranged to meet Mr. Shepard at the library yesterday. Were you there?"

"Not in the library, no. I watched her go in. I would have followed if Mr. Shepard had arrived. He didn't. She came out shortly after."

"And went to the Shepard home. You saw her go there?"

"Of course. She wasn't there long. She went back to the Butterworth."

"You didn't have a room there. Why is that?"

Martin chuckled. "She didn't want to pay for it. I don't suppose she told you that. She thought she was already overly generous with my salary. Initially, Miss Headley did not want to be associated with me, and she would have me believe that was the reason I needed to take a room here. That changed following her meeting with Mr. Shepard."

"Why didn't she want to be seen with you?"

"She did not want Mr. Shepard to suspect I was with her because she was afraid of him."

Roen's eyebrows lifted, skepticism carved in the curl of his lip. He schooled his features when Ben shook his head almost imperceptibly as Martin Cabot looked away.

Ben said, "You used Frankie Fuller to communicate with each other."

It was not a question, but Martin responded anyway. "Yes. It surprises me she told you that. She could never recall his name."

"Actually it was Mr. Shepard's son who knew that. Frankie is his best friend. The boys don't have secrets."

"Ah. Just so."

"When did you last see Miss Headley?"

Martin frowned deeply. "That question is concerning. Has something happened? Did she leave without me?"

Ben pressed on without responding to Martin. "When did you last see Miss Headley?"

"I told you." He paused, reflecting. "I suppose I wasn't clear. She returned to the Butterworth after visiting the Shepard home and went straightaway to her room. I waited to see if she would go out again, and she didn't. I had dinner at the hotel. She did not come down for the evening meal while I was there. By that time it was dark, and as it is not her practice to leave the hotel at night, I returned here. Mr. Shepard can confirm. That's when we met outside."

"Then it was happenstance that you crossed paths."

Confused, Martin's brow furrowed. "What else would it be?"

Ben nodded to Roen.

"Miss Chen thinks you watch her," said Roen. "It occurs to me that perhaps your arrival at that precise time was no accident."

"We were coming from opposite directions. I had just left the hotel."

"I only have your word for that."

Martin appealed to the sheriff. "Ask your mother. She knows when I left." To Roen, he said, "I have enough to do watching Miss Headley. Miss Chen is mistaken. It's likely she is sensitive to people's eyes on her. I saw the stares she drew when she worked at the hotel. She would have to be blind not to notice them."

"She noticed you."

"That doesn't speak well of me, does it? I do not know if I am more offended personally or professionally. I regret whatever I've done that's given her this wrong impression, but it *is* a wrong impression. I was appropriately concerned, I thought, when I discovered a threatening note outside her door. Perhaps she misinterpreted my response. I addressed the other boarders rather forcefully. Do you know about the messages she receives, Sheriff?"

"I do."

"And what are you doing about it?"

"At the moment, I'm speaking to you."

"That's why you're here? Miss Chen?"

"Yes."

"You raised so many questions regarding Miss Headley, I just assumed . . ."

Ben prompted, "Assumed?"

"Assumed your visit had something to do with her. Mr. Shepard's presence supported that assumption. It occurred to me he had registered a complaint with you."

"He did, on behalf of Miss Chen."

"Oh, I see. I hope you are satisfied that I have done nothing untoward."

Ben did not say one way or the other. "Do you still have the note you found outside Miss Chen's door?"

Martin shook his head. "I destroyed it."

"Did you write it yourself?"

"No! It was vile. Did she say I wrote it?"

"She did not. Did anyone step forward to

admit authorship?"

"Not to me. Has anyone ever claimed responsibility?"

"No."

"Humor me, Sheriff. Why the questions about Miss Headley?"

"You're misremembering, Mr. Cabot. The majority of my questions were about your work for Miss Headley. Your presence in town has given rise to speculation."

"I'm aware. Mrs. Springer thinks I have something to do with Victor Headley's railroad enterprise. I imagine she's not alone."

"No, she's not," said Ben. "My mother thinks you're spying on Mr. Shepard."

Martin's smile was regretful. "If only I had been hired for that task, but no. I have nothing at all to do with Mr. Headley. I've never met him."

"I believe that will change soon. He's informed Mr. Shepard by telegram that he will be arriving within a few days."

"Oh?"

"He will very much want to know how his daughter came to be murdered under your watch."

Chapter Thirty-Eight

Lily was studying the wanted notices in Ben's office when Ben and Roen arrived. She turned when the door opened and regarded them expectantly. "Well?"

"Let us take our coats off first," said Ben. "What are you doing here anyway?"

"Isn't it obvious? I want to know how the interview went with Mr. Cabot. When Roen didn't return home, I thought he must be here. I'm sorry, but I couldn't wait any longer."

Roen shrugged out of his coat and passed it to Ben to hang up. He closed the distance to Lily in a few strides and kissed her on the cheek. "Come. Sit with me over there." He pointed to the two visitor chairs. "Ben just concluded the interview. We didn't discuss it on the walk here."

"Too damn cold," said Ben. He looked in the coffeepot on the stove and made a face. It was empty. He decided coffee could wait but the fire needed attending. He tossed in some kindling, and when it blazed, he added coal from the scuttle. When he turned around, he saw Lily scooting her chair closer to Roen's. She leaned her shoulder against his. It was a small gesture, but an intimate one, and all the residual doubts Ben had about their unconventional marriage vanished.

Ben sat behind his desk and asked Roen, "Do you think Cabot was genuinely caught unaware when I told him Miss Headley was murdered?"

"I can only say that he seemed so."

"Hmm. I had the same thought. Appearances aren't necessarily fact. He asked all the right questions. I couldn't tell if he was preparing himself for Mr. Headley's visit or simply satisfying himself about the progress of the investigation."

Lily held up a finger to forestall Roen from speaking. "Mr. Headley is coming here? I didn't think you'd had a reply from him, Roen."

"I haven't," he said. "Ben lied. He's quite good at it, too. For a moment, I believed him. He convinced Cabot that he was there solely on Fedora's account, and when the man was lulled into believing his answers were satisfactory, Ben dropped the other shoe. Cabot was struck dumb but not paralyzed. He jumped to his feet and would have left right then if Ben hadn't blocked him."

"It helped that he stumbled over your foot. Well done."

Roen shrugged modestly. "No taste for physical altercations, I'm afraid."

"Neither, apparently, does he," said Ben. "He returned to his seat easily enough."

"Did he say where he wanted to go?" asked Lily.

"He wanted to see her. He wanted proof." Ben leaned back in his chair. "It's not an unusual reaction to learning about a death when it's unexpected. Still . . ." He fell quiet, musing.

"Still?" asked Lily. "What else?"

Roen said, "He's thinking, Lily."

"Then he can do it out loud. You do."

Roen gave her a look that was wryly amused and put a finger to his lips.

Lily clamped her mouth closed and waited. She wasn't sure that Ben had even heard their exchange. Ben finally made a sound at the back of his throat that seemed to signal the end of his thinking. Lily leaned forward just a little.

"I hope you're not expecting an oracle,"

Roen whispered out of the side of his mouth.

She tapped him on the forearm. "Hush."

"Still," said Ben, "there was something not quite right about his presentation."

"I told you," said Roen, still whispering to Lily. "Not an oracle."

"I can hear you, you know." Ben's tone was dry as dust.

"What are you saying?" Lily asked. "It sounds as if you're considering him a suspect. You didn't go there with that in mind."

"I went there with an open mind," said Ben.

Roen said, "He can't prove he was in his room all evening."

"No one who lives alone can provide proof of staying indoors."

"You're right," said Ben. "It doesn't mean much that he can't account for his time, but there was something about his reaction to the news that struck me as false. I'm trusting my gut here, but it seemed calculated, as if he was preparing to jump before I'd finished telling him the news. He set his feet and leaned forward. It was subtle. God knows I might have imagined it."

"Did you see that, Roen?" asked Lily.

"Not that I'm consciously aware, but

perhaps I did. I only said that it seemed he didn't know about Victorine. I trust Ben's gut."

Lily nodded. "So do I. I suppose this means he's not leaving. You'll want him to stay. Fedora will be unhappy. *I'm* unhappy."

"I know," said Ben, "and I'm sorry. I would have escorted him to the station myself if it weren't for Victorine."

"You asked about her pregnancy?"

"Not directly. In fact, I never told him she wasn't pregnant. He spoke of it several times, each time as if it were real. I decided not to challenge him about it."

Roen said, "He wants to see Victorine's body, so he is going to meet Ben at Ridley's surgery. I'm going to go to see the station agent about that telegram. I told him I wanted to know right away about a reply, but perhaps he forgot or he's busy."

Both Ben and Lily chuckled at the idea of the station agent being busy. Except for those times when a train was due to arrive or depart, Mr. Winslow napped in the back room or read a newspaper at the counter.

Lily explained to Roen why they'd laughed. "Why don't I go to the station and inquire about the telegram and you go with Ben?" She added hurriedly, "Unless you'd rather not. I thought you might like an opportunity to revise or confirm your suspicions."

"That's a good idea, Lily," said Ben. "Roen? What do you think?"

Roen nodded. "I'll go with you. Lily, if Victor's telegram is there, bring it to me straightaway."

"And if there's none? Do you want to know that as well?"

"Yes. Come to the surgery regardless."

"Of course. Should I compose a reply?"

"If he requires one, I trust you'll know how to answer him."

"All right." She stood and retrieved her coat. Roen helped her with it, angled her hat just so, and then wound her scarf around her neck and the lower half of her face. She yanked it down so she could speak then changed her mind about telling him anything. Careless of Ben's presence, she kissed her husband instead.

Grinning crookedly, Ben watched her go. Under his breath, he said, "I'll be darned."

"How's that?" Roen handed Ben his coat.

"Talkin' to myself." Ben took the coat; his smile didn't fade. "Just talkin' to myself."

Lily stopped at home to inform Fedora that she would be a while longer. She didn't share details that she'd heard from Ben and

Roen, but she did say that Mr. Cabot would not be leaving soon. Fedora was more resigned than disappointed, and Lily tried to reassure her that Mr. Cabot would not trouble her again in any manner. "He's meeting Ben and Roen at Ridley's surgery and there will be more questions for him to answer. I imagine he will be occupied with matters concerning Miss Headley's death. Her father will require explanations that only Mr. Cabot can provide."

"He's coming, then?" asked Fedora. "Mr. Headley, I mean."

"We don't know yet. I'm going to the station to see if a response to Roen's telegram has arrived. Either way, I have to let Roen know. Will you be all right?"

"Lizzie and I will be fine. We are changing the beds and washing sheets."

"Oh, Lord. Don't let her be *too* helpful." Lily was encouraged by Fedora's lilting laughter. Everything would be fine. There was truly no reason to believe that Fedora was in any danger; it was only that there was a tightness in Lily's stomach, a wretched feeling that had been coming on in small increments that she associated with impending threat.

Lily stepped outside. She was halfway to the end of the flagstone walk when she heard Fedora close the door behind her. She had an urge to look back that she forced herself to ignore. Victorine's murder, Fedora's injuries, this violence against women; Lily understood it was related to why she was finding it difficult to draw a full breath and why her skin prickled even though she was not cold. She hadn't been fully honest with Ben and Roen about why she went to the sheriff's office to wait for them. Yes, she wanted to know what they had learned from Mr. Cabot, but it was truer that she wanted the comfort that was her companion in Roen's presence.

It was a short walk to the train station. Hank Ketchum, owner of the livery, tipped his hat to her as she passed, his normally taciturn expression brightening momentarily as he greeted her. She smiled in turn and was relieved to know it wasn't forced. Perhaps the fist around her heart was beginning to loosen ever so slightly.

Solomon Winslow, the station agent in Frost Falls for as long as Lily could remember, smoothed the broadsheet he was reading across the countertop when Lily's entrance blew the corners back. He did not trouble himself to hide his annoyance at the interruption, but he did have the grace to look abashed when he saw who it was crossing his threshold.

"Lily Salt," he said, folding the paper and pushing it aside. "As I live and breathe."

"Lily Shepard now, Mr. Winslow."

"And so it is. Seems it was just a week or so ago that you were Lily Bryant. Can't figure out if change comes too quick or my brain's too slow. Probably a bit of each." Solomon slid off his stool. Long legged with a short torso, the agent was the same height on the stool as he was off it. "Now what can I do for you, Miss Lily?"

Lily unwrapped the scarf around the lower half of her face. "Has there been a reply to the telegram my husband sent this morning?"

"Ah, I thought that might be it. I promised I'd get word to him as soon as I heard, but I reckon he's anxious, her being who she is and all and him working for Northeast. Damn shame, if you'll pardon the language. 'Course I only met her the once. That was the night she arrived, and I can't say I was pleased to make her acquaintance. A woman like her, she doesn't breathe air the way you and I do. She *sniffs* it." Solomon put his sloping nose in the air and sniffed to demonstrate Victorine Headley's expression of disdain.

"She's dead, Mr. Winslow," Lily said. It

was not an admonishment, simply a matter of fact.

"So she is." His haughty countenance vanished. "Did you notice the car on the side track? It's down a ways. You'd have to step outside to see it. That's her private car."

Lily hadn't noticed. "What will happen to it now?"

"I expect there'll be some instruction from New York. Mr. Shepard ain't the only one waiting to hear from Mr. Headley."

"Have you spoken to anyone about this?" asked Lily.

"Not a soul. Mr. Shepard asked me not to and I haven't. Couldn't if I'd wanted to. No one's been around since your husband was here. He told me to expect the sheriff sometime, but Ben hasn't shown himself either."

Lily had not asked Roen exactly what he had communicated in his telegram to Victorine's father, but she felt confident that murder had not been mentioned. Mr. Winslow, therefore, knew that Miss Headley had died and nothing at all about how she had died.

"Not sure what Ben's business is," Solomon said. "Do you know?"

"I imagine he wants to send condolences, what with Miss Headley being all alone here and her father being a man of considerable reputation."

"Was it the babe?"

"I couldn't say," said Lily. "But I agree with you, it's a shame. Do you mind if I sit a spell? Perhaps the telegram will arrive while I'm waiting."

"Suit yourself. That chair by the window is more comfortable than either of the benches. Here, I'll give you my paper to read. I've looked it over twice already." He slid it across the counter.

"Thank you."

"Would you like a cup of coffee? I have fresh in the back."

"No, thank you." She removed her mittens, stuffed one into each pocket, and took the paper. The heat from the woodstove in the corner was insufficient for her to be able to remove her coat, and she kept her scarf draped around her shoulders. She carefully folded the paper and then sat. "When do you expect the morning train?"

Solomon pointed to the slate board behind him. "Eleven forty. Evelyn Gray should be on it. At least that was her plan when she left to see her daughter and new granddaughter in Denver. Not expecting anyone else I know. Can't say what strangers will show up and stay. There's usually a drummer or two come to town. Guess it won't be long before we'll be getting folks looking for work with Northeast. Word's got around that your husband's already interviewed the locals."

Lily murmured a reply, but it went unheard as the telegraph machine began to tap. Mr. Winslow plucked the pencil from behind his ear and a piece of pale yellow paper from a notepad and began to record the message as it appeared on the alphabet dial. Lily sat up straight and looked on anxiously. When the agent caught her posture out of the corner of his eye, he gave a small negative shake of his head. She relaxed, shoulders slumping slightly.

When he'd finished, he placed the message in an envelope, wrote the name of the recipient on it, and sealed it. "Message is for Harrison Hardy."

"Do you need to deliver it?"

"Not an emergency. Frankie Fuller can ride out to the Double H with it after school." Solomon examined his pocket watch and then came out from behind the counter to look out the front window. When he wasn't satisfied with the range of his view, he opened the door and briefly stepped outside.

"Looking for anyone in particular?" asked

Lily when he returned.

"Fella bought a ticket early this morning for the first train out. That's the one Mrs. Gray will arrive on. Thought he'd be here waiting. I wouldn't say he was eager to leave town but he was definite about his intentions."

Lily merely nodded and turned her attention to the newspaper.

Martin Cabot surreptitiously checked his pocket watch before he followed Roen and the sheriff into Dr. Madison's surgery. The pair stood back to allow him to approach the table where Victorine Headley's body was laid out. A sheet covered her. Ridley stood on the opposite side of the table and folded the sheet back to Victorine's shoulders.

"She looks at peace," said Martin. He'd given serious thought as to what he should say when he confronted Victorine. What he said was the best that he could manage. He did not want to give the impression that he was grieving because he certainly wasn't. She had been his employer. He believed that making their arrangement seem something that it wasn't would cast suspicion his way. Martin was not confident that the sheriff, and especially Roen Shepard, did not already harbor misgivings where he was concerned. The reason for it was not clear to him, except perhaps that it had something to do with Fedora Chen. How one was related to the other remained a mystery, but he knew from his own years as an investigator that a straight line did not necessarily connect the dots. Leaps of intuition sometimes trumped linear reasoning.

Ridley raised the sheet so it covered Victorine's face. Martin's gaze swept the outline of the body beneath the sheet. He took a step back, feigning confusion and surprise.

"Did you remove the child? What happened to the child?" Martin lifted his eyes to Ridley first then looked back at Roen and Ben. "I don't understand."

Ben asked, "What were your traveling arrangements on your journey here?"

Martin frowned. "My traveling arrangements?"

"Yes. Did you share Miss Headley's private car?"

"Share it?" He chuckled humorlessly under his breath. "I never stepped foot in it, never was invited to. She offered to pay for a sleeping berth for me but I refused and accepted the additional recompense instead. Our only contact came when she left the train in Chicago to send a telegram to Mr.

Shepard. I advised her against it. My interference, though it was hardly that, was not appreciated it. I believe she wanted to let me go. I cannot say why she didn't."

"You never questioned her pregnancy?" asked Roen.

Martin raised his eyebrows. "No. Why should I? Did you?" He looked at the doctor and the sheriff in turn. "Did any of you?" His frown deepened and furrows appeared on his brow. "What are you saying? That Miss Headley *wasn't* carrying your child?"

Ben spoke up before Roen could. "She wasn't carrying any man's child."

Ridley said, "She was using a bolster to simulate pregnancy."

Martin opened his mouth, closed it again.

Roen asked, "Do you have knowledge of anyone with whom she had a disagreement? Someone who had given her offense?"

"Someone other than you?" Martin asked baldly. "No. As you must know, she was a disagreeable woman, more likely to give offense than receive it. People in her employ or those who served her tended to grit their teeth and bear it. I know I did. Think what you will of me for that."

"Did she make the acquaintance of anyone in particular?" asked Ben. "Assignations?

Trysts?"

"None. It was my job to know where she was, what she did. There was nothing like that. She arranged to meet Mr. Shepard at the library yesterday, but he was working out of town."

"We're aware," said Ben.

"You have no suspects?" asked Martin. When his question went unanswered, he went on. "You've questioned everyone at the hotel? Mr. Butterworth? Fedora Chen? What about Mrs. Shepard? Perhaps she thought she had motive."

At his sides, Roen's hands clenched. He said nothing.

"We've been thorough, Mr. Cabot," Ben said. "I'm still not clear why you were not staying at the Butterworth if you were hired by Miss Headley to look after her."

"It was a combination of her preferring that we maintain a distance and her unwillingness to pay for the more expensive room. As with her car on the train, I was never invited to her room. I took my meals at the Butterworth, which allowed me to attend to Miss Headley's whereabouts and plans."

"Miss Chen's also," said Roen.

"I suppose," Martin said, shrugging. "She worked there."

"My mother said you specifically asked

for Miss Chen to wait on your table."

"That's true. She didn't chatter, didn't spill things. She came and went silently. I appreciated that. Forgive me, but I fail to understand what one has to do with the other." When no one responded, Martin said, "I've satisfied myself as to the truth of Miss Headley's death, and I will be making my own inquiries. Mr. Headley will expect it of me even though my contract was with his daughter. And although it is wholly inadequate, it is also the only way I have of making amends for what appears to have been a tragic oversight."

"Oversight," Ridley said under her breath. She bent her head to hide the derisive curl of her lip.

"I cannot stop you from looking into the circumstances of Miss Headley's murder," said Ben, "but not only is it unnecessary, you could easily complicate and compromise our investigation."

Martin gave this the consideration he thought it was due, which is to say he gave it none at all. "As you said, you cannot stop me. Gentlemen. Doctor. If there is nothing else, I assume I am free to leave."

"Yes," said Ben. "Yes, of course."

Martin tipped his hat to Ridley and bade them good day. When he was out of sight of the surgery window, he consulted his pocket watch again. Pleased that there was still time for him to gather his bags and get to the station, Martin Cabot proceeded to the boardwalk, whistling softly. It was some time before he realized the tune was "The Band Played On."

Roen, Ben, and Ridley retired to her office adjacent to the surgery. Ridley sat at her desk while the men took seats opposite. The housekeeper appeared to ask if they required refreshment. Since none of them had eaten, Ridley asked for coffee and breakfast rolls.

Roen sat back in his chair and stretched his legs to the side so his boots did not touch Ridley's cherrywood desk. Ben did not show the same consideration. He set the toes of his boots against the ornate scrollwork that bordered the bottom edge. Ridley set her elbows on the desktop and steepled her fingers so her chin rested on the tips. She looked from Ben to Roen and then back to her husband. "Well?" she asked. "Mr. Cabot was either wholly inadequate to the task of watching over Miss Headley or he did the deed himself."

Neither man spoke to her assertion. Roen said, "Did you notice he was carrying?"

Ben nodded. "Don't see many shoulder

holsters like that around here. You might be the only other person I know who has one."

"You still have it in your office?"

"Sure. You want it back?"

"Yes. I think I do. Cabot wasn't wearing his when we spoke to him earlier. What do you suppose changed?"

"We surprised him before."

Ridley's eyebrows rose. "What did he expect this time if he felt the need to be armed?"

Ben shrugged. Roen shook his head.

"I don't like this," said Ridley. When silence followed her observation, she knew it was the same for them.

Roen said, "I'd like to look around Victorine's private car. I don't feel especially confident that I'll find anything, but it can't hurt."

Ben nodded. "Good idea. I'll go with you. You can pick up your shoulder holster on the way."

Mrs. Rushton appeared just as the men were getting to their feet. They looked at each other and then at the tray with coffee and a pyramid of sweet rolls. Without a word or a glance between them, they sat down again.

Ridley chuckled. "You'll think better with something in your belly."

■ ■ ■ ■

Lily read several stories in the broadsheet before she set the paper aside. Solomon was sorting mail. Since there had been no train since yesterday morning, his deliveries were already a day past due. Lily smiled to herself. Nothing moved particularly quickly in Frost Falls.

She came to attention when the telegraph machine began to tap out its code. Solomon dropped the half-dozen envelopes in his hand and took the pencil from its resting place behind his ear.

"This is what you've been waiting for," he told her.

Lily stood and went to the counter, where she set the newspaper aside. The rhythmic tapping meant nothing to her, but she observed that it was a language Solomon Winslow understood very well. He scribbled on the notepad, his fingers ceasing to move only after the machine had stopped communicating in a series of dots and dashes and the letters appeared on the dial. She leaned over the counter, trying to read Solomon's scrawl upside down. "Is it from Victor Headley? What does he say?"

Solomon read: " 'Express train arranged.

Arrive the 18. Bring daughter home.' "

"The eighteenth," Lily said under her breath. "That's only three days."

The station agent shrugged philosophically. "He does own a rail line. There're benefits to that."

Lily ignored him. "May I?" she asked, holding out her hand.

Solomon folded the paper and placed it in her palm.

Lily removed her mittens from her pockets and put the note in one of them. "Thank you."

"No reply?"

She shook her head and began to put on her mittens. Turning to go, she stopped suddenly as a figure crossed in front of the station window. "You have a customer, Mr. Winslow."

"Been expecting him. That's Mr. Cabot. That's the fella I told you about who came in first thing this morning for a ticket on the earliest train out."

Lily turned back to the counter. "First thing?"

"First customer of the day. Only customer, come to think of it. Your husband was the second but that was later. And you're my third. Slow day."

Martin Cabot opened the door and

stepped into the station. He dropped his bags on one of the benches and approached the counter. "The train's running on time?" he asked the agent.

"Haven't heard otherwise. It's been known to show early. Afraid you were going to leave it until too late."

Lily wound her scarf around her neck and the lower portion of her face and backed away from the counter. She ducked her head slightly, turning away from Mr. Cabot, and made for the door. He was a stranger to her. For all that she had heard about him, she had never laid eyes on the man, but she doubted the reverse was true. If he gave her any attention at all, he would be able to identify her. At the moment, she was unimportant to him, not worthy of notice. That was precisely as she wanted it.

Roen and Ben would be very interested to know that Martin Cabot had already arranged to leave town before they ever spoke to him this morning. As far as Lily was concerned, there was only one reason for him to prepare for a hasty departure. He had murdered Victorine Headley. It was his misfortune that today's earliest train wasn't arriving until just before noon. If he had been the least bit familiar with the countryside, he would have been better served to hire a mount from Hank Ketchum and head out. He would have had a decent start, although his chances of not being run to ground by Ben and a posse were slim indeed.

Lily had one foot out the door when she heard her name. He spoke it softly. There was nothing menacing in his tone, nothing that should have alarmed her, and yet experience with exactly that sort of tone warned her she *should* be alarmed. The skin at the back of her neck prickled and blood drained from her face. She was cold. She recalled moments when she had been this cold before. The last time was the night of the fire that destroyed her home and almost destroyed her life.

Lily considered pretending she hadn't heard, but she had already paused and the length of that pause had certainly given her away. She stepped back inside, turned, and closed the door. "Yes?"

"You are Mrs. Shepard, aren't you?" Cabot asked.

Lily looked past Cabot's shoulder to Solomon. The station agent was watching them curiously. "Excuse me," said Lily, "but you are . . ."

"Oh, of course. Where are my manners? Martin Cabot. I imagine your husband's spoken of me."

Frowning slightly, Lily feigned thinking it over. "Not that I recall, Mr. Cabot, and I believe I would remember."

"Hmm."

Lily couldn't help but notice that his genial smile did not touch his eyes. "Was there some reason you stopped me?"

"Only to make your acquaintance. I spent time with your husband this morning. Twice actually. Once at Mrs. Brady's rooming house and again at Dr. Madison's surgery."

"Mm." She nodded in Solomon's direction. "Thank you again, Mr. Winslow. Good day." Opening the door for the second time, she managed to step outside with both feet before she was abruptly pulled back. Mr. Cabot blocked her exit.

"Hey!" Solomon Winslow called out, starting to come around the counter bent on aiding Lily.

"Stay where you are," said Cabot. He took a threatening step forward but did not draw his weapon. He pushed Lily toward the chair. "Sit there. Don't move."

Lily stumbled over her own feet but stayed upright. She dropped into the chair, tugged at her scarf, and breathed in deeply. "I don't understand."

"Yes, you do. Don't play me for a fool,

Mrs. Shepard."

"Well," said Solomon, "I sure as hell don't understand." He looked at Lily for an explanation.

"Back behind the counter," said Cabot.

Solomon hesitated but not long. When he turned to retrace his steps, Cabot clubbed him with the butt of his gun. Solomon was momentarily draped over the counter until Cabot pushed him over it and let him drop to the floor. The station agent moaned, got clubbed again, and then lay silent, still, and out of sight.

Cabot turned. Lily hadn't taken the opportunity presented by his distraction to try to leave. She sat pale and motionless in the chair. It was as if he had clubbed her. He slipped his gun back into the holster under his jacket. "You know why I can't let you leave, Mrs. Shepard."

Lily did not reply.

"I am paying you the high compliment of being a perspicacious woman. Please do not offend me by pretending otherwise. I should like to hear the reason for your visit here. You have no bags, so I can safely assume you have no travel plans."

Lily kept her gaze fixed on the large slate behind the counter with the train schedule recorded in neat block letters. The letters turned fuzzy the longer she stared. She remained mute.

"Was it your husband's idea to send you here?" asked Cabot. "Why? What are his suspicions?"

Lily did not respond to his question. "May I look after Mr. Winslow? You have no idea how badly you may have hurt him."

Cabot looked over the counter. "He's breathing. Your concern is unwarranted." He took a step toward her, and although it was not done in a threatening manner, it still struck him as curious that she did not flinch. "Are you fearless, Mrs. Shepard? Is that it? A fearless woman. Such a rarity. I don't believe I have ever made the acquaintance of one such as you." He consulted his pocket watch. "Twenty minutes."

Lily removed her mittens again and stuffed them in her pockets.

"You dropped something." Cabot pointed to the floor beside her chair, where a neatly folded piece of pale yellow paper lay. Lily started to bend sideways with the intention of picking it up with her fingertips, but Mr. Cabot stooped and swept it up. He held it out to her without opening it. Lily took it without comment and carefully slid it back in a pocket.

"Telegram?" asked Cabot. When she said

nothing, he merely shrugged. "Do you imagine I intend to hurt you, Mrs. Shepard? Let me set your mind at ease. I do not. Your continued silence is an annoyance, nothing more."

"You hurt Mr. Winslow."

"He had violent intentions. I know. I've seen his kind before. Thinks he's half his age and twice as strong as he was then. It doesn't end well."

"Why did you murder Miss Headley?" asked Lily.

Cabot blinked. "Just like that? You have nothing to say and then you ask me that? I'm not admitting anything, you understand, but answer me this: Why do you care?"

"She was a human being."

"Barely."

"Deserving better."

"Again, barely."

"You'll be caught and charged and hanged for it."

"You sound very sure. I admire your confidence in your sheriff."

"And my husband. And Miss Headley's father. They are a formidable triumvirate."

"That remains to be seen." The station floor vibrated under his feet. "Feel that? That's the train approaching. Still a ways off but definitely on its way. About time for you to stand up now. Take my bags. They will occupy your hands. Stand here. In front of me."

Lily stood and hefted a valise in each hand then stood where he indicated, her back to him.

"No hesitation? No questions? Perhaps you are not fearless after all, Mrs. Shepard. Perhaps you know nothing but fear. Is that it?"

"Yes, Mr. Cabot. You have it exactly."

Roen pointed to the lone car on the side track as he and Ben rounded the corner of the station. "That's hers. That's the Headley crest on the wrought iron rails at the back."

"Pretentious," said Ben.

"Victor Headley can trace his family to the New Amsterdam settlement, or he says he can." Roen stepped on the track. "I can feel the train coming on."

"Then we should cross here before it pulls in."

"Shouldn't we let Mr. Winslow know we're going to search her car?"

"Solomon will make noises for five or six minutes and then he'll tell us to go ahead. I aim to save those five or six minutes for kissing my wife. I'm doing you the same favor."

Grinning, Roen nodded. "I think I'll enjoy kissing your wife."

Far from taking offense, Ben gave a bark of laughter. It was largely swallowed by the oncoming train's whistle as it approached the station. The men hurried across the tracks and over the rough gravel on the side beds.

"I doubt it will be open," said Roen as they climbed onto the small balcony at the rear of the car. He twisted the handle. The door didn't budge. Shrugging, he pulled on the sleeve of his coat so it was tight around his arm and jammed his elbow hard into one of the window panes in the door. Glass shattered. He cleared it out of the frame then stuck his arm inside and jiggled the knob and opened the door. "There."

Ben smiled, amused, as he followed Roen inside. He stopped once he crossed the threshold and whistled appreciatively while Roen walked deeper into the room. "Ain't this something?"

"Indeed," Roen said wryly. The car's appointments were spare owing to the size of the space, but every piece was quality, from the ornately carved walnut headboard of the three-quarter bed to the round dining table and four matching chairs with the same cabriolet legs and ball and claw feet. The vanity had a large gilt-framed mirror and was cleared of everything except a fine layer of dust. Women's fashion magazines, apparently the only publications that Victorine read, were scattered on the golden yellow damask divan.

Ben began searching the small drawers in the vanity while Roen looked in the drawers that were built into the base of the bed. They moved methodically around the room, examining the narrow wardrobe and linen closet and the inside of an upholstered bench that stretched the length of two side windows. There was no writing desk in the car, but there were papers scattered on top of the table. Roen divided the papers and gave half to Ben to look over.

"Correspondence to her father," said Ben. "Nothing about the pregnancy. She writes here that you proposed and the wedding will be in January."

Roen shook his head. "When is the letter dated?"

"It's not." He handed it to Roen.

"It would appear she was keeping her options open. Planning for every eventuality. The correspondence I was reading informed her father the marriage had already taken place. Again, no date. I think she was amusing herself."

Ben nodded. He picked up something else to read. "Here's the contract between her and Mr. Cabot. I wonder why she left it here."

"Perhaps it's a draft."

There were no papers of any consequence and they left the correspondence and contracts in a neater arrangement than they'd found them. Roen stood in place and slowly turned, his eyes taking in the interior space, top to bottom, side to side. He stopped suddenly, arrested by the neatly made bed. "Victorine never made a bed in her life," he told Ben. "And she had no travel companion to make it for her. Help me with the mattress."

Ben lifted it while Roen swept an arm under it. Two sweeps and he found what he was looking for: Victorine's palm pistol. It was loaded. Ben dropped the mattress back in place.

"Not a convenient place to keep it," said Ben. "Under her pillow would have made more sense."

"Not if she thought she might blow off her own head." Roen tucked it into a pocket. "Nothing in here to suggest that Cabot was ever a visitor."

Ben nodded. "It would have been a good

beginning to catch him in a lie." The car rattled and shook as the late morning train pulled into the station, snorting and squealing and steaming until it finally fell silent. "Let's go. I have to send my own telegram to Victor Headley, and you can explain the broken window to Solomon."

Roen chuckled. "Thanks."

They stepped out of the private car and jumped down to the gravel bed. Rather than walk around the train, they took the shortcut of climbing aboard and getting off on the other side. Roen was the first to hop to the platform; Ben was on his heels. Greeted by the sight of Lily standing as if rooted in place, a valise in each of her white-knuckled fists, neither of them moved. At first, Lily took up the whole of Roen's vision and he didn't see Martin Cabot at her back, but Ben had no such problem. He saw Cabot as part of the whole from the beginning.

A porter appeared, stepping down from the adjacent car. The man had a paisley carpeted valise in one hand. He held out the other hand to the passenger standing on the lip of the stair. It was Evelyn Gray come home from visiting her daughter and new granddaughter in Denver. Mrs. Gray landed lightly on the platform and kept her balance, thanks to the porter. Seeing nothing at all untoward in the tableau near the station entrance, Mrs. Gray waved gaily at Lily.

"Set down one of the valises," Martin Cabot whispered in Lily's ear, "and wave."

Lily did as she was told. "How are your daughter and the baby?"

"Fit as fiddles, both of them. Now I'm anxious to see that my husband hasn't starved while I was gone. He can boil water and make an egg seven different ways, but that is the extent of his skill in the kitchen."

Lily knew she was expected to smile and she did. She was grateful that Mrs. Gray's thoughts were so occupied with getting home to her husband that she didn't think to ask where Lily was going with the valises or why there was a man standing at her back while her husband and the sheriff stood some ten feet distant.

"I feel confident he has survived," said Lily, and she bade Mrs. Gray good day. Ben and Roen did the same. Mr. Cabot nodded in her direction. Mrs. Gray took her valise from the porter, thanked him, and began walking down the platform toward town.

The porter took a step toward the station house, but Mr. Cabot shook his head. "Mr. Winslow stepped out to deliver a telegram. You can take my valises, though. I'm just saying farewell to the Shepards and Sheriff

Madison."

"Very good, sir." He approached and lifted the valise that Lily had set on the platform. She held out the other one for him to take. "Train'll be leaving in a few minutes. We're not crowded. You can take a seat anywhere."

Cabot nodded. "Thank you. I'll be along directly." When the porter boarded, Cabot directed his attention to Ben and Roen. "I intend to board this train. I had no plans for Mrs. Shepard to accompany me, but your presence here has changed that. I will gladly let her go at the next stop if there is no sign that you've followed; otherwise I cannot guarantee her safety. It is all around unfortunate that you arrived when you did. I saw which way the wind was blowing when you questioned me at Mrs. Brady's. I decided then it was best for me to leave. There is no evidence of wrongdoing on my part because I committed no wrong, but I am a stranger here and I am familiar with how that stacks the most circumstantial of evidence against me."

"He's lying," said Lily. "He bought his ticket before you interviewed him this morning. I have the time from Solomon, who is lying unconscious behind the counter. He wouldn't allow me to exit the station because he suspected I was going to find you and tell you he was planning to leave town. What reason does he have to hurry off except that he murdered Miss Headley?"

"She makes an excellent point," Ben said calmly.

"My arrangement with Miss Headley was concluded," said Cabot.

"Odd you didn't mention that when we spoke," said Roen. "We read through several drafts of your contract with Miss Headley. According to what was set down, your arrangement would be concluded with the birth of her child. That must have amused her because there could be no other reason she would insist on it."

"Drafts," said Cabot. "The final agreement had no such terms."

"Do you have it?" asked Ben.

"In one of the valises that the porter just put on the train."

"May we look at it?"

"I'm feeling reasonable, gentlemen, because I truly do not wish to be burdened by Mrs. Shepard's presence. I do not trust her in the least. Yes, you may look in my valises. The agreement is in an inside pocket. I suggest you hurry. Mrs. Shepard, tell them what I have pressed to your back."

"I believe they know you have a gun, Mr.

Cabot. My husband knows I would not be standing here otherwise."

"Just so." He waved his free hand toward the train. "Go on. Quickly."

Ben indicated that Roen should investigate. Ben kept his gun hand hovering near the butt of his weapon. They all knew he wouldn't use it while Lily was Cabot's hostage. While Roen followed the route the porter had taken and disappeared in the car, Ben said, "You're right not to trust Lily Shepard. You have no idea what she's capable of. If you board the train with her, I cannot guarantee that you will arrive safely at the next stop."

"She's a deep one, I'll give you that."

Ben nodded, smiled reassuringly at Lily, although he wondered if he didn't require more reassurance than she did. "Where do you imagine you can go, Mr. Cabot, that you won't be found? Victor Headley has vast resources."

"Your mind is made up that I am guilty. I'm not. Your slim resources would be put to better use questioning your deputy."

"You'd make a better case for yourself if you were to let Mrs. Shepard go."

"I only want to make certain I can leave Frost Falls. Everything you have said and done makes that a very large question in my mind."

"Why do you think I should question Hitch?"

"He had motive."

"Really? He only knew Miss Headley to see her."

"He knew she disliked the China girl, had a vicious temper, and unleashed it on her."

"You probably should explain yourself since this is nothing you shared earlier."

"Miss Headley is responsible for Miss Chen's bruised face."

"I thought you said Miss Chen fell."

"I said that she *told* me she fell. Miss Headley told me that she slapped Miss Chen. For insolence the first time, and simply because she wanted to the second. I told you I kept an eye on Miss Headley. I followed her to the Shepard home. Afterward I observed she was upset in that cold, contemptuous manner of hers. I asked her what happened when she went inside. She told me."

"Hitch didn't know about it."

"Is that what he said? Of course you'd believe him. This is what I meant about a stranger having none of the advantages of a resident, especially when that resident is a lawman and the son of one of the pillars of the community. Is it any wonder I want to leave town?"

"Wouldn't you agree that purchasing your ticket before you claim you knew Miss Headley was dead is suspicious?"

"When you read my contract, the one that we agreed to abide by, you will see that I had the right to terminate my employment in the event Miss Headley engaged in — or expected me to engage in — behavior which I determined was morally repugnant. When Miss Headley struck Miss Chen in such a spiteful manner, she effectively ended our contract. I had no reason to kill her. I knew last night I would be leaving this morning and I told her so."

Ben features remained expressionless as he listened to Cabot's facile explanation. "Allow Mrs. Shepard to step aside. You don't need her. If you are innocent as you say, then you are complicating your defense by using her as a shield."

Cabot shook his head. His gaze shifted to the car where Roen had disappeared. "Mr. Shepard is taking an inordinately long time."

Ben shrugged. "He's probably reading the agreement." Although his eyes did not stray from Cabot's, he could see past the man's shoulder and through the station's large front window to where there was movement near the counter. He recognized that it was Roen and not Solomon Winslow that he was seeing. Ben doubted Roen had even looked for the valises. Instead, he had used the opportunity to leave the train on the far side and circle around to enter the station through the rear door.

The porter appeared again at the car entrance and gestured to the trio on the platform. "Better come aboard who's ever comin' aboard. Our girl here doesn't wait for stragglers." Having said his piece, he stepped back inside. A moment later his announcement was punctuated by the long ear-piercing whistle signaling the imminent departure of No. 462.

The sudden and deeply disruptive notes of the whistle made the very air shudder and had a similar but not identical effect on those standing nearby. Ben gave a start. Lily winced. Martin Cabot recoiled.

As soon as Lily felt the barrel of Cabot's gun shift away from her back, she threw herself to the ground. There was no benefit to Cabot in shooting her. She had only ever served as a shield and a threat. Now she was neither. The private investigator had an advantage over Ben. His gun was drawn, while Ben's was only now coming out of its holster. Ben, though, had an advantage over

Cabot that the investigator could not imagine: Roen Shepard had the sheriff's back. The train's signal had covered the sound of the station door opening and the vibration concealed Roen's long stride toward Cabot.

Ben was only surprised that Roen did not fire his weapon. Instead, he used Victorine Headley's palm pistol to clobber Martin Cabot hard at the base of his skull. Cabot was felled like a tree. "Timber," Ben said under his breath. He settled his gun back in its holster and rushed forward to drag Cabot off Lily so Roen could help her to her feet.

Roen slipped his weapon inside his jacket pocket and took Lily in his arms. He held on tight. She held on tighter.

Ben gave them a measure of privacy by examining Cabot's injury and determining the man would live. The irony of Victorine's pistol being Roen's weapon of choice was not lost on Ben. The size of the pistol was likely the reason Cabot was still alive. Roen's blow had been pitiless. Ben's attention was drawn back to the train when the porter appeared on the steps of the car yet again. This time he was holding one of Cabot's valises in each hand and looking at Roen for direction. Roen loosed one hand from Lily's back and pointed to the platform. The porter tossed both valises. They thumped in quick succession at Ben's feet. When Ben looked up, the porter had disappeared and No. 462 was beginning to roll on wheels of steel.

Shaking his head at the mystery of it all, Ben announced he was going to look in on Solomon.

"He has an egg-sized lump on his skull," said Roen, "but I'll wager the one I gave Cabot is half again that size."

"Well done." Ben squeezed Lily's shoulder as he passed her on his way. "Quick thinking, Lily, you dropping like that. What happened that you seized the chance?"

Lily turned her head so she could see Ben but kept it solidly against Roen's shoulder. "He recoiled when the engineer blew the whistle. I felt the gun move so I went down."

Ben nodded. "Bet you gave Roen a few gray hairs."

"More than a few," said Roen.

"Silver," Lily corrected. "Angel's wings."

Ben didn't understand, but he saw Roen's indulgent smile and knew that Roen's comprehension was all that mattered. Ben left Roen and Lily alone on the platform and went into the station. Solomon Winslow had pulled himself into a sitting position on the floor and was leaning against the counter.

"The bastard," he muttered when Ben hunkered down beside him. "Caught me unawares. How is Mrs. Shepard? He was grabbing at her when I interfered. Shame I didn't get my hands on him."

"Mrs. Shepard is fine. Better, in fact, than you. Mr. Cabot, on the other hand, is worse. You can thank Mr. Shepard for that. You think you can get to your feet?"

"Sure can."

To be safe, Ben supported Solomon with an elbow and shoulder and helped him up. "How about sending a telegram for me? Can you do that?"

Solomon flexed his fingers. "Right as rain. All ten." He sat at the telegraph machine. "Victor Headley, I presume."

"That's right."

"I gave Mrs. Shepard a telegram from him right before that Cabot fella came in and made a fuss. Doubt Mr. Headley's left New York yet, but he's taking an express train here."

"Good. You send this to him." Ben gave him the message. "Make it from Ben Madison, Sheriff, Frost Falls."

"Official like," Solomon said, nodding as wisely as his namesake. "He'll be sure to take notice."

Ben waited for the telegram to go before he walked outside. Roen and Lily were no longer in a clinch. They were sitting cross-legged on the platform with one of the valises open between them. Roen was rooting through it while Lily waited patiently for him to produce what he was after.

"You looking for that agreement?" asked Ben.

Roen shook his head. "Found something better."

Ben stepped closer and looked down past their bent heads into the contents of the open valise. "What?"

"Proof," said Roen. He continued rummaging through Cabot's belongings until he came across the item he had pushed to the bottom of the valise after discovering it. When his hand closed over it, he held it tightly and then lifted it out of the case. There was a modest measure of triumph in the way he raised up the glossy black lacquered box with gold Chinese characters painted so exquisitely across the top and along all four sides.

"What is it?" asked Ben. "Besides a box, I mean."

Roen opened it up to reveal the red silk lining. The box was empty. "Victorine kept some of her jewelry in here. This is hers."

"How do you know?" Ben asked.

Lily glanced up at him, frowning. "Truly, Ben, it's obvious that Roen's seen it before. They were intimates, you know."

Ben flushed. The curse of a redhead. "When did you become so forthright? It's Ridley's influence, isn't it?"

Lily smirked and turned her attention back to the box. She held out a hand. "May I?"

Roen passed it to her. He spoke to Ben. "Lily's right. I have seen it before, but what she is about to learn is that it was a gift I gave Victorine on the occasion of her birthday. The characters on the lid represent the Chinese year of her birth. Oddly enough, the year of the red fire rat, although it should not be interpreted through a Western lens. The characters on the sides — if I recall correctly — are harmony, joy, happiness, and prosperity."

Ben hunkered beside Martin Cabot and produced a pair of handcuffs that he fitted to the man's wrists behind his back. "So evidence, then, that Cabot was in her suite on at least one occasion."

"She didn't give that to him," said Roen. "He took it from her."

"Her jewelry was loose in the top drawer

of the chest in her room," said Ben. "I found it there when I searched her room."

"Victorine was not careless with her belongings. She didn't trust the help in her father's house. She would have never trusted the staff at the Butterworth."

Lily finished examining the box and passed it to Ben. "I think what you have there trumps your circumstantial evidence, Ben, and brings all of Mr. Cabot's lies to light. He is your murderer. As Roen said, 'Proof.' "

Chapter Thirty-Nine

It was the middle of January before Martin Cabot's trial came before Judge Miner. Victor Headley was not in attendance. He stayed in Frost Falls long enough to collect his daughter's body and thank Ben and Roen for their diligence and speedy resolution. He asked to know the details of her murder but his countenance remained as unyielding as granite while Ben described the circumstances of Victorine's death. Victor did not evince any surprise when Roen told him that Victorine had used the pretense of a pregnancy to provoke a proposal, but it was the first time he revealed a hint of grief, though whether it was because of the loss of a child that never was or that his daughter had demeaned herself in such a manner, neither Roen nor Ben could say.

Victor asked to see Martin Cabot. Ben would not allow Victor to step into the cell with Martin, but he did agree to give them privacy. It was a brief meeting, no more than five minutes, and whatever was said left the private investigator with a pasty face and a tremor in his hands.

While Cabot awaited his day in court, professing his innocence to the *Ledger* and a reporter sent up from Denver for the *Rocky,* as well as his lawyer and whoever happened to be in the adjoining cell, usually on a Friday or Saturday night, the people of Frost Falls went about their business, which at this time of year was most notably preparations for Christmas and the annual New Year celebration at the Butterworth.

Ridley Madison decided Christmas Eve was the ideal occasion for the dinner party she wanted to host. Lily helped her select a menu agreeable to the palates of the adults and children, though she assured Ridley her children would eat whatever was put in front of them. At Lily's suggestion, Ridley delivered the invitations personally, thus assuring Fedora's attendance.

One of the reasons Martin Cabot's incarceration elicited so little comment among the town busybodies was that the busiest body of them all was taking the high road for the time being. By anyone's measure, it was a fine path that Amanda Springer was walking, and it was frequently whispered outside of her hearing that she could not maintain the straight and narrow for long. What even her closest acolytes did not take into account was her considerable pride, and rather than air her frustration and disappointment that her son was courting Fedora Chen or remarking on Miss Chen's unsuitability as a match for Hitchcock, Amanda kept her head up and acted as if there was nothing at all extraordinary about the pairing. It was Amanda's rather significant insight when she realized that the longer she acted *as if* there was nothing extraordinary about the courtship, there *was* nothing extraordinary about the courtship.

Ridley's dinner party was a success, which surprised only Ridley. Ellie had nothing but admiration for the dining arrangement and enjoyed herself fussing over the children, who had their own table and comported themselves so beautifully that Lily was moved to wonder if Roen had bribed them.

"Of course I did," he said when she asked him that night. "I promised them a sleigh ride. It's all been arranged with Hank Ketchum for tomorrow afternoon."

"You must have been sure they would do very well if you had the sleigh reserved."

"I set rather low expectations. Ham had

to keep his shoes on. Lizzie had to keep her bottom on her chair and not climb up on her knees. Hannah had to help Lizzie cut her food into small pieces, and Clay had to keep his napkin in his lap and direct passing of the food."

"I am in awe," she said. Lily leaned over and kissed him on the mouth. "Merry Christmas, my love."

As joyous as Christmas Day was with its candy-and-fruit-filled stockings and exchange of presents, the days leading up to New Year's Eve grew increasingly somber. Roen was sensitive to the two-year anniversary of Jeremiah Salt's death but uncertain what he should do, or even if there was anything he could do. Lily's efforts to remain emotionally even were forced and Roen was not alone in noticing it. He observed Clay and Hannah watching their mother more closely. Lizzie and Ham took their cue from their older brother and sister and were clingy and needy. Roen had to remind himself it was not necessarily their father's death they were remembering and mourning, but the trauma of the fire when they lost their home and almost lost their lives.

"Am I right that you will not want to attend the New Year's Eve party at the Butterworth?" Roen asked Lily when they were alone at the table after breakfast, finishing their coffee.

She nodded. "The children can't attend and I will not leave them alone."

"I understand. Don't look at me as if you think I'm disappointed. I'm testing the water here, trying to figure what the right thing to do is, or if not the right thing, then the best thing."

"You probably wish I could help you. I can't. I don't know."

"What did you do last year?"

"Nothing," she said quietly, staring into her coffee cup. "We survived it."

"We can do better than that."

Lily's smile was wan, but she did not dismiss the idea. "I'd like that."

"What do you think about a party for the children?"

"A party?"

"Nothing fancy. My parents used to allow us to invite a friend to sleep over. We never did it on New Year's Eve, but it's really the perfect night for it so now I'm wondering why we never did. Clay can invite Frankie. I'm sure Hannah and Ham will have someone in mind."

"Who would Lizzie ask?"

"Her best friend. Fedora."

Laughter bubbled on Lily's lips. It felt good. "What about Hitch?"

"He'll come, too. I don't think they're ready to go to the Butterworth as a couple. And Hitch is probably working tonight so Ben can have it free. He'll be able to come and go. We'll bring blankets and pillows down to the parlor and spread them out. I'll make ice cream punch and you'll make little jam sandwiches. We'll play games and tell ghost stories and —" He stopped because Lily was frowning. "All right. Maybe not ghost stories, but you get the idea. They'll all try to stay up until midnight and they'll all fall asleep by ten."

"Optimist."

"We'll give them breakfast in the morning and send them home." He waited for Lily to give him an indication that she was on board or preparing to throw him off the train. She did neither. Though she had not moved, it struck him that she was suddenly far away, so deep in thought that she was oblivious to her surroundings, to the cup she clutched tightly, to the tremor of the saucer, to him. When she spoke, it was so softly that he wasn't certain that she meant for him to hear.

"I killed him."

Arrested, Roen stared at her while she

continued to stare into her cup. "Lily?"

"You heard me. I can't say it again. I promised Ben and Ridley and Hitch I would never say it once, and now I have. To you. I've said it to you." A tear leaked from her right eye and rippled the smooth brown surface of the coffee. "It's yours now. My guilt is your burden, too. You must do what you think is right. Not what is best. What is right."

Roen took the cup away from Lily and then he took her by the hand. "Come with me. We can't talk here." He tugged and without any real effort brought her to her feet. He led her out of the kitchen, down the hall, told the children they were going upstairs and not to be disturbed, and nudged Lily to take the first step. When they were in their bedroom, he closed the door and leaned against it. Lily stood alone, all at sea, and then slowly sank to the edge of the bed.

"He was drunk," she said. She spoke quietly, without inflection, a storyteller with nothing vested in the story she was about to tell. "As drunk as I'd ever seen him. I was sleeping when he came in, but I woke when he closed the door. He stumbled toward the bed. Toward me. He was carrying a hammer in one hand and tongs in the other. He brought them from the forge. I could only imagine he was going to use them on me. Why else would he have them? I flung myself out of bed but not away from him. I went at him. He dropped the hammer. I picked it up. I hit him with it like Mr. Cabot clubbed Solomon, like you clobbered Mr. Cabot. He went down. Sprawled on the bed. I think I must have stared at him for a time. I seem to remember that I did. Then I dropped the hammer and ran. I knew what I had to do, where I had to go."

She stopped abruptly.

Roen waited for her to go on. She didn't, and he realized there was not time enough in the world for her to continue without prompting. "What is it that you had to do, Lily? Where is it that you had to go?"

"Turn myself in, of course. I went to the jail. I left my children and went straightaway to the jail."

"But the fire . . . what happened?"

"I don't know. I swear I don't know. I was sure I killed him. I hit him so hard. Swung the hammer as if I were John Henry. Hitch and Ridley and Ben say no. They say he wasn't dead and that he must have tipped the bedside lamp struggling to get up. Ridley says a burning beam struck him in the head when it fell. She says she could tell because she and Hitch found his burnt body buried under it. I'm supposed to believe her. They want me to believe. It's supposed to be my story now, the way I'm supposed to remember it and retell it if I have to. But I don't know, Roen. I hit him so hard. He didn't stir and I knew he was dead and I ran. I might have knocked over the lamp myself. The fire. That could be on me. I left my sleeping children with their dead father and there was a fire and they might have died if not for Hitch raising the alarm, and Clay's quick thinking to save Ham, and Ben risking his life to save Clay in turn and then risking everything again to save my girls. I was safe, asleep in a cell, and they might have died, and that would have been because of me, because of what I'd done."

Roen pushed away from the door and knelt at Lily's feet. He took her hands in his. "Oh, Lily. My sweet, courageous Lily. The burden you have shouldered. I know of no one who would not be stooped under the weight of it. That is not you. You are brave, Lily. You are . . ." He paused, searching for the word that would show her the truth that was in his heart. "You are *heroic.*"

Lily lifted her downcast eyes from Roen's beautifully capable hands enfolding hers. She stared into his eyes, lost herself in them.

His face blurred, but it didn't matter because she knew the angle of his cheekbones, the slant of his eyebrows, the slope of his nose, and the cast of his jaw. She knew the elusive dimple that would appear at the left corner of his mouth when he smiled at her. It was not there now. Roen was not smiling. His features were marked by earnestness, by gravity. She was heroic. That's what he'd said, and he meant it. Whether or not she believed it about herself, it was the truth he held.

Lily caught her breath on a dry sob. Her lower lip trembled. She sucked it in and bit down until she knew she could hold it steady. "Mr. Cabot asked me why I cared that Miss Headley had been murdered, and I said it was because she was a human being. His voice was positively arid when he replied. 'Barely,' he said. And then I told him she deserved better, and he said, 'Again, barely.' " Lily's shoulders heaved on a second dry sob. It ended with a hiccup. "It reminded me that I thought of Jeremiah in precisely that same way. Barely human; barely deserving better. Mr. Cabot is in jail awaiting trial and I have been free these last two years just as if I weren't guilty of the same crime."

"But you haven't been free, Lily." Roen

squeezed her cold hands. "You haven't been free a single day, and you don't know that Ridley and Ben and Hitch were wrong. If they have an explanation they can accept, why can't you? You survived. You *deserve* to survive."

"But —"

Roen stopped her with a look. He removed one of his hands from hers and reached under the blankets to give her one corner of a sheet to dry her eyes. She accepted it, sniffled, and touched it to each eye in turn.

"Lily," Roen said gently. "It is an honor you've given me, allowing me to hear your story. A great privilege. I'm not sure you can appreciate that now, but someday I hope you'll know how heartfelt the sentiment is. To entrust me as you have, that is a great gift, and I mean to prove to you that I am worthy of it."

"Oh, but you are. You *are*!"

His faint smile caused the dimple to appear and vanish in the blink of an eye. "You'll have doubts from time to time. That's to be expected. But you mustn't close me out, Lily. Come to me with them."

She regarded him with something akin to wonder. "I thought . . . that is, I was afraid . . . I thought you'd put me away."

Roen's brow puckered as he frowned

deeply. "Put you in jail, you mean?"

"No. Put me away from you. I couldn't bear that, but I also couldn't bear you not knowing who I am and what I did."

"I know who you are and now I know what you think you did, and that is all I need to know. I will never put you away from me, Lily. That talk of divorce was just talk, a way for you to feel at ease because you'd believe there was a way out. There never was a way out. Do you understand?"

She nodded.

"Say you understand," he said. "I need to hear you say it."

"I understand you'll stand by me. There is no way out."

Roen's chuckle rumbled pleasantly. He got to his feet and sat beside Lily on the bed. "You know you said that as if it were a life sentence handed down by a judge."

She looked at him askance, smiling faintly. "Wasn't it?"

"All right," he said agreeably, nudging her shoulder with his. "Maybe it was."

Lily nudged him back. It seemed wildly inappropriate that she should have an urge to laugh, but it was exactly a laugh that was tickling the back of her throat. Roen was right when he said she hadn't been free a single day since Jeremiah's death, and the laughter she felt bubbling against her lips was proof that her life was different now. She would live it unburdened by oppressive guilt and relieved of secrets that sometimes made it difficult to draw a breath.

Lily leaned into him, kissed him full on the mouth, her hands cupping his face. "It is a happy talent you have, Roen Shepard, making the ridiculous seem reasonable, but I will never regret listening to your nonsense and somehow hearing the sense in it." His cheeks grew warm under her palms. "You're blushing. Are you blushing?"

Instead of answering, Roen removed her hands and folded her fingers. He pressed his lips to her knuckles and then to the soft undersides of her wrists. "I would very much like to see you blush." It wasn't what he said but the way he said it that brought pink to Lily's cheeks. Roen chuckled. He kissed her lightly on the mouth. "We have a party to plan, children to invite, little jam sandwiches to make, but you keep entertaining wicked thoughts and I will make every effort to oblige you tonight."

Lily pushed at his chest and stood. She stepped away from the bed before he could pull her back. His deliciously roguish chuckle followed her all the way downstairs.

■ ■ ■ ■

The guests at the annual New Year's Eve party at the Butterworth arrived in their finery to celebrate with their neighbors and friends. They danced and drank and ate dainty triangle sandwiches with no crusts and elegantly iced cakes topped with pink and yellow rosebuds. They all laughed, some sang, and a few revelers congregated in the lobby to share jokes too ribald for mixed company. There were only two fights, and only one of those drew blood, so all in all, as the midnight hour approached, the evening was already judged to be a splendid success.

Lily and Roen were equally pleased with the outcome of their celebration. They stood arm in arm on the threshold of the parlor and regarded the sprawl of blankets and bodies carpeting the floor with satisfaction. Lizzie had been the first to succumb to sleep, not at all disturbed by the giggling and teasing of her siblings and their friends. Fedora had stayed awhile longer to be sure Lizzie did not wake and find her gone, but when Hitch showed up on his last round through town before midnight, Lily helped her on with her coat and gave her no choice but to accompany the deputy. Ham and his rascal friend were sure they would be awake when the church bell announced the new year, but they carried on too energetically in the early hours to make it until the late ones. Frankie Fuller arrived bearing good news in a telegram for Roen that Solomon Winslow had received earlier in the day. Northeast Rail had accepted his proposal for the new route that bypassed the questionable property lines of the Frosts and the Hardys by using Thunder Point. He was given authorization to proceed with hiring, purchasing, and finalizing land contracts. Now Frankie was snuffling softly in his sleep, his face turned precariously close to Clay's stocking feet. Clay was lying on his side in the opposite direction, and equally undisturbed by the suspicious odors emanating from Frankie's feet. Hannah and her friend Sarah lay cuddled on cushions that they had pulled from the sofa and chair, exactly as Roen had done his first night in the house. Hannah looked up when Roen turned back the last lamp and smiled drowsily.

"Thank you," she whispered, and then promptly closed her eyes and was asleep.

When the church bell struck its first note, Roen and Lily were on the stairs. On the second note, they were on the landing. Lily was in Roen's arms for the third, fourth, and fifth as he carried her to their bedroom. On the sixth he was laying her down, and on the seventh, he was following her. He kissed one corner of her mouth on the eighth and the other corner on the ninth. On the tenth she clutched his head, wound her fingers in his hair, and kissed him back in the manner she thought she deserved. He apparently thought so, too, because that kiss lasted through the swell of the eleventh and to the very last echoes of the twelfth.

And so they greeted the new year as they meant it to go on, loving well and most often wisely, sharing what was mutually satisfying and deeply held in their hearts, and finally finding the ridiculous to be sublime when even Roen couldn't make it seem reasonable.

ABOUT THE AUTHOR

Jo Goodman is a *USA Today* bestselling author of numerous romance novels, including *A Touch of Flame, A Touch of Frost, The Devil You Know, This Gun for Hire, In Want of a Wife,* and *True to the Law;* and she is also a fan of the happily ever after. When not writing, she is a licensed professional counselor working with children and families in West Virginia's northern panhandle.

CONNECT ONLINE
jogoodman.com
facebook.com/jogoodmanromance

The employees of Thorndike Press hope you have enjoyed this Large Print book. All our Thorndike, Wheeler, and Kennebec Large Print titles are designed for easy reading, and all our books are made to last. Other Thorndike Press Large Print books are available at your library, through selected bookstores, or directly from us.

For information about titles, please call:
(800) 223-1244

or visit our website at:
gale.com/thorndike

To share your comments, please write:
Publisher
Thorndike Press
10 Water St., Suite 310
Waterville, ME 04901